WOLF'S ENDGAME

USA TODAY BESTSELLING AUTHOR
EVE L. MITCHELL

WOLF'S ENDGAME

Foreword

This is a continuation of The Blackridge Peak Series. This is the final book in this paranormal romance series, and cannot be read as a standalone.

Book Description

Just when I thought I could finally find my place and *belong* in a pack, fate had other plans. The sting of betrayal cut deep.

As the dust settled from the devastating blow that threatened to shatter the fragile trust between Cannon and me, we both struggled to confront the harsh realities of our world. Fueled by a thirst for revenge, my heart was torn between the hunger for retribution and the longing for reconciliation.

As I prepared to fight for my pack, I knew the stakes had been raised, and everything was on the line. At every turn, danger threatened, and with each step forward, uncertainty hung in the air—not only ahead, but also within.

Knowing I had yet to face my most formidable adversary, I realized it was time to reclaim what was rightfully mine. I wasn't running anymore.

It was time to fight...and win the ultimate endgame.

Content information: Wolf's Endgame is a paranormal romance, and is the final book in The Blackridge Peak series. Recommended reading age is 18+ due to sexual content, mature language, violence, and some mature themes.

CHAPTER 1
Kezia

Darkness greeted me as I opened my eyes, and I swore to myself as I lay there on a hard dirt floor with a musty smell surrounding me, that at some point in my future, I was going to make a concentrated effort to stop waking up in cells.

It was getting old and repetitive.

My dry attempt at humor did little to quell the panic and fear I felt. Moving slowly, I sat up. The overpowering scent that Landon had drugged me with lingered in my nostrils, making me feel nauseous.

Landon.

That treacherous bastard had drugged me and threatened me.

He threatened my *family*.

Anger made me surge to my feet, my earlier caution fleeing as my temper rose within me. I wanted to scream for him. Demand he show himself to me. Reaching out, my hands sought to learn the confines of the place where I was being kept. Fingers brushed against the cool stone. Smooth.

I knew this place.

I was in the cells under the hall.

He'd brought me back to the Anterrio Pack. The hall was in the center of the town. How had he gotten me here without being seen? Where was Kris?

Moving to the left, I felt for the cot that I used the last time I was in here.

I *really* needed to stop getting locked up.

After a thorough search of the space, I realized there was no cot. Once more, I sniffed the air. The scent was familiar. Dropping to my hands and knees, I tested the floor. Hard compact dirt.

Getting to my feet, I brushed at the knees of my leggings reflexively. I wasn't in the cell I was in before, the one that Kris had locked me in when I first went into heat.

Was I on the other side of it? Or worse...under it?

Panic swelled within me. What if I was trapped here? Cannon wouldn't find me.

Would he even come looking? I'd left him and I hadn't even told him why. Would he know? Would he guess I left to protect my brother?

Luna, I hoped so.

A noise above made me freeze. Cocking my head to hear better, I counted the steps as someone walked back and forth above me. The rhythm felt familiar. My body sagged with relief as I counted the steps. There was only one other person I knew who paced that fast when they were thinking, my brother.

Clapping my hand over my mouth in time to muffle the shout for Kris, I prayed no one heard my stifled yell. I was being foolish. If Kris wasn't alone, I'd alert whoever was with him that I was awake.

Moving stealthily, I began a frantic search of my surroundings. If there was someone above me, that meant I came in another way. I needed to find it.

Stretching above me, my fingers knocked briefly against something small and metallic. On raised tiptoes, I stretched, reaching for it, hoping it was a way out.

I jumped back when the rush of cold air coated my fingers, and a hissing noise filled the room. It wasn't a way out; it was a vent of some sort, spewing out gas into my small room. With my arm over my nose and mouth, I struggled not to breathe.

I was a shifter. Most things that hurt humans didn't hurt us. But, I wasn't invincible.

Sinking to my knees, desperate to cough, I squeezed my eyes shut as I fought the gas designed to knock me out. I knew I wouldn't succeed. I was losing a battle I couldn't fight.

The hissing stopped and I opened my eyes in time to see a solo blink of a red light, high in the corner of the room. Or what I assumed was the corner.

They were watching me.

It was my last thought as I passed out from the fumes.

"Kezia?"

Cannon's arms surrounded me. I was safe in the warm cocoon he provided me. Sleep tugged at my awareness, bringing me back down to the warm slumber I had been in, with my mate curled around me.

"Kezia! Will you stop moaning and wake up?"

"Mm-hmmm...Cannon, shhh."

"Oh for fuck's sake, Kezia. This is your own fault."

The sharp sting of water washed over me as I jumped up,

confused and disoriented but awake. The blue eyes of my captor watched me warily as I took a step back from him. Glancing over my shoulder, I saw the bed I was lying in was empty; Cannon wasn't there.

I'd been dreaming, and now I was faced with the ugly reality that I'd been betrayed by one of my oldest friends.

Taking in the room, I didn't recognize it. This wasn't where I had been when I woke up the first time, they'd moved me? "Where am I?"

"Home." The glare I sent Landon's way made him take a step back.

"You kidnapped me."

He rolled his eyes. "You came to me."

"You drugged me.

Landon let out a long sigh. "*After* you came to me. Willingly."

"You *threatened* my family, you sociopath!" As I lunged forward, a sharp yank on my arm halted my progress, and I looked down at the handcuff around my wrist and the chain that led from it to the nail in the wall. "What the fuck is this?" I growled, yanking on the chain, hissing in pain as it dug into me.

"It's a precaution."

My head snapped so quickly to the sound of the other voice in the room, that I hurt myself. "Bastard!"

Bale was leaning against the wall, his arms folded, his dark stare fixed on me. "'Pack Leader Bale' is how you will address me."

"You're right, bastard is too good for you." Looking him over with disgust, I sneered. "'Fucking asshole' is much better." My attention flicked to Landon. "Where's Kris?"

"It's unfortunate, but Beta Kris is indisposed," Bale answered calmly.

"If you've hurt him, I'll—"

"You'll what?" Bale looked me over once, much as I had done him only moments before. His smile was cold and chilling. He straightened, his arms relaxed, one slipping into his pocket while he walked towards me. "You'll glare at me some more?" Hate filled his eyes. "Call me more names?" he mocked. Leaning forward, his face inches from mine, he laughed. "You will do *nothing*. You *are* nothing. You live because *I* say you can." He lost his smile, his face cold and emotionless once more. "You're mine now, bitch."

"Dad."

I'd forgotten Landon was in the room, but I dared not break eye contact with the pack leader in front of me.

I saw the sneer on Bale's face when Landon spoke, but it was gone when he turned to look at him. "Yes, I know, you want her." He glanced back at me. "Fuck her and be done with it."

Landon moved into my line of sight as he spoke to his father. "Dad, you said you would think about allowing the marriage."

"No. She's rabid."

Speak for yourself, psycho.

Bale glowered at me. "She's like her mother," he spat. "Her mother was a whore as well."

I bit my tongue so hard it bled. Landon's head was lowered, his face pale, but I saw the tight clench of his fist at his side. "She can be taught."

Bale threw his head back and laughed. A sound with no joy. "*That*?" He pointed at me. "*That* cannot be taught. You cannot teach a feral wolf, son. Use her how you want, then make her disappear."

Landon nodded his head, and with one more baleful look at me, his father left the room. I opened my mouth, but the almost indiscernible whisper reached me. "Say nothing, Kezia."

But I wasn't scared of Landon. Until today, I had never been scared of Bale either. The male who had just stood in front of me had not been the male I knew as Pack Leader.

How well he had hidden his hate.

"Where's my brother?"

Slowly Landon raised his head to meet my glare. "Kris is on pack business."

Hope surged within me. "Where?" I took a step forward. "Is he here?"

Landon wet his lips, breaking eye contact. "Kris is on pack business."

My stomach plummeted and I was about to demand more answers when something made me look to where Landon had turned his attention briefly before looking back at me.

A small red light blinked.

They were watching. Someone was watching. Me? Or *both* of us?

I stiffened when Landon stepped into my space, fighting revulsion when he reached out, a finger trailing over my collarbone. "You need to be smarter," he murmured. Not low enough not to be heard. "I told you, you will be my mate, but you need to prove to Dad that you can obey." His finger left my collarbone, moving over the curve of my breast. I jerked away from his touch, but he grabbed my hair, pulling me into his body as he held me tight. "Obey, Kezia. Obey me and you can live."

Every cell in my body reacted violently to his touch, but the look of panic in his eyes stayed my hand. The memory of his tears, his beg of forgiveness as he followed me to the ground as he drugged me, resurfaced.

He has my mom. I remembered the plea before I passed out. Was it true?

Landon's hand cupped my hip, pulling my lower body into his. His breath caressed my ear. "Fight me," he breathed. "But not too much. I need your help, Kez."

The words confused me. His words contrasted with his actions. I needed to move away; his touch was making me ill.

"Take your hands off me," I growled as I jerked away from him. "Touch me again, I'll remove your hands." My wrist burned and I looked down, ready to tear the metal off when I saw the thin trail of blood. "Silver..." Looking up at him, I held up my wrist. "You hold me with *silver*?"

His head dipped slightly. "It will help tame you."

"Tame me?" Fury burned so fiercely inside me it almost dulled the pain of the silver on my skin. "*Tame* me? I will skin you alive for this."

Landon stepped back, the usual wide smile I was used to spread across his face. "There she is. My girl. My fighter." He looked pleased, but his expression didn't match the sadness in his eyes. "You need to rest, babe. Someone will bring you food." He pointed at my wrist. "You resist, Kez, we have more than one of those."

He left me in the room. I was handcuffed to the wall, with the threat of more silver to use against me. Sitting on the bed, I tried not to react, but the truth that I was alone and scared, with only the occasional blinking red light for company.

What the hell was I going to do, and how was I going to save my brother, never mind myself?

~

I WAS ALONE FOR DAYS. No one came to feed me. No one came to even give me water. There was no bathroom, only a bucket in the corner of the room, and after one use and nowhere to empty it, the smell became nauseating.

I'd fallen asleep once. No matter if you were a shifter or human, your body needed sleep. When I awoke with a start and panic in my heart, I realized I had another silver cuff around my other wrist.

They'd also sliced my arm open, and the burning pain of the silver as it rubbed constantly against the shallow wound had me curled in a ball on the floor as I fought the agony.

I heard the footsteps approach. Black boots that were far too polished to be those of an honest shifter faced me. The kick to my stomach knocked the wind out of me, and I was gasping for air when Bale grabbed my hair, forcing my head back to look at him. An ugly sneer marred his face as he looked at me with loathing.

"You look like her."

I said nothing. I wasn't sure what I could say even if my throat wasn't too dry to speak. I could smell the scent of liquor on his breath, and my fear intensified.

"She thought she was too good for me." He pulled my head back further, my back arching to try to alleviate the unnatural angle. "Opened her legs wide for an *alpha* though." The sheer intensity of his hate oozed out of his pores. "Just like her whore daughter. My boy's not good enough? You just want to fuck an alpha? Like *her*."

I spat in his face. It seems I had saliva left after all.

Bale backhanded me across the face, and it knocked me back. He was on top of me, hands around my throat, and I no longer had the strength to fight back.

But *she* did.

Moonstar burst forward, her strength weakened from the silver rubbing into our flesh, but she bucked our hips, and Bale's grip loosened. Scrambling to our feet, we swayed as we stood. My fingers clutched the band of silver around my other wrist, tugging at it, trying to get it free.

"Bitch!"

Bale's punch knocked me off my feet, my head banging off the floor as I fell. Another punch and I felt my cheekbone crunch.

"*Dad*! Dad, *no*! *No*!"

I heard them scuffling as I rolled away, my hands too shaky to be stable enough against the floor to push myself up. I heard voices, but I couldn't concentrate. The pain in my head, my face, my wrists—every part of me hurt.

Using the wall for support, I struggled to my feet. Turning cautiously, I saw I was alone with Landon, and it showed how much my life sucked that I felt relief when I saw my abductor.

"Kezia..." Landon moved towards me, and I flinched. With his hands up, he approached me. "I won't hurt you."

"Again. You won't hurt me again." My voice was hoarse and croaky, but I saw the pain I felt reflected in his eyes. "Stay the fuck away from me."

"Kezia, you're hurt. I need to help you so you can heal." He took another step. "I'll take one of the cuffs off," he said as he glared at my wrists. "I didn't know you had two."

"Right."

"Kezia, I *didn't* know."

I watched him. My cheek was throbbing. My wrists were on fire, the agony constant and relentless. My scalp burned, and looking past Landon, I saw a clump of my hair on the floor. It hurt to talk. It hurt to breathe.

Everything hurt.

"I'll take the cuff off. You can heal."

"And then what?" I swayed on my feet, but I'd rather fall than let him touch me. "Your dad can use me as a punching bag again?"

Anger burned behind Landon's eyes. "That won't happen again."

But he couldn't promise that. I knew that and so did he. The overwhelming urge to cry welled up inside of me. I wanted Cannon. I wanted my mate, my alpha, to come and tear this hateful pack to the ground. I wanted vengeance.

I wanted a lot of things.

"Where's Kris?"

Landon looked at me with pity. "Let me help you first. Then I'll answer one question." His eyes flicked to the side so fast I thought I imagined it, but then I remembered the camera in the corner.

"I don't need help."

"Your cheekbone is broken."

"I know, asshole, I can fucking feel it."

Landon rubbed his hands over his hair in frustration. "You're my worst fucking nightmare sometimes," he hissed. Striding forward, he grabbed my arm, right where the cuff dug into my bloody and wounded wrists. Unceremoniously, he pulled me forward, and when I tried to resist, he pushed the cuff into torn flesh. "*Stop it, Kezia!*"

Dragging me to the bed, he pushed me onto it. "Stay there and don't fucking move."

He left the room, coming back moments later with a tray of bandages and another male from the pack. I couldn't remember his name; he hardly ever spoke to me, being one of the Anterrio Pack who was convinced I was feral and wild. His hypocrisy stank more than the smell of shit from the bucket.

"Clean up the floor and take that bucket out of here," Landon demanded.

"Pack Leader Bale—"

Landon turned on him so quickly that I gasped. Landon's hand was around the male's throat. "Clean up this room, take that shit out of here, and get my mate food. *Now.*" Landon watched him for a few minutes before he turned back to me. "Your face looks like a car crash."

"Because I got punched in the face. What's your excuse?"

He bit back his smile, but the glance he gave me strangely settled me. Carefully, Landon took the first handcuff off me. When I held up the other wrist, he gently but firmly pushed it back down onto my thigh.

"Afraid?" I murmured so low that only he could hear.

"Fucking terrified, babe."

His simple admission scared me far more than anything that had happened since I woke up here.

He cleaned my wrist and then bandaged it before putting the cuff back on. He did the same with the other, leaving it off longer, and we watched my skin sluggishly heal itself.

"You always were a quick healer." He spoke softly but loud enough to be heard by whoever was listening.

"Good thing."

Landon took my hand, ignoring my attempt to pull away. "I have something to tell you."

"I don't think I can take any other revelations from you." My voice was heavy with bitterness, and I took small satisfaction when Landon flinched.

"It's about the Blackridge Peak Pack."

Everything inside me froze. I was sure my heart stopped beating. "What about it?"

Landon cleared his throat. "It gives me no pleasure to tell you this..."

"Landon!"

"Alpha Cannon is dead."

The words hovered in the air between us with a finality that I couldn't quite comprehend. Eventually, I found my voice. "You're lying."

Landon looked at me with pity. "No, Kez, I'm not. He was attacked. They took him out with a silver knife."

The room was spinning. I was on my feet, and the room spun around me in a frenzy. I stumbled, my knees giving way as I crashed to the ground.

A knife?

Silver?

He was dead.

No.

"No." Panting on the floor, I fought for breath to fill my lungs. "No. He wouldn't... No! He isn't, you're lying!"

Landon knelt beside me, his hand smoothing over my hair.

"He's gone, Kez. They held a service for him. That's where I was, paying my respects on behalf of the pack."

"Respect?" My teeth gnashed together as bile rose in my throat. "You didn't respect him!"

I lunged for him, but Landon caught me and tried to soothe me. "I know, I know you're hurting."

Tears poured down my face, and somehow, I was sobbing into his chest. "Tell me it's a lie."

I felt him take a deep breath. "I wish I could," he whispered, "but I can't. They burned his body yesterday."

I couldn't stop the tears. At some point, Landon left me.

It didn't matter.

Nothing mattered. Not anymore.

My mate was gone.

CHAPTER 2

Kezia

THE DAYS PASSED IN A BLUR. I COULD HAVE BEEN here one day, one week, one month. I no longer knew. Landon had bandaged my damaged wrists, but somewhere between then and now, someone had removed them, and once more, my skin was torn and blistered where the silver cuff rubbed against it.

I'd stopped eating. Cannon would laugh at the miracle of me refusing food, I had no doubt.

Cannon.

My mate.

My mate who I had *left*. Who I hadn't trusted enough to help me.

I was dehydrated, but still, the tears came. My body hurt. My heart was destroyed. I'd fought him so much, so determined not to accept the fact I was his mate, and just as we were both open to accepting it, I'd run away in the hopes of saving my brother.

Now Cannon was gone, and no one had told me if Kris still lived, and I had lost the strength to fight.

I knew I needed to be fighting, trying to escape. I couldn't do anything. My body was weak; it was as if learning of my mate's fate sapped all the strength out of me.

The bed dipped and I no longer moved away from the feel of Landon beside me. Bale hadn't returned after the incident where he lost control, and I knew somehow that I had Landon to thank for that. The idea of thanking Landon for anything upset me.

Landon upset me.

The touch of my old friend made me stiffen as he smoothed his hand over my hair. I stank. I knew I did, but he didn't flinch from touching me. Maybe he thought I needed consoling. Soothed? Hell, maybe his touching me soothed him—I didn't know, and I would never care.

"Kezia, you need to eat."

I found the strength to move away, no more than an inch, but it was enough when I heard his unhappy sigh.

"Kezia, you're not helping."

Had I the energy to lift my head and bite him, I would have.

"Can you hear me?" His voice was lower than a whisper, but I heard him given how close he was to me. "Kris is alive." The weight of his hand stroking over my hair got heavier, pressing my head down slightly as if he anticipated my reaction to his words. "Kris doesn't know you're here. He's with my sister. They locked them *both* up. Kez? Help me, I can't do it alone."

Help him.

Why would I help him?

Bale took Cass?

Slow, burning anger ignited within me. Cassandra was the apple of her father's eye. Or so I thought.

Landon let out a loud sigh. "You're proving them all right, Kezia. They told me that you were too wild and feral to accept pack life. I hate that they're right."

I felt him leave the bed and walk away.

"Who's *they*?" My throat was so dry my voice was unrecognizable. My head remained on the mattress, my matted hair covering my face, but it was enough to stall Landon's exit.

"Dad. Some of the other older pack members." Landon gave a dramatic sigh. "The Pack Council, you know, the usual."

I did *not* know, and he was telling me. Telling me his father had the backing of the Pack Council. This was so much more than the loss of Cannon, and I thought...perhaps Landon was as trapped as I was.

"I'm thirsty." The wobble in my voice was more than a lack of hydration—true fear gripped me.

Landon moved back to the bed where I lay unmoving. Once more, his hand stroked my hair. "I'll get you some water," he told me gently, "if you stop this silliness and show me that you can behave."

For the first time in days, my stomach churned, and I feared I would vomit.

"Can you do that, Kezia? Can you behave?"

"I don't know." It was the most honest answer I'd ever given. But it seemed it was the right one as I heard a huff that was too far to be Landon.

"She's broken?"

Landon's fingers dug into my hair, and I tried not to wince. "Not yet, she's smart," he spoke in a low voice. "Give me time. She'll see reason."

Footsteps approached and I curled into a tighter ball. Bale stood over me. "She stinks."

"Well, Dad, you won't allow me to wash her."

The sigh was long and loud. "Don't let a pretty face and a warm cunt fool you." A touch that was not Landon's ran over my hip, and I shrank from the unfamiliar hand. "She's poison, like her mother."

Landon's voice was calm and even as he spoke. "You've known Kezia since she was brought into this pack," he told him reasonably. "She's rebellious, but after this, she will understand, Dad. Trust me. This is the best plan. You said it yourself."

"You're letting sentimentality rule you," Bale grunted in disappointment.

"Am I?" It was Landon's turn to snort. "I coerced her to leave that fucker, Cannon. I got her here. She's been chained to a wall with silver for three weeks. My sister is under lock and key too. Have I not done everything you have asked of me, Dad?" A sigh of disappointment followed. "Why do I still need to prove myself to you?"

"Because you still cling to this whore. She humiliated you."

Landon withdrew his hand from my hair. "He was her mate. She had little choice."

"And now he's dead."

Pain stabbed at my abdomen.

"And now he's dead," Landon spoke with a coolness that was chilling. "Kezia will remember that being *my* mate is what she wanted all along."

There was a long silence, and I hardly dared to breathe. Landon's words contrasted with his actions. Bale filled me with fear, and I could practically feel his hate surrounding me.

"Wash her. Feed her. Fuck her—see if it gets her out of your system. Then we'll talk."

"I'll wait to have sex, Dad," Landon said with a laugh that

17

caused my churning stomach to roil once more. "I like a little participation, not an almost dead half corpse."

Bale sniffed loudly. "Keep the cuffs on. If she's no use, give her to the men. They're strung tight waiting for the retaliation. She'll give them some relief."

Lurching to the side of the bed, I threw up all over the floor.

"Fuck!" Bale yelled. "Get the bitch washed and this room cleaned. She's a disgrace to this pack."

His footsteps faded, and when they were gone, Landon crouched beside me. Lifting my head, he forced my eyes open to look at him. His concern was genuine, but his voice was hard and brutal.

"You heard your pack leader! Get this shithole cleaned up," he yelled to the corner of the room where the red light blinked incessantly. "You can't run yet," he murmured in my ear as he lifted me as if I weighed nothing. "Let's get you cleaned up."

I never saw who came into the room, scared it would be a pack member I knew and liked. I couldn't handle any more betrayal. Landon seemed to know that and skillfully kept my head turned into his chest. The cuffs fell from my wrists, and I gasped with relief.

"Don't fight me," he whispered. "I need you to act the part of broken."

Act? I wish I were acting. I *was* broken. My heart was shattered, and my soul ripped open. Cannon was dead. My mate was gone, and I knew I had to fight. I knew I had to get to my brother. Hell, even Cass. But it was as if knowing Cannon was gone meant I was gone too.

Landon carried me down stairs that led to rooms that I didn't recognize the scent of.

"We're not in town." He kept his voice so low I had to

strain to hear him. "There's a whole other level of fucked up you're going to have to learn." His grip tightened. "Try to trust me." My body jerked at the thought, and he let out a soothing sound. "I know, I know, it'll come back. I hope."

He lowered me to my feet, and I staggered. Landon caught me in his strong grip. For the first time in days, I looked at him properly, and had I not been a shell of myself, I would have hidden my reaction better.

His blond hair was dull and uncared for. His once golden skin was pale and ashen, and his normally bright blue eyes that sparkled with mischief were dull and lifeless.

"Landon?" Instinctively, I reached for him.

He grabbed my hand like it was a lifeline, pulling me to him. "There's cameras everywhere. They're always watching. You need to play the part."

He stepped back, his voice firmer, his face stern. "Strip."

"Fuck you." It was automatic, but Landon looked almost relieved.

"We'll get to that," he said with a wink that held none of his usual humor. "Right now, you stink, like so bad, Kez. Let's get you washed."

Breaking his stare, I saw we were in the washrooms. I'd never seen this place in my life. Concrete block walls, several simple showerheads, and an open drain in the center of the room. There were no stalls. It was completely open.

"Strip," Landon commanded one more time. He was angled in such a way his back was to the camera, but I wasn't. Landon let out a sigh. "We're shifters, Kez. Get naked. I've seen it all before."

He had. There was no issue, usually, with being naked between shifting to wolf and back, but it wasn't the same as being vulnerable in a shower block with someone you thought you knew, in a pack you knew you would never belong to but wouldn't have thought they'd turn on you so completely.

"I have no problem taking your clothes off," Landon warned, his eyes flicking to the side to remind me of the cameras.

As if I could forget.

Footsteps made me back up, and I saw Landon frown as he turned to the newcomer. A male I didn't know and had never seen before walked in with a wide grin.

"She putting on a show or what?"

Landon laughed. "She's putting on a show of defiance," he said with amusement. He looked back at me, his tone light as he spoke, but his eyes were pleading. "I'm letting her have her moment of rebellion," he said with another good-natured laugh.

The newcomer walked closer. "She's too thin for my tastes." He came closer. "I like something to grab onto."

He reached for me, and Landon had his arm twisted up behind his back. His other arm was around his throat. "Let me make this very fucking clear, because you're new. You don't touch my fucking mate. *Ever.* Unless you want me to remove your head from your shoulders."

The stranger tapped Landon's forearm. Landon glanced at me once, and I saw his reluctance to let the male go, but he did. He stepped away as the stranger rubbed his throat.

"No touching," the stranger said with a laugh. "Got it." He looked me over. "I can watch though, right?"

Landon's smile was brittle. "Make yourself comfortable."

I had no time to process as my once best friend stepped into my space. He refused to look at me as he quickly and efficiently stripped me of my shirt and leggings. Cold water hit my skin, and I jerked forward, and in doing so, Landon was able to reach around me and unclip my bra.

"Looks like she's more eager than she lets on," the stranger said.

"Aren't they all?" Landon pretended to be easy and casual, but I noticed that he avoided looking at me or at my body. "Under you go." A gentle push, and I stepped back under the lukewarm water.

Waking up in the back of Bullet's truck hadn't made me feel as vulnerable or as exposed as this. Tears of helplessness welled, and I tipped my head back under the spray to hide their fall. A warm hand grazed my hip, and my eyes flew open to see Landon semi-naked in front of me.

"I'll help."

My instinct was to push him away, but the stranger moved, and I realized, in his way, that Landon was covering me with his body. Shielding me under the pretense of being intimate with me.

"What's real?" I whispered as he began to use the soap to lather his hands.

"Me." Then louder, he spoke with easy familiarity. "Never smelled a shifter smell like a wet dog before." His joke caused the stranger to laugh. That's how he washed me. Making jokes and laughing with a stranger as he helped me get clean. Landon was clever though, so much smarter than I ever thought. He never touched me intimately, only on my arms and back. He helped lather my hair, and slowly, so slowly, I began to trust him.

No matter what he said or how he acted in front of this stranger, his touch was gentle and respectful. Or as respectful as someone could be in these circumstances. He wrapped me in a towel before he stood back and wiped himself dry quickly with another.

I saw the warning look in his eye as he once more stepped in front of me, his lips brushing mine gently. "Good girl, Kezia. Let's get you back to bed."

I ignored the stranger's lewd comments because Landon was already scooping me into his arms and carrying me back through this strange compound.

His father blocked the way to the stairs. He was leaning against the wall, an apple half-eaten in his hand. "Did she bite?"

"She's not an animal, Dad."

Bale scoffed as he took another bite of his apple. "Now what?"

Landon stiffened but tried to hide it, and perhaps had he not been holding onto me, I may not have noticed it. "I thought a change of scenery might help."

"She's not going into the pack."

"Duh." If I had been watching him, I knew he would have been rolling his eyes. "My room. I meant my room."

Bale looked speculative. "You think because she lets you hold her, wash her, shield her..." Okay, so he had been watching. That creeped me out more than the stranger in the washroom. "You think she's compliant?"

"Or maybe I'm exhausted," I spoke quietly, feeling Landon's grip get tighter. "Maybe I'm tired and lost. Maybe the fact I don't know why you're doing this, why my pack leader beat me, said such ugly things to me. Hurt me. Maybe it's taking a long time to process that I don't know why any of this is happening to me."

Bale watched me, his eyes narrowed, but I dropped my stare as a good pack member would. I had to be careful.

For me.

For my brother and Cass.

For Landon.

"War makes us all unpredictable, Kezia," Landon said.

"War?" I dared look up, but the pack leader's attention was on his son.

"It's not for you to worry about," Landon soothed me. "Can I take her to my room, Dad? I'll keep her chained."

He would?

"Fine." Bale waved him away with a careless shrug. "Keep your trophy. One ounce of trouble from her, she's gone. Understand?"

"Of course." Landon dipped his head in acknowledgment.

"Of course," Bale sneered mockingly. "Remember I'm watching."

He walked past us, his shoulder knocking into his son's like he was an enemy.

"Even you?" I whispered. Bale was watching his son also?

"Yeah," Landon grunted and slowly climbed the stairs. "Especially me."

CHAPTER 3

Kezia

LANDON LET ME GO ONCE I WAS IN HIS ROOM. I SAID nothing when I saw the chain nailed to the wall, the glint of the metal too shiny to be anything but silver. Wordlessly, Landon attached my left wrist to the wall and made a show of how long the chain was, as if the length of the chain mattered when it still gave me no freedom. His room was not much bigger than the one I had been in. His bed was wider, his blankets clean and fresh. He had a chair in the corner of the room, and when he told me to sit on the bed, I took the chair.

Landon didn't make a comment on my small act of defiance, and I felt it was for the best. I feared that if I started screaming and demanding to know what the *hell* was going on, I would never stop. Maybe he knew that too, which is why he didn't say anything.

He left me in his room. Sitting in the chair, chained to the wall, with only the small red light in the corner of the room for company—again. The fact he had a camera watching him in his room was enough to curb my anger towards Landon.

I mean, was he dick? Absolutely.

Would I punch the shit out of him when I was free? I could guarantee it.

Was he in over his head as much as I was? Perhaps he was.

And I didn't know what to do with that.

He'd taken me. Tricked me into leaving Cannon. Landon had been so vile and toxic that day in the study, I'd believed he was the worst thing I was facing. If he'd told me... I wiped tears away as I thought about the last time I saw my alpha. If Landon had been *honest*, Cannon would have helped him. I know he would.

We would have done it together.

And maybe...just maybe, Cannon would be alive.

The tears fell freely as I slowly retreated into my misery. This is how Landon found me hours later, curled in a ball in the seat, worn out.

"Kez," he sighed, stooping to pick me up. Carrying me a few feet to the bed, he placed me gently on top of the covers. "What can I get you?" he asked gently, stroking my hair back from my face.

"My brother."

His smile was pained as he watched me. "You know I can't." Landon gave a half shrug. "Kris has not cooperated well."

"Is he hurt?"

He looked insulted that I'd asked. "No! Luna, Kez, it's Kris! He's with Cass." Landon appeared relaxed as he leaned backward. "They're mates, remember?"

"For how much longer?"

Landon didn't meet my eye when he answered. "For now."

I didn't think I could cry anymore, but the tears spilled over. "You're going to kill him?"

"No." He didn't sound convinced, and truthfully, I wouldn't have believed him anyway.

Not for this.

His father, Bale, had shown unrivaled hate when he struck me; how would he be different toward Kris? Kris was an alpha, whereas Bale wasn't. Kris, my father's son, was mated to Bale's daughter. It must have been the final thing to make Bale snap. I had no other reason for his behavior. It was so contrary to everything I knew about him. Sure, he was a dick at times, and he had forbidden my shift until I was fourteen, but I'd never thought he would be *this*.

"Where are we?"

"Not far from the pack," Landon answered easily. "If you'd gotten off that chair, you could have looked out the window."

"I could do a lot of things." Turning onto my side, I stared at the closed door. "The door's a sham like everything else."

I felt Landon move on the bed, no doubt looking at the door as I faced it. "What makes you think that?"

"It gives the illusion of privacy, but what is the point when the camera sees it all anyway?"

Strangely, I felt his reaction, and despite his attempt to hide it, the small jerk of his body as he caught himself from turning to look at the camera told me more than he intended.

Landon never knew his camera was switched on.

"Do you want food?" he asked me as he got off the bed.

"No."

"Kezia, you need to eat, babe."

"Don't call me babe. I told you that before." Closing my eyes, I wished for sleep. An escape from the nightmare I was living. "I'll eat when I'm hungry."

I heard his sigh, but wisely, Landon said nothing, and

moments later, he left me in the room again. For hours, I lay on the bed and watched the door, the faint glow of the camera in the corner watching me.

Where are you? Moonstar? Where are you? I need you...

Silence was my answer.

The slow burning on my wrist reminded me that I was contained far more effectively than simply chained to the wall. The silver wouldn't allow me to shift. It also kept Moonstar subdued but not contained.

I was weak. For weeks, I had let my grief consume me, I hadn't eaten, and my strength was gone. What chance had I left myself to escape? Cannon would be furious with me for lying down and accepting what had been done to me.

A cramp in my lower belly caused me some discomfort, and I knew my mind was listening to my body now. That *I* was listening to my body. I needed to eat.

Landon needed me to play along. For me. For Kris. For Cass. For his mom. His family needed me as much as I needed my brother.

Needed me? What did he think I could do? I was just...*me*. If I had the strength, I could fight, but I couldn't rely on Moonstar. Even though I had called for her, I had little doubt that my *passenger* wouldn't take my form and save only herself.

Or was I being too harsh?

I wished Cannon was here. Or the shaman.

The shaman. Where the hell was the shaman?

There was no way he related to this, I knew that. I hoped that. I had to have hope.

And I needed answers.

I lay awake, anticipating Landon's return, and the subtle movement of the bed made me realize he had joined me while I was asleep. I felt him curl his body around me, spooning me, and I forced myself not to react.

"What time is it?"

I felt his start of surprise. "Too late for you to be awake."

His fingers tangled in my hair before smoothing out to glide his hand over my hair. It was a new habit he seemed to have developed, and I hated it. Moving away from him, I felt his hand fall to the thin mattress. "Don't do that." My voice was barely a whisper.

I expected him to listen; I didn't expect Landon to pull me into his body or for his hot breath to be on my neck. "Fight me, but not too much," he breathed into my ear. When his hand moved under the shirt I was wearing, I reared off the bed, my legs shaky as I spun to confront him, my fists raised.

"I said don't fucking touch me," I snarled at him in the semi-darkness.

Light flooded the room, and I squinted at the sudden brightness. Landon moved from the door where the light switch was and walked around the side of the bed until he was in front of me. Even with my nerves strung tight and my body prepared for the unexpected, I still saw the familiar gleam in his eyes as he watched me. I also noted he stood with his back to the camera.

With easy insolence, Landon crossed his arms across his chest. "Kez," he said with firm disapproval. "Why are you being like this?"

I almost lowered my hands in shock. "What?" I gaped at him and was pretty sure my mouth was hanging open. "Are you joking?"

He gave a half shrug. "Look, I get it, you liked the alpha

28

bastard's dick. But he's gone. You're here. I'm here. We've fooled around before."

My tongue was stuck to the roof of my mouth as he casually spouted lies. My eyes flicked to the camera once. Landon followed the movement and grinned.

"Ah, you're worried my dad didn't know about you and me?" His eyes held a warning that I wasn't sure I was reading properly. "He knows. I mean, I told the whole pack you're my mate, babe. Stop this. It's silly and you're fooling no one."

"I was with Can—I was with the alpha of Blackridge." I swallowed hard past the tears that threatened, the thought of saying his name too much for me.

"Yes, and like I said when I came and got you, that's over. It was time for you to come home." Landon looked me up and down. "I *am* your mate, Kez, it's *my* children you will have, and it's *my* son who will be an alpha."

"Son? Alpha?"

Landon looked me over critically. "You'll need a few more pounds on first. You're practically scrawny." He walked around me, and although I flinched from his touch when his hand cupped my ass, he didn't stop until he was in front of me. "When you're healthy, which won't take long, not the way you eat, Dad has said if you continue to be no trouble, we can mate."

"Fuck off."

Landon took a step forward, his thumb pressed against my bottom lip. "Lose the attitude, or lose the right to be my mate. Which is it?" When I went to speak, he spoke over me. "It's always been me and you, Kez. Sure, I've fucked around, you've fucked around, but it's me and you, *babe*." Hard blue eyes watched me. He'd angled himself to give his side profile to the camera. When I didn't answer, because I couldn't answer, he rolled his eyes. "I mean, I didn't fuck a human—"

"Neither did I!"

Landon moved into my space, his hand around my throat, and it was so similar to the day in Cannon's study, that I froze at the similarity. "Your human friend wasn't quiet when he boasted about parting those thighs, Kez, so be very careful what you choose to lie to me about."

Did he know about Vance? Searching his eyes, I forced myself not to look past him to the camera. "I've never slept with a human," I said carefully, hating how vulnerable I sounded. "I kissed one. Once."

Landon snorted and made a big show of turning away from me. "A human? A filthy human? And yet you reject *me*?"

"I've never rejected you!" I blurted and stumbled back at how quickly he turned around, looming over me. I froze as he pressed his lips to mine.

"See, Kez," he said when he drew back. "This can just be a stumble in our road. We're meant to be together."

I almost told him he was batshit crazy, but I felt the small nip at my hip as Landon pinched my side before he stepped back.

"I need more time." I licked my lips as I watched him, trying to rid the taste of him. "After everything, I still don't know what's happening. I need time...to come to terms with this."

It wasn't a lie. I would need time. Hell, I'd need eternity.

"How much time?"

"I'm not a machine," I snapped more testily than I intended. I felt a surge of relief when I saw his lips twitch, but I forced myself not to react to him. "I need time."

"Fine."

"And my brother."

Landon cocked his head and shook it slowly. "You were doing so well, Kez. Time to grieve? I get it. Time to adjust to the new pack life? Fine, I can give you that. But you don't make demands of me, understand?"

This was the same character he had played in Cannon's study. Once more, I was reeling, not sure who I was seeing in front of me. The character Landon the Asshole or my friend Landon? I shouldn't push it until I knew which one was the real one.

Good mature advice, I told myself.

"He's my brother." I was also shit at taking advice.

Landon let out a long sigh and flicked the light switch off. "Get in bed. I need to sleep."

I stayed on the spot until I was lifted off my feet and dropped onto the bed. "You weigh nothing," he grumbled as I felt the bed dip. "Three weeks of starving yourself has not made you attractive, babe."

My foot connected with his shin at the same time as my fist dug into his gut. I heard Landon's *oomph*, but I realized a moment later it was laughter.

"You hit like a newborn pup." Pulling me across the mattress, Landon curled me into the shape of his body, spooning me, careful never to touch the chain or cuff of silver at my wrist. "Kiss goodnight?"

"Fuck off."

Landon laughed loudly, tugging me closer. "Go to sleep."

Lying stiff and unresponsive in his arms, I almost sobbed with relief when I felt his lips at my ear. "That was good, Kez. Stay strong for them."

I don't think either of us slept. I was too alert, my body

31

wired for anything else fucked up to happen to me. I knew from his breathing that Landon was awake too, but neither of us acknowledged the other, and I hoped whoever was watching was fooled. At some point during the few hours that we lay there, Landon moved onto his back, and I curled tighter into a ball, relieved not to be touching him anymore.

When the first rays of morning shone through the window, Landon rolled out of bed and stretched. He let me pretend to be asleep as he slipped out of the room, and only when he was gone, the door closed and the sound of a key turning, did I succumb to a fitful sleep.

He was back in the room when I woke, and watched me avidly as I sat in the chair and ate the broth he had brought with him. If what he said was correct, he wanted out of this situation as much as I did, and to do that, he needed me strong. So, I ate. The soup felt heavy and greasy in my belly, but I kept eating, and having known the male in front of me for so long, I recognized it when the tension left his shoulders.

"Where's the shaman?" I asked when the soup was finished.

Landon looked surprised that I asked. "With the pack, where he always is."

He was still here? Alive?

"Do I get to see him?" I asked tentatively, scraping the spoon along the bottom of my bowl, making Landon wince.

Landon shook his head, watching me with more attention. "Not yet."

I nodded, placing my bowl on the floor. Straightening, I smoothed my hands over my bare legs. "I have herbs I take..."

"That suppresses your heat." Landon sat back on the bed, completely at ease, his elbows propping him up as he held my gaze while I sat across from him. "You won't need them with me."

The soup turned sour in my belly. A reminder that I had only needed them to keep me and Cannon from completing the bond. With my first full heat passed, the others wouldn't be as intense, not without my mate near me. Pain clutched at my heart, and I forced myself not to cry.

"Everyone in this pack knows you do not touch what is mine," he added, interrupting my thoughts. "Next time your heat comes, we'll lock the door and come out when it's over, and your belly will be full of my kid." He winked at me, and I resisted the urge to swipe the bowl from the floor and smash his face with it.

Landon stood smoothly, bending to scoop the bowl from the floor, almost as if he could read my mind. "You did well," he said, pressing his lips to my forehead. "This is real progress, Kez." Walking to the door, he looked over his shoulder at me, his smile wide. "Dad will be pleased."

He left me with the stark reminder that we were never alone. Despite my best efforts not to, I stared at the camera in the corner. I wasn't Landon. I had never been good at acting, but he and his sister excelled at it. I would know, I'd been their best friend.

What did I used to do when they were both putting on a show to get what they wanted? I played along, by *not* playing along. Mainly because I was shit at hiding my reaction. Hoping that Landon was performing for someone other than me, and only I knew he was acting, I tried my best to be who I used to be in this pack.

Landon had a small bathroom adjoined to his room, and I walked to it, still not sure there wasn't a camera in there too.

After washing my face, brushing my teeth, and using the toilet, I walked back into the room, the tightness of the silver chain lessening as I walked back.

On the bed, I examined the chain. The links rubbed against my wrist when I examined their strength with my other hand, hissing in pain as the silver burned my tender flesh.

Curling into a ball, I gave the camera my back. Stretching my arm out in front of me, I studied the links.

Moonstar?

Tears slid down my cheeks as I felt the emptiness within me.

Moonstar, please?

Silence answered.

A while later when Landon disturbed my sleep by pulling me into his body, I felt more than his presence.

Child?

CHAPTER 4
Kezia

W<small>HEN</small> I <small>WAS SURE THAT</small> L<small>ANDON WAS ASLEEP</small>, I cautiously got out of bed and made my way to the bathroom, maneuvering the chain under the door and cursing inwardly when it didn't fit. I closed the bathroom door as much as I could with such care that it only caused my anxiety to peek. The click of the chain against the wood sounded like a crack of thunder in the quiet of the room, and I held my breath as I waited for Landon to wake and ask me if I was okay.

No, dickhead. I would *never* be okay again.

Moonstar?

She answered instantly. *The silver burns.*

Her voice was faint, but it didn't matter. A relief so intense washed over me, and I slipped down the wall as my knees gave way. Pulling my knees to my chest, I rested against the wall as I fought to control my emotions. All I needed was to start sobbing again.

Child?

I'm here. Licking my lips, I wasn't sure how to do this. This was one of the first times I had spoken to her knowing she wasn't just my wolf spirit.

She was *just* a spirit.

A shudder ran through me, and I pushed that thought aside. I needed to deal with the things I *could* control. Like Moonstar. Because I was so good at controlling her...

I snorted so loud in the quiet of the night, that I froze once more, terrified that Landon would wake at any moment.

Where have you been? It was a stupid question really and merely highlighted to me how messed up I was. Where had she been? Nowhere. If she could leave me, then I had no doubt she would be gone.

The alpha, his Will is strong. The sleep we enter is deep.

I could hear her resentment. Yeah, she wasn't a fan of Cannon. *They killed him.*

I felt her presence a little more, and I braced myself for her joy at my mate's death.

The alpha? Is dead?

She sounded confused, and despite myself, I felt the tears spill over once more. I couldn't say it again, so I nodded.

What makes you think he is dead?

It wasn't what I was expecting, and I was stumped on an answer for a moment. *Landon told me that they killed him.*

Moonstar was silent, and the more I listened to her silence, the more I realized I knew she was thinking. Had I ever known it this clearly before? I could feel her weighing her words before she spoke.

Why would you believe this?

What?

Why would you think he was dead?

Frowning, I looked inward to where my wolf lay, amber eyes watching me. *Because if Cannon were alive, I wouldn't be here, chained to a wall. And every one of these fuckers would be dead.*

The wolf's head tilted to the side as she considered me. *Can you not feel him?*

Bitterness swelled within me. *You don't need to hammer it home. You didn't like him. He's gone, don't be cruel.*

I think she rolled her eyes at me.

You are older to know better.

Something I hadn't felt in days surged within me. Hope. *Moonstar? Are you saying...? Is he?*

Your alpha lives.

I was on my feet so quickly I made myself dizzy. *Are you sure?*

She gave a huff, resting her head back on her paws. *You are mates. If he dies, your agony would be more than a throbbing in the arm, child. That kind of pain would have brought me back a lot sooner.*

He was alive? Oh my Luna, he was *alive*?

I need to get to him!

Moonstar yawned and then jerked her head towards my wrist. *Get it off.*

I don't know how. It burns to touch.

I felt her presence even stronger as she lifted my arm to inspect my wrist. *No burn marks on the flesh. It only feels like it burns.*

Still reeling from the fact Cannon may be alive and the fact that I just felt my body be used by my *passenger* for the first time, it took me longer than it should have to hear what she said.

37

What does that mean? It's not silver?

It is. We feel it binding. It should mark the flesh. You only bleed.

Only? Inspecting my wrist much like Moonstar had done, I saw only redness, some scabbing, but mostly open welts and blood. *It hurts.*

We have felt worse.

A memory of Cannon shooting me resurfaced. I could see how guilty yet determined he looked as he watched me when I cursed him out for using me as an experiment. Being shot was unlike anything I had ever felt. Wrong. It was unlike anything *I* remembered. My *passenger* had felt a lot more.

Can you break it?

We are weak. The wolf stood, shaking her head as she did as if she had just woken up, and from the sound of it, she had. *We need to eat. Hunt.*

We're chained to a wall, I reminded her. *Bale has cameras everywhere. He is watching me.* I thought of Landon. *He is watching Landon too.*

Moonstar considered me. Had she always looked at me like that? Like I was annoying her?

What is it? I asked.

Which male has the key?

It was an excellent question. One I should have known the answer to. *I don't know.*

She gave me a side-eye with such an attitude I genuinely didn't know how I ever thought she was my wolf. She was so clearly her own person. Was she a person?

Focus.

Startled, I met her heavy gaze.

Now is not the time for these questions.

"Sorry."

I see how you were tricked, she told me with another huff. *You should have called for us.*

I did call for you! You didn't answer.

You called for me? How many times?

Twice.

Only twice, child?

I was ashamed to admit it, but she looked at me with such knowing, I knew she already knew why I had only called for her twice. Cannon had told me his thoughts about the inner spirit who hitchhiked in my body, and in truth, I was scared of her.

Admitting it to myself, I looked up to meet her steady gaze. *I don't want to lose myself.*

You are always with me, child.

A sliver of fear trickled down my spine. I didn't want to be *with* her, I wanted to *be*. Just me.

You need us.

I did. I wasn't strong enough to break free on my own. I wasn't clever enough to fool Bale. Moonstar had broken free from the cell before. She had almost bested Cannon, and it was only his Will that was able to control her. Bale would not hold that power over her.

I would have given her control there and then, but I remembered being shot. Bale may have no alpha Will, but he had silver. Lots of it, and being captured and held here, I knew he wasn't afraid to use it either.

He will shoot us with silver.

Moonstar paced in my mind, and once again, I was struck by how blind I had been to the obvious fact that this was no ordinary wolf.

Get us free of this. As soon as we are free, no wolf will be able to catch us.

Her words caused more than a shiver of fear this time. *And we go back to Blackridge Peak?*

Get us free of the binding, child.

The wolf closed her eyes, and I felt her fade. On shaky feet, I stood in the bathroom, going over everything that she said. I was scared. I knew if I gave Moonstar control, I may never get it back. An hour ago, that would have been doable.

Now?

Now that she had told me that Cannon could still be alive, I had no desire to lose myself. More than ever, I needed out of this place. Studying the cuff on my wrist, I wrapped a towel around my hand and tried to push the cuff over my wrist.

The pain brought me to my knees. Fighting back tears, I pushed again, my mouth opening in a silent scream. Nausea churned in my belly as I gave another shove of the cuff, wincing in new pain as I saw my flesh break open and bleed as I tried to force the band over my hand.

My stomach churned again, and I heaved into the toilet. Gagging, I felt Landon's cool hands on my shoulders when he swept my hair back.

"Hey, you okay?" he asked, and I heard his genuine concern.

"Yeah." Straightening, I wiped my mouth on the towel, seeing the bloodstains from my hand and hoping he hadn't. No such luck.

"Kez!" Landon hissed, grabbing my arm and looking at my bleeding mess of a wrist. "Did you try to take this off?" he whispered furiously.

"Would you be more surprised if I hadn't?" I snapped, clambering to my feet.

"We're being watched." Landon was seething, his words no louder than a murmur, but his fury was so loud he may as well have been shouting.

"I tripped."

Landon's scowl matched his temper. "I'm not fucking stupid, and neither is anyone else here." His look was meaningful, but I was pissed off.

"What do you want from me?" Turning on the faucet, I rinsed my mouth and tried to clean up my wrist. He was right to be freaked out; there was no hiding what I had tried to do. With the silver slowing my healing process, there was no way this would escape Bale's notice.

"I want you to remember what the fuck we're trying to do," he hissed in my ear. Throwing his hands in the air, he spoke louder. "I want you to be my mate. Like we thought we would be." Seeing my skeptical scowl, he made a carry-on gesture, and I knew he was telling me to go with it. "I thought you wanted this as much as I did. We spoke about it enough when we were younger."

Bullshit.

Swallowing my temper, I tried to relieve the tension in my shoulders by rolling my head from side to side as I forced myself to pretend his lies were real. "We were children."

Landon let out a relieved sigh, quickly masking it to sound like exasperation. "Children? We were seventeen."

I almost told him I was four years older than him, but I didn't want Bale to know I knew his murderous secret. "A lot changed." Passing him, I dragged my chain behind me, sitting in the seat across from the bed.

"Did it?"

Holding up my wrist, I gave him a mocking look. "Well, you never used to cuff me to walls, so I'm saying, yeah, it did."

"I thought you wouldn't mind a little light bondage." Landon's smirk was wicked—and so achingly familiar to how we used to be, it hit me like a blow.

Pointing at the cuff, I leveled him with a flat glare. "I'm all explored out."

"You need to behave," he scolded with an easy smile, lying back down on the bed. "Trying to take the cuff off gives the wrong signal, know what I mean?"

"How can I be your mate if you want to keep me cuffed to the wall?" Tilting my head, I ignored the camera in the corner. "Mates mean trust. Any relationship is built on trust."

"We'll get there," he said with confidence. I watched him as he settled into a comfier position, his hands resting behind his head as he stared at the ceiling. "You need more time."

"I do? Or you do?"

Turning to look at me, Landon watched me with a seriousness I didn't expect. "Maybe we both do?" he admitted. "Things aren't how I thought they would be. We both need to adapt to the new ways."

Picking at a scab on my wrist, I kept my eyes lowered as I spoke. "You never knew any of this?" I gestured to the room. "You didn't know about this place?"

"No. I wasn't ready." His voice was soft, gentle, like he was confiding in a friend. "Dad's been so smart, keeping this a secret. It's impressive."

The secret? Silver? Or the hidden bunker full of soldiers?

"Kind of scary." Lifting my head, I spoke clearly. "I don't understand why it has to be hidden. We have security at the pack. Why do we need this?"

Landon's cheeks puffed out before he expelled a loud breath. "I could tell you, but then I'd need to kill you."

With a huff, I returned to picking at my scab. I heard him move on the bed, and then his hands were pulling mine from my wrist.

"I'll tell you everything you need to ever know," he promised as he led me to the bed, "soon."

"Tell me one thing?" I asked as I got onto the bed and only resisted slightly when he tugged me into his body.

"About eight inches."

It took a moment before I realized what he meant, and then despite myself, I smiled, my elbow digging into his ribs. "Don't be a dick."

Landon laughed loudly, turning me in his arms and curling around me, which seemed to be his favorite position. "Good to see you laughing, babe."

My smile dimmed in the semi-darkness of the room. "Not had much to laugh about."

I felt him playing with the ends of my hair. "I'll change that. Soon."

"You keep saying soon—how soon?"

"When you stop trying to hack your hand off trying to remove the cuff," he snapped angrily, and I hoped he was once more playing for the camera.

We lay in silence for a few minutes before I spoke again. "Can I ask my question?"

"Sure." His dramatic sigh almost made me smile again.

"Who killed Cannon?"

Landon's body went still behind me. I think he may have stopped breathing. "You don't need to know."

"Maybe not," I told him while screaming internally that I

absolutely *did* deserve to know. "I want to know."

"You won't like the answer."

Half turning in the bed to look at him over my shoulder, I hoped he could see my glare. "*Tell* me."

Landon sighed as he turned away, and I almost pulled him back to look at me until his words caused my heart to stop.

"Who killed the alpha?" Landon asked, his voice low and uneven. "You did."

CHAPTER 5

Kezia

"Me?" I couldn't move my limbs. I couldn't reach out and grab him and haul his face in front of me and demand he say it again. I couldn't do anything. Stunned, I lay immobile as Landon shifted on the bed to face me.

"Told you that you wouldn't like it."

"You're lying."

I heard his snort. "I've never lied to you, babe, you know that."

"Why would you say this? It's not true." Finally, my brain connected with my body, and I pushed myself up. "You think I killed him?"

"Not physically." Landon yawned. "But was it because of you that he died? Yes." Grief gripped my throat, and I wasn't able to speak. Landon either didn't notice or was still playing for his audience. "You made him vulnerable." He gave a half chuckle as he stretched out on the bed. "It seems the alpha was so busy screwing you he forgot to watch his back." Landon yawned again. "Dad says thanks for that by the way."

No, this wasn't real. He was lying, he *had* to be lying. My heart was racing too fast in my chest. I couldn't get breath. I didn't make Cannon vulnerable. Was this another of Landon's acts I had to play along with? I tried to focus. "He says thanks by chaining me with silver?"

"Ahh, your good friend sarcasm is back." Landon reached over and squeezed my hip. "You're getting better."

"Stop touching me."

"For fuck's sake, Kez, I'm hardly licking you out while you sleep. You're no virgin, stop acting like one."

The sound of my fist connecting with his jaw was music to my ears. In seconds, we were full-on fighting, kicking and biting, until Landon was on top of me, straddling my chest, my hands pinned over my head, and I could feel his hot breath on my cheek as I turned my head away. The room was still dark, but wolf sight meant we could see each other better than I would have liked.

"Hey, baby." Landon grinned down at me. "While I love that your fight has returned, let's keep the tangling between the sheets to more pleasant things." Dipping his head, he kissed the corner of my mouth. "Play along," he whispered.

"I'm grieving!" I snarled.

With an exaggerated sigh, Landon rolled off of me and flopped onto his back. "You hardly knew this guy. He's dead. Move on already. I've been your best friend for years."

Friend. Not this. Never this.

Landon rolled onto his side, propping his head onto his hand as he loomed over me. "Remember the day we fought in Dad's training room and they caught us?" he asked with a small smile. "You think you can lie to me that you weren't checking me out?" Once more, his head dipped, and I felt his lips brush my cheek. "This was always the plan for us, Kez. You know it as well as I do."

Only I didn't, and as I stared up at him, I wasn't sure if this was another part of the act. I remembered Cannon telling Bale in the cells the day I went into heat for the first time, that they had to knock Landon out twice. Before any of this happened, he had tried to get to me on the day of my heat. When I returned to the pack, he was keen to start something with me.

As he leaned over me, that small cocky smile playing about his lips, I suddenly wondered who Landon was acting for.

His father? Or me?

Drawing in a shuddering breath, I moved onto my side, my back to him as I closed my eyes tight. "I'm tired."

His hand skimmed over my hip with a familiarity I resented. "Me too, we'll talk more later." I felt his lips pressed into my hair, and I willed myself to not turn around and punch him again.

You there?

We are.

Is he lying?

We do not know. We don't trust him.

I caught myself from nodding in agreement.

I don't trust him either. It hurt to admit it to myself, but Landon was proving a very good actor, and I was no longer sure who the performance was for.

Trust no one. Moonstar agreed with me, and that eased my paranoia a little.

When we leave... I hesitated and then surged on as I thought of Cannon. *When we leave, we won't take him with us.*

We never were.

My savage passenger.

For the first time since I had woken up here, I knew I was going to be all right. Moonstar was here, and with her by my side, I would be unstoppable.

Nothing was going to keep me from returning to Cannon.

Nothing.

I fell asleep wrapped in that belief. Although I was only allowed a few hours of sleep, it was undisturbed.

I woke to the sight of Bale staring at me. Pushing myself up into a sitting position, I looked around the room for Landon, but it was just me and the pack leader.

"Pack Leader Bale." Tugging the sheet over myself, I tried to appear demure. "Can I help you?"

He sat and watched me in silence until it was so drawn out that it was no longer uncomfortable, it was excruciatingly awkward. Gloves that had been on his knee were pulled on slowly. They weren't latex and he had no need to hide his tracks if he killed me, so why he was pulling on leather gloves was as random as him sitting there.

I eventually snapped. "Bale? Do you want something?"

His slow smile and the way he ran his eyes over my body made me want to hide more of myself, but I willed myself to remain unfazed, even as my heart started racing. Moonstar came forward, and I felt her soothing presence.

He is testing us, child. You must remain calm.

Easy for you to say; he isn't looking at your body like you're a piece of prime rib.

Isn't he?

Now I wasn't sure who I was scared of most. The unhinged pack leader in front of me, or the spirit who wanted her independence within me. Unsure of them both at that moment, I pushed the sheet off me and got out of bed.

"If you're here to stare and be creepy, Pack Leader," I walked towards the bathroom, "you've achieved it. I need to pee." Dragging the chain around the door, I took less care with the door this time as I closed it behind me, conscious that the man who openly hated me sat a few feet away as I forced myself to relax and empty my bladder.

After washing my hands, I stepped back into the bedroom. Bale remained where he had been, and as I had no experience with this kind of thing, I had no idea what to do.

What would Cannon do? Punch him and kick his ass. It was a tempting thought.

"My son is so desperate for a taste of your pussy. I'm surprised he hasn't fucked you yet."

Wow.

"Maybe he respects me too much to force me into something I'm not ready for." I stood across from him, the bed between us, my back to the open door of the bedroom.

Bale's lips twisted into a sneer. "Respects you?"

I matched his sneer. "I know it may be an alien concept for you, but most men like their partners to be willing."

Bale leaned forward, his eyes narrowing into slits. "I see you."

"I'm standing right here."

"I *see* you're as much of a teasing bitch as your whore mother was." He leaned back. "She spread them for anyone as well."

"But not you." I should have stopped myself, but fuck him and fuck that. "Right, Bale? She rejected you each and every time." Cocking my head, I looked him over with disgust. "Desperate, jilted psycho is not a good look for you."

I watched his jaw clench before he looked at me with amusement. "So you know about your mother?"

Why lie, there was no point. "I do. I know you ran her and my father from the Anterrio Pack when she rejected you for the final time. When did you realize Kris and I were her children?"

"Kris? The minute I saw him." He spat on the floor. "You? You took longer."

"Because you never realized the wolf pup you shot was a shifter, did you?"

He scoffed. "No. I thought you were a pet. A stray. Andrea was always collecting fucking strays."

Holy Luna, he just admitted that he killed my parents. I felt the tightness in my chest as the realization that the killer Kris had been looking for, for our murdered parents, had been right in front of him the whole time. Moonstar stood ready and waiting, and it took every shred of willpower not to succumb to her right then.

"Why did you accept us into the pack?" My voice sounded hoarse, even though I wanted to be strong.

Bale shrugged. "A moment of guilt? Kindness?" He broke eye contact for a moment, his eyes on the camera. "A weakness."

"Making up for that now, aren't you?" I raised my hand with the cuff of silver around my wrist. "Is my brother chained like this?" I took a deep breath. "Is Cass?"

Bale surged to his feet in anger. "She carries his young!" he seethed.

Cass was pregnant? I was both happy and terrified at the same time. "You need to let us go."

He laughed, walking around the bed until he was in front of me. "Let you go? I don't have to do jack shit, little girl. I rule these mountains. No one gives a fuck about a white-haired human killer or her mutt brother."

"They care about Cass though," I challenged. "The Pack Council cares about me." It was a risk, and I wasn't sure what made me say it, but I saw the flash of bitterness in his eyes, and I had the wild hope I was right to guess.

"They'll see you're nothing but a whore whose recklessness threatens us all."

"Yet you're the one who killed my parents, you're the one who chains the members of his pack to the wall with silver, and you're the one who killed an alpha. A *true* alpha." Scratching my jaw, I shot a look of loathing towards the pack leader. "Sounds to me like there's only one threat on these mountains, and that's you."

I expected the punch, but it still knocked me off of my feet. As I scrambled to stand, Bale kicked me in the back, and when I was down, I felt his hands on my shoulders and then burning as he wrapped the chain from the wall around my neck.

"Burns, doesn't it?" he hissed in my ear. "What have you got to say for yourself now?" He squeezed tighter, and my fingers clutched at the chain, ignoring the pain in my hands as the silver burned my flesh. "What? No words? You finally quiet, you little bitch?"

Child?

I grappled with the pack leader, trying to get free, but he held me too tight, and the silver made me weak. Tears ran down my cheeks as the pain increased. I couldn't breathe. Spots floated in my eyes, and I knew the fucker was going to kill me today.

Child! We don't have much time!

Screwing my eyes shut, I tried to fight him, because if I gave in to Moonstar, would I ever come back? So many people needed me.

Promise me you'll find out if he lives. If you can...save Cannon. I felt her hesitate. *Moonstar, I will never give you what you want unless you promise me this.*

Bale tightened the chain at my neck, and I felt dizzy. *Moonstar? Promise me.*

If he lives and we can heal him, we will.

"Yeah, you've nothing to say now, do you?" I felt his spittle on my cheek as Bale pulled even tighter on the silver links. "I like this look on you. On your knees, ass pressing into me. Maybe your cunt will feel like hers. Hey? What do you think?"

I felt his hand move over my side, his intent as clear as his words, and my eyes snapped open.

Make it hurt, Moonstar!

The male was nothing for us. He had overpowered the child, but the child was weak. We enjoyed his look of shock when we threw him off us like the annoyance he was. As we rose above him, his look of confusion as it changed to fear also pleased us.

He was right to fear us.

Taking the chain from our neck, we looped it into coils in our hands, watching him as our skin burned from the cursed metal. Crouching, we searched his pocket, our foot on his throat when he tried to move. His strength was not our strength. The key we needed was in his pocket, and when we had it, we unlocked the cuff, the force of our foot grinding his face to the floor.

It was only fitting that the male screamed when we put the chain around his *neck, the links squeezing tight as he struggled for breath. We took his gloves off him and tossed them aside. As the male panted and whimpered at our feet, we went over to the camera and ripped it off the wall. A final hard yank on the chain, and the male lay still.*

We heard the running footsteps and prepared to fight, no time to check if the male was dead. The first one through the door was her friend. The child did not fully trust him, and we trusted him even less, but still, for her, we let him live. She would mourn him and be difficult if we killed him.

The next three males we did not let live.

Walking down the stairs, we took in the surroundings. It was a large log cabin. We could sense more rooms and more people, but they weren't coming for us. Not yet. Knowing we had to be quick, we ran down the corridor, sensing fresh air. We met two more of the males that camped here. We dealt with them.

Outside, we turned to the highest peak and longed to be free. We felt the whimper of the child. She was faint, but she was there.

Running along the side of the cabin, we saw the large doors, chained and bolted, that would lead to underground. We hesitated, and when we felt another pulse from the child, we ran to the doors.

Metal bent like tin when we pulled the chains free. Concrete stairs and a bad smell awaited us behind the doors. Once more, we looked to the high mountains. We desired to be there, not here. Not underground. Quickly we ran down the steps, and the smell and the sound of hearts thumping led us to the two who were kept here.

"Come."

The male was weak, and the woman was almost dead.

"Kezia?" The old male became unnaturally still as he scented the air. "You are Moonstar?"

The woman moaned low on the ground, and we could hear her death rattle. "She will not survive this."

The child would want the male freed. He moved back when we opened the bars with our magic. "There is not much time." *We could sense them coming.* "Shift and run."

We shifted to the wolfskin. The male did not shift, and we saw the silver band on his wrist. Fluidly we shifted back to the human form, pulling the band free from his arm, ignoring the tearing burn on our flesh.

"It does not bind you?" he asked in wonder.

"Shift."

We took the wolfskin one more time. The old one shifted to his wolf, and with a nudge to the she on the floor, he looked up at us. We shook our head. The scent of death was already seeping from her. The male hesitated once more, but our low growl made him move.

We ran. There were ones who would chase us, but we fought them, shielding the old one.

The old one was weak, but his Goddess aided his escape as we ran. Soon we saw the packlands of the alpha. We did not trust the alpha; he used his Will on us, but the child asked this of us.

For the child, we would save him.

CHAPTER 6
Cannon

THE CLAMOR OF RAISED VOICES JOLTED ME FROM MY slumber, though it took my groggy mind longer than I would've liked to register that the angry exchanges had been echoing around me for longer than I realized.

It hurt to move, but still, my stubbornness caused my teeth to grind as I fought the screaming pain that had been a constant presence in my body since the night I was stabbed.

Stabbed by a traitor on the command of the woman I was falling in love with.

"For fuck's sake, Mal, I told you, you open him up again and he'll die. I thought you were a fucking doctor!"

Royce. I recognized my beta's furious tone as I lay there trying to see who he was talking to. *He must be pissed. He only curses like this when he's pissed. Not like him to be pissed at the Doc. They must not have had much success with the last surgery.*

It hurt to lie like this. Which pissed *me* off. Tev stabbed me in the back. Literally. But he left the silver knife in, and as the silver worked its way into my system, it hit my brain stem and basically fucked me up. The magic of Luna fought it, my shifter nature fighting to heal me, but silver didn't give a fuck if I was an alpha or had alpha power. It killed shifters and I was a shifter.

I wonder if it was worth it for her? It was a recurring thought that circled within me whenever I was awake. That Kezia hated me this much, it didn't sit right with me. But I knew what Tev told me, and I had been conscious long enough for Royce to tell me that the pack had received a condolence card from the Anterrio Pack with Kezia's name on it.

My mate. My murderer. It tasted bitter on my tongue, and my heart still refused to believe it.

I did not doubt that I was dying. Doc had done everything he could, and although I could hear my beta arguing *against* any more surgery, I knew Doc would never give up. I appreciated it. I did.

But I was done.

I knew it. Doc knew it, and I knew he did because he wouldn't look at me anymore when he spoke.

The sign of someone unwilling to lie to a dying man's face. I respected that.

Royce had *not* accepted it, but although he knew when enough was enough, he was still willing to put his faith in his Goddess and the magic within us to heal me.

"Nikan?" I asked when their argument trailed off.

The sound of silence filled the room. At least it stopped them arguing, but it also meant my brother was still in more denial than Royce. *Denial* was being kind. Nikan refused to acknowledge any of us. Myself the most. He spent his days and nights skirting the Anterrio Pack intent on grabbing Kezia and...I don't know what he planned to do when he caught her.

Kill her?

Drag her back here and let her see what she had done? I didn't want to see her.

I wanted nothing to do with her. For the little time I had left, I wanted to forget her.

If only she would stop haunting my every waking thought, I could die in peace.

"How are you feeling today?" Royce came into my sight line, and with relief, I was able to turn my head back and stare at the ceiling.

"Still like I've been stabbed with a silver blade." I saw him nod out of the corner of my eye, and I tried to smile.

"We'll find her," he promised. "She *will* pay for this."

"Or she's as much a victim as you are," Doc muttered. I didn't need to look to know Royce was glaring at him. I would be too if I could turn my head again. "There's no sign of her. No one has seen her. Everyone we've asked thinks she's *here*. Stop glaring at me Royce. Before we know for definite that Kezia is against us, let's leave room for doubt."

"He's right."

Huh, I hadn't known Hannah was here. The grunt of pain that left me when I tried to move again caused her to step closer. "Stop it," she admonished gently. "You don't need to look at me to speak." With a cool cloth, she wiped my brow. "But Mal's right. Until we know for certain Kezia was working with Tev and that the Anterrio Pack is rising against us, we need to remember exactly *who* your mate is."

She was right. They both were. But I still remembered the pain of betrayal when the knife went in, and it was nothing to the slice to my heart when Tev said, "Kezia says fuck you."

"Water?" I asked and within seconds, Hannah was placing the straw in my mouth as Doc tipped my head gently, giving me support to drink. I was drinking through a straw. A fucking straw. I managed two sips before another wave of fatigue crashed over me.

"You need to rest, Alpha." Hannah took the straw away, and Doc placed my head back on the pillow.

I wanted to tell her that all I had done for weeks was rest. Honestly, what I needed to do was die and stop being this burden on my pack.

"Let him sleep," Hannah murmured to the others. "The more he rests, the more his body can heal."

Another one in denial.

I could have slept for minutes or hours, but again I was wakened by the shouting in the room. Much louder this time. It startled me awake.

"You fucking touch him, bitch, and I will slice you open."

Nikan. Finally.

"Move, or do you wish the alpha to die?"

That voice. I knew that voice. Kezia? How did she get here? Struggling to move, I felt the crest of pain rise within me.

"Cannon, no," Hannah whispered urgently beside me. She pressed me into the mattress and then swiftly turned her back to me again.

She was protecting my prone body with her own. This was bullshit.

"We can save him."

"Fuck you. You're the reason he's like this."

"You are stupid."

Not Kezia, I realized. Moonstar. *Shit, I really would have preferred Kezia.*

I heard a scuffle, and then the face of my dreams appeared above me. Or were they nightmares? I no longer knew.

Brace yourself, Alpha, this will hurt.

I screamed as white hot pain erupted within me, and then there was only blissful darkness.

THE PAIN EBBED AND FLOWED, leading me through moments of lucidity and others of utter disorientation. It was within every inch of my being, yet remained elusive, shifting like sand through my grasp. At times, my blood seemed to ignite and burn within me, while at others, I felt as desiccated as an ancient husk.

But everywhere, shafts of golden light pierced the darkness. It wasn't sunlight—there was nothing natural about the light that bathed this empty room.

Pain swept over me again, and my muscles clenched tightly as if they were desperately trying to shield me once more from its assault.

You need to be stronger.

I knew her voice. I knew her touch. I knew the imposter that wore my mate's skin.

Let her go. My voice was weak, even in the mindlink. My Will was as depleted as my strength.

She knows what she asked of us. For her, we will heal you.

Her words were washed away when a torrent of suffering once more engulfed me, wrenching sounds from me that I wouldn't recognize as human. The sound of my suffering seemed to linger, hanging in the dead air as if mocking me for my weakness.

As I lay gasping for breath, I felt her cool hands on my body. One on my forehead, the other on my chest over my heart.

It runs deep. Brace yourself.
That was all the warning I got.
Bitch.

SOMEONE WAS BURNING SAGE.

Sage was a scent I'd never cared for.

If I didn't know any better, I would have sworn they were burning it directly under my nose. Reflexively, I grabbed at the arm of the fool who seemed intent on fumigating my nasal passages with the foul stench.

"Holy shit, it worked!" The burning sage was dropped, and I opened my eyes to stare into Doc's wide-eyed wonder. "Oh fuck, you're alive."

"You sound disappointed." My voice was hoarse, my throat dry, and my tongue felt thick and heavy. "Water?"

He stared at me for a few more moments, seemingly immobile, and then he burst into action. He screamed for Royce and Hannah, the nearness of his shouting deafening me, causing me to wince. Pushing myself up the bed into a sitting position, I watched as Doc fell over his own feet trying to get me water, spilling more than he poured into the glass. When he went to pick up the straw, the sound of my voice made him jump.

"I don't need a fucking straw."

A raspy chuckle sounded from my left, and turning my head, I was astonished to see the shaman in the bed near me. He was sitting up like me. His body looked very frail, his eyes cloudy, but his skin had a good color.

"Welcome back," he greeted me. "Luna graced you."

Taking the water from Doc, I took a grateful gulp and then

another. Nodding thoughtfully, I looked between the two of them. "Where is she?"

"Cannon!" Royce came barreling into the room, and I knew how lucky I was to be seeing him again. Hannah was close on his heels, and she didn't even try to stop him when he engulfed me in a bone-crushing hug. I could hear Doc berating him, I could hear Hannah sniffling, and I was reminded how very lucky I was to be alive.

"Luna's grace, Royce," Nikan snapped as he approached us. "He just woke up and now you're smothering him!"

Royce took a step back, unashamed of the tears in his eyes. "Fuck, Alpha," he said, blowing out a huge breath. "Don't ever do that to me again."

"Die?" I asked him, but my eyes were on my brother. "You okay?"

He nodded, but I could see that he was not. Nikan looked haggard. Dark circles sat under his eyes. He was both bulked up and gaunt at the same time; it didn't suit him. It seemed I wasn't the only one being haunted by my mate.

"Where is she?" I repeated.

"Kezia?" Royce asked as he took a refilled glass of water off of Doc. "Gone."

"I know it was Moonstar who was here with me," I corrected him. "Where is she?"

Hannah stuck something in my ear, and when I jerked away, she *tsked* at me. "It's a thermometer, stay still."

She read whatever the reading said and made a note on a chart. I had a chart. I'd never had a chart before. Sucking my teeth, I looked between my beta and my brother. "Why are you avoiding the question? Where did you put her?"

Running a hand over his face, Royce shook his head slightly. "She's gone."

Gone? "Gone where?" An unsettling feeling was rising within me.

"The she was not Kezia," the shaman spoke quietly. "You know that, Alpha."

I was already agreeing with him before he finished talking. "I *do* know that, but that doesn't explain where she is or why you're telling me that she's gone."

Nikan gaped at me. "Because she's unstoppable?" He walked closer. "Because she covered you in some blanket of swirly gold stuff that came from *nowhere* and barricaded herself in here with you for *days*."

"You are very blessed," the shaman told me sagely. "A great gift has been bestowed on you."

Was he joking?

"A gift?" I asked him. Pushing the blanket off me, I swung my legs over the side of the bed, ignoring everyone's protests. "A gift?" My legs weren't steady; they felt like Jell-O, but after a moment, they felt stronger. I met the old man's almost sightless eyes. "A gift at what cost?"

Pulling off the white sleep shirt they had me in and pushing down the shorts, I flexed my neck. My wolf was waiting, and I sank into the familiar form, feeling the healing power of my wolf run through me. It took two shifts, but after the second, I almost felt normal.

As I redressed in the sleepwear, I looked around the room.

"Someone better start talking."

"Is it too soon to wish him back in the sleep stasis?" Hannah murmured to Royce, who pulled his wife into his side, kissing her temple. "I'm joking," she added when she met my eye.

"Shaman? What's happening at Anterrio? Why are you in..." I looked around the empty white room. "Where the hell am I?"

"Medical ward."

I wasn't sure Doc was joking. "*What* medical ward?"

"Remember when you told me I'd never need one?" he said with a cocked eyebrow. "Guess the joke's on you."

"Huh." I turned back to the shaman. "You can shift?" He nodded. "And you're not shifting because?"

"When I shift, I leave a trace. By Luna's grace, I am her eyes and ears in this world, and because of that, any shifter can find me. I am easy to find."

"You have less presence in human form." I nodded in understanding. "Were you here when she came?"

"Not when she was healing you. No one was. But she broke me free, and she ran with me here. She defended us. Your pack has treated me well."

"Free?"

The shaman turned his head away as he spoke. "Anterrio Pack is in grave danger."

"Because we're going to annihilate them," Nikan growled from behind me.

The shaman turned back to look at me. "There are too many innocents in this, Alpha. Do not let it become a war. Have mercy."

It was Royce who stepped forward to speak to the shaman. "They lost that right the day they struck my alpha down."

"There are too many innocents," the shaman protested softly.

"Then they should have chosen a better leader," Nikan snapped.

When the shaman went to speak again, I spoke over him. "Has your pack missed you?" His head bowed. "Did any of the pack fight for you, shaman? Even you won't expect me to believe that no one in the pack didn't notice you're missing. And they did *nothing*."

"I can't answer that."

Sharing a look with my brother and Royce, I turned my back on the shaman, walking to the door of the *medical ward*. "I can. No one's fighting for you. You were as good as dead." Opening the door, I turned back to look at him. "That pack lost its innocence a long time ago, old one. There will be no mercy."

"And Kezia?" he called after me.

I hesitated, my eyes closing briefly before my resolve hardened within me. "She's already gone."

CHAPTER 7

Cannon

IT SEEMED THE MEDICAL WARD WAS PART OF THE bunker, and Doc had merely repainted it. I remained quiet as we walked down the hall to the doors that led outside.

"I need to run," I told them as I walked ahead. "I need fresh air. I need to run and fill my lungs. I know how much there is to talk about—I need this first." I didn't want to look at any of them. I didn't want to see their pity.

"I'll follow," Nikan said. "You're never to be alone until this is over."

At the doors to the outside, I turned to look at my brother. "And when is it over?"

"When every one of them who knew about this is dead."

My lips tightened into a firm line as my eyes flicked to Royce, who looked back at me, stone-faced. "We'll talk when I come back."

I'd shifted before any of them could answer, blocking the mindlink, and as the breeze teased me, washing away the smell of the lingering sage, I ran.

With every stride, my paws sank further into the terrain.

EVE L. MITCHELL

Stronger. I felt the healing magic of the Goddess as I picked up speed. The wind whistled past. Dipping my head lower to the ground, I pushed myself further. Faster. The heaviness of my human body left me as I ran.

Days of lying motionless. Still. Unable to move. Were shed as I ran up the mountain. I *never* wanted to feel that again.

At a stream, I paused and drank the fresh water of the mountains. I sensed my brother behind me, but he never came too close. He was giving me space, I knew.

Plus, I'd been outrunning him all his life.

Movement amidst the sparse copse of trees caught my attention, and swiftly I took off after the rabbit, the familiar thrill of the chase calming my inner being.

I shared my catch with Nikan, and when I was fed and soothed within, I opened the mindlink.

You are angry.

My brother looked at me before turning his attention to the east. *Angry? I could rip the bastards apart with my hands.*

I knew anger like that. It burned deep and strong within you, until it either engulfed you entirely or extinguished your flame. My brother burned too bright for that to be his end.

I feel your rage, brother. Trust me, I do. I commiserated. *But hate only takes us so far, Nikan, don't let it consume you.*

You almost died. Twice.

I stood, then stretched. *I felt every moment of it.*

They will pay.

Trotting over to the slightly smaller wolf, I bit at his ear playfully. *They will—all of them who were involved in this.*

Nikan swiped at my nose when I nipped him, and I breathed a sigh of relief at seeing some of the lightness returning to my brother. We ran side by side back down the mountain, the wind behind us, our footing sure, and our speed almost reckless.

My return to my pack was them seeing me approaching them at great speed, racing my brother to an imaginary finish line, and both of us feeling better than we had in weeks.

As I walked the streets as my wolf, I let the pack in, humbled at the outpouring of love and support they sent. In my boot room, I shifted, pulling on jeans, and then I went back outside, walking the streets of our home, letting my pack see me, giving them the reassurance they needed that their alpha was ready to fight for the attack on our pack. Because to strike an alpha was a strike to the pack.

We were ready to retaliate.

Nikan walked beside me, and at some point, Royce flanked me, the three of us being seen together, united, and ready for vengeance.

Because I *would* have my vengeance. The more I thought about it, the keener I was to be back in my study with my men, getting up to speed. But the pack came first, and I could school my patience just as they had waited for me to be healed. I needed to be there for them now. Reassure them. Ease their concerns and worries.

It went well, and it was when I was heading back to the house that I saw them waiting for me at the gate.

"Well, this is going to be interesting," Royce muttered.

"Willy, Barbara," I greeted. "How are you both?"

Barbara was as timid as I remembered, and Willy as blunt as always. "Where's Kezia?"

"Not here," I answered with a polite smile.

"Is she in danger?"

"Where is she?" Willy asked at the same time.

"Yes."

Royce and I both turned to Nikan, who shrugged at our glares of warning. "What? She is."

"From who?" Barbara asked, stepping forward. "Bale?" Her timidness was gone as she met my eyes. "Or you?"

Nikan went to speak, but Royce cut him off. "Kezia is not our immediate concern. She's with someone who will protect her at all costs."

Willy noticed his slight hesitation over *someone* but said nothing, her gaze locking on me.

Barbara was still watching me. "Aren't you the one who should protect her at all costs?" she asked quietly. "She is your mate."

"Landon," Royce grunted. "She is Landon's mate."

Barbara looked at Royce as if he was an idiot. In fact, both women were wearing identical expressions of *who do you think you're kidding?*

"I changed your diapers, boy," Willy reminded me.

"She's safe," I told them, relenting under the disapproving frown of the older female. Willy was right, she was no fool, and I learned a long time ago that she saw right through all my bullshit. I also had my inner voice nagging at me, questioning whether Kezia was actually safe. "As Royce said, she's with someone who would do anything for her."

Even heal me. A pull in my belly caused me to look up the mountain. Where would Moonstar go? How long would it take before Kezia came back?

Would she come back? Unease sat deep within me.

"Alpha?" Royce nodded towards the house. "You ready?"

"Yes." Looking at the two women, I said my goodbyes and headed inside the house. I wasn't surprised to see Doc and Leo waiting for me. When the doors to the study were closed, I turned to everyone in the room. "Where is she? Who followed her when she left?"

Nikan was the first one to speak. "No one. She was gone before we knew she'd finished doing whatever it was she did to you."

My gaze darted over the four of them. "No one? At all?" I knew my surprise showed. "You left her alone with me?"

Royce snorted. "You say it as if we were given a *choice*. There was none. The thing that inhabits her body acts with a primal force. She parted her hands, made a gesture that forced us apart, and then simply walked between us. In a few strides, she was at your side. By the time we were able to move again, she had already pushed us out of the room, locking the door behind us."

"She is strong," I conceded. *Why was there no guard outside?*

"Anyone we left outside, on guard, including us, couldn't stay awake long enough." Leo's eyes were narrowed in remembrance. "I don't know what the fuck she is, but I was glad she was on your side."

My eyes met Royce's heavy gaze, and I didn't correct Leo. Moonstar was *not* on my side. I don't think she was even on Kezia's.

"We need to find her," I told them as I turned to look out the window. I expected the protests, my brother being the loudest, but I waited for them to calm down, which they did when I didn't immediately answer their questions. "Kezia has not betrayed me," I told them when their protests had reduced to grumbles of discontent.

"Tev said—"

"He told me what any liar would. A lie." Turning back to them, I addressed them all. "The thing that would hurt most? Apart from the silver," I added with a quirk of my lips, "would be to tell me that my mate had betrayed me." I ignored Leo's surprised look at the others when I called Kezia my mate as I carried on. "He wouldn't have known the silver hadn't stopped all my power. I was lucky—"

"Lucky?" Nikan was on his feet, rage twisting his features into a mask of anger. "You have no fucking idea what we found!" He started to pace, and I let him vent his anger. I didn't know, but I could imagine. To see their alpha brought low would have been a worrying sight.

"I know I was dying," I spoke bluntly. "I never heard Royce's answer. When I passed out, I thought that was it. It was too late. I knew, as I lay in the bed and the surgeries I went through, that my days on this earth were over." The four of them avoided my eyes as I spoke. "I also know I wasn't ready to go," I added softly. "Thank you all for agreeing with me." Nikan wouldn't look at me still, and I directed my next statement to him. "And I know she wouldn't do this to me. Kezia *loves* me. As I do her."

"Then where is she?" Leo asked quietly. "Alpha, I've never doubted you, not once. But...if she's your mate? Where is she? Why did she leave?"

"There is no *if*, she *is* my mate." My voice was sharper than it should have been, given what they had all been through. I met Nikan's glare. "She will *always* be my mate. And she's in danger."

My brother snorted, looking away from me.

"Moonstar," Royce spoke for the first time. "I knew it was her when she used magic. Kezia will come back on her own."

He didn't look happy about it. "Like she always does. And, *Alpha*, I'm telling you now, I am *not* chasing the mountains looking for her." His look was steady. "You and I are needed right here. Anterrio has made its move. It's time to counter."

"Kezia won't come back."

Doc looked at me. He had been quiet throughout the exchange. "Why?"

Anxiety spread through me. I didn't like it. "I need to find her. Sooner rather than later. Just...trust me on this."

"No." Nikan stood. "Because *she* can't be trusted."

I understood my brother was angry, but his attitude towards Kezia was surprising. "Nikan, I know you're pissed, *I'm* pissed. She should never have left, but she did, and I believe, *truly* believe, she left because she thought she had to. She wasn't part of the attack on me."

His cold stare was a look I had never seen in my brother before. "If she hadn't left, you wouldn't have been out looking for her. You wouldn't have been blind to the danger in front of you, but you were, and it's *because* of her."

My temper picked up to match his. "No. It isn't. The reason Tev stabbed me is *my* fault. Because I gave a poisonous old fucker a pardon when I knew how much he hated me. I should have killed him the day I killed Rek. I allowed Tev to strike me. I gave him the means to have access to me. Access and familiarity in *my pack* that it wouldn't have mattered who I was out on the street for, or even if I was walking home from the food hall. He stuck a knife in my back because he believed I did the same to Rek when I never told him I was an alpha."

Nikan dipped his head, not meeting my eye, the same as he always did when our father was mentioned.

"I hid my scent and my power, and I only came back to the

pack when I knew I was strong enough to take it." Nikan's anger was cooling, but mine was not. "Tev told me the day Rek lay at my feet, dead. He said I only succeeded because I had blindsided our father as if I had *stabbed him in the back*." I shook my head. "Kezia is not part of that. Tev wanted to hurt me like I hurt him when I betrayed his alpha and killed him." Running my hand through my hair, I tilted my head back to look at the ceiling. "What happened with Tev *is* my fault because *I* allowed him to live when he should have died the same night our father did."

Nikan sat down, still refusing to look at me. Royce watched me carefully and I couldn't stop the huff of laughter. "And yes, Royce, you can say *I told you so*."

It was the first smile I had seen on my beta's face for a while. "Well," he said solemnly, the smile fading. "We are all at fault. I advocated for his death that night, but over time, I no longer saw him as a threat, just a bitter old bastard. So I won't say I told you so, I will apologize for not sticking to my gut."

"We were *all* blindsided by Tev," Doc spoke up. "We are all to blame." He also wouldn't meet my eye, and I made a note to find out why later. "Why are you so worried about Kezia? The being inside of her has her, and we all know what she'll do to protect her. We've seen it before."

I watched him shake his head as he remembered walking into the room where he had kept Vance a prisoner and seeing what Moonstar had left of his body.

"But you're not worried about that, are you?" Leo was frowning as he watched me. "I know that look, Alpha. Served with you too long not to know when you're worried."

"I need to find her."

"Why?" Leo asked. "I don't know what's fully going on. I

know I thought, like we all did, that she was part of it, and therefore I was ready to do what we needed. She came back, she healed you, or something that looked like her did." Leo hesitated. "From the magic I saw and the power that she had...she doesn't look like she needs your help, Alpha."

"She does!" I growled angrily. "Because she *isn't* Kezia. My mate is inside still, and she needs me to get her out." Fear gripped my heart. "I hope I am strong enough."

"You've done it before," Royce said gruffly.

I nodded in reply, but the feeling of panic, now that I had addressed it, was slowly climbing up my insides, hooking itself into my throat and making my mouth dry.

"Tell us?" Doc prompted.

"Moonstar, the spirit inside her," I explained for Leo's benefit, "hates me. I've used my Will on her before to bring Kezia back." I swallowed. "I think Anterrio was holding Kezia as a prisoner, and Moonstar broke them free. She took the shaman, someone very dear to Kezia. You saw the state of him; he's in a hospital bed for fuck's sake. Something's happening in Anterrio that's beyond fucked up if they are hurting their shaman. Moonstar brought him here to safety, and she *healed* me. She told me she did it for Kezia." Fear prickled low in my gut. "I remember, right before the pain of her healing, she said *she knows what she asked of us. For her, we will heal you.*"

Leo looked at Nikan, whose head was down, then to Royce who was tight-lipped, his stare worried as he watched me. "Alpha?"

"She's not coming back?" Nikan's rage was simmering, his look uncertain, and I counted it as progress.

"I don't think so," I admitted. "I must find her."

"You think she did it?" Royce spoke. "Don't you?"

"I do." Turning back to the window, I looked out at my pack. "And I want revenge on Anterrio Pack as much as you all do, and we will get it. But..."

"What do we think she did?" Leo asked behind me.

"She gave up control," I whispered, scared that giving voice to my fear would make it even more real. Looking over my shoulder, I confessed, "She gave it up, and I don't know if I can get her back."

"For her freedom? For her and the old shifter?" Doc asked, his forehead furrowed in thought.

"For me." I knew it in my heart. My mate had surrendered her soul to the spirit that resided in her body so that Moonstar would heal me. "My life, for hers."

CHAPTER 8

Cannon

Royce was the first to speak. "You don't know that."

Wetting my lips, I turned back to the window. "Don't I?" I could feel the wolf inside me, prowling, eager to go find his mate and rip out anyone's throat who got in the way. I was on board with that plan.

"Cannon," Leo began, blowing out a low breath as he searched for the right words. "I get it. I do. Your mate is...everything, but—"

"There is no *but*." Keeping my eyes on the streets outside, I stubbornly refused to turn around. I didn't want to see reason. I didn't want to hear *but*s. I didn't want to be here. I wanted to be running up that mountain and finding where that bitch took my mate.

"Of course, Alpha." Leo didn't hide his sigh of disappointment, and I knew there was more than him in the room who didn't like my answer.

I also knew not all of those in the room would stay quiet, and Royce didn't disappoint me.

"You're alpha in this pack, Cannon. Every shifter in this pack is your responsibility. So, yes, there is a very big *but*."

Nikan snorted and I heard the *oomph* as someone elbowed him, but my brother's snort of inappropriateness eased the tension. Turning to them, I saw Leo smirking and Doc shaking his head.

"You're such a juvenile," I chided him with a small smile. Nikan cleared his throat but couldn't hide his grin.

Royce's attention was all on me. "How long do you think it will take you to find her?"

"I don't know," I told him truthfully.

"It took us five months last time," he continued as if I hadn't spoken. "And she was Kezia the whole time. Five months," he ground out. "You think Moonstar doesn't know how you hunt by now? You think she doesn't know how to evade you, if you even knew which direction to look in?"

"I have to find her," I told him.

"We will, Alpha." Royce was solid. Steady. He didn't let emotion overcome him or rule him. Until Kezia, neither had I.

I hated that he was right. I *knew* he was right; I knew I was letting the need to protect my mate rule my emotions. "Ever since I met her, she's made me irrational," I mumbled, and I saw my beta dip his head to hide his smile, knowing that I had heard him. "After Tev stabbed me, what happened?"

Nikan leaned back, mockery in his eyes. "Finally! You ask the questions we can answer."

Dragging my hand over my face in frustration, I accepted all their criticism. They were right; I wasn't acting as I should. "Start talking," I ordered them. "Tell me everything."

"I heard your call," Royce began. "Faint. But I heard, and I found you. Nikan wasn't far behind, and you were..." They exchanged a look. "It was bad. We got Doc, and Nikan and Leo enforced lockdown." I watched him scratch his cheek. "Put the pack in panic, but too many had seen you injured by then. Rumor spreads quicker than wildfire after all."

"Lockdown was in place. Patrols were in place within twenty minutes of Royce finding you," Leo told me, and I could hear the pride in his voice.

As he should.

We were a well-disciplined pack, and that was reflected in how quickly they had responded to the threat. The pack had rallied without me telling them to—that's how well communication ran through my pack. They didn't need the mindlink to gather them. We had systems in place for all eventualities.

"Vic saw Tev try to leave despite lockdown," Nikan carried on the retelling. "Contacted me immediately." My brother looked at me with steely determination as he spoke. "*Only* for him did I leave your side that night."

"Good." I knew what he was telling me. "The answers to what was happening weren't going to come from me," I added. "Did he break?"

"Like a twig." Nikan's fierce satisfaction should have worried me, but I'd recognized a long time ago that the fire in our veins ran hotter than most. It wasn't always a good thing, but the very moment that Rek became our father, our DNA was against us. "He folded within a few hours," he said smugly. "Do you remember, in the food hall, he had said he had been in Anterrio Pack, and it was him that told everyone that Landon was missing a *mate*. I didn't remember it, I'd been distracted that night..." I watched the flush on his cheeks, knowing it was because he was remembering his hurt at finding out Kezia was my mate.

"We all forgot it," Royce grumbled. "I meant to ask the prick why he'd been there, but I was more focused on trying to keep Cannon and Kezia apart."

"Apart?" Leo asked in confusion. "Why would you want to be away from your mate?"

"We haven't completed the bond," I answered gruffly. "At the time, we didn't think we wanted it." His eyes widened in surprise, and I knew I was scowling in return. "It's complicated, okay?"

It was Doc's turn to scoff, but he kept his mouth shut.

"What did Tev have in common with Anterrio?" I asked my brother and knew the answer before he told me. "Stefan, right?" The old pack leader, Bale's father, knew about silver bullets. "He wanted to know if Bale was carrying on his father's practices?"

Nikan was nodding. "Pretty much."

"The apple never falls far from the tree," I grumbled. I met my brother's look. "What the fuck that says about us, I don't know."

"It says we're adopted," he quipped with a wink, and I grinned in return.

"I wish." Growing serious again, I motioned for him to continue. "What did Tev tell you?"

"Bale's building something, I don't know what. I've scouted that pack for days, but it looks like it did when we were there last. I can't see anything that looks out of place. They're like they always are. Blind and ignorant."

"Not so ignorant they didn't almost kill our alpha," Royce murmured. "We're missing something."

Leo was nodding in agreement. "Nikan interrogated the traitor, and I've been with him when we scouted after. I've been back alone because something didn't fit. The pack looks the same with two exceptions."

"Which are?"

"The pack leader is not present. I realized the second time I went back alone. The pack looks *better* and...happier. I don't think he's been there for a while."

"Which means he's somewhere else," I concluded, following Leo's train of thought. "We need to know where," I said, stating the obvious as I once more looked out the window, trying to sort through everything that was happening while my whole being screamed at me to find my mate.

"That's one thing," Royce spoke to Leo. "What's the other?"

Leo sounded almost nervous as he spoke. "His beta and his daughter are nowhere to be seen either."

I spun to face Leo. "His beta? *Kris* is gone?"

Leo nodded slowly. "I got as close as I could, but I never saw him. Their security is slack too, something it never is when he is there."

"How often do you scout the pack?" Doc asked curiously. When Leo gave him a flat stare, Doc huffed out a laugh. "Right. Always. Forget I asked."

"Shifters fight," I reminded him. "Anterrio Pack may be our nearest neighbor in these mountains, but they are not our allies. And they have no alpha," I added. "Their pack is prime to be overtaken by rogues."

"Unless you have silver weapons in your arsenal," Leo added gruffly. "Then you might just have the advantage."

"Why would he want you dead?" Nikan asked. "Bale's never bothered with us before, not even when Rek was alpha."

"Kezia?" Royce suggested. "No, that makes no sense. He doesn't even know she's your mate."

"Why would that make a difference?" Doc asked. As a scientist, he kept his opinion about the mate bond to himself these days.

"It wouldn't." I agreed with him. "Unless..." Royce and I shared a look.

"Kris," we both spoke at the same time.

"The *alpha* in the pack." I closed my eyes as it became clear. "It's not about Kezia, not to him. *Fuck*. We've been blind!"

"Her *brother* is an *alpha*?" Nikan asked, looking at us both incredulously. "And you didn't *tell* us?"

"It's complicated."

"It really isn't, Cannon," Nikan snapped, and I saw Leo nod in agreement. "An alpha in the next pack, undeclared, is a threat to us all."

"I only figured it out recently," I countered defensively. "Kris doesn't want the pack. He was working his own angle."

"Which is?"

The question hung between us.

"Cannon?" Nikan pressed.

"I don't know." I avoided all eye contact as I admitted how badly I'd dropped the ball. "But I do know we need to find him."

"Find him, find Kezia, we're not fucking scavenger hunters!" Nikan was on his feet. "*Bale* is the threat to this pack. *He* needs to be eliminated." Nikan and Leo exchanged a look before my brother looked back at me. "Then we deal with their alpha."

"Kris is *not* their alpha," I reminded them sharply.

"Yet," Royce amended.

I stared at Royce in disbelief. "Kris is no threat to us."

"*Yet*," Nikan echoed Royce. My brother's temper was overriding his common sense.

"And he won't be, because his little sister is *my* mate." Inhaling deeply, I looked around the room. "He keeps her safe, he would never hurt her. Hurting *me* is hurting Kezia." I gave them a shrug. "Plus, he likes me. We get along well. There is no fight there. Trust me."

"Oh fuck, we're doomed," Nikan groaned, dropping back onto the couch. "Our alpha is testing pack safety on how popular he is."

"We'll be annihilated," Royce kidded back.

"I thought it was only Tev that stabbed me in the back," I grouched as I glared at my brother and my beta.

The reminder sobered them both.

"What next?" Doc asked the suddenly quiet room.

"If Bale has acted against Kris, we need to move. Removing the threat of someone who can control him with their Will is the first thing I would do," I reasoned. "Kris is his daughter's mate, so he wouldn't hurt him...I don't think." I wouldn't bet my life on it, but I never said that. "The shaman was hurt?" When more than one of my companions nodded, I chewed my inner cheek. "Retaliation? Or a move to strike?"

"A shaman is the Goddess's power on earth," Leo mused. "Remove an alpha and the influence of the Goddess, it evens the odds in your favor."

"Add in an armory of silver, and you've got one hell of an advantage," I added grimly. "What a fucking mess."

"You know," Doc piped up, looking uncertain. "The more we talk and the more I hear, I don't think this has anything to do with you."

"What?" Nikan turned his full attention to the Doc. "You saying my brother isn't as popular as he thinks he is?"

Doc gave him a flat look. "I think it may be a benefit, but honestly? It sounds like a coincidence."

"How so?" Royce leaned forward, his elbows on his knees.

"It seems the focus is on the siblings. Kezia was taken or tricked into leaving. Her brother, we think, has been taken. Only Tev struck against this pack."

"Our alpha has been brought down for weeks." Leo leaned back in his seat as he thought about it. "Plenty of time to wage an attack, when we are at our weakest."

"We're a strong pack," I countered. "They don't need me as much as you think."

"We still need our alpha," Royce corrected quickly. "We *are* strong, but we are strongest with you among us." He shifted in his seat as he thought about it. "What if they didn't make their move because *they* were waiting on *us* to make ours?"

"And in that time, they moved against the ones Bale *actually* wanted rid of," Leo concluded. "We've played right into their hands?"

"Why take Kezia?" Nikan asked.

I knew the answer immediately. "*Landon,*" I breathed. "That little prick wanted her. Bale wouldn't care. I get the impression Bale's never cared about her. Why start now?"

"Moonstar?" Royce asked.

I shook my head. "No. Kris kept that secret very close to his chest. He never told his sister; he wouldn't risk anyone other than the shaman knowing."

"Which means Bale never knew his biggest threat was the one he wasn't paying attention to?" Leo said. "Pity Kezia escaped."

My rage erupted so quickly that I'd taken two steps towards him before I got a hold of it. "*Never* say that again." I watched the younger shifter nod his head rapidly, eyes wide as I fought for calm.

"You okay?" Royce asked quietly as they watched me rein my temper in.

"Yes." I shared a look with him. "No," I conceded. "I could be slightly on edge." I felt the tension ease as more than one of them relaxed. "Just don't..." Taking a deep inhale, I looked at Leo. "Try not to be careless in what you say. The bond, it's riding me closer than I thought."

"Understood, Alpha," Leo said. Nikan nudged him. "Sorry, Alpha."

"We need to strike Anterrio Pack." I knew they were all staring at me. "What? This is what you wanted when we walked into this room. Why so surprised?"

"And it wasn't what you wanted," Royce reminded me. "Why change your mind? Kris?"

"Yes." Looking at Doc, I addressed him. "You said you thought you could break the bond, with your science." He nodded as I spoke. "It's not just this pack that seems to have embraced science and technology. Bale's manufacturing silver weapons. What else has he been able to make?"

"You think he will try to break the bond between his daughter and Kris?" Royce realized.

"I do. The pain of a mate's death is allegedly so powerful that the one who remains fades rapidly. He's a prick and a pile of shit, but he cares for his children. He won't want her to suffer. When we searched, we never found a recounting of a broken bond. There's no way to tell if it has the same effect as the death of a mate."

"Because we don't think it's possible," Royce reminded me.

"I think it is," Doc spoke quietly. "In this world, anything is possible. You think he will break it and then kill Kris?"

"I do. I think we need to act as if this could happen at any moment. We need to move and move fast."

"An attack?" Leo asked. "Or a rescue mission?"

Excellent question. A stealth grab and take, or an act of war? "We go to war."

Their eyes met briefly before shifting to me. Three stood up, their heads inclined in deference. My gaze lingered on Doc, who remained firmly seated.

"Never could agree to causing death." He kept his eyes on the floor as he spoke. "I *heal*, not kill."

"I have a council," I spoke calmly and clearly. "But this is not a democracy. We go to war with Anterrio, make no mistake about it." With my eyes on Nikan, he straightened when he saw my look. "How soon can they be ready?"

"They're ready. They've been waiting for you to wake, Alpha."

He took my tight-lipped smile for what it was, approval. "Good." Turning to Royce, I saw my beta was more than ready.

"The ones who remain with the vulnerable are all armed, and we have enough food stocked."

"Hannah?" I asked him about his wife, a fierce fighter but also the mother of his children.

"Will remain with the girls."

I nodded even though my lips quirked. "And have you told her that yet?"

"No, Alpha." He swallowed. "That's a conversation for later."

Nikan failed to hide his snort.

"Nikan?"

My brother straightened his shoulders. "Perimeter is secure. We'll leave two full units behind to protect the town. Weapons stock was low; it's been replenished."

I gave him a look. "Do I need to know?"

My brother glanced at Leo before giving me a half shrug. "Maybe later."

Right, I wasn't touching that one with a ten-foot pole right now. I had enough problems.

"We leave in two hours," I told them. The three of them headed to the doors, while Doc remained seated. Royce glanced back once, but seeing my look, he left, closing the doors firmly behind him, the room once more spelled.

"You want to tell me?" I watched him as he kept his focus on the floor.

"If I say no?"

"I'm not asking, Mal."

Doc raised his head and looked at me. "I hate when you call me Mal, reminds me of the man I used to be." He shifted his focus from me to the window behind me. "Maybe I was a fool, maybe I will always be *Mal*."

"What have you done?" I waited, unmoving and patient.

"I fucked up." He took a shuddering breath. "I never meant to betray you."

CHAPTER 9

Cannon

Doc didn't turn his head from where his gaze lingered out the window. I didn't want to look at him right now anyway. When he began to speak, I cursed my instincts.

"I mean it, it was never my intent to betray you or..."

"Or put Kezia in danger?" I scoffed. "Talk faster, *Mal*, I have a war to fight."

"A war to *start*," he corrected sharply.

"Watch your tone when you speak to me right now," I warned quietly, folding my arms across my chest.

"The bond *can* be broken," he stated bluntly. "I've been researching it ever since you two realized you didn't want it." Still not looking at me, he huffed out a laugh. "We all knew it was bullshit. You two were drawn to each other, and some mumbo jumbo *bond* had nothing to do with it."

"Your lack of faith in the Goddess is going to get you in trouble one day." Tilting my head, I regarded him. "If it hasn't already." I urged him to continue. "Speak."

With a loud, resigned sigh, Mal sat back in his seat, finally meeting my stare. "As you are more than aware, information about shifters is hard to come by." Mal rubbed his jaw. "I've read everything. You know that. The need to know *how* I exist has been my—"

"Obsession."

He glanced at me. "You say obsession, I say passion."

"Both equally dangerous when it gets out of control," I countered.

"Yeah, well." His focus shifted to the bookcase. "How the DNA of a shifter and a human *worked* to create me, and the few like me, remains my torment," he added bitterly. "The bond between you and Kezia was almost as much a mystery to me. Everyone knows chemicals, pheromones, and adrenaline cause attraction, but you and her, it's more than that. It's almost beyond science."

"Or things in common?" I added dryly. "Physical attraction, attributes, recognizing similar likes and dislikes. You know... personality." His questioning look made me want to shake him. I recognized that gleam in his eyes; I'd seen it before. There was a reason I used the word *obsession*. His next sentence jarred me out of my inner musings.

"You told me her brother was making contact with the Pack Council..."

He wouldn't. The more I stared at him, I realized that he had. "You reached out to the *Pack Council archives*?" I asked him incredulously. "About breaking a *mate* bond? A sacred *gift* from the Goddess Luna?" Mal nodded. "Any request to the archives is public knowledge!"

"I know that...now."

"Why the *fuck* would you be so reckless?"

"I was researching!" he bit back.

I watched him as he glared at me as if it was *my* fault he was unhinged when he became focused on his work. "You put my pack at risk."

"*Unintentionally.*"

"Mal...you don't want to be pedantic right now, not if you want to walk out of here." I focused on what he said. "Hold on...are you saying you *intentionally* put Kezia at risk?"

"No! Never!" He stood and crossed the room to the bookshelves. "I like her, she's perfect for you," he told me as he looked at me over his shoulder. "But she can resist silver. And... is your mate. Both of these things are rare. Put them together in one girl, and..."

I hated to admit that I could see how that would be the ultimate puzzle for someone like the Doc. "It's a coincidence."

"I'm a scientist. We don't believe in coincidences," he muttered. "It's either you or her."

"What is?"

"The anomaly." He walked back to the couch. "One of you is powerful enough, but together? You talk all the time about Luna creating a mate for an alpha for *balance*. Kezia didn't balance you out; she didn't calm you down or make you rational. Nor you her. You're both volatile, overly aggressive, and hated each other." He pulled at a thread on his shirt sleeve. "So, it had to be the being inside her."

"Kezia and I were volatile to start with, but that changed. *We* changed."

"Well, I know that now," he grumped at me. "But by then, I had already made inquiries about breaking mate bonds and if they could be broken."

My eyes were wide with horror. "Tell me that you worded it more subtly than that. *Tell* me that you never asked it that bluntly?" He didn't look at me. "Luna above, you stupid fucking idiot!"

"I know!" Mal shouted back. "I wasn't thinking."

"Who did you tell?" I was seething. "I know you. Who did you tell when you realized that you had fucked up?"

Mal wouldn't look at me, then finally whispered a name, "Koda."

Fuck. "Why?"

"Too much whiskey, self-loathing, and...a pretty face."

"You're gay."

He shrugged. "She was an attentive listener."

I bet she was. "You stupid bastard."

He stood, his posture one of a defeated man. "I never meant to harm Kezia. Or you."

I knew that. Mal was a genius, but when his obsessive nature took hold of him, he let it. He'd been down too many dangerous paths before, and we'd made the inner joke a long time ago that he was like *Dr. Jekyll and Mr. Hyde*. The obsessive-don't-care-what-happens persona was Mal, and the doctor, the *healer*, was Doc.

"Tev?" I asked him.

"Wasn't me," he assured me quickly. "I only told Koda how a bond could be broken."

"Get out."

I watched him leave, and after a moment to calm my rage, I left the house to find my ex, connecting through the mindlink to Royce to let him know what had happened. Koda was in the food hall, doing as little as possible to help the others. Watching her from the shadows, I wondered what I had seen in her. Sure, she was pretty, her hair perfect even while preparing for a fight. Her clothes were chosen carefully, simple jeans and a shirt, but on closer inspection...the jeans sculpted her ass, the shirt a deep V that accentuated her chest. She was attractive, she knew it, and I never judged her for flaunting it.

It was the look of superiority she wore that turned my stomach. I watched her as she practically sneered as Willy struggled past her with a burden too heavy for an older woman, even a shifter, to carry, and Koda merely glanced at her nails rather than help.

Koda was shallow. I hadn't lied to Kezia the day I told her that Koda and I used each other to scratch a mutual itch. Nor had I shied away from the fact I knew that Koda pretended it was more. It wasn't because she *cared* for me, like Kezia thought, it was because she enjoyed letting others think she was better than them.

I may be alpha, but my shit smelled like any other. A fact Koda never grasped. I wasn't a better shifter than anyone in my pack; I was the best shifter I could be *because* of my pack.

Nikan took the box Willy was carrying from her, his comment too low for me to hear, but I saw Koda's flushed reaction. However, it was her knowing smug smirk at my brother's back that caused me to move forward.

Come for me, I'll fight you if that's what you want. Come for my loved ones, I'll kill you, no questions asked.

The pack stilled around me as I approached her. No one spoke when my hand wrapped around her throat and I practically lifted her off the stool.

"Who did you tell?" Koda made a show of looking innocent and outraged at once, but my temper was barely hanging on.

Koda.

She stopped clutching at her neck. Her eyes filled with hate as she met my glare.

My lover.

"Seems like you've been collecting them," I mocked as I dropped her. "Don't even pretend you slept with Doc. So... Landon would be my guess? Who else have you been trading pillow talk with?"

"Are you jealous, *Alpha*?" The sultry look she gave me made me laugh.

"No. I don't care who you fuck, Koda, I never did." I saw the effect my words had on her, and I didn't care. "How long has Landon known how to break the mate bond?" I ignored the whispers around me. "I won't ask again, Koda."

"A few weeks."

"I've been in an infirmary bed for more than a *few* weeks... try again. This time, tell the truth."

"A month, maybe more." She didn't look at me.

"You told Landon over a month ago how to break the mate bond?" When she nodded, I glanced at Nikan, who was rigid with fury, but he nodded once. "Why did Landon want to know?"

"*Her.*"

Figures. "And?"

Koda tossed her hair. "His sister." Gaining confidence because I wasn't acting on what she was telling me, made her cocky. She shrugged carelessly. "Why he would need to know for her, I don't know."

"Because, you stupid bitch, she's mated to an alpha," Nikan snapped.

Koda looked at me in confusion. "No! Landon said *Kezia* was your mate!"

I was in her face, my snarl quieting the cacophony of sudden voices. "She *is* my mate. Landon's sister, Cass, is mated to Kezia's brother, Kris." Koda searched my face as I loomed over her. "Did he tell you *he* was an alpha? Is that it, Koda?" I saw the truth in her eyes, and I stepped back. "You thought Landon was an alpha and would want you?" I snorted. "You're an idiot. Get her out of my pack."

"Where will I go?" Koda wailed.

"I don't give a fuck. As long as it's nowhere near me, my mate, or my pack, I don't care."

Royce stepped up beside me. I had seen him enter, but he'd kept his distance. "Willy?" He gestured to the older female and another male. "She leaves but not until we're back. She's betrayed us already. Let's not allow her to do it again."

As I left them, Willy was already putting binds around Koda's wrists, as deaf as everyone else to the sound of Koda's pleading.

"What did we miss?" Royce asked as the three of us left the food hall. I filled them in that Doc had alerted the Pack Council to the fact I had a mate and wanted to break the bond. A fact that could sign my death sentence for heresy against my Goddess. I told them he had told Koda, and she in turn had told Landon, whose father *actually* wanted to break the mate bond between his daughter and his enemy's son.

"If Bale has the Council on his side..." Nikan shared a look with Royce. "Cannon..."

"I know," I told him. "It's going to take more charm than I have to dissuade them."

"What do you want to do?" Royce asked hesitantly.

"Nothing's changed." I kept walking. "Kris is our priority. Everything else can come after." I hesitated. "If we pick up the treacherous little fucker as we go, I'm okay with that."

"Doc really told her?" Royce muttered. "He gets so blind sometimes."

I said nothing as I prepared my pack to go to war.

WE ADVANCED AT NIGHT, keeping to our human forms. Shifters were more inclined to pick up on the scent of a fellow shifter. Human scent was much subtler, and it wasn't until you were very close to one, that you would know if they were a shifter or not.

A fact that had fascinated Doc in the beginning. I met him in the army. He was, as his name suggested, a doctor and was the medic on duty the night my unit took me into the medical tent after shrapnel had ripped into my body from an unexploded mine. My unit never knew that if they'd just left me alone, I'd have been fine. But it's hard to explain miraculous recoveries in the army.

I knew within a few minutes that Doc wasn't one hundred percent human, but it took too many nights to realize he was half shifter.

When we both realized there was more to us than met the eye, he conceded to hide my recovery if he could watch me shift. I had no issue with nudity; I was naked more than I was dressed sometimes. Doc took my hesitancy as homophobia. Idiot. I remember his face when I laughed so hard I cried. I ended up telling him that I hesitated because there was a moment during the shift when I was at my most vulnerable.

He had moved to the other end of the room, his hands raised at all times. An act of trust from us both. A friendship was born. It had been rocky at times, but it was a friendship nonetheless.

"It really pisses me off because," Royce murmured as we moved through the night, "he wouldn't have meant harm."

"I know."

"He still caused harm," Nikan grumbled at my other side. "Why didn't Hannah notice his tells?"

"Because my wife is not his babysitter."

The edge in Royce's voice shut my brother up. We approached Anterrio Pack two hours before dawn, and as we had on the run-up to the Luna Ball, we circled the perimeter and we watched.

Leo had been wrong. Their security wasn't slack. It was non-existent.

I was just about to give the signal to move forward when my signal changed to *hold*. If the shifter who fell out of the house, more likely the bed, of his lover knew he was being watched by an army of shifters, he showed no sign as he staggered towards the trees to the north.

Leo and Nikan were already following him, as he obliviously tucked his shirt into his pants, swaying unsteadily before setting off again.

What's there? I asked through the link.

Nothing. Abandoned barn. Searched it before, Nikan replied.

Search it again.

I ignored the image of the hand gesture my brother sent back. We waited. My pack never moved. Even as the dawn began to break, we held position.

Alpha. Come.

Twelve of us broke off and headed in the direction of my brother and Leo. We found them a distance from the dilapidated barn. They stood around two doors in the ground. The long grass hid the doors from visibility.

"A cell?" Nikan asked.

Looking around, I realized at the same time as Royce did. "A trap!"

They burst from the soil like ants from a disturbed anthill. Shifters I didn't recognize were ready to fight us. Their element of surprise was short-lived when my pack quickly recovered.

Nikan pulled the doors open of the bunker that hadn't opened. "Let's see what's behind this."

My yell of warning was lost when he disappeared into the darkness, and I hurried after him, reaching him in a few strides. "Let's not jump into any more underground tunnels," I whispered angrily when I caught up to him.

We both slowed when we realized how extensive the tunnels were. We were faced with a fork ahead of us, and Nikan looked over at me.

"They've utilized old mines and made them structurally stronger."

He nodded as he looked around. "Who do you think they are hiding down here?"

Cautiously we moved forward. Keeping the mindlink open, Royce and the other unit leaders kept me updated with the skirmish above. I heard the noise first, my pace increasing as I led and my brother followed. As the tunnel split into two, I walked forward, the noise leading me to it.

When the tunnel ended abruptly, I almost didn't notice, because all I could see were the two wolves that lay on the floor of a cell, heavy collars of silver around their neck.

"Fuck," Nikan hissed. "Is that them?" When I nodded, he cursed again. "How do we get them out of that?"

"Painfully." I approached the cells, careful of Kris's tawny wolf. His body lay protectively over the smaller gray wolf. The protection he offered was little. He was half-dead, the she beside him more dead than alive, I feared.

"Cannon? How do we get them off?"

"We need a human."

"Well, I'm fresh out of carrying humans around in my pocket!" Nikan snapped.

I sent the command. "They're bringing Doc."

He gaped at me. "That will take hours." Both of us turned to the sound of running feet behind us. "And them?"

"Something to pass the time?" Rolling my head on my shoulders, I stretched my arms over my head. "I came here for a fight. You?"

Nikan's answering grin was wicked.

Four approached us; two shifted just as the other two attacked. They were skilled fighters. They weren't me or my brother.

It had never been a boast to make Kezia feel belittled. My pack was a pack of superior fighters. We trained extensively, and when I killed Rek, we had *all* thought that there would be retaliation from other packs. A pack with a new untested alpha was just as vulnerable as a pack without one. My pack wanted me as alpha, and for that, every single one of them had gone through emergency combat skills. It was one of the reasons we had been so eager to attend the Luna Ball. I'd put them through the training, and then no one had challenged us.

It was ironic.

The games at the Luna Ball were their outlet, or they were

supposed to be. Right up until Kezia went into heat and I knew she was my mate, and all thoughts of the games vanished like smoke on the wind...the same way my mate did.

Bale had filled his pack with fighters, I could see. But they weren't *my* fighters.

They didn't stand a chance.

CHAPTER 10

Cannon

Nikan looked at me as the pile of shifters finally stopped growing. "You think that's all of them?"

Surveying the bodies of the fallen, I glanced over my shoulder at the two wolves. Kris had tried to get to his feet, but he was too weak and was lying back on the ground, his body as close to his mate as possible. "No, there will be more. Once they've realized we're not moving from this cage, they'll have us where they want us."

"We need Doc," Nikan muttered.

Turning, I looked at the locked cell that held the two wolves. It was sealed shut with a chain wrapped around the door and the bars. The chain was made of silver, but the cell door was not.

"That look sturdy to you?"

Nikan eyed the heavy silver chain and then me. "Yes. It does. Don't even think about it."

He was right, what shifter would try to open a silver lock... when you could kick the door down instead? You needed strength to kick the door down. Not much strength in you if you were wearing a collar made of silver.

"Cannon!"

My brother's cry of protest was lost in the noise of my kick against the bars of the cell. I aimed my kicks at the iron hinges. They were sturdy, but nothing spectacular, in a cell that had been created in the tunnel of an old mine. When Nikan saw I wasn't going to stop, he joined me.

I grinned at him when the metal warped, and I grinned even more when the force of our kicks loosened the bolts, and then between us, with more luck than strength, we managed to pry the door open, enough that the she would get out. I had my doubts about Kris, but where there was a will, there was a way.

"Strip them," I commanded my brother, jerking my head towards the fallen members of Bale's pack.

"Why?" He was already doing it. That was his way—he followed orders, asking his questions as he did so.

"We'll use their clothing to shield our hands," I explained. "The collars are wide, but they don't look that thick." Stretching my arm through the gap we'd made, I tried to reach for the fallen she. "What's her name again, Nikan?"

"Cass," he answered, throwing shirts at me. "This is weird by the way. I mean, I know why, but I don't like undressing unconscious people."

"Would you prefer them dead?"

"Shut up."

Kris was on his feet again, and between the weak shoves with his head moving his mate across the dirt floor, I managed to snag a hold of her leg. Gently I pulled the young wolf towards me.

"She won't fit," Nikan murmured.

"I know." With great difficulty and extreme care, I managed to maneuver Cass into a position where my hands would fit around the collar at her neck. "Keep an eye on that tunnel." Wrapping a shirt around each hand, making sure they were as thick as possible but still allowing me to move, I reached out for the collar.

Even with the protection of the shirt, I felt the burning on my skin. Painful but not enough to stop me. There was no way to tell where the catch was; the clothing didn't allow for such intricacies. Instead, I hooked one hand under each side of the collar and pulled.

The she whined pitifully at the pressure on her neck. I knew it would be hurting her, and I tried to soothe her with soft words. Kris was hovering protectively, and I knew that had he had the strength, he would have been pacing to and fro in this cell.

"Is it working?" Nikan asked from behind me.

"I think I loosened it." Grunting, I pulled again. "Goddess, I thought it would be easier using these shirts." Gently I rotated the collar and pulled again. The warped silver wasn't loose but was definitely not as snug around the wolf's neck. Sweat gathered on my brow as I tried to stretch the metal again. The little wolf opened her eyes and met my stare. "Hey there," I murmured. "You're feeling better already, aren't you?"

Pulling my hands free of her collar, I drew my hands away, discarding the shirts I'd been wearing for protection. Scorch marks marked the clothing. Nikan and I exchanged a wordless look while I rewrapped my hands.

Four shirts later, and I had enough room made for Cass to almost get her head free. She was on her feet, her eyes a lot brighter, her concern for her mate getting stronger, which was making her careless. Gripping her snout, I pulled her head down to meet my eyes.

I was not her alpha, but I was *an* alpha. "Cass, look at me, I need you to focus. I almost have it, but this last bit will hurt, okay?" A low whimper in her throat, and I was reassuring her even more. "I'm going to hold it as steady as I can, and I need you to back up. Do it slowly and steadily." A huge ask when she had been almost dead a short while ago. "When I say *now*, I need you to jerk your head back with everything you have."

"If it hits her eyes, you'll blind her," Nikan murmured behind me.

"You must keep your eyes closed, Cass." I saw her wariness as she looked at me. "Trust me, okay? It's a big ask, I know, but Kris trusts me. Trust *him* if you can't trust me."

As she dipped her head slightly, I inhaled deeply. Carefully, slowly, I maneuvered the distorted collar over the wolf's neck. Cass held perfectly still, muscles taut from tension. During my time in the army, I'd watched children on the base engaging in a game involving a buzzer. Participants used tweezers to extract items from simulated human cavities, and touching the sides meant triggering the buzzer, and you lost your turn.

This was very much like that game. Only a red-nosed buzzer didn't sound. Instead, the wolf in front of me either flinched or whimpered when the collar touched her. Firming my grip on the collar, I braced myself.

"You ready?"

She looked back at me, apprehension clear in her gaze.

"Close your eyes, keep them closed. On my count, Cass." Nikan was practically on top of me, ready to offer support should I need it. "One, two...*three!*"

She jerked back as I pulled forward. Stunned, I looked at the empty collar in my hands, then immediately flung it away from me.

The wolf shifted to human immediately and then back to her wolfskin. Three times, she did it before turning to us and accepting a shirt from Nikan. It had scorch marks, but Cass donned it quickly. Dropping to her knees, she pressed her forehead against Kris.

"You're next, my love," she whispered. Looking up at me, she glanced between us both before getting to her feet. "Help him."

"That's the plan."

Nikan handed me a pair of pants. "You used all the shirts."

Kris stumbled closer, his ears pricking upward as he looked past me.

"Shit, they decided to come and investigate." The pants were thicker, so I didn't need as much protection against the silver, but they were harder to grip.

"Sounds like a few," Nikan muttered.

Kris held his head up, and I saw the collar and the lock on it. "Thanks." The running was getting closer. More than my brother could handle. They weren't coming closer, and I prayed they took the other tunnel *away* from us, but I knew our luck wouldn't hold much longer.

"Fuck." Ripping the leg of the pants off my hands, I tossed them aside. "Come here!"

"Cannon! No!" Nikan shouted just as I wrapped my bare hands around the silver collar and pulled against the locking mechanism of the collar.

The pain was excruciating. I tried to keep the agony contained—I didn't want to encourage our enemies to move faster. Strong hands wrapped around my wrists as Nikan crouched over me, adding his strength to mine, and the two of us pulled. Curls of smoke rose from the palms of my hands, and just when I thought it would never work, the collar snapped in half.

Kris danced backward, careening into his mate as he tried to regain his strength. Nikan was already grabbing my damaged hands, mumbling so fast I couldn't hear him over the roaring in my ears.

"Fuck, that hurts." Gritting my teeth, I let my brother help me out of my shirt. Kicking off my pants, I shifted to my wolf, a yelp of pain escaping as my damaged paws hit the packed dirt. Shifting once more, I knew I had no more time. The footsteps had slowed on their approach.

Give the clothes to Kris. We protect them at all costs.

"I'll shift too?"

No. Stay as you are. You protect them until they are stronger. I called for my beta. Hearing his answering call, I charged down the tunnel.

When we made it out of the tunnels, Kris was almost half-recovered, and seeing my pack weary but intact, I ordered the retreat. We had what I came for. There was no reason to over-stay our welcome.

We met Doc halfway down the mountain. He was on a dirt bike, and one of the younger males of the pack was on another. The young one shifted to his wolf as soon as he saw Cass and Kris. Nikan took over his bike, and Cass climbed on behind him, with Kris taking up position behind Doc.

We raced down the mountain. There was no sound of pursuit, but just because I didn't hear it, didn't mean it wasn't coming.

Back on packlands, I waited until every shifter who had

gone with me had passed me, returning to the shelter of their home.

My beta brought up the rear, along with three others of my pack. He gave me an angry scowl, and I knew I would be getting yelled at later. But I got what I wanted from Anterrio—Kris was safe and that was all that mattered. I'd need him soon to help find his sister.

MY HANDS WERE STILL TROUBLING me, but they were better than they had been. I rubbed the ointment that the shaman had made me into them while ignoring Doc's scowl at my use of the shaman's salve. We were in my study— Nikan, Royce, Doc and myself—waiting for the shaman to join us.

"You really hate this salve," I mocked, enjoying Doc's flush of annoyance.

"I've given you hundreds of medicines and remedies, and you've never used them once. He gives you a watery thin lotion, and you use it religiously twice a day."

"Your lotions don't soothe the burn of silver; the shaman's does."

"The shift isn't helping?" Royce asked me curiously.

"It does, but the ache, it's deep... It's hard to describe."

The sound of knocking on the study door made me turn my attention to our visitor. When Kris walked through the door with the shaman, I smiled widely on seeing him.

"Two days in a row you're up," I noted. "Better?"

Kris inclined his head to the others, letting out a slow exhale when he met my eyes. "I can't explain it, I feel..."

"Weary," the shaman told us all. "It aches down to your bones and feels like it will never stop burning."

I saw Doc frown, and he caught me looking. "You got a lotion for that?" I asked him.

"The salve will work," the shaman told me. "Shift at least three times per day too. Find someone who can rub the salve in your wolf form. It will help."

"My wife's been doing that for him," Royce told him. "Your mate aiding you?" he asked Kris.

"She'd have to be talking to me first," he muttered, sitting beside Nikan on the couch.

"Our next steps are not your decision," I reminded him. "This is my pack, and it is my choice how we proceed."

Kris was already nodding. "I know, I told her. But she thinks I can overrule you. She just wants us to rescue her twin." He didn't meet my gaze this time, looking past me to the window.

"I'll believe he needs saving either when he's in a silver collar like his sister was or when my mate returns and declares his innocence." I had more chance of the moon falling from the sky than my mate returning to me anytime soon.

"Shaman?" Kris asked his old friend.

"This is not my pack," the shaman spoke in a reasonable, calm voice. "You know better, Kristoff, than to use the Goddess to overrule an alpha." The old man turned his head to look at me. "I have thought over my most recent conversations with Landon as you asked, Alpha." The old shifter looked puzzled. "He spoke with clarity."

"Was he lying?"

"I have known him for a very long time." The shaman paused. "He was always skilled with strong conviction and—"

105

"Showmanship," Kris grunted. "He's a skilled performer. Don't believe a word he says."

Royce's eyebrows rose upward in surprise. His look to me spoke volumes. "Your mate is his sister."

"I know." Kris was on his feet. Making his way amongst the outstretched legs, he walked to the bookshelves. "Luna, Kez would have died when she saw these."

I moved over to see what he was talking about. "Crime novels?"

"She loves this author. Goddess, I don't know how many suppers I've sat through, listening to her retelling me the entire book." He looked at me over his shoulder. "No wonder you're mates."

I wanted to tell him it was more than a shared love of the same genre of books, but when I saw his look, I knew he understood that it was *so* much more than that.

"If she ever comes back, I'll gift her the whole collection."

Kris gave the books his back as he looked over the occupants of the study. "I need to hear it all again."

And so I listened to the retelling of Kezia leaving the pack and the return of Moonstar. I sat silent throughout it.

Some would call it brooding. *Some* could kiss my ass.

When they were finished and Kris had asked the same questions, silence fell around us. Looking up, I saw the shaman looking right at me.

"Shaman?"

"You have been quiet for too long, Alpha." Leaning back in his seat, he tilted his head to the ceiling, his stare so focused it was as if he could see through it. "The anger burns deep. Not all that scorches your bones is silver."

Bowing my head, I heard what he said. "I need to know

where she is," I admitted quietly. "I can't think, I can't focus. All I can *feel* is her absence."

"Yet you sit here," the shaman chided, "with the books."

"I committed an act of war on a neighboring pack. We have one of the pack leader's children, his beta, and the pack's shaman in my pack. It could be said that I kidnapped them. Bale has not retaliated, why? *Why*? Because he is within his rights to call for Pack Council. And I lost the advantage when..."

"When you rescued me and Cass."

It wasn't fair to blame Kris. It was my choice to get him and his mate to safety, and I would make it again. Even if it meant I had lost my advantage. Which I had.

Kris shuffled his feet. "I could go back." He met my stony glare. "She's my mate, he's her twin."

"And they would take you prisoner again." When he went to argue, my temper rose higher. "You will stay in my pack until we have a better plan than you going back and handing yourself over for that limp dick little shit."

Kris stared at me, his body still. "I *will* stay?"

My gaze swept over *my* mate's brother, reminding myself she would kill me if I put him in the cells, even if it was for his own protection. "You are my guest."

"Am I?" We held each other's stare until Kris looked away. "Sorry. But..."

"There should be no but." Royce's glare was just as hard as mine. "We offer you shelter; don't fuck it up by betraying our alpha's trust."

Kris was pacing again. "Just listen. Okay?" When no one spoke, he looked at the shaman, who gave a slight nod. "Right. Well...so, I've been digging. Ever since we knew...things."

"What kind of things?" Royce asked warily.

Kris tugged at his ear. "For years, we"—he gestured to the shaman and himself—"have suspected that Bale has been bribing the Pack Council." I noticed that my own wide-eyed shock mirrored those of the others. "As I dug deeper... He's not bribing them, he *owns* them."

"Owns them?" That was Doc. "What does that mean?"

Kris was shaking his head. "He owns them. He's got so much dirt on them, and they've earned so much money off his *extra income*, they'll do whatever he wants."

"What's the extra income?" Nikan asked, glancing at me.

"I didn't know," Kris blurted. "Landon told Cass. Just before we were taken. I see no reason for him to lie about it, not to her."

"Told her what?" I asked. "That he knew they were going to put a collar around her neck?"

"No, he's a dick, but he would never have rested with his sister locked up. Definitely not with silver on her." Kris looked at me, his eyes begging me to see reason. "He's a dick, but he's not that kind of dick."

"So just their father, then?" Nikan quipped sarcastically.

"Then what is it he *did* know?" I snapped irritably, and I saw his face and I already knew. It made so much sense. *So* much fucking sense. "The fights."

Kris nodded. "Bale organizes the fights that Kezia was fighting in. It's where all the extra men have come from. He sends his shifters there to train and to earn money for the pack." He cleared his throat. "His other pack."

"*Other* pack?" Royce demanded, his attention on me now.

"He knew where she was the whole time?" Nikan asked at the same time.

Kris was nodding, his anger evident. "He was keeping tabs on her. I think it was Bale who covered up the death of those humans."

"It was *Bale* who gave the order to kill her. He told them to shoot her with silver." I was on my feet, rage rolling off me in waves of fury. "Why her? Why Kezia?"

"I don't know, but I think..." Kris's head was lowered, and he raised it to meet my anger with his own. "That he's always wanted her...us? Dead."

"There's a woman here; she knew your parents. She told us Bale was obsessed with your mother." Kris looked interested, but my thoughts were already racing. "But that makes no sense for him to obsess over Kezia." Running a hand through my hair, I closed my eyes. "What am I missing?" I was asking myself more than them.

"A psychotic break."

Opening my eyes, I looked at Doc in question. "It's a human term. Who knows, it may occur in shifters too. It's when a person has a medical condition that affects the mind, or experiences something so traumatic that their mental health deteriorates." His eyes flicked to mine. "They lose touch with reality. It makes them delusional. Sometimes dangerous."

"And this is relevant to who?" I asked cautiously.

Doc shifted in his seat. "What if Bale isn't fixated on Kezia like we think?" He looked over at Kris. "What if it's you?"

"Me?" Kris turned to the shaman as he spoke to Doc. "I've known him most of my life. Why would I be the reason he's suddenly gone mad?"

"Cass." Royce rubbed his jaw as he thought about it. "His daughter. You turn up at his pack as a child, when you're supposed to be dead, and you have a wild untamed sister with

109

you. He takes you in, the son of his former obsession. He keeps you close so he can watch you."

"And you hide the fact you're an alpha from him." I knew where Royce was going. "I did it with Rek; I understand why you did it. But then his daughter has her first heat and finds her mate. You. Alerting Bale that you've been lying to him all along, and now the son of his enemy—"

"Enemy?" Kris questioned.

"Your dad got Bale's girl. I was told he sent his pack to fight him the night your dad and mom went back to see her family. Doesn't sound friendly to me." I waited until he had a moment to think about it. "And then you're revealed as Cass's mate. Because you are an alpha. And she's his only daughter. And he... breaks." Nikan looked at me with a *what the fuck* look. I agreed with the sentiment entirely.

"That would do it," Doc agreed.

"You think we're right," I realized as Kris stared wordlessly at the shaman. "Don't you?"

"I think so." Kris's concern matched my own.

"He's been building this for years," I mused. "That compound, those males there, they don't happen overnight."

"The mate bond accelerated his plan?" Royce asked doubtfully.

I sighed long and loud. "I don't know," I admitted, banging my hand off the wall in frustration. "But it feels...right. He's been building and preparing for something, but what? Just to feel prepared as he isn't an alpha?" I looked around at them all. "And if we're right, none of us are safe. Plus, he has the Pack Council in his pocket."

Kris's hands were in his hair. "We're fucked."

"And Kezia is in even more danger out there alone," I

added. "Because he won't rest if she's free. She's your sister, so she's your weakness." She was mine too, but I saw her brother's eyes harden, his jaw clenched.

"Yeah, she is." He began to pace. "Fuck it all to hell."

The study was once more in total silence until the shaman snorted in a most undignified manner. "Well, there will be none of that. Alpha Cannon, isn't it time you found your mate?"

CHAPTER 11

Kezia

IT FELT LIKE I WAS ENCASED IN MUD.

No. Mud wasn't right, it was heavier than mud. The feeling clung to my skin, weighing me down.

Everything was muffled.

Sensation lost.

Touch forgotten.

Again and again, I pushed to reach the surface of whatever it was that was forcing me down, but as hard as I tried, I couldn't climb any higher.

I needed to breathe.

Where was the air?

What was suffocating me?

Struggling to know what was happening, fighting to escape this feeling of helplessness, I blacked out.

~

WHERE AM I?

Opening my eyes, I saw only blackness.

Maybe your eyes are still shut?

I tried to look again. It was the same blackness. Placing my fingers on my eyelids, I checked to see if my eyes were shut.

I felt nothing.

I felt everything.

What the actual fuck is happening?

≈

I WAS FLYING.

I can fly?

No, you idiot, you can't fly. Great, now I was answering my own questions. *And now you're just talking to yourself.*

I waited. Quietly. No voices.

Not even mine.

It definitely felt like I was flying.

Soaring.

Weightless.

Wait...not flying. Floating?

Where the heck am I?

≈

I WAS DRIFTING.

So I was still going with the floaty theme, great.

Turning around—

I turned? Did I turn?

I stopped drifting. I could stop drifting?

I'm treading water? No, that couldn't be right. I wasn't wet.

I checked my clothes to see if I was wet. There was nothing to check.

Holy shit, I have no body! Who took my body? Is this a dream? Where's my body?

And then I remembered.

I blacked out.

IT WAS STILL BLACK.

Used to the feeling of depersonalization, I turned in a circle to look around.

Do you even have eyes?

The idea of me being *just* a pair of eyes freaked me out, and I squeezed my eyes shut.

How can you squeeze your eyes shut if you are only *eyes?*

Kris was right. I was really annoying with all the questions I asked.

Kris.

My brother. An alpha.

Cannon...

My *alpha.*

Panic welled within me.

Where was my alpha?

WHEN MY CONSCIOUSNESS returned this time, I didn't waste time worrying about whether I was real or not. I was already turning, searching, desperate for a way out.

Spinning fruitlessly in a black hole abruptly stopped when I saw, in the distance, the faintest of lights.

Lights.

I needed to get *there*.

How the hell do you move when you have no body and no limbs?

Think, Kezia.

THINK.

I may have no actual body, but I can still *feel* my body, and if I can feel it and I can still think, then I can still walk.

Right?

I could already hear Kris tearing through my logic, but like I usually did when my brother was critiquing me about my *whimsical thoughts*, I ignored him.

I willed myself to put one foot in front of the other.

I moved.

If floating around in a disassociated thought was moving, then I moved.

I moved again.

Holy Goddess, I'm walking.

Swallowing, I moved faster. If I could walk...then I could *run*.

It seemed to be very sudden that the light grew brighter. I ran towards it, ignoring every sarcastic thought in my head saying *not* to run towards the light, and as I got even closer, I slowed down.

Squinting against the sudden brightness, I crept forward and promptly fell over.

I was me.

I wasn't me.

I mean I *was* me, but I also wasn't.

Holy shit, these are my eyeballs. I'm looking out through my eyeballs, but I'm not seeing with my eyes in my body. I'm seeing with my eyes. The floating ones.

Wait.

What?

I needed to calm down.

Where am I?

I'm inside my body. Obviously.

But I wasn't in control of my body.

Moonstar was.

Moonstar.

I gave her control.

I gave up.

I never give up. Why would I do that?

The alpha.

Where was my alpha?

I WAS BACK in the darkness.

This is getting old.

There were no pinpricks of light this time. I was back to floating.

Ugh, enough with the floating!

I channeled my thoughts to my feet. Ah-ha! I could walk again. *Fuck you, floating!*

Time to explore.

I found nothing. *Are you sleeping?*

It made sense. I could be asleep. *Moonstar* could be asleep.

Is this how she felt inside me?

I giggled.

You're a child, Kezia, Cannon is already rolling his eyes at you.

Cannon...

I WANT MY MATE.

Bitch.

He better be alive, or I will skin you alive from the inside out.

WE WERE RUNNING.

I was already in front of my eyes—behind my eyes?—when I became aware again.

I was my wolf.

Thank you, Luna.

I could feel more. I could do more.

I *was* more.

Stop running.

The command did nothing.

Focus, Kezia.

Stop.

I felt the hesitation in my being.

Oh Goddess, you can hear me.

Stop *running.*

The wolf slowed down. *I* slowed down.

Look around. Show me where we are.

My wolf shook her head, snow falling off her muzzle.

It's winter?

The landscape came into view. A scattering of trees. Dark gray mountain. Barren land.

I'm on the Peak.

Turn around, look down, show me how high we are.

Holy hell, that was a long way down.

A force hit me, knocking me away from the sight.
Sleep, child.

∾

I WAS WRAPPED in something soft and warm. I was so comfy.
I could stay here forever, and nothing would bother me.

I was so tired.

I was happy to snuggle down and sleep.

∾

You BITCH.

Let me out, you crazy demon.

Let.

Me.

OUT.

∾

MY WOLF WAS MOVING.

Running.

I could taste the scent of autumn in the air as I chased the
wind.

No, not the wind.

Hare.

I loved to hunt.

∾

WHEN I WAS aware once more, I was already using my wolf's eyes to look around. Thicker trees, sturdier, I was lower down the mountain.

My head jerked as I scented people nearby.

Shifters.

Anxiously I watched my wolf edge closer to the settlement.

Friend or foe?

My wolf's head snapped to the side as a familiar scent caught its nose.

Alpha.

THE HUNGER WAS RAVENOUS.

The need ruling my body.

My skin itched with want.

Lust burned through me.

Scorching me with its heat.

Alpha.

COLD AIR NIPPED at my bones.

Shivering, I moved my hair out of my face.

I froze when I saw my hand.

I had a hand.

I had hair.

I could *see.*

"Fuck." My eyes widened and I waited a moment before I realized it had been me that I heard. "I can swear! I can speak!"

My arms were weak, but I managed to push myself off the ground and scrambled to my feet.

"Where am I?"

I was naked and disoriented. Turning and turning in a circle, I tried to get my bearings. Hearing noise from what I hoped was a town, I forgot stealth as I stumbled toward the noise.

"Stop! Don't come any further. We'll shoot first and ask questions later."

I froze mid-step.

Familiarity brushed against me. I knew that voice.

Slowly I walked forward.

Two women stared at me in varying shades of shock. One older and wirier, the other redder in the cheeks and younger, but long past her youth.

"Angels save us, I'm seeing spirits."

"Lottie?" I looked at the other woman. "Maggie?"

"Zia?" Lottie moved towards me, shotgun still pointed at me. "If you're a spirit, I swear on the good book, I'll haunt your naked ass."

"I'm me."

I *was* me. I was back. Holy Goddess, I was in my body...and it was fucking cold.

"Can I get a coat? It's freezing."

CHAPTER 12

WITH MY HANDS WRAPPED AROUND A STEAMING MUG of tea, I watched the two women, who were openly staring at me while pretending they weren't.

I should have been hurt that Lottie's hand didn't stray far from the shotgun, but considering I had been gone for over a year, had been a wanted killer, or at least a fugitive, which was then a case of mistaken identity, I wasn't holding it against her.

"You need to eat?" Lottie asked me.

"Yes." I looked at her as I sipped my tea. "Can you cook better yet?"

"I can cook fine." Her glare was the same, and it made me smile.

"In that case, I'm not hungry."

"Lost your damn clothes, not lost your smart mouth, I see," she snarked, but I saw her lips tug upwards before she pretended to scowl more.

"He told me you were both dead." Okay, so I was going right there. "The guy..." How did I explain this?

"I think we need to call the police," Maggie tried to whisper to Lottie.

"I don't need the police." My voice was a little too high, a little more high-strung sounding than normal. "I can kind of explain to you both, kind of."

"Why?" Lottie's hand inched closer to the shotgun. "Why no police?"

"Do you have silver bullets in there?"

Lottie looked at Maggie quickly, her finger now on the barrel of the shotgun. "Maybe we should call someone."

"Lottie, I'm fine."

"You're not fine!" she snapped. "Sitting here as bare as the day you were born, gone for months, and now asking about silver bullets. You think you're a damned werewolf or something, girl?" Her snort was loud. "You need help." Maggie was nodding along with every word. "Let us help you."

"You *are* helping me. I have a blanket and a cup of tea. I just need time to warm up." Which was a lie as I was already toasty. "I can be gone so quick you won't even know I was here." I watched them share a dubious look. "I thought you were both dead." Lowering my cup of tea to the table, I knew I needed to explain. "I can't tell you how happy I am to see you are both alive and well."

"Wouldn't say well." Lottie sniffed. She took a seat, her hand no longer so near to the gun. "Your disappearance and then manhunt"—she grunted out *man*—"aged me about ten years, I reckon."

"Did you kill those men?"

I met the fear in Maggie's eyes, and I knew there was no point lying. "I did. They were going to rape me, then murder me. I fought them and I won." She looked worse after the explanation if that were possible. "If you could let me finish my tea, I'll go. You can call the police and never have to see me again."

"You'll stay where you are." Lottie gave me a meaningful look before she turned to Maggie. "Never heard you argue against self-defense before." She slid the shotgun across the counter to Maggie. "Hold onto that if it makes you feel better."

It shouldn't have made me sad when Maggie pulled the butt of the gun closer to her.

"Where have you been? Why *are* you naked? Who can we call?" Folding her bony arms across her chest, Lottie waited for me to answer. "I'll know if you're lying."

"I was taken." Not a lie. "I was held prisoner." Also not a lie. "I escaped." Still not a lie. I'd escaped so many places now, it was almost funny. "I didn't have any clothes, which is why I'm naked." Truth. "I need to call my brother."

"You have a brother?"

"Yes. He's older. He needs to know I'm okay."

Maggie's hand flexed on the gun. "He'll be worried? He knows you are missing?"

"Yes, I'm worried about him too. May I use a phone?"

"You're not telling us it all."

Lottie. Luna, I'd missed this woman, but I hadn't missed the fact she was almost shifter-sensitive when it came to sniffing out bullshit. "I'm telling you what I can."

Still not lying.

Digging into her pocket, Lottie handed me an old and battered cell phone. "Know his number?"

Taking it, I felt the wry smile as I punched in his number to make the call. "It's the only one I know."

Anxiety twisted inside me as I waited for Kris to answer. What if something happened to him? What if he no longer had this phone? What would I do if he never answered? How much had I missed? Was anyone hurt? Was he alive? What if Bale answered?

Panic surged through me. *Shit!*

"Who is this?"

Tears spilled down my cheeks as I heard his gruff voice. "Kris?"

"*Kezia?*"

"Yeah, it's me. Are you okay? Are you free? I need you to come get me."

"Kezia?" I could already hear him moving. "Kezia, is it... *Fuck*. Is it you? Tell me you're okay."

I was sobbing now. "Is he alive? Are you hurt? Is he okay?"

"He's fine. I'm fine. *Where* are you?" I heard the phone move and a muffled shout, realizing Kris had covered the phone. "I shouted for him. Where are you? Are you hurt? Is she there?"

She? I understood.

"I'm fine. I'm with old...friends." Both of whom were watching me with a mix of curiosity and suspicion. "They found me in the woods. They took me home—"

"Home?"

"To their home," I corrected quickly. "One of their homes. I got a cup of tea, a whole lot of explaining to do, and a phone call. I can't get to you as I am," I told him, hoping he would understand that I was scared to shift. I couldn't explain more with the women both listening, so I asked what I needed to know. "How is he?"

"Furious."

I laughed. It felt as if I hadn't laughed in so long, but my brother's blunt one-worded answer made me feel *light*. "Good, I am too."

"Cannon isn't nearby. He's...busy with pack stuff. Tell me where you are. I'm coming for you."

Busy? Lowering the phone, I asked Lottie. "Can I tell your address to my brother?"

"Is he coming?"

"Yes."

"He dangerous?"

"Yes." I saw the scowl again. "But not to you." My eyes flicked to Maggie, who had a death grip on the gun, and I put the phone back to my ear. "On second thought, I'll wait on the edge of town. I'm in Baywater Creek; it's not that far really." It was pathetic how close I'd stayed to the mountains of my home when I thought I was "running away." "When will you leave?"

I was eager to see him. I was eager to be back on the mountain. If I shifted and lost control, who knew how long it would take for me to come back.

"I'm leaving now, Kez." His voice was soft, but I could hear his urgency.

"Kris, how long have I been gone?"

Lottie's eyes widened with sympathy, and even Maggie looked less likely to shoot me. I looked away from them. I didn't want to explain anything, but I knew I had to tell them *something*.

"Seven weeks."

That was almost two months.

"Three days short of two months," he added gruffly.

"You counting?" I tried to tease him, but I was too emotional.

"Cannon is."

Tears dripped off my chin. "He's really okay?"

"He's really okay. She did it."

I heard more muffled talking, and then an engine roared to life. "You're driving?"

"Royce is. I'll be there soon." I heard a door closing. "Don't move from there. Don't shift. Stay out of sight."

"I will."

"I'll see you soon. I love you."

"I love you too."

As I handed Lottie back her phone, she handed me a tissue. "Reckon we'll need more tea." Looking between me and Maggie, she nodded to herself. "I'll get you a change of clothes. Maggie, put the kettle on."

"Why were you in the woods?" It had been bothering me. It was so random for them to be out there.

"Seen a white wolf lurking on the edge of town," Lottie told me with a gleam in her eye. "Not seen it for a long time. Not since you were last here."

I swallowed hard. Did they know?

"Been out looking for it for a few days, finally convinced Maggie to come look with me." She slapped the other woman on the shoulder. "She must be my lucky charm."

"Did you find it?" I was shaking. "The wolf?"

"Nope. Found you." Lottie started to walk to the stairs. "I'll get those clothes. Maggie, we need more tea." When the other woman didn't move, Lottie came back and snatched the gun off her, startling her. "Make tea." Looking at the gun in her hand, she shook her head. "I'll keep this." Lottie glanced back at me. "I'm ready to hear more of your story, Zia."

The problem was, was I ready to tell it?

I watched as Maggie made tea and Lottie handed me a pair of jeans, a sweater, and underwear. It was all mine from before. The fact that she had kept my stuff made me teary-eyed. She'd gestured to the bathroom wordlessly with another meaningful look at Maggie as she did. I understood she wanted five minutes alone with her, and in the bathroom, I pulled on the clothes, splashed water on my face, and did my best to tame my hair.

I looked like a wild woman. No wonder Maggie had been holding onto that gun.

Lottie rapped her knuckles against the door to let me know it was time to come out. Taking a deep breath, I pulled the door open and joined them in the kitchen.

"More tea, Zia?"

"That would be great, thanks." I watched Maggie as she buttered a thick slice of white bread. When she put it in front of me, I murmured my thanks.

"Are you still on the run?"

It was Maggie who spoke, and it surprised me she went straight to it. Why it did, I wasn't sure; she'd always been forthright. "No. I believe they dropped the case."

"But you said you killed them."

"I did." I took a bite of the bread, my mouth watering in appreciation. "This is good."

"No need to sound surprised," Lottie grumbled. "I *buy* the bread."

Maggie and I shared an amused look as I took another bite until she realized what she'd done and looked away hastily. "It's delicious." I ignored my disappointment.

"You human?"

I gaped at Lottie. "If you cut me, I bleed."

"If I cut a fox, it bleeds too."

"I'm human." I took a smaller bite of bread. "Mostly."

Lottie sucked her teeth as she watched me chew. "Mostly?"

"I'm something else, too."

"What is it?" Maggie asked, and I heard her nerves as she spoke.

"You don't need to know." Putting the bread down, I looked between them. "I won't hurt you. Ever. I give you my word..." I knew I was doing the right thing. "But I can't tell you. It's dangerous for you to know, and I won't put you in danger."

"Are we in danger with you being here?"

I held Maggie's stare. "Possibly."

She looked at Lottie, and Lottie nodded at the unspoken question she saw in Maggie's eyes. "Go. I'll be fine here. Zia would never hurt me."

Maggie's head dipped. "I want to stay, I do, but..."

"I killed three men, I disappeared, I turn up naked and confused, and I just told you I'm not fully human and it could be dangerous me being here." I smiled at her. "Honestly? You're crazy if you stay."

"You sure?" she asked Lottie, and when the older woman nodded, Maggie squeezed Lottie's hand and hurried to the door. She hesitated on her way out. "I won't tell anyone I saw you, Zia."

I swallowed past the lump in my throat. "I appreciate that."

Her eyes turned soft as she looked at me. "I really am glad you're okay. Stay safe."

The door closed behind her, and I turned to look at Lottie. "Stay safe but not here." I picked my bread up again. "I can go."

"It's cold out. You can stay here. I reckon your kin knows how to find you." She was slicing more of the bread. "Want some bacon to go with this?"

"Well, now I do."

As I finished my first slice, we were quiet as I watched her fry the bacon to a lovely crispness and then carried on cremating it even when I tried to politely tell her it was ready. Nevertheless, when she placed the four formerly-known-as-bacon slices in front of me, I added them to my new slice of bread, folded the slice in half, and ate my sandwich. Lottie ate her own slice of bread, and we sat in comfortable silence. It was familiar and it settled me.

"You a werewolf?"

I almost choked on my meal. When I recovered enough to answer, I shook my head. "I told you I won't tell you."

"Okay." She took a large swallow of tea. "Nod, don't speak. Are you a werewolf?"

Sneaky. I liked sneaky, so I nodded and saw her eyes widen a little. "Shifter, not a werewolf. We prefer shifter." I sniffed. "We don't need the moon to shift."

"Ah, I wondered." Lottie looked down at her plate and then back up at me. "So you are both?" When she saw my confusion, she elaborated. "Wolf and girl."

"Yes."

"Just a wolf?"

Her question made me smile a little. "There's no *just* about it."

"You don't *shift* into anything else?" I shook my head. "I have questions. Questions I know I shouldn't ask, and even if I did, you'd shut up quicker than a clam." Leaning back in her seat, she shook her head a little as she looked me over. "Did they deserve it? To die?"

"Yes."

She looked out the window, her gaze thoughtful. "Knew you were different the first night I saw you slipping outside that cabin into the woods naked." Lottie ignored my startled look.

"Thought you were one of the new-age pray-at-the-moon people." She harrumphed. "I've always been too straightlaced to be a hippie. Free love in the sixties meant being a little too freer than I was comfortable with." She sniffed with disdain. "All manner of diseases going around. No siree. Not for me."

"You thought I was a hippie?"

"You were a drifter. Young. Carefree. Forgive me that I thought that before I thought *werewolf*." Her dry tone made me grin.

"Shifter."

"Whatever." Lottie got up, crossed to the sink, and poured her tea away. "Think I need whiskey." She pulled a tumbler down off the shelf, looking at me in question, and didn't wait for an answer before she took another one down. Sitting back down across from me, she handed me my drink. "Saw you do it a few more times, and then more than once, I saw a white wolf in the trees, and it would disappear and then you'd be there. Still naked...but happier." She blew out a breath. "Which is when I started thinking you were more than a hippie." She grinned at my eye roll. "Tell me what you can."

I sipped the whiskey, the burn at the back of my throat making me cough slightly. "Holy Luna, woman, that's lethal."

Lottie's grin got wider. Taking a drink, she hissed in appreciation. "Puts hair on your chest."

"I don't want hair on my chest," I reminded her as I took another drink.

"Why? You got yourself a man?"

I nodded, my smile breaking free and loving that it did. "He's..."

"Let me guess, *perfect*..."

"Yeah." I frowned as I thought of my alpha. "He's also a

dick. Sometimes." I scrunched my nose up as I thought of Cannon. "Most times."

"The best ones usually are a good blend of both." Lottie grew serious again. "As I said, Zia, tell me what you can. I won't repeat a word of it. Not even to Maggie." Her hand had a slight tremor the next time she spoke. "When they came asking for you last time, I ran them off, but it took a while before I was able to sleep right through the night."

Vance. The bastard.

Reaching over, I squeezed her hand. "I'm sorry."

Lottie patted the hand that held hers. "You did nothing wrong. I never spilled anything about you then; I won't do it now."

Taking a drink of my whiskey, I avoided her stare as I considered what to say. "We're born under the grace of Luna. Humans with a little bit of magic in them, a little bit more bite." I winked at her as I spoke. "We keep to ourselves. It is forbidden to tell humans. For our protection, I think." I remembered Bullet and his friends. "Your kind can be so cruel." I thought of Bale and the abuse I had suffered with him. "My kind too." I finished my whiskey. "We're faster, stronger, and can heal ourselves from most wounds."

"Handy." I wanted to laugh at her expression, eyes wide with wonder.

"We still get sick." I held my glass out for more when she poured her own. "We can still die."

"What did they want with you last time?"

"To hurt me." I sighed. "I'd been participating in illegal fighting rings. They didn't like my winning streak."

"You cheated?" Lottie looked surprised.

"I didn't think I did, but I was able to heal after a match,

131

and I went back too quickly for more. My need for more money meant I grew careless." Pushing my hair off my face, I shrugged. "Not grew, I *was* careless."

"They caught you? Is that where you've been?"

"No." A pull in my lower belly had me turning in my seat, my attention on the door. "My mate did."

"Mate? Who's he?"

I wanted to race to the door and fling it open, but I forced myself to remain sitting in place. I wasn't sure if Cannon was as eager to see me as I was him. That kept me in my seat. "You're about to meet him."

"What?" Lottie was off her chair, slightly panicked as she looked between me and the door. "When?"

"Now."

CHAPTER 13

I WATCHED THE DOOR WARILY. THE SHARP RAP against the wood made me jump a little even though I was expecting it. Lottie moved into my line of sight, and I knew without looking at her, she was waiting for me to tell her to open it.

"Do I need my gun?" she whispered.

"No."

We both watched the door handle push down. My mate was never one for patience.

The door swung open, and when my brother stepped through, joy erupted at the sight of him, but I still pushed away the disappointment that he wasn't Cannon. I was off my seat and across the room, and he crossed the space to sweep me into a hug.

"Luna's grace, you are a sight for sore eyes," he muttered as he squeezed me close.

I squeezed him back as tightly as he held me. "It's so good to know you are okay." I looked up at him. "How are you here?"

Kris stepped back, and I saw Royce over his shoulder. I

shouldn't have been surprised when Royce simply nodded in greeting, but I had to admit that I was expecting more than a nod.

"Cannon got me and Cass out," Kris told me gruffly.

Looking back at the door expectantly, I saw it was closed. "Where is he?"

Royce's attention flicked behind me, and I turned to see Cannon standing there. A part of me knew why he'd come in the back way, and that same part knew that would piss me off later, but for now, I drank him in. In a pair of faded denims, bare feet, and bare chest, he'd obviously just shifted from his wolf. His hair was messy, the way I liked it, his jaw was clenched, and his eyes hard.

He was alive.

Holy Luna, he was alive. Pissed off but alive—and *healthy.*

My chest tightened with emotion, and I already knew I was crying.

"He told me you were dead." I felt like I was frozen in place as I watched him watch me. I saw a flicker of emotion in his eyes, and it was seeing that break in his armor that snapped my control. I ran to him and threw my arms around him, my tears flowing freely as I sobbed against his chest. "Thank you, Luna, thank you," I whispered over and over. Looking up, I met his cold, hard, green eyes. Fear gripped me. "Cannon?"

His arms hadn't embraced me. His mouth hadn't met mine. He hadn't reacted to me.

Backing away, I shook my head. The way he was looking at me was for the same reason as he covered the back door exit.

He didn't trust me...

"No. *No!* You can fuck off. Do not even *think* of doubting me. I have been in misery. I have been beaten, threatened, all of it. I wanted to die, thinking you were dead. You do *not* come into this house and *doubt* me." I shook my head in denial. "You don't get to fucking do this to me, Cannon!"

Looking at my alpha, I wanted to cry again. He was alive. He was standing in front of me and *breathing*. As angry as I was at his reaction to me, I just wanted to hold him. "I never thought I'd see you again."

Cannon broke our stare, looking down at the floor. "You almost didn't."

His voice did something to me. The anger faded as quickly as it came. More tears escaped as I stepped forward, my hand reaching for him. "I should have never left. I knew it as soon as I was halfway up that mountain. I'm so sorry, Alpha."

Cannon tilted his head back slightly, his eyebrow arching. "Alpha? Sorry?" He glanced at Lottie. "I can smell the whiskey. How much has she had to drink?"

I coughed out a laugh, hope rising within me as I took another step forward. "He told me you were dead." I started sobbing again, and I angrily brushed the tears away. "I couldn't move, I couldn't eat, it was horrible. I thought you were gone." I hiccupped and took another step towards him. "I don't care if you think I'm drunk, please, Cannon, they told me you were dead. I need to hold you."

His face gave nothing away, and I felt he would say no, but just as I was ready for rejection, he gave a slight nod, and I closed the distance with a speed that surprised us both. I heard his *oof*, but I didn't care, because this time my mate was hugging me back.

All the weeks that we had been apart, all the horribleness we had both endured, it all faded away as his arms tightened around me, and I used them to lift myself onto my tiptoes as I hung onto him like the lifeline he was. Silent tears coursed down my cheeks, and when Cannon lifted me higher, I wrapped myself around him, while his head nestled into the crook of my neck.

And he held me.

And he didn't let go.

And for the first time, in so long, my heart didn't hurt.

"I've missed you so much," I whispered into his shoulder. "I thought I lost you."

"I think you almost did."

His words were sobering enough to make me lift my head and look at him. "Bad?"

I heard Royce grunt and had completely forgotten there were others in the room. "Bad?" he bit out. "I don't think any of us thought he would be standing again."

Reaching up, I brushed the hair off Cannon's face. "Tell me everything."

Cannon let me down, and realizing I wasn't letting go of him completely, he wrapped his arm around me. "Introductions first?" He looked at Lottie, who had remained silent the whole time, her back against the wall as she watched us all.

"Oh shit, Lottie." I gaped at her. "Um, this is my brother, Kris." He nodded in greeting. "Royce. He's usually more cheerful, but harmless." Royce growled under his breath, and Lottie's eyes widened. "He's harmless to you!" I corrected. "And this is..." I turned my face up to look at Cannon, who was watching me, and when I reached up to touch his face, he leaned into my palm. Our eyes locked, my pulse racing, and I marveled that he was in front of me.

"This is your fella," Lottie deadpanned. "I'm Lottie."

Cannon looked away from me, and I saw the question.

"Vance lied. Lottie and Maggie are fine. He didn't kill them like he said," I told the males in the room. "They found me earlier." I saw Cannon and Kris exchange a look, and I wasn't sure what it meant. "What? What was that look?"

"It's not safe for you here," Kris told me. "We need to move."

"I can be trusted," Lottie told them, understanding the look far quicker than I did. She walked back to the counter. "Zia has explained a little of what she is." I felt Cannon's arm tighten on my waist. "I may not have known her as long as you all have, but I'd give my life for this girl. Almost did last time," she added. "I trust her, you should trust me."

"Lottie, you said it wasn't... He hurt you?"

Her eyes gentled when she saw my concern. "I'm fine." She scowled at Kris. "No harm will ever come to your sister through me, and I don't like the implication it would."

"Ma'am." Kris had the grace to look abashed at the reprimand. "But we're exposed here, and we need to be gone."

Lottie looked at me, and I was already turning to Cannon. "Can we take Lottie?" His reaction was a slight widening of his eyes. "Please, Cannon. If they come back..."

"No." Cannon pressed a kiss to my forehead to soften the blow. "Do you have family you can visit?" he asked Lottie.

"No."

"See!" I seized on it. "No one will miss her."

"Geez, thanks, Zia."

"Shh," I scolded her over my shoulder.

"Kez," Kris muttered, and I could hear his warning.

"She knows I'm a shifter." This time, Cannon's eyes narrowed. "She knew before today, saw me last time. Never

137

mentioned it to anyone." I prayed to the Goddess that Lottie wouldn't mention Maggie. "Please, I need to know she's safe."

"I'll make this easy for you all," Lottie said as she poured herself another whiskey. "This is my home. I run a business here, and I have no intention of leaving it."

"But—"

She took a drink as she watched me. "You come visit me. You are always welcome, but I belong here." She gestured at the man beside me. "You belong where he is. It's the twenty-first century; technology will allow us to keep in touch. I know you have phones," she added with a slight smile. "I think you need to go with your family."

"I think that would be best," Cannon said to her softly.

"But—"

"Shh." Cannon pulled me into his body tighter. "We need to move."

"But..." I felt lost again. "I can't lose anyone else." I knew I was crying again.

"You haven't lost anyone," Royce reminded me gruffly. "Your friend here is fine, Cannon is fine."

"I still thought I'd lost them," I snapped at him. "My grief was real. My loss was real." Staring at my hands, I shook my head. "I don't want to go through that again. I can't go through that again," I added, looking at Cannon. "I broke."

"I'm here," he told me, and the way he was looking at me had me turning into his body again, feeling comfort when his arms wrapped around me.

Sooner than I was ready, we were in the Jeep Royce had driven to get them here, and Lottie's place was behind us. I was in the back with my brother, Royce was driving, and Cannon, being the biggest, was in the passenger seat.

"She'll be okay," Kris reassured me, patting my hand.

Wiping my eyes, I tried to convince myself she would. "Tell me what happened to you."

Cannon turned in his seat and met my gaze.

"I came home, and you weren't there," he started. "I thought you may be with Nikan or Barbara. When I went to look for you, I passed Tev, and when I went past him, he stabbed me in the back. Twice. The second time, he left the silver blade in my back where I couldn't reach it."

My eyes were wide, I knew that, but I was still reaching for him, and he turned, leaning forward so I could see his back. A thin scar was evident in the low light of the car, and I glared at the mark on my alpha's body. "Tell me you killed him."

"Nikan took care of that," Royce said gruffly. "After he... interrogated him."

My head cocked as I looked between the two of them. "You mean tortured?"

Royce shrugged. "It's done."

"He's dead?"

"He is."

Turning back to Cannon, I fought my urge to crawl between the seats and sit on his lap. "How long did it take to cure you?"

Cannon's eyes flicked to Royce. "A while."

Royce was watching me in the rearview. "Why don't you tell us why you left?"

They were all waiting for me to speak. "I should never have left that day. But Landon, he told me Kris was in danger and if I told anyone, he would die. I left for my brother." Kris grunted, but I kept on talking. "And then when I met Landon at the meeting point, he told me he had to trick me as Bale had his mom. And then he knocked me out, and I woke up in a cell." I glared at the thought. "Which I am sick of, by the way. They knocked me out again—"

"Who's they?" Royce asked.

"Bale." I spat his name with venom. "That sick fucker has lost his mind. He put me in a silver cuff and chained me to a wall and beat me. And Landon tried to get him to believe I could be his mate, which I could never be his mate, and they made me shower in their compound, and this guy watched, and Bale said if I didn't cooperate with Landon, I was to die. And then Landon told me Cannon had been killed, and I..."

The tears were falling again as I remembered the fear, and I was choked up and my breathing was fucked as I relived it all. "I couldn't fight them anymore. They told me Cannon was killed, and I broke. Bale said I was broken, and I was to be given to the men, and then Landon told me I had to play along so his dad would believe I was tamed," I snarled. "He left me and then Bale was there when I woke up, and he said, he said..."

I was breathing raggedly, too far gone to realize I was having a panic attack and not realizing Royce was no longer looking at me with distrust or that he had stopped driving. "He was going to force himself on me, and Moonstar had come back, and she had said Cannon wasn't dead because I would feel more pain than the silver cuff, so when Bale went to touch me...like that...I let her take control."

I refused to look at any of them, my eyes stinging and snot running as freely as my tears. Wiping my nose on the back of my hand, I stared out the window.

Royce blew out a breath. "Fuck, that was a lot." He looked over at Cannon. "I think she's telling the truth."

"I have no reason to lie," I snapped. Cannon opened his

door and left the Jeep. I followed him, hearing the others do the same. "You think that I'm lying?" I asked him incredulously.

"When he stabbed me, Tev said 'Kezia says fuck you.'"

I stared at him, knowing my eyes were as wide as saucers. "You really think *I* did this?" My guts were churning with anxiety and rage. "That's why you didn't come for me?" My laugh was sharp and bitter. "Now I get it."

"You get it?" Cannon asked, his own anger riding close to the surface.

"No. I don't. I'm lying." I refused to look at anyone but Cannon. "Why wouldn't you come and get me? Why would you let me think you were dead?"

"Because until Moonstar walked into the bunker, I was as good as dead."

I blinked. Cannon didn't. A quick look at Royce confirmed what he had said. "What?"

"I was dying. The silver was in my bloodstream. In my heart. Kidneys. Lungs. Tev almost succeeded in his revenge."

"How? How are you here?" I swallowed. "Moonstar?"

"She used magic. It hurt like hell, and I passed out." Cannon looked over at Royce. "Royce can tell you more than I can."

Royce rubbed his hand over his face, as if the very idea of repeating it caused him distress. "We'd been arguing," he began. "Doc wanted more surgery. Hannah knew it wouldn't make a difference. Nikan...well, Nikan was...busy looking for answers. Cannon was in a bad way. Barely conscious. The pain he was in was a lot. Then when I thought it was really it, I was going to lose my alpha, I heard her." Royce took a deep breath. "The door burst open, and you stood there. I didn't know what to do; we were so sure you'd had a hand in it. I almost killed you there and then, and then Moonstar spoke. I knew it was her. She told us she could help. Doc refused to let her near him. She told us you were dying, like we didn't fucking know that. Then she just walked past us, *through* us, and told Cannon it would hurt. He screamed and blacked out and..." Royce shook his head as if he still didn't believe what he had seen. "This light, this ball of light she created from nothing spread out over his body and sunk into him, and his whole body arched off the bed, and he screamed again, and then...she pushed us out of the room, and when she was done, she was gone."

I gaped at him. "She was gone?"

Royce gave me a flat look. "You're giving me attitude?"

"I can't believe you let her go."

"You say it like I had a choice." Royce sniffed.

My head was reeling, but one thing hurt me more than anything they had said. I looked over at Cannon. "How could you ever think I would do this?" I looked between him and Royce. "I know you didn't trust me to begin with, but I thought we were past that." I felt both sad that they thought so little of me and happy that Cannon was saved, and I knew I was going to start crying again.

"My alpha was struck down. The male who struck him told him 'Kezia says fuck you.' You had already fled. We got a condolence message for our loss sent from *you*."

"You got what?" I asked in outrage.

"A card."

"A *card*!" I was gawking. "You believed a *fucking* card?" I was furious. "He's my *mate*. I was heartbroken."

"Don't give me attitude," Royce growled. "If it walks like a duck, it's a duck."

"If it... *What*? Why are you talking about ducks?" I asked in confusion.

Cannon's rumble of laughter startled me. Turning to him, I saw him watching us, and at the expression on my face, he laughed harder. "It's a duck," he said through his laughter.

Royce started laughing too, and I was sure they'd both lost their minds. "Why are you laughing? What's funny?" My hands rested on my hips as I glared at them both. "Why is there a duck?" Turning to my brother, I glared at him too, but he simply shrugged.

Cannon had seen the exchange, and that caused him to laugh harder, and it was so good to see him alive, laughing, that I found myself smiling, and then I was laughing too.

Luna, it was so good to laugh again.

CHAPTER 14

Kezia

CANNON SOBERED THE QUICKEST, CROSSING THE small space to me. Bending his knees, he came down to my eye level. "I'm going to kill them all." His stare was so intense it made my mouth dry, and I licked my bottom lip. Seeing his fury turned molten, I itched to reach for him.

"My heat," I blurted. "I remember when I was aware..."

"When you were aware?" Kris asked. "Did you really let her take control?"

My eyes wouldn't leave Cannon's, but I needed to be honest. "I didn't *let* her... I gave her control." I saw the question in his eyes. "I had thought you were gone."

Cannon took a step back, confusion on his face. "You gave up?"

"I thought you were *gone*..." I remembered the fear I felt when Bale held me down. "So I was weakened. I had no strength," I whispered, avoiding his look. "She told me you may live. I knew I couldn't fight him." I drew in a shuddering breath. "I made her promise if you were alive and needed help, she would give it."

"And I would lose you in the process?" Cannon's voice was as hard as the look in his eye. "What good would that do?" He ran his hand through his hair in frustration. "Sacrificing yourself isn't the answer. Have you learned nothing? You run off to save Kris, giving yourself up to that fucker, Landon. You give *yourself* up to Moonstar for me—why do you continuously make the stupid choice?"

My anger flared. "Fuck you!" I pointed wildly at my brother. "Landon told me they were going to kill him. Sever his bond with Cass—what would you have me do? Sit back and make a plan?" I sneered.

"Yes!" Cannon roared, his temper breaking. "I *want* you to come to me and let me help you."

"You want to control me!" I snapped back.

"If it means I keep you alive, then yes, I'll control you."

My lungs expanded as I sucked in air, and I knew I was going to explode. "You may be my mate, but you are not in charge!" I snarled in fury. "You don't *own* me!"

"That's what you think," he barked back at me, his eyes changing to turquoise. "You *are* my mate. I *am* your alpha, and I swear to the Goddess, if I have to keep you contained every day from now on to know you're safe, I will."

"Shall I call you Bale?" Tossing my hair over my shoulder, I stood with my hands on my hips. "He liked to chain me to the wall to keep me *contained*."

The anger dissolved from Cannon as he looked at me, stricken. "Kezia..."

I wasn't having it; my temper was still high. "Kris is my brother. Severing the mate bond was so Bale could kill *him* and not kill Cass. I had a limited time to stop that. You, you pigheaded idiot, *are* my mate, and I knew *if* you were alive, she could save you." Angrily, I wiped away a tear. "I will always fight for the ones I love. *Always*."

Cannon and I stared at each other, emotions high, and I saw him struggle not to argue with me. He took a deep breath, and I could almost see him counting it out to calm his temper. "I know you will, and it is commendable, and it's why you are you, but—"

"There doesn't need to be a but."

He gave me a long-suffering look. "*But* we as a pack could have planned an attack much better than you rushing into capture." When he saw me about to protest, he threw his hands in the air. "For Luna's grace, Kezia! *I* saved Kris, not you! You did *nothing* by handing yourself over to them."

"That's so unfair," I whispered.

"It is unfair." Kris's voice broke our stare off as we both swung to look at him. "You stood against Bale's pack to fight for me and Cass, Cannon," Kris spoke quietly from where he stood. "You and your pack, against how many?"

"I wasn't counting," Cannon answered gruffly.

"There were too many to *count*," I demanded, outraged. "You're a complete hypocrite sometimes, you know that, don't you?"

"Okay. We can all admit we made mistakes, and lessons have been learned." Royce stepped between us, ignoring the three answering grunts. "You two are giving me whiplash. Pick an emotion, will you, and go with it, at least until we're back in the pack." He turned to look at me. "What about your heat?"

He was right, but it wasn't that easy. I wanted to lose myself in Cannon, but I also wanted to punch him for thinking I would betray him. I wanted to scream in frustration that he thought I'd given up fighting because I had surrendered to

Moonstar. I wanted to bash his head off the nearest hard surface, that he thought I was to be controlled, and I wanted to tell him how much I loved him because he would do anything to keep me safe. My emotions were all over the place, and looking at Cannon, I could see he was struggling as much as I was.

"I went into heat," I said. "I think. I remember being aware that I felt"—I glanced at my brother, my cheeks flushing—"that way. I think you were near."

Cannon sniffed. "I caught your scent a week ago." He was looking at the peak. "Been chasing it down for days."

"Your heat and his scent would have pulled you forward," Kris mused. "She is strong, but even she can't fight the Goddess's Will."

"The sooner you two complete the bond, the better for everyone," Royce grumbled. He looked at me with a speculative gleam in his eyes. "You feeling—"

"If you're about to ask me if I'm in the *mood* in front of my brother, I will cut your balls off."

"Two visuals I don't need," Kris said with a grimace. "Have you both settled down?" When we both nodded, he smiled as he looked between us. "Royce is right, you need to complete the bond, but let's get back to the pack. We're still too exposed here."

My gaze drifted to Cannon's bare chest. He was exposed in more ways than one, and I wasn't complaining. He caught my stare, and I saw the corner of his mouth lift in a knowing smirk.

He watched me as he spoke to the others. "Kris is right in that we need to return. The pack is vulnerable without us."

As I followed them to the Jeep, Cannon wordlessly slipped into the back seat with me, and we both pretended we didn't hear Kris's muttering about the journey being awkward.

We drove in silence. Cannon's hand rested lightly on my knee, and I was grateful for the barrier of the denim. If he'd been touching my skin, the car ride would have been a lot less comfortable for the two males in front. When Royce hit a bump in the road, causing all of us to lift off the seats at the impact, Cannon's hand moved off my knee and landed further up my thigh, causing me to fight back the groan. I expected him to move it, but he merely slipped his hand further in between my thighs, and I wondered if this was his method of punishment. To touch me but not *touch* me.

I couldn't concentrate. I was trying so hard to focus on anything but his hand. It was all I could think about. I felt his gaze shift from the front of the Jeep to mine, and his hand inched its way higher. Pressing my thighs together caused him to let out a small huff of amusement, and the bastard dug his fingers into my thigh.

"You two okay back there?" Royce broke the silence, and I nodded quickly, not trusting myself to speak. "We're almost on packlands."

"If you can resist for longer, we'd appreciate it," Kris grumbled from the front, but he let out a sigh. "Though I know if it was Cass…"

I could feel Cannon's heavy stare, and I knew if I looked his way, I'd be a goner. Still, when his fingers flexed on my inner thigh, I relaxed them slightly, and this time, he didn't care who was in the car. His hand slid up and cupped me, and my cheeks burned when my scent flooded the confines of the car.

Royce cursed and slammed on the brakes, and I felt the cold air rush in when Cannon pulled me from the Jeep. I didn't even look to see them drive off. The two of us stared at each other, suspended in stasis for a moment before we crashed together.

His lips claimed mine, his hands on my ass, lifting me, my legs wrapping around his waist before I was pushed against a tree. Cannon's mouth was everywhere—his mouth sucked at my neck, then was back at my mouth, his tongue stroking mine, his hands already pushing my jeans off me.

"You need to be taken over my knee one of these days," he scolded, pulling my sweater off. He kissed his way down my body, tongue laving over my nipple before biting the other one. I cried out when his fingers slid through my wetness, my fingers digging into his shoulders as he pushed inside me.

"You can't spank me," I protested, my hips rolling against the rhythm of his hand. "I'm not a child." His thumb was pressing against my clit, his fingers curled inside me, and I was losing my mind.

"I *can* spank you," he told me, spreading my legs further with his shoulders. His tongue replaced his fingers, and my cry of pleasure was drowned by the sound of my heartbeat, which sounded as if it were in my ears. When he stopped, I mewled in protest. "I can spank you, fuck you, eat out this pussy, make you choke on my cock." Cannon kissed his way down the inside of my thigh. "I can do it all because you're my mate. *Mine.*" His possessive growl fucked with my head.

My snappy retort, if I had one, disappeared on a moan when he went back to licking and sucking my clit. The orgasm started everywhere at once, causing my eyes to roll back in my head. My fingers tightened in his hair, and my scream of ecstasy echoed in the woods.

I was still coming down from my high when I was turned and pressed against the tree, my feet kicked apart, and Cannon buried himself inside me in one smooth motion. My back arched as my body adjusted to his size, and he held still for a moment, his lips on my neck, his breathing uneven.

"You feel so good."

He began to move, and anything I'd been about to say died on a groan as I felt him deep inside me. Desire and need were racing in my blood, making me crave this man. I moved my hips in time with his thrusts, fucking myself on his cock. I was lost in the sensation and feeling of Cannon, taking what I needed from him and being what he needed. "I'm close."

Cannon's fingers dug into my skin as he fucked me faster, his teeth and mouth on my neck, sucking at my pulse as he fucked me. "Come for me, Kezia." His hand slid around the front, dipping down, circling my navel before traveling further, his thumb pressing my clit. "I want to feel you come all over my cock."

Fuck. My alpha had a dirty mouth, and I loved it.

I was a million things and nothing at all. I could feel everything, and it was almost too much.

"You're gripping me so tight." Cannon's groan of approval tipped me over the edge. My orgasm ripped through me, and I heard his answering moan as his thrusts became wilder. Cannon's hand circled my throat, pulling me back into his chest. His lips met mine, his tongue thrusting against mine in time with his hips.

Tearing his mouth away, he burrowed his head in the crook of my neck. Cannon reared back and slammed into me one final time. His cry of release surrounded me as he spilled inside me, fingers pinching my clit, causing me to come with him.

Thank fuck for the tree. It was the only thing holding us both up.

Sweat covered my body, and I whimpered in protest when I felt Cannon pull away from me. I was lifted and carried to a mossy patch. Neither of us spoke. Cannon lowered me until I was flat on my back, his body covering mine, kissing me more thoroughly than before. I opened wider for him, and he kissed me deeper.

I felt his cock stiffen as we kissed, and then he was sliding inside me again. Pulling him close, I hooked my legs around him and fell into the rhythm that he set.

Cannon's hands were buried in my hair, tilting my head back, giving him access to my neck. I moved my head further away, exposing more of my neck in a move of submission, and my nails bit into his skin as I felt his fangs grow against my throat.

"I want it." My whisper was so low I wasn't sure he heard me, but when I felt his bite, my body once more rode the wave of my orgasm. Cannon licked at the newly made mate mark on my neck, the blood spilling into his mouth, causing him to fuck me harder.

"More," I panted, feeling him fuck into me. "Make me yours, Alpha."

As he threw his head back, I saw the blue eyes of his wolf and felt the change in my own eyes as the bond intensified around us. It was tighter than a vise as it wrapped around us, and I doubted we'd be able to separate until it was complete.

"Kezia..." He said my name like a prayer, and I spread my legs wider, giving him all of me.

Pulling his head to mine, I claimed his lips. "I want every drop of your cum inside me."

Cannon roared as he came. My fangs emerged and I bit my mate in the crook of his neck, shuddering around him as his blood flooded my mouth. Cannon was still hard despite his recent release, and he was fucking me again. I pulled at his neck, drinking his blood as he fucked me faster and faster. His mouth was on my mark, doing the same.

The frenzy of the mating bond took control of us both as we kissed, bit, and fucked like animals in heat.

I don't know how long it lasted, but I knew when it had passed, and my awareness seeped back into my exhausted body. My body felt hypersensitive, and I ached all over. Cannon was big and we had not been gentle, and the random thought that I may never walk straight again popped into my sex-addled brain.

Cannon, my alpha, curled around me, spooning me, his arms wrapped around me protectively.

I could feel his presence inside me. We'd mindlinked before, but this was the next level. He was there. Just *there*. A sense of him that I knew I would have for the rest of our lives.

"Are you okay?"

The question caught me off guard. I wasn't sure how to answer it. Was I? *Yes.* I was more than okay, I felt amazing.

I felt his lips on my shoulder. "I feel amazing too."

"Did I speak?" My throat was hoarse. I'd screamed his name so many times it was a wonder I had a voice left at all.

"I can feel your emotion." He exhaled, his breath tickling my ear. "I think it's safe to say we completed the bond."

I giggled at such an overwhelming understatement. I felt his answering rumble of laughter, and I turned around so we were facing each other. I saw the scar of my mark on his neck, already healed. My fingers traced over it. I jumped when he did the same to mine.

"I didn't know we did that," I whispered, meeting his green-eyed stare. "Marked each other."

"Sorry." He didn't look sorry at all. "I couldn't resist it."

Pushing myself up to meet him, I brushed my lips across his. "I didn't want you to resist. Does it fade?"

Cannon shook his head, a soft smile playing across his lips. "No. The mark is my claim on you. And your claim on me. That okay?"

I nodded eagerly. "More than okay." Reaching for him, I kissed him again. I couldn't get enough of him. The kiss became more, not the frenzied fuckfest we'd just had, but a slow, leisurely kiss that messed with my emotions.

Cannon drew his head back and stared down at me. "We will fight this war together. As mates. As one."

"As one?"

"You are my equal and I yours. It's you and me, Kezia. For life."

I felt the tears run down the sides of my face into my hair. "I really want that with you." I was feeling so emotional, and I knew it was because of everything that had happened as well as just being with Cannon. Completing the mate bond felt so right. "I want a life with you."

"You have it."

This time when he took me, it was slow and gentle. Gone was the rush and fever of my heat, of our need to complete the mate bond, and I realized that we were making love.

I'd claimed him and he had claimed me, and it felt like the most natural thing in the world.

We were complete.

CHAPTER 15

Kezia

THE JOURNEY BACK TO THE BLACKRIDGE PEAK packlands was quicker than I thought. Royce hadn't been exaggerating when he said we weren't far, and the thought of anyone having come across us made me squirm with embarrassment.

We walked back, neither of us willing to admit out loud the threat of Moonstar, although since forming the bond, I felt different. More secure. Which was weird, as I had always been somewhat confident. Even in the Anterrio Pack where most of them treated me like I was an outsider, it had never made me feel insecure about who I was. It was probably *because* of them that I had a thick skin.

But now, I knew I was different. It may have been the Cannon effect; he oozed confidence and perhaps, with the bond completed, that was coming through our connection to me.

"I can feel you thinking," he said, and when I looked up at him, he was smiling.

"I feel different."

"Yup."

"You too?" I watched him with curiosity. There was something about him that was changed. "You look weird."

"Your charm, as always, leaves me speechless." He was still smiling, so I knew he wasn't offended. "How do I look *weird*?"

Good question. He was smiling, but he smiled before. He looked sure about himself—no change there, really—he was always an arrogant dick. He looked good, well...when did he not? "I don't know, you just look..."

"Happy?"

My mouth opened and I shut it again. "Are you happy?"

Cannon looked down at me. Reaching out, he took my hand and interlinked our fingers. "Aren't you?"

"Um..." Yes, I felt content. He was here beside me, and we'd accepted the bond, and I felt...good. No, not good, *great*. I realized my cheeks were sore from smiling. "Oh Luna, I'm going to be an idiot like Kris and Cass are."

Cannon laughed loudly in the quiet of the night. "Don't worry, I won't let you." He was far too amused for me to believe him.

"I'm not a hearts and flowers person."

"You shock me."

"Will you be serious?"

His smile faded and he wore the stoic expression I was used to seeing from him. "You regret it already?"

"No!" My quick answer pleased him, and he looked all smug and conquering again. I elbowed him in the ribs. "You don't need to look so smug."

"I can't help it," Cannon admitted sheepishly. "I just feel good about...everything." His sudden frown matched my own from a moment ago. "I'm also not a hearts and flowers person. You're right, this will become annoying."

"Maybe it fades?"

Cannon shrugged and we walked on in silence together, both pretending that nothing had changed when everything had changed.

"Okay, this is stupid."

The corner of his mouth tugged upwards. "Agreed."

"So maybe we just have to accept we may be hearts and flowers people."

"How about I promise to never give you flowers?"

"Well, I mean, it's not like I have anything against flowers..."

Cannon was laughing under his breath, which earned him another dig in the ribs. "I suggest we take it each day at a time and see how we go. Thoughts?"

"One day at a time sounds good." His fingers squeezed mine, and I was glad that neither of us had mentioned the whole hand-holding thing. Which felt completely natural, and I wasn't a hypocrite at all.

"I need you to give me a full debrief when we're back. Are you ready for that?" He was staring straight ahead, but I could feel the tension in him. "I need more than the jumbled mess you shared in the car." He pulled me closer. "You need to tell me it all."

"You're not going to like it." Taking a deep breath, I tried to loosen my fingers, but he held onto them. "You want to hear it first?"

"I do, but only because I don't want you to have to tell it twice and cause unnecessary upset."

"I'm not fragile." I turned my head so he couldn't see me. "I already told you before, you know, what happened."

Cannon huffed out a laugh. "I never said you were fragile." He tugged playfully at my hair. "But while I don't want to hear what happened to you, I need to hear it once more. I need to be able to ask questions and not the word vomit you gave earlier when you were upset." He saw my look and pulled me closer. "Which was understandable, but I need to hear it again, slower. Once for me, and I can tell the others if you need."

"I can tell it twice if you want." This time when I tugged at my fingers, he let me go. "But you're right, I think you may be better off hearing it properly first."

Cannon's frown deepened, his eyes darkening. "Why?"

"Because I know you won't like it, and you're going to over-react, and it's bad for you to do that in front of the others, and…" I blew out a breath. "Let's just do it."

"Do you want to stop?"

"Nope." Shaking my head, I looked towards the town where the houses were within sight but still slightly hidden from the way we were approaching, and the feeling of returning home was strong. "We're almost home and I'm eager to be there."

A hand on my upper arm pulled me to a stop. Cannon turned me into him, and his finger under my chin tilted my head back to meet his gaze. "Home?"

"Yes." My voice was confident, sure. I no longer had doubts —they were my pack. They'd been my pack the first night in the food hall, and I was desperate to return to them. "They're my pack."

His smile was breathtaking. "It sounds good, hearing you say that."

"Feels good saying it." Rising on tiptoes, I kissed him softly. "Hold onto that feeling of happiness; you aren't going to like what I tell you next." We resumed walking and I spoke with a low voice. "I went to Landon, as you know." I ignored his scowl; it was only going to get worse. "Landon told me he knew what had happened to my mom and dad and he could help me find the ones responsible."

Cannon was trying hard to keep his face clear of emotion, but I saw his jaw clench. "And you believed him?"

"Not really," I admitted. "But he told me that Bale knew how to break the mate bond, and I needed to stop that. He also told me that Bale planned to kill Kris, but we could stop it, but I had to renounce you and the bond and marry him instead. If I did, then Kris would be safe." I ignored the angry vibes coming from Cannon as we walked. "I know it means little now, but before I even got there, I knew I should have told you what I was doing. But it was too late." Glancing at him, hearing his scoff, I forged ahead. "Tev was involved."

"With your decision to leave?"

"I was in your room, I knew what Landon wanted me to do, and I sat in your chair, thinking through my options—"

"So you *did* think and *still* chose to believe not telling me was the best choice?"

"Just let me do this, you can fight with me later. Tev was outside, and he tapped his watch, and I realized he was telling me that time was running out. When I left, he was waiting on the outskirts of town." It was me who pulled Cannon to a stop this time. "I never thought...if I'd stayed...you wouldn't have been hurt."

"*What ifs* are a fool's game, Kezia." Cannon resumed walking. "Keep talking."

"I got to the meeting point, and Landon was worried."

"Worried how?"

"Biting his nails, fretful, anxious." Pushing my hair off my face, I shrugged. "I've known him a long time, I know when he's nervous, and he was nervous. When he saw me, he looked *relieved*."

"Well, you did just walk into his trap."

"Sarcastic comments won't make this better."

"Probably not, but too bad."

"He knocked me out with some horrible chemical smell he put over my nose and mouth. When I was going under, he apologized and said *he has my mom*."

Cannon glanced at me. "Bale?"

"No, the Easter bunny."

"I thought sarcastic comments wouldn't make this better?"

"Shut up."

Cannon grumbled but was once more quiet.

"I came to in a cell. I recognized the smell. It was the hall cells where Kris put me that time during my first heat, but it was *under* them."

"He must have tunnels that run under the town itself." Cannon was frowning, but he gestured for me to continue.

"There are cameras everywhere," I told him. "When they realized I was awake, they gassed me."

"They did *what*?"

"They filled the space with some kind of steam, and when I realized it was gas, it was too late." We'd slowed in our approach to the town, but Cannon was in no hurry since I was talking. "When I came to *again*, I was in a bedroom, chained to a wall, with a silver cuff on my wrist."

"Openly using silver?" Cannon raised his eyebrows as he thought about it. "Seems like things have gotten worse since Barbara's days." My mate was pissed off but trying to keep it together so I would finish, but I knew he was furious, I could feel it.

"I wasn't in the town anymore either. They have another place, a camp of some sort." I swallowed hard in remembrance. "Landon was there when I woke, Bale too. Landon was trying to convince his father that I should be his wife."

"Bale needed convincing? So taking you wasn't Bale's plan?"

"I don't believe so," I admitted. "They kept me chained to the wall, and Landon was advocating for me to be his mate. Bale wasn't having it." I stopped, wrapping my arms around myself. "I'd already realized that Bale didn't care if I was mated to you. The need to break the bond wasn't for me, it was for—"

"Kris."

"Yes."

We shared a look and Cannon looked to the town where his pack was. "It would be agony." His voice was barely a whisper, and I wasn't sure if it was because we'd so recently formed our own mate bond, but I also felt sick at the thought of him being taken away from me.

"It would." We stepped closer to each other, and I took comfort in his presence. "Landon told me you were dead. He was gone for a few days, and he said he was at your death service, paying his respects." Cannon was already shaking his head.

"Bullshit. I was close to it, I won't lie, but no one was ready to send me to Luna yet."

I told him the thing I hated admitting. "I don't know if Landon can be trusted."

"What gave it away?" Cannon drawled with a roll of his eyes.

"He *protected* me in that place. When Bale beat me the first time—"

The alpha had me in front of him, fury rolling off him in waves, his hands curled around my biceps as he stared down at me, fire in his eyes. "Say that again, very *slowly*."

"He went crazy. Bale said horrible things about my mom. He beat me and if Landon hadn't dragged him off me, I don't know if he would have stopped." I touched my cheek. "He broke my cheekbone... Landon was allowed to take the cuff off to let me heal, but I had silver in my system and it took a while."

"I'm going to kill him."

"Landon stopped him." I hated recounting this. Cannon was right, I wasn't sure I could tell this story again. "I was allowed to bathe when Bale told Landon I was broken." I looked away from the steady green gaze of my alpha. "I couldn't stop crying at the thought you were gone. I wouldn't eat or drink. You were dead, and I'd never see you again."

"You're so quick to write me off, pup." He cupped my face gently. "You couldn't feel me?"

"I was numb. I had an ache in my belly—"

"That was me."

Startled, I stepped back. "Wh-what?"

"Have you never felt me before?" Cannon was genuinely surprised. "It's how I know where you are and how to track you. I can feel you. You tug at me like an annoying little gnat."

His gentle smile softened the blow of his words, but still...a *gnat*? "A gnat? Really?"

"Meh." Cannon acting playful when I knew how angry he was, soothed my anxiety. I knew he was angry, but he was taking care not to further upset me with his emotions. "Where was she during all of this?"

Looking away from him, I shrugged. "She wasn't present for a long time, not until I started calling for her. I asked her for help." We shared a look and Cannon gave a nod of understanding. "Moonstar told me you weren't dead. She said I'd feel even worse than I did if you were gone."

"You felt my pain. The silver did its job." Cannon pulled me into his arms. "That ache that you felt? It was the bond straining to get us together, I think."

"When Landon told me his plan, for me to give him an alpha child—"

"A child?" I could feel his rage through the bond. Gone was his forced calm, and his anger pulsed through our connection. "Did he *touch* you?"

Swallowing hard, I forced myself to look him in the eye. "We slept together." When Cannon reared back, I grabbed for him, placing my hands on either side of his face. "*Slept*. That is all. I *slept* in his bed. Nothing else. We needed to show Bale I could be tamed."

Shaking free of my touch, Cannon stepped back. "Nothing you're saying to placate me is making me feel less murderous."

"Well, let's rip the Band-Aid off," I muttered. "Bale tried to force himself on me." I hurried on. "I'd finally felt Moonstar, and she told me you weren't dead, but I was too weak to escape." Cannon was still as stone, and I spoke quickly. "Bale hates me—it's frightening how much he hates me. He knew who Kris was from the second he took us into the pack. He told me Cass is pregnant..." I saw Cannon's eyebrow rise in surprise. "And he called me a whore and said... It doesn't matter what he said; it was horrible, and all that matters is that he was going to...assault me. I was weak. I was terrified. I told her that if you lived, she must heal you, and in turn—"

"In turn, you gave up on us."

It was like a slap to the face. "No!"

"Yes." Cannon was stony-faced, but his eyes were wild with emotion. "You gave up."

"I was weak! He was going to take something that didn't belong to him, and I used the only weapon I had! *Moonstar*. And before I did, I made sure she would heal you. She did, didn't she? I gave her control for you! I needed you to be okay, Cannon."

I watched him turn away from me. "They fed you a lie to make you weak, and you let them."

"Cannon..."

With his head tilted to the sky, he let out a deep sigh. "I'm sorry." Looking at me sideways, he was still furious, but I could see he was sincere in his apology. "You're mine to protect. You're mine and we need to be smarter than this. They played you, pup, and I *am* grateful Moonstar came and healed me...but it shouldn't have been at your expense." The way he was looking at me made me relax slightly. His words stung, but I knew he was being honest. "But I understand that you have weaknesses. Your brother. Me. Fuck, even that lying fucker Landon." Crossing the short distance to me, he wrapped his arms around me, squeezing me briefly. "I'm angry at them. At myself. Everything."

"Yourself?"

"I should have killed Tev when I came back. I let him stay, knowing he hated me. I never expected the hatred to run that deep. That's my error."

We stood slightly apart, both frowning at what had happened. "We both made mistakes," I reasoned softly. "But it's mistakes we can learn from, right?" Pulling back, I looked up at him. "The question is, how do we stop this?"

Cannon's glare was emerald fire. "Easy. We kill them all."

CHAPTER 16

Cannon

ROYCE WAS WAITING FOR US AT THE EDGE OF TOWN. His look of anticipation turned sour as we approached. "Seriously? Again with the misery and the sad faces? Didn't you just complete the bond?"

"Royce—"

"You don't have to Royce me," he snapped with frustration. "The whole pack felt it." Kezia spluttered as she choked on fresh air, which made Royce laugh out loud, easing the tension in his shoulders. "Your privacy is intact, Kezia. We didn't get any sordid details, but we all felt our alpha get stronger. It was...a good feeling." He beamed at us both, the smile turning into a scowl as he ran his gaze over me. "For fuck's sake, don't tell me you've screwed it up already?"

I gaped at him. "Why are you only asking me if I've screwed up? Do you remember *who* I'm mated to?"

"Nuh-uh, I'm innocent!" Kezia protested loudly.

"Really?" I jerked my thumb over my shoulder. "After what we just did?" I teased her. My laughter at her bright blush was cut short when she punched me in the gut.

"That's better." Royce looked at us both with delight. "*This* is what you present to the pack, not the faces of doom you just met me with."

Sobering, I met Kezia's worried frown. "It's a serious time."

"I know," Royce agreed, sobering with me. "But if there's no moments of joy, what are we fighting for?"

"Bale tried to rape my mate."

"He tried to kill *my* mate," Kezia added angrily, glaring at me for Luna knows what this time. "And my brother."

Royce let out a long sigh as he rubbed his forehead tiredly. "Right. Moments of happiness can wait. Let's get to work."

Kezia and I exchanged a look, and although we both shared the same feeling of urgency, when we met pack members on our way through town, we accepted the well wishes, blessings, and congratulations. We took our time to get to the house, ensuring that the pack saw their alphas.

"I don't think we fooled anyone," I muttered to Kezia once I realized there were too many of my pack who weren't in the least surprised Kezia was who I was mated to.

"Maybe the thing Royce spoke about told them?"

"Both still living in denial?" Royce asked over his shoulder. "Let me be blunt: you're both shit at being subtle. This pack knew who your mate truly was months ago."

I caught Kezia's flushed cheeks, and with a laugh, I pulled her closer to me. Bending, I kissed her openly in the middle of the street. It felt good not to hide the fact who she belonged to anymore.

When I pulled back, we walked hand in hand to my house. In the study, Nikan, Kris and Doc waited for us. Kezia gave her brother a sheepish wave, but his answering eye roll had her grinning, and I loved seeing her look so at ease.

"How do we know she can be trusted?" And just like that, Nikan sucked the atmosphere out of the room.

"She's my mate."

"She was your mate the night she left you too."

"She is my *bonded* mate."

Nikan snorted and Kezia stepped in front of me, no doubt thinking I was going to punch him.

"You have every right to be mad at me," she told Nikan, her voice low but steady. "I shouldn't have left. But he threatened my brother." She held Nikan's angry gaze calmly. "Glare at me all you want, Nikan. I know, if it was Cannon whose life had been threatened, you would have done the same as me."

"I wouldn't have."

Royce's cough sounded a lot like *bullshit*, and Nikan spun to him.

"Nikan!" My voice stilled the words of anger on my brother's tongue. "Mistakes were made. Things we all regret. We need to focus on what's in front of us. Now we have sight of the bigger picture." Tucking Kezia under my arm, I looked at all those gathered in my study. The door opened and we all reacted as if we were about to defend ourselves, but the three shifters who came into my study had me momentarily speechless.

Leo led the shaman into the room, and much to my surprise and Kris's, Cass made up the trio.

"Cass?" Kris was at her side, a worried glance my way letting me know he wasn't sure what to do next.

"The shaman said we all needed to be here." Her eyes met Kezia's, and she looked away quickly, looking up at Kris with wide eyes. "I don't want to be here."

Kezia spoke over her brother, and she wasn't giving a shit

whose mate it was. "Tough, Cass. No one wants to be here. Not for this. But you're an *alpha's* mate. Act like it."

Cass whirled on her best friend, the first fire I had seen in her...ever. "Because *you're* so perfect?" Her screech was almost deafening.

"Goddess, Cass, hardly!" Kezia marched forward and jabbed a finger in her friend's chest. "But this isn't a chore you can bat your eyelashes at to get out of! This is serious! Your father's lost his mind!"

"Says you!"

"Says the silver collar around our necks," Kris reminded her.

Cass's eyes filled with tears, and with a sob, she burrowed her head into Kris's chest and wept. Noisily.

It didn't help that Kezia rolled her eyes or that her brother looked ready to throttle her when he saw her do it. The shamans weary sigh lessened the tension in the room.

"Kezia, why don't you tell us what happened, and then we can fill you in on what you've missed."

I saw the change in how she held herself. She went from fiery to uncertain in the blink of an eye, and when she looked back at me, I slipped my hand into hers, squeezing slightly to let her know I had her covered.

"I can tell you." Quickly I relayed Kezia's ordeal. Cass cried more, but her worry for her brother made her focus, and eventually, her anger at her father dried her tears.

When I was done and my mate was leaning against me, carefully avoiding looking at anyone, the shaman told us what had happened to him. "They took me from my bed. I knew something was coming. There had been signs for days. I'm ashamed to say I was looking outward for a threat. I never thought the threat would come from within so soon. Not yet. They took me by surprise."

"Moonstar got you out?" Kezia asked as she pressed into me more.

"Yes." He looked over at Cass. "I'm sorry, Cassandra, but it was too late for your mother."

Cass collapsed onto the floor, her grief overwhelming her. Kezia stepped away from me when Cass pushed Kris away, and I watched as Kezia crossed the room to console her, lowering herself to the floor. She wrapped her in her arms as Cass wept for her loss.

"Does Landon know?" Cass asked Kezia through her tears. "You were with him, Kez, does he know?" When Kezia shook her head, Cass's misery turned to anger. "Don't lie to me. Did he look like he knew?"

Kezia licked her lips, her tell when she was nervous, but once more, she shook her head. "I don't think so. I think he believes you're both being held with Kris."

Kris crouched down beside Cass, murmuring too low for me to hear, and when Cass nodded, he scooped her up and withdrew from the room.

"He is too gentle with her," I said to no one in particular.

"She just found out her mom is dead," Kezia said with a sigh, her eyes on the closed door. "She needs some time."

The shaman sensed my stare. "You are both right. She needs to understand this is not a game, but she should be allowed to grieve."

"There's a time and a place for mourning," Leo mumbled.

"There is," I agreed. "But, we also need to be more understanding."

"What's the plan?" Nikan asked brusquely. "We need to retaliate and we need to do it soon."

"I'm aware, thanks," I snapped at my brother, and I saw Kezia's frown. She said nothing but pressed into me again, her arm slipping around my waist. It was remarkable how much her being beside me soothed me. Before, I would have felt restlessness when she was near, and now I realized it was the pull of the bond needing to be completed that had caused that feeling. Blowing out a breath, I met my brother's stare. "We're on edge. We've heard a lot tonight that we weren't expecting. I think it's best to take a moment to absorb everything we have learned."

"I don't need a moment," Nikan snapped. "I've absorbed all I need the weeks you lay dying."

"Nik—"

"I'm sorry, Nikan."

I looked down at Kezia in surprise at her apology. "I know it's me you're pissed at. I also know Tev would still have made a move against your brother, even if I had been here. Me leaving worked in their favor to allow doubt to be spread between us, but the attack itself, I couldn't have stopped that. What *Moonstar* would have done is heal Cannon quicker. That is all. I couldn't have done that either."

"You shouldn't have left."

"I know."

Nikan's glare was focused on the bookshelf, but he glanced at my mate as she stood beside me, her gaze calm and steady. "You trusted none of us," he added.

"I trust you all," Kezia said quickly. "I trusted you all to stop me."

His eyes flicked back to hers in understanding. "Which is why you never told us."

"He's my brother." Kezia shrugged almost apologetically. "Saving him was the only thing I could focus on."

"And I have already pointed out to my mate," I cut off Nikan's next words, "that *I* saved her brother. We did."

"Because the semantics are what's going to win this war," Kezia drawled, but no one missed that her head dipped or that her smile was forced.

"We both have things to learn," I reminded her softly, pressing a kiss to her forehead. "Right?"

"Right." As she tilted her head to look up at me, I leaned in and gently pressed my lips against hers. To my delight, she responded by lifting herself slightly, meeting my kiss with a touch more urgency, deepening the connection between us.

"The Goddess is happy," the shaman declared. Kezia and I both turned to look at him. "I feel her presence, and she is content that the bond is strong." The old shifter leaned back in his chair. "But her anger is equally as strong."

"At us?" Nikan asked, glancing our way.

"At Bale," I corrected. "He strikes against the packs, against pack law. A pack leader is not an alpha, no matter how downtrodden his pack is."

"Not all of the pack are guilty," the shaman reminded us.

"None of them are innocent," I reminded him. "They are complacent with the way he runs that pack. They have been complicit in the treatment of Kezia for years. None of them can be called innocent."

"Cannon," Kezia murmured. "Not everyone is strong like you."

"You're too kind, Kezia," Royce told her. "Your life there was not a happy one, yet you still defend them."

"I had Cass," she answered simply. "And Landon."

"Hmm, tell me how that worked out again, the *friend* who wishes you to give him an alpha child."

"You make it seem sordid."

"Because it is!" Leo and Nikan were both nodding in agreement with me. "If you are only friends, then where does the idea to impregnate you come from?"

"I think he was trying to save me," she countered. "I don't think he wants that any more than I did." She wasn't looking at me when she spoke, and I think my mate forgot about our bond. I could *feel* her uncertainty. Kezia had expressed her doubts about Landon, confiding in me that she wasn't certain she could trust him. However, I also knew now wasn't the time to press her. We had a pack war on our hands, and that was where our focus needed to be.

"Kezia?" Leo spoke from his position on the couch. "Can you tell me about this compound? How many shifters are there?"

"There were rooms, some with a bathroom, some like mine, where there wasn't. Cameras all over. In rooms, in the shower block."

"Shower block?" Royce asked.

"Landon took me there. Another shifter came to..." She swallowed hard. "To watch."

"Watch you shower?" Nikan asked gruffly.

"Yes." Rolling her head on her shoulders, Kezia tried to loosen herself up. "Bale said that if I didn't cooperate, Landon was to give me to the men." She paused to wet her lips. "I don't know how many men there are, and when I got free, I..." She looked at me for support, and I sent it through our bond. "I wasn't myself when I left."

"I understand." Leo was frowning as he thought. "How many stalls?"

"What?"

"In the shower block, how many stalls?"

Pushing her hair off her face, Kezia closed her eyes briefly. "There weren't any. But there were showerheads... Fifteen?" Opening them, she looked at Leo. "Five on three walls, one wall was bare."

"Bare? Or were there lockers?" he pressed.

"Um..." Again she closed her eyes. "Not lockers, open compartments for...towels?" She looked between Leo and me. "Does that help?"

"Fifteen means his pack is big." Leo spoke to Kezia, but his attention was on me. "We need to assume fifteen men per shift, eight-hour shifts..."

"Forty-five pack at least," Royce grumbled in agreement. "Separate from his main pack. Kezia, how many can fight in the pack?"

The doors to the study opened, and Kris came back in. Leo quickly told him his thoughts, and I watched the other alpha pale, his gaze darting to his sister's frequently.

"The females of the pack do not fight," he told us all, shame tinging his cheeks. "Kez can, Cass as well, although she is not proficient in it." Kris rubbed a hand over his face tiredly. "The pack numbers are seventy-three. Forty of those are males, who have been trained by me."

"Eighty-five fighters." Royce and I shared a look. "At least," I added.

"We have those numbers," Leo reminded me.

"We do, but it's all our numbers..."

"And we have to assume that Tev has told them everything."

"Fuck, I knew I would regret letting him live."

"You should never regret mercy, Alpha," the shaman corrected me.

"When it hurts my mate, he can," Kezia bit out. "We can't leave the pack here vulnerable." She began to pace, her frown matching her brother's. "You don't know their numbers, and you don't know if where I was held is the only place they have. We know so little, and as Royce said, we need to assume that traitor told them everything about Blackridge Peak."

"And they have the Pack Council," Kris added. "Which means Bale has our law in his pocket."

"So the odds aren't good," Royce said with a shrug, a knowing look in his eye. "Right, Alpha?"

"Right." I grinned at them all. "But when has that stopped us?"

CHAPTER 17
Kezia

CANNON AND THE OTHERS WERE PLANNING, AND THEY looked like they would be there all night. My knowledge of planning a strategic attack was very much limited to one-on-one combat, and I managed to leave them to it on the pretense that I was going to the bathroom. I knew that I hadn't fooled my brother, who knew exactly where I was headed, nor my alpha who had dropped a kiss to my temple as I walked past him.

Climbing the stairs, I wondered what room Cass was in, but I needn't have worried—I followed the sound of crying.

She was in one of the guest rooms I hadn't been in before, decorated in gray and white. I hovered in the doorway before making the decision to go in. She was curled in a ball, her back to me, and while so much had changed, familiarity made me climb on the bed beside her and scoot in until I was lying on my back, staring at the ceiling, knowing she knew I was there.

"I'm sorry about your mom."

"Were you telling the truth?"

It stung a little that she asked, but I kind of understood. If she had told me Kris had acted like her brother or father did, I would have doubted her too. Only, my brother would never have done that. But...when I thought about it, wouldn't Cass say the same about Landon?

"I was." Clearing my throat, I said with more conviction, "I am. You can ask me anything."

"Dad hit you?"

"Yeah." We lay in silence while she digested it. I didn't think she would speak, but I felt her move until she was on her side, facing me.

"What happened to him?" Her voice was a soft whisper, causing me to turn on my side too.

"You're pregnant?" Her eyes widened in shock that I knew, but she couldn't hide the smile. "Does Kris know?" When she shook her head, I bit back a sigh. "Your dad does."

"How?"

"I don't know. Tell me what happened."

She lay on her back, her turn to stare at the ceiling. "It was all so...odd," she began. "Landon was acting *so* weird. I mean, even for my brother, he was being extra." Cass pressed the heels of her hands into her eyes. "I can't forget the feel of the silver clicking around my neck." Tears ran down the sides of her face, and I wanted to comfort her, but I knew it was best to let her get it out. "They came for us at night. Kris was downstairs. He was making me a tea. I felt nauseous, and I wanted something to soothe my tummy. I was in the bathroom, and I just *knew* what was wrong with me. I opened the door to tell him, and I heard him shout. I ran to the stairs and there was a male on the stairs, someone I didn't know. I heard Kris shout for me to run, but I had nowhere to go." Cass took a deep breath. "Where would I even go?" she asked me bitterly. "I would never leave him."

I hated to admit that I really needed to hear her say that, and when she did, a knot in my chest I wasn't aware I had, loosened.

"You've never seen the guy before?"

"No. I stupidly thought we were under attack." She snorted with contempt. "I couldn't speak when I realized he was with my dad. I still thought he was there to *protect* us, and then..." Her face crumpled as emotion overcame her, and through much sniffling, sobbing and inability to speak, I figured out she realized how bad things were when she saw Kris.

"They beat him?" I asked quietly. "You realized that you were being taken prisoner when you saw my brother?"

"He was on the floor, and there was so much bl—"

Cass dissolved into tears again, and I had no option but to let her sob. I knew hormones had a lot to do with women's emotions during pregnancy, and I had no doubt that a shifter would experience the same. It was a long time later when the door cracked open and Kris poked his head around the door.

Cass was on her side, but her head was on my shoulder, and when he saw her fast asleep, he opened the door fully, coming into the room, his face tired. But when he gave me a soft smile, I returned it.

"Is she okay?"

Was she? I had no clue. "She will be." I eased myself away from her, both of us waiting for her to wake when I moved her head onto the pillow. "She has you."

Getting off the bed, I welcomed the hug my brother gave me. "She has you too," he reminded me. Kris motioned for me to follow him, and in the hall, I waited until the door was closed and he faced me. "I need to know about Landon."

"Cannon told you."

"Kez..." I hadn't missed that look of reprimand at all. "Tell me."

With a sigh, I pulled his arm, taking him to Cannon's room and closing the door firmly behind us. Kris felt the soundproof spell the moment the door was closed and looked at me in surprise.

"He's full of surprises, your mate." Kris looked around the room, taking in the simple décor, eyes lingering on the hole in the wall. "Do I want to know?" he asked me with a rueful look.

"Always so quick to assume that it's my fault." I didn't add that it *could* have been my fault. I wasn't sure why there was a hole in the wall either.

"Known you all your life, Kezia," Kris joked as he took the seat across from the bed. "I'm going to say there's a strong possibility you were the reason the alpha wanted to punch something."

"Unfair." Sitting on Cannon's bed, I pushed myself back until I had enough room to cross my legs and wait for my brother's questions. "What do you need to know?"

"I'd like to know how you are." I hadn't expected that, and it was obvious that my reaction had told my brother that when Kris laughed. "You're my sister," he said, turning serious again. "You've been beaten, kept a prisoner, thought your mate was dead, and been through hell. Yes, you're mated now, but you're still my little sister."

Turning my head, I tried to hide the emotion from my brother. He had Cass; he didn't need to see my emotion too. "I'm better now that I'm back with my pack."

"Your pack." Kris looked thoughtful. "I never thought of that. Of course they would be." His expression remained neutral. "How do you feel about that?"

"I belong here," I told him simply. "I wanted to be here before I ever accepted who Cannon was to me. Everyone's treated equally, they all contribute to the system in place, and, Kris...they're *happy*. It's so refreshing. They fight, they train, they stack dishwashers wrongly..." I saw his puzzled frown and I gave a light laugh. "I'll explain another time."

"I tried to make Anterrio that for you," Kris said, his focus on his hands. "But they are stubborn, single-minded and... stupid."

"You want to stay there?" I asked him. "You are an alpha, you deserve your own pack, is Anterrio the pack you would fight for?"

I didn't think he was going to answer when he shook his head. "Once, maybe I would have. But..." He looked away from me, anger creasing his forehead. "The way they turn a blind eye to all the wrongs, their impassiveness and lack of empathy. I don't doubt that there will be many of them who fight against us. Against me."

"I'm sorry."

"I'm not." Kris gave me a genuine smile. "We can start a new pack. Once we're clear of this business, we'll have options."

"I hope so," I told him honestly. "You deserve happiness."

"Thank you." We watched each other for a moment before I sighed, and Kris let out a low chuckle.

"You can be nice to me all you want, Kez, but you know me better than to think I will let this go."

"I know, I don't know what I was thinking," I told him dryly. "He told me the Pack Council knows how to break the bond. I thought he meant mine and Cannon's." Kris was stony faced and I carried on. "But they mean you and Cass." He said nothing and I wasn't sure what to say. "I'm sorry." My brother still said nothing, and I didn't take it personally; it was a hard thing to know. "She would never go through with it, you know that, don't you?"

"I do."

His voice was clipped, and I knew better than to push. "Um..."

"Use your words, Kez," Kris murmured, his brow still furrowed in thought about the fact Bale wanted to break the bond.

I took a deep breath. "He admitted it," I said softly. "Bale. He told me he killed them. That he killed our parents." I felt how still my brother was. "He thought I was a stray. He never knew I was your sister when he shot me that day." Rubbing my nose to stop the tears, I couldn't look at him. "He told me, so *easily*, that he killed them, and I could do *nothing*." I felt my chest tighten as I spoke. "Landon told me that Cannon was dead." It was my turn to break eye contact. "I believed him. The pain was...a lot. I didn't care about anything. I'm sorry, I should have been fighting for you and me." I hesitated. "I gave up."

"I'm going to kill that bastard," Kris vowed, his voice a tight whisper. Looking at him, I saw his pain and anger. "You did *not* give up. You were beaten, and your mate was full of silver. The pain would have been excruciating," Kris reasoned. "Even without the bond fully made, you would have felt your mate's suffering."

"Bale called me broken," I remembered. "Landon told him I needed time."

"Time for what?"

Puffing out my cheeks, I blew out a loud breath. "To be his mate. He was spinning a story that he and I were *more* than we had pretended previously. There are cameras everywhere, even in Landon's room, and he would whisper in the dark that I had to play along. He said he was being watched more than anyone."

"Watched for what?"

"I don't know." I debated whether to tell him my fears and then decided that Kris needed to know. Kris would understand. "I don't know if he was always honest," I admitted. "He seemed too eager for me to be his *mate*." Pulling my hair over my shoulder, I tugged at the ends as I told him all the ways in which Landon had confused me. "He was *too* good at acting, if you know what I mean? He said I could give him an alpha son."

"What the fuck?"

"That's what I said." We looked at each other, and I saw my brother's anger rising. "It was little things like that, that made me wary, and then other times, he was reminding me we had to play the game." Checking the door to the room was closed, I turned back to my brother. "I don't know if he's alive."

"Moonstar?"

"I don't know who she killed and who she let live." Biting my lip, I confessed my worst fear to Kris. "I don't know how to tell Cass."

"We don't," he said firmly. "She's too delicate right now. This will tip her over the edge."

"Delicate?"

"Her mom's dead and her father's trying to kill her mate," Kris said with exasperation, and I took the reprimand, grateful that was all he meant and I hadn't told him something I wasn't supposed to know before him.

"Right, of course, I knew that."

Kris's fingers drummed on the arm of Cannon's chair. "We have to treat him as an unknown," he told me after a while.

"What?"

"Landon," he confirmed. "He's not a threat, but right now, he isn't an ally."

Shit. That was a very clear line in the sand. Even for an unknown, Landon was still...well, Landon. "You sure?"

"I am."

He had his *you can't talk me out of it* face on, so I let it go, pleased he was the one who had to tell Landon's twin.

"Will you tell Cannon?"

Kris gave me an eye roll. "Who do you think suggested it first?"

"Ah." I should have known. "I guess you strategized a lot?"

"We all knew what was to happen; it was just the first time we were all in the room together since getting you back."

"Right." He was looking at me, and I recognized the look so well. "You're wearing your *you're not going to like it* face."

"I have a face for that?" he asked me with a smirk, and I stuck my tongue out at him.

"Just tell me."

"We need to fight Bale and the Pack Council and win."

I nodded. "I knew this."

"There are two battles to plan for."

"Anterrio Pack and the Pack Council—I'm not deaf."

"No, that's one and the same," he corrected me.

"It is?" I frowned. "So what's fight number two?"

"You are."

Kris said it so matter-of-factly that I doubted I had heard him correctly. "Me?"

"Moonstar. She needs to be handled."

"And how do you plan to do that, brother?" My voice was

low, almost a hiss, senses on full alert in case he called her forth. "She's *inside* me."

"We're aware." Kris was nodding.

"We are? Who is we?"

The flat look my brother gave me was enough, but I wanted to hear him say it, and with a resigned sigh, Kris threw his hands in the air with exasperation. "Luna, Kez, you know this is all Cannon will fixate on. To him, getting rid of her is more of a priority than Anterrio Pack."

"Stopping Bale is all that matters."

"Not to your mate."

Pushing myself off the bed, I crossed the room to the door. "Well, he's stupid. Let's go fix his thinking."

"Kezia, wait." Kris was on his feet, and I hesitated at the door, looking back at him. When he held up a phone, I felt my mouth drop open. "He already knows."

"What the heck?" Looking between the phone and my brother, I wasn't sure whether to laugh or erupt. "You...you're... he's *listening*?"

The bedroom door opened, and I stepped back automatically, letting Cannon into the room. "Before you lose your sh—"

"Too late. Ship's sailed. Train's left the station. Rocket's launched. Shit's lost." I walked to the corner of the room, eyeing both of them. "You two are cozier than I thought."

"That feels like an accusation," Cannon murmured.

"Good, it was supposed to."

"Kezia—"

"You're *my* mate," I snapped. "You're bonded to *me*. Equals? Right?"

"Yes, but—"

"There is no *but*. Me and you. Equals. That's what you said? Am I wrong?"

Cannon sighed. "No."

"Then what in the name of the Goddess is this shit?" When I saw my brother start to speak, my glare cut him off. "You, you can shut up until I tell you that you can speak." For once, he did as he was told, and on any other day, I would have had a smart comment for that. But my focus was all on the male in front of me.

"I needed you to be open and relaxed." Cannon saw my disbelief and he raised his hands. "I appreciate that it was probably stupid."

"Probably?"

"Fine, it was stupid." He looked at Kris. The look was one of expectation, and I gave my brother my full attention.

"This was your idea?" Pointing at Cannon, I knew my voice had risen. "Him? Him I expect this crap from! You..."

"You needed to be relaxed—"

"Both of you get out."

"Are you going to listen to us?" Kris demanded, getting to his feet.

"Like you listened to me?" Kris dipped his head, and I opened the bedroom door. "Out, both of you."

"This is my room," Cannon murmured as he walked past me.

"Tough. You've pissed me off. Stay away before I lose it completely."

"Kez..."

"Save it, Kris. I don't want to hear it from either of you."

When the door was firmly closed behind them, I shook my head in disbelief. Just what I needed, my mate and my brother to be cut from the same cloth and be in cahoots with each other.

Glancing upwards, I sent a look of reprimand to the ceiling and the Goddess beyond. "Just once, I would like a break. Just once."

The ceiling didn't answer, and neither did the Goddess.

Typical.

CHAPTER 18

Cannon

"I guess she's right to be annoyed with us." I looked at Kris with expectation. "After all, it does seem like a crazy idea when you say it out loud."

"You saying you learned nothing from it?"

"I'm saying that it wasn't worth the price." Looking over my shoulder to my bedroom door, I turned back to Kris with a raised eyebrow. "I really wanted to sleep in bed with my mate tonight."

Kris grinned as he walked away towards the bedroom where his own mate slept. "You're mated to my sister. Trust me, this won't be the first night that you spend locked out of your bedroom."

The door closed behind him as he walked into his bedroom, leaving me in the hallway, alone. Glancing at my bedroom door, I thought about knocking, but in the end, I opted to go downstairs. If I was honest with myself, I understood where Kezia's temper had come from. The idea to get her to open up and talk about the last few weeks with Landon had been Kris's idea, and

I knew she had held back from telling me it all, but the way we had gotten her to open up...yeah, I'd be pissed too.

In the kitchen, I poured myself a glass of juice and drank it while looking at the ceiling, hoping my mate saw it in her heart to forgive me for being...me. When Kris suggested that he talk to his sister, I was offended. The idea that my mate wouldn't open up to me was abhorrent. Kezia and I had been through a lot together, we'd *just* completed the mate bond, and there were supposed to be no secrets between us.

But then Kris reminded me of who my mate was.

Kezia was stubborn and loyal. Although Landon had duped her, she would still protect him because she was a good person. Kris argued that she would only open to someone who knew the twins as well as she did. Enter the ridiculous idea of having an open phone line so I could hear everything that she said firsthand.

And it worked—I never knew about her reservations regarding her friend or the liberties he took with touching her. She wouldn't have approved of that. Kezia may have resisted our bond, but she was my mate, and that meant something to her.

I meant something to her.

Realizing what a fool I had been to listen to her brother, I contemplated creeping into the room and asking for forgiveness. But I knew my mate well. She would be more likely to punch first and listen later.

Resigned to a sleepless night, I headed to the study. If I was going to be up all night, I could be productive.

In the study, I pulled old books from the shelves that chronicled our ancestors and pack laws. I needed to know every detail about our Pack Council and find evidence to demonstrate that Bale had them in his pocket.

With every turn of the page, my determination grew stronger as I delved deeper into the rich history of pack law. A weight of responsibility settled on my shoulders, because exposing Bale's manipulation wasn't just about justice for Kezia —it was about preserving the integrity of pack governance. With each crisp page I poured over, I unearthed clues and insights into the intricate workings of our Pack Council. As I read each word, my determination to confront Bale and the Pack Council grew stronger, driven by the desire to reclaim the autonomy that rightfully belonged to us.

Sitting back in the chair, I felt doubt begin to gnaw at the edges of my resolve. With each new discovery, the burden of responsibility seemed to weigh even heavier, leaving me uncertain about my capability to challenge Bale's actions. The Pack Council was law, and to challenge that and their integrity left me feeling torn between my duty to my pack and the fear of the consequences of my actions. Despite my determination to do the right thing, self-doubt lingered like a shadow, threatening to undermine my resolve at every turn. I knew that by not acting, I was letting my pack down, my mate down and myself. Turning back was not an option. I had to see this through, no matter the personal cost, but that didn't mean I couldn't fear the consequences.

"You look lost."

Looking up, I saw Kezia in the doorway, watching me. She was in simple cotton sleep shorts and a black tank that sculpted her body, highlighting how frail and thin she looked. Her white-blonde hair was harsh against her pale skin, making her appear frailer than she was.

"You should be sleeping," I countered, watching her as she closed the door behind her, the spell enclosing us in privacy.

"The bed is too big without you."

"You were the one who said I couldn't sleep there," I reminded her.

"You were the one who fucked up," she reminded me simply, walking across the floor. She took the seat nearest me. "What's with all the reading?"

"Pack law." I flicked through a book beside me, opened it to the page I had marked, and handed it to her. "I remembered most of it, but there were some intricacies that even I forgot."

Kezia took the book from me, her frown deepening as she read.

I spoke to her as she read. "I've been digging into pack history, trying to find evidence to expose Bale's control over the Council. But the more I uncover, the more I realize how deep his influence runs. Confronting the Pack Council might lead to...repercussions."

"Repercussions? What kind of repercussions?"

"Well, for one, they could deny it all, I could prove nothing, and they could exile us."

Kezia looked up at me as I spoke. "They can try to do that, but even if they do, our voice will have been heard, and other packs will listen and ask questions."

"You think it's that simple?"

"No, none of this is simple. It's a shitshow. Fighting Bale and his love of silver torture is one thing, but challenging the Pack Council for being corrupt is a whole other level." She got to her feet and walked over to me. "It's a level that needs to be confronted though, and I can't think of anyone better suited to the task."

I drew her nearer, settling her between my legs, feeling her warmth against my skin. With each upward stroke of my hands along the back of her legs, I paid special attention to the gentle caress of my thumbs against the skin beneath her buttocks, causing her to let out a small gasp.

"And if I am exiled?"

"Then we'll be exiled together. But it won't come to that. I believe you will win this fight."

Looking up at her, I found strength in her unwavering belief in me. I felt undeserving of it, unsure of how I had earned her trust after everything I had done to her, yet seeing it swelled me with pride.

"I don't think I deserve you."

"I know." She smiled down at me, her fingers stroking through my hair. "You could have had such an easier time if you had stuck with someone like Koda."

With a growl, I picked her off her feet, and laying her down across the couch, I climbed on top of her. "You are the only one I want," I reminded her. "I don't want easy, I don't want complacent, I don't want a mindless fool who agrees with every-thing I say." Peppering her jaw with kisses, I nibbled on her ear. "I want you. Someone who challenges me, who tells me when I'm being a dick—"

"So, you admit you're a dick?"

Grinning, I hid my smile against the crook of her neck. "I admit that you make me act like a dick."

Kezia's fingers tightened in my hair. Tugging my head upwards, she scowled at me playfully. "I think you're a dick even without me."

Kissing her roughly, I groaned into her mouth when my mate took my cock in her hand and gave it a gentle squeeze. "Is this my punishment?" I asked as she began to work me over slowly.

"No. It's my pleasure," she whispered against my lips. "You're just the tool I'm using to get off."

"Is that right?"

"Mm-hmm."

Kezia wiggled underneath me, and somehow, I was on my back and she was on top, pulling my pants down, freeing my cock. I had no control when she ran her tongue over the length of me. Looking down, I watched as she took the head of my cock into her mouth and sucked. Desire raced through my veins as I watched my mate fuck her mouth with my length. Kezia opened her eyes and met my stare, her hunger evident as she worked her tongue over me.

"Fuck, Kezia, I need inside you."

Pulling herself off me, she used her hand to maintain a steady rhythm that made me weak. "No. You come like this or not at all."

The dominance in her tone made my balls quiver. "I'm going to come too soon," I muttered even as her mouth enveloped my cock once more. A gentle tug on my balls, and I started pumping into her wet and willing mouth. "Fuck, Kezia, I don't want to know where you learned these skills." My fingers threaded into her hair, gripping her hair tight as my mate worshipped my cock.

Teeth nipped at the base of me gently and then scraped over the length of me, and it was the last straw. With a twist of her hand and a final hard suck, I erupted into her mouth. Waves of pleasure coursed through me as Kezia swallowed me down.

When my breathing was normal again, I opened my eyes to see her cleaning the head of my cock with her tongue, a smug look in her eyes as she watched me. Tucking me back into my boxers, she got off me and stood over me.

"You taste delicious." Kezia laughed as she danced away from me when I tried to grab her. "Nuh-uh! I told you, it was for my pleasure, not yours."

"I just had my pleasure right down your throat," I reminded her. "Let me return the favor."

With one arm outstretched to hold me back, Kezia shook her head playfully. "No. You were a dick, and I told you, this was all about me." Her smile faltered a little when she looked away from me. "Was it...okay?"

"It was better than okay." Moving forward, I caught her hand, our fingers linking almost automatically. "I was your first time?"

"You are all of my firsts."

Fuck if that didn't make my chest puff out like a peacock. Kissing her hard, I worked my hands under her sleep shorts. "Let me fuck you, Kezia," I whispered between kisses. "I want to hear you scream as I make you come."

"You're a narcissist," Kezia gasped as I slid a finger through her wetness. "You just want to hear me scream your name."

Stroking her clit, I nipped her bottom lip. "I do. It's the only thing I want to hear as I fuck you. You begging me for more as you come all over me."

Kezia's head tilted backwards as my fingers picked up their pace. "Luna, help me," she groaned when I slid a finger inside her. "You have such a dirty mouth."

"You love it." Kissing along her collarbone, I resisted the urge to rip her clothes off her. "Say yes," I pleaded, prepared to take her shorts off, but she stepped back.

Panting, Kezia shook her head. "No. I told you, this is your punishment." Backing away, she watched me lick my fingers clean of her essence.

"You sure it's me that's being punished?"

Kezia nodded. "Yes, you will stay here and think about your actions"—I watched as she fumbled for the door handle—"knowing that I'm upstairs, out of reach, getting myself off."

Growling, I stepped forward, halted by her hand raised to stop me. "Kezia..."

"No. You don't get to be all growly and possessive. You want me? Well, tonight you can't have me." She smiled wickedly. "I realize this may not be the best way to communicate, but you pissed me off earlier, and now it's your turn to be frustrated." She slipped her hand under her shorts, and I could smell her arousal as her eyelashes fluttered, her tongue wetting her lip. When I stepped forward, she backed up. "Not tonight," she warned, teasingly.

With a light laugh, she turned and left the study, closing the door firmly behind her, leaving me lusting after her like a newly whelped pup.

Alone in the study, I had no choice but to respect my mate and go back to the books. I hadn't lied to her. We really could be exiled and shunned from pack life if things went badly.

Within all packs, the Council held sway, a body of thirteen esteemed members entrusted with the governance of our community. Their authority was absolute, their decisions binding, as they upheld the ancient laws passed down through generations. Our pack's existence revolved around these time-honored laws, which shaped everything from resource distribution to conflict resolution and the preservation of harmony. To challenge the Council was to challenge the very foundation of our pack's unity, a risk few dared to take lightly. Yet, beneath the surface of said unity, I'd heard whispers of discontent, fueled by suspicions of corruption and manipulation, and I hadn't paid them any mind, too intent I had been on wrestling control of this pack from my father.

As I explored the history records, I felt even more determined to uncover the secrets hidden in the Council's meetings. I knew that revealing these secrets was crucial for securing our pack's future. Not just my pack, but all packs.

When the first rays of daylight pierced through the night's darkness, I leaned back in my seat, feeling the exhaustion wash over me. The path in front of us was a long one. Or, I could bypass all traditions and openly challenge them. It was a crude method, but it meant I could get results quicker.

Or banished quicker.

The outcome wasn't guaranteed.

But then when did a fight ever have a guaranteed outcome?

The door to the study slid open, and I watched quietly as the shaman walked into the room, closing the door behind him.

"You smell of rebellion."

I didn't hide my grin. "I should, I've been planning one all night."

The old man nodded as he took a seat. "What have you planned so far?" When I hesitated, I saw his frown. "My loyalty is to the packs," he reminded me.

"It wasn't your loyalty I was thinking of," I answered honestly. "It was whether or not I was ready to share my rather desperate plan."

"Saying it out loud makes it real," he said with a knowing smile.

"You know it."

"Try it anyway," he encouraged.

"I need to overthrow the Pack Council. I was merely going to highlight their corruption, but it needs to be more than that." When the shaman nodded, I continued. "To overcome the power of the Pack Council, I need a comprehensive strategy. My first task is to gather evidence of the Council's corruption and manipulation. This must be irrefutable. Next, I need to build alliances with other packs. Knowing who else thinks like I do is crucial. If I can rally them behind a common vision for change, I think others will be more receptive to my message. A strategic communication plan is necessary to effectively address the Council's misconduct and call into question its legitimacy, highlighting their wrongdoing."

Seeing the shaman was still listening, I continued. "I'll talk to influential pack members who agree with me and get their help to push for change from inside the packs. I'll also need to have contingency plans ready to tackle any resistance that may arise, which may mean mobilizing support from nearby packs and asking them to fight." I sighed loudly. "And to navigate this effectively, I need to demonstrate transparent and accountable leadership, which I thought I had until the moment you put a white-haired female in front of me, and then I become irrational."

"Sounds like a good strategic plan."

"But?"

"A plan like that takes time." The shaman may be hindered in sight, but still, his gaze felt piercing.

"Time we don't have."

"Agreed."

Running my hand through my hair, I sighed loudly. "I have an alternative plan."

"Let's hear it."

"We go in, take out Bale's pack, gather whatever evidence we can find, and when the Council comes asking for answers, we deal with them then."

"Risky."

"Yeah."

"I like it."

I grinned. "So do I."

In the early hours of the morning, I joined my mate in bed. Feeling the warmth of her body against mine brought me a peace I never knew I needed. While Kezia slept in my embrace, her muttered words about me cheating couldn't dampen my contentment as I held her close. She nuzzled against me, seeking comfort, and soon returned to her deep slumber.

This was what I was fighting for. My mate's freedom. Knowing what Bale had done to her, had been about to do to her, and what he had done to others, it was time to put a stop to it all.

Kezia deserved better, all pack members did. No matter how I waged this war, there was no point denying it anymore, the time to fight was now.

CHAPTER 19
Kezia

I WAS IN THE KITCHEN MAKING NUT BREAD WHEN Cass found me. Her golden blonde hair was pulled back into a perky ponytail, her cheeks were flushed like she'd been running, and her smile was dreamy.

"You're not the poster child of a rebellion," I told her dryly as I kneaded the dough.

Cass immediately looked guilty, glancing over her shoulder to ensure there was no one listening. "I know and I feel terrible, but I have so much *joy*, Kez," she told me as she rubbed her belly. "I never thought that this is what would make me feel so... complete."

"Have you told him?" I sprinkled some nuts into the dough, watching her carefully. Cass's lower lip trembled as she shook her head. Glowering at her, I punched nuts into the dough, ignoring how I was overworking it. "He needs to know and he needs to know *now*."

"I'll tell him when it's the right time," she hissed at me. Coming forward, she lifted my hands from the mixture. "You're going to overwork that, and it will be denser than an old boot."

"There isn't a right time for this," I reminded her. "We're in the preparations of war. Kris needs to know everything before he jeopardizes it all."

"You think he won't fight if he knows," Cass asked me, brown eyes wide with doubt.

"I don't know," I told her truthfully. "The idea of Kris being a fa—" Cass made a noise and I corrected myself. "Being *that* is something I've never thought of before. I don't think he has either."

Cass blew a raspberry at me. Leaning over, she took a handful of nuts. "Are you crazy? He's raised you, hasn't he? The man was born to do this."

"I'm different." Was I? I'd never thought of it that way. Kris was responsible for me when our parents died, but had he raised me? I ate a walnut absentmindedly as I considered it. He really was the only father figure in my life.

Cass was grinning at me. "Cat got your tongue?" she teased.

"Shut up."

I went back to making my bread, and she went back to grinning like a fool and rubbing her belly. At this point, it was unlikely that she'd *need* to tell my brother...he'd figure it all out on his own.

"Do you think Landon is innocent?"

The question took me by surprise so much that I choked on air. When I had stopped spluttering like an idiot and taken several mouthfuls of water, I met her questioning look. "What makes you ask?"

"He's Landon," Cass said with a shrug as she looked away from me. "You know as well as I do how clever he can be."

I did know. It was something I'd been struggling with for a while now. "I know. He plays the part very well."

"Do you think he is playing now?"

I could lie. I could. She was my brother's mate, my brother's *pregnant* mate. She was also my best friend. "I no longer know what to believe."

"Oh." Cass's eyes filled with tears that she was trying hard not to let spill over.

"When he told me that if I didn't go to meet him, then Kris would die, I believed him. He was so horrible, so unlike himself, I was too stunned to react. To even think properly." Giving up on the dough, I stepped back. "When I got there, he overpowered me and told me they had his mom. He never mentioned you." My tone was hard, but it had to be if I was to get through this. "He touched me in ways he shouldn't, ways he had never been interested in before. In the compound"—I took a shaky breath—"after he told me Cannon was dead, I couldn't keep up with him. One moment he was *we're in this together,* other moments, he was *this isn't as bad as you think it is.* But it was. Cannon was dead, my brother a prisoner, your father was trying to break the mate bond, and Landon was trying to convince me that me giving him an alpha son was the answer...I"—I inhaled deeply—"I no longer know what to believe."

"I knew he hated that I was mated."

I looked at Cass in surprise. "To Kris?"

She shook her head. "I don't think it would have mattered to who; it was something I had that he didn't." Cass ran her hands over her jean shorts as she spoke. "He's always been competitive. It's a twin thing," she added with a shrug. "But he couldn't beat me at this. I had something that he didn't, that he could never have."

Wow. Just wow. That explained so much, but I wasn't sure if Cass knew what she was implying.

"If they could break the mate bond, it would mean I was the same as him again," she added.

"Did he...did he ever talk to you about it?" When she turned her head completely away, I sensed she was hiding something from me. Walking around the counter, I stepped into her line of vision. "Talk to me, Cass."

"He said..." I watched the tears spill over and handed her a tea towel as she tried to stop crying.

"He said what?"

"He said that just because I had an unused pussy didn't make me special." She sniffled a little. "He *did* apologize almost immediately afterwards."

My anger flared within me, and I grabbed my best friend by the shoulders. "Your brother is an asshole." Cass laughed despite her tears. "I love you both, I do, but he's a jealous little prick with a tiny dick."

"And how would you know about the size of my brother's dick?" Cass tried to joke, but her eyes widened as she looked over my shoulder, which only meant one thing, and I closed my eyes briefly.

"Yes, please enlighten me, *mate*, how *would* you know?"

I did what I always did when caught in an awkward position. I went on the defensive. "Don't judge me, Mr. I-Have-An-Understanding-With-Someone-For-Mutual-Benefits."

"He has a what now?" Cass looked between us in confusion.

"A fuck buddy."

"Oh." Cass was still looking between us. "Past tense?"

I saw Cannon roll his eyes. "Obviously," he grunted as he walked into the kitchen. He was wearing dark jeans and a dark blue T-shirt today. It made his green eyes pop, or maybe his eyes popped whatever he wore. The black boots on his feet had thick tread, yet he made no noise. I really needed to learn that skill.

Cannon kissed me briefly, pausing as he pulled away. "I'll ask one more time, how do you know about his dick?"

Pushing him away, I glared at Cass when she giggled. "Because we're shifters. I've seen him naked hundreds of times."

Cannon pulled me into his body. "Is that right?"

"You're being ridiculous."

"I'm your mate."

"You're my ridiculous mate." Pushing him off me, I returned to my bread. "Nudity is common in the pack; you know it as well as I do."

"Doesn't mean I need to like it." Cannon popped a walnut in his mouth, his attention on Cass. "You need to tell him."

"You told?" she accused me.

"Yes, he's *my* mate!"

"We all know, *except* the one person who *should* know," Cannon told her. "We think it's why your father has gone insane." He saw Cass look at me quickly in confusion. "Humans call it a psychotic break. It seems that Kezia's mother was the object of your father's obsession. It was your father who killed Kezia's parents and tried to kill her children. Years later, her son turns up at his pack, seeking refuge for himself and his little sister. Fast forward more years, and the son of his enemy is an alpha. Something Bale nor his son can be. Add to that, his daughter is this male's mate. It's a lot. Add on to that she's pregnant—and it's the last straw and he loses his shit."

"I don't..." Cass shook her head. "I think that's a little far-fetched."

"Which part?" Cannon asked casually as he ate more

walnuts. "The fact he took in his obsession's children or that he put collars made of silver around your neck?"

"You don't know he was obsessed with her!"

Cannon went to speak, but I quieted them both.

"I do." I dared not look at my mate as I spoke. "I know he was obsessed with my mom." Avoiding looking at both of them, I spoke to the dough, once more left unattended, and scooping it up, I put it in a bowl to proof.

"Kezia?"

I ignored the questioning concern of my mate as I got the wrap for the bowl. "He told me I was just like her, that all I wanted was to be fucked by an alpha, like *her*. My mom." Quickly I wiped away the tears. "He said that I didn't think his boy was good enough, I only wanted an alpha."

"Dad?"

I nodded. Putting the bowl aside, I had nothing to do with my hands, so I grabbed a towel to wipe them. "That was when he beat me, broke my cheekbone." I felt sick as I said the next words. "The final time, when he was going to kill me, he told me"—I cleared my throat—"he told me that he was going to see if my cunt felt like hers."

I heard the bang, and glancing up quickly, I saw that Cass had knocked the stool over as she stood. I didn't need to look to see her repulsion; I could feel it surrounding me.

"Kezia..."

Strong hands took mine, their grip gentle for someone so tall. "Look at me, Kezia." Angling my head back, I looked into the deep green eyes of my alpha. "Why didn't you tell me this?" Cannon asked softly.

"You didn't need to know."

I saw his anger, but his touch was still gentle when he

cupped the side of my face. "I need to know everything that he said and did to hurt you," he told me.

"Why?" I tried to pull away, but Cannon held me tight. "You don't need details, the actions speak for themselves."

"Bullshit." He dropped his head to kiss me softly. "The words can cause more pain. Is there anything else you haven't told me?"

I shook my head.

"Kezia, I swear to the Goddess, I will love you no matter what you tell me."

Blinking, I looked up at him. "You love me?"

Cannon's eyes closed briefly before he rested his forehead against mine. "Luna's grace, Kezia, what the hell do you think we've been doing?"

"I didn't know you loved me."

"You think I want to set the world on fire for just anyone?"

Biting the inside of my cheek, I shrugged. "You do give off strong hero-complex vibes."

Cannon's laughter reverberated through me. "Your smart mouth is going to be the death of me." He pressed his lips to mine, and I almost forgot to check that Cass was still in the room as I fell into my mate's embrace. "She's gone."

Cannon scooped me up without breaking our kiss and carried me up the stairs, his mouth owning mine the whole time. I was sure there was someone we passed on the way there, but the alpha never slowed. In his room, he laid me on the bed, and slowly, torturously, he removed items of my clothing as he made sure every inch of my body was kissed.

"Aren't you supposed to be organizing a revolution?" I said between gasps as he parted my thighs.

"My mate's hurting, I'm soothing her," he told me as he licked along my seam, parting my folds with his tongue.

"I'd really prefer if you were planning revenge." My protest was weakened as I moaned his name when his tongue circled my clit.

"Mm-hmm, I think you protest too much." Cannon's mouth did something wondrous, and my whole body arched off the bedspread.

"Holy shit, do that again."

With my fingers tangled in his hair, I held him close as he focused on making me feel so good, and he made me forget all about my capture at Anterrio Pack. For now, it was just me and my mate.

When we were done, I lay on the bed, my body worn out and my mind a fogged mess as I lay exhausted on the comforter. Cannon was pulling his jeans on, and I didn't know where he got his energy from. I was dead. Okay, I wasn't, but I felt lifeless.

"How are you standing?" I grumbled as I watched him pull on a shirt. "After all"—I waved my hand over the bed—"that."

"Because I have better stamina," he told me with a grin. "I told you that you needed to train with Leo."

"I don't want to train with Leo, I want to train with you," I pouted. "Oh, for fuck's sake, am I pouting?"

His laughter surrounded me, and I fought my grin. "You look so cute." Cannon kissed me long and slow, and I was already reaching for him when he pulled away. "No, greedy little mate," he scolded. "I have to go. There's a pack meeting. I'd really like it if you could join me."

"You want me to be at a pack meeting?" I asked with surprise.

"You're my mate," Cannon said reasonably as he put his boots on. "We're equals, my pack is your pack."

Pushing myself up to a sitting position, I looked him over. "You just screwed me seven ways to Sunday, and now you want to be all 'let's go have a pack meeting'?"

Straightening, he grinned wolfishly at me. "Seven ways to Sunday?"

"It's a human term," I said while trying to fight the blush.

"I like it."

"I'm shocked," I deadpanned. Wiggling my ass up the bed, I leaned against the headboard. "You really want me there?"

Cannon rested his palms on the bed and then crawled up until he was hovering over me, caging me in. "I want you wherever I am," he told me, his voice all kinds of husky sexiness.

"You keep looking at me like that and using that voice, and there's a danger that I may never wear clothes again."

The look in his eyes became predatory. "I can live with that."

"I bet you could, Neanderthal." Pushing against him until he was sitting back on his heels, I got off the bed. "I need ten minutes."

"For what?"

"To get clean, you ass." Piling my hair on top of my head, I turned to look at him. "How does this look?"

"Like birds are ready to nest in it."

"Leave!" I ran to the bathroom, ignoring his laughter as I turned the water in the shower on. Despite it all, I was smiling. He had taken a horrible memory and made me forget it as he devoted himself to me this afternoon. Now, when we were being serious, he was still making me smile with his silliness.

Silly is not a word I would have ever described my alpha as.

Opening the door of the bathroom, I caught Cannon straightening the bedcovers.

"Hey."

He looked up, saw me still naked, and smirked. "Hey yourself."

"I love you too."

The smile vanished as he looked at me. "Yeah?"

"Yeah." His smile would have lit the room, it was so bright, and I smiled back. "Now give me ten minutes, and we'll go talk to the pack together."

"Sounds good."

Was it so wrong to be so happy when the world was turning to shit? I hoped to Luna it wasn't.

CHAPTER 20
Kezia

THE FOOD HALL WAS CLEARED OF TABLES AND CHAIRS when we got there, and I wondered who had done it and how long it had taken them. It was standing room only in the hall, and I felt self-conscious right up to the moment Cannon reached back and took my hand. His strength and belief in me came through the bond so strongly that I felt myself getting teary-eyed. Had I been anyone else, I would have rolled my eyes so hard at the lovesick fool that I was.

Cannon walked with purpose to the front of the hall, where Royce, Nikan, and Leo were already waiting. Kris was standing to the side, not apart, but not included at this time. I almost asked why until common sense told me it was because my brother was not part of this pack.

He was an alpha, and in time—hopefully, not too much time—he would have a pack of his own.

It was probably wrong that I hoped it wasn't Anterrio Pack that he took over. That pack didn't deserve the alpha my brother would be.

"Hey, folks, glad you could all make it." Cannon began the

meeting without any fanfare or preamble. Just right in there, direct and to the point. Like he was.

"Not a lot of notice," Willy grumbled from the front. "If it's to tell us about you two"—she looked around at several of the pack, who were grinning back at her—"trust me, we know."

"Willomenia, have I ever boasted about my sex life before?" Cannon asked with a dry tone that made the desert seem lush. When the woman shook her head, he looked over at me. "Well, I could start now, but I'm worn out." Several of the pack laughed at his playfulness and my reddening cheeks. "Kezia, as you all know, is my mate." He pulled me into his side. "My true mate. And I am delighted that we have made it official." Cannon bared his neck, showing the silvery scar of my bite. "Kezia?"

Blushing furiously, I moved my hair aside to show my own mate mark. Causing the hall to cheer loudly.

"Well, thank Luna for that," Willy said loud enough for everyone to hear. "If I had to listen to either of you naysaying it one more time, I was going to paddle your behinds myself."

Cannon faked a wince, which made the hall laugh, but as he grew sober once more, so did his pack. "I would love to tell you that was the only reason we were here...but I've never lied to my pack." Cannon's hand took mine and we stood together, united, when he told his pack we were at war. "As you know, Pack Leader Bale of the Anterrio Pack took my mate and her family hostage. They recruited one of our own pack to betray me, and with the inadvertent help of another of this pack, they sought to break the mate bond."

There had been a low rumbling when he told them I was taken hostage, but there was outright fury at the fact they sought to remove a mate bond.

"An alpha's mate is a gift from the Goddess," Cannon told them. He tugged on the end of my hair, causing me to look up at him. "A fact that this one tried to deny for the longest time." He grinned as there was a general chuckle around the room. "But the bond is sacred. We all know that, and even thinking of breaking it is a crime against Luna."

Confused, I looked up at my alpha. "Weren't we thinking of breaking it?" I whispered quickly.

"And don't you think she has punished us for that?"

I had nothing to say to that. It was all very well and good for me to accept that the mate bond itself was a gift from Luna, but all the bad stuff that had happened? Was that my punishment for thinking I could run from my mate?

To be honest...I didn't want the Goddess to be watching me that closely.

"Anterrio Pack has lost their way," Cannon spoke above the murmuring of voices. "Not only did they take my mate, they caged her brother, their head of security and a trusted beta, along with his mate. When we found them and *broke them free*, they both wore collars of *silver* around their wolf forms."

The murmuring this time was more of a rush of anger that swelled around us.

"The pack leader of the Anterrio Pack conspired with Tev to strike me down. He gave him the blade that struck me, knowing the damage that silver can do." Cannon let that sink in, and I wondered how many of his pack knew that he had been stabbed with silver. "They have threatened us. They have struck against your alpha, they have chained your alpha's mate and her brother with silver, they have tried to assault my mate. This needs to end." He looked around the room. "Too many of us have turned our heads in regards to this pack. They are *not* different, they are *not* an anomaly. They are dangerous and manipulative, and they need to be stopped." He looked at his pack, meeting their curious or angry glances head-on. "You are my pack. Will you fight with me?"

"I'm insulted you ask us, Alpha," a man at the back spoke, his voice filled with amusement. I recognized him from somewhere but couldn't quite place where. The moment our gazes met, a wave of familiarity swept over me. It wasn't until he crossed his arms over his chest that I remembered where I knew him from—the fighting ring. He had been beside Royce the night that Cannon faced me in the ring.

Cannon wasn't insulted by the male's forthrightness, and he shared a grin with him that spoke volumes. "I wasn't asking the likes of you, Ned; you're with me regardless."

Ned laughed and I noticed several others did too. The more I looked at the pack, the more I realized there were several males like Ned scattered throughout it, and knowing the sneakiness of my alpha, I wondered how random their randomness actually was.

"You be needing us all, Alpha?" The male who spoke this time was the one who had a limb missing, and I struggled to remember his name.

"I will." Cannon held his stare. "This is my pack, and while I am an Alpha, I will listen to your concerns. If the will of the pack is to stay out of this one, then I will do everything in my power to keep my pack from my fight." His eyes swept the room. "But I *will* go forward with my plan to bring the pain to Bale like he has to me."

The male nodded. "I understand," he said, his attention shifted to me. "And for Zia, I think we all do. Silver collars sound like a whole lot of hurt, and we don't want any of that here. But..." He rubbed his limb, and I saw the flush to his cheeks.

Vic. His name was Vic, I remembered now.

"I grew up in the Anterrio Pack." I stepped forward as I spoke. "I didn't know pack life could be so different until you welcomed me in." Taking a deep breath, I continued to share my story. "I was shunned most of my life. I mean, who wants a white-haired girl, who had to be forced not to shift, around their kin? I was considered unstable, unpredictable, wild." My voice held a bitterness that I thought I had left behind me. "I shifted as a babe."

Looking at my brother, I beckoned him forward. "This is Kris, my brother, he's an alpha. Bale took us both in, and he knew when he did so who my brother was. He told me recently that he realized who I was not long after. You see, our parents were nomads. My mom came from the Anterrio Pack. You may have known her. Her name was Andrea." I heard the slight murmurings.

"Your mom's hair was darker than yours," Vic said gruffly. "Was always in trouble too, if I recall," he added with a wink.

"It runs in the family," I said with what I hoped was a care-free shrug. "I learned recently that Bale was quite keen to secure my mom as his wife. I guess us standing here tells you he was unsuccessful. My mom met her mate and together they opted to be nomads. They had Kris and then me." Swallowing hard, I watched the faces of the pack as they listened. "Bale murdered my parents. He shot them with silver, then shot their son and the wolf pup that was with him." I pointed at myself as tears spilled over. "Only I wasn't *just* a wolf pup. Through the grace of the Goddess, I lived, and so did my brother. Kris tried to raise me, but I am mischievous like my mom, I guess." I smiled at

Vic. "And so Kris went to the nearest pack and asked them to let us join them. He didn't know that he was seeking refuge from the very male who took our family from us. He didn't know that he was a beta in a murderer's pack until the night he realized that *his* mate was Bale's daughter."

There were more rumblings amongst the pack.

"Not only did Bale have his lost obsession's children in his pack, but one was also an alpha and mated to his daughter." I took in a shaky breath. "I've done bad shit in my life. I fought in human fighting rings for money, never knowingly using my wolf strength, but I wasn't fighting fair, I know that now. I've stolen from humans, disrespected pack law, and done it all to survive." Deadly silence greeted me. "But my brother hasn't. My brother is *so* good it's...well, it's kind of sickening." A few of the pack chuckled. "He's the kind of male who'll let you have the last of the meatloaf even if it's your second helping and he's had nothing. He'll stay up all night with you if you think there's a monster in the shadows under your bed, even though he's worked a double shift and must do the same the next day. He's the kind of male who worked tirelessly to make us fit into a pack that didn't want me. And it was that same pack that Luna mated him to."

Kris stood beside me, his expression solemn, but when he glanced at me, I saw the emotion in his eyes.

"Yes, Bale took me, yes, he beat me and almost raped me." I ignored the gasps. "And yes, Bale told his son that if I wasn't going to be *tamed*, then I would be given to the men to ease their stress." I heard the low growl from beside me and plunged on, knowing if I looked at Cannon now, I'd be too emotional to continue. "But I am not here in front of you for *me*. Those bastards put a silver knife in your alpha, not once, but twice.

They left him to die. Those fuckers put collars of silver around my brother's neck for being an alpha and a mate to that sick, twisted fuck's daughter. Don't fight for *me*."

I met every one of their stares as I continued, "I'm not worth it; I deserve what Luna punishes me with. I don't deserve your alpha, but he *is* mine and I will die before I let him fight this alone, and I hope you feel the same. Fight for Cannon, avenge *him*. Fight for my brother and his mate. Fight for what you know is right. The Anterrio Pack has evil within it, and it needs to be stopped. Fight for that, for justice, and for Kris, an alpha who deserves to lead. For his mate, who did nothing other than be mated to the son of an enemy long dead."

The silence in the hall was heavy, and I decided it was now or never to purge my soul.

"I killed three humans." If anything, the silence got quieter. "I fought in fighting rings for profit. I needed money to survive in the human world, and lacking patience, I chose the easy route."

"Kezia," Cannon murmured beside me.

"No, this is my pack now too." I stood straighter. "You deserve to know who your alpha is mated to." Pushing my hair back, I steeled myself for the backlash. "I thought I was clever, disguising my bruises with makeup, when in reality, I had already healed myself. I wasn't clever enough. A man tracked me down, shot me three times with silver, and when I came to... well, it wasn't going to be a party I wanted to be invited to, if you know what I mean. I fought them. I won't say I won, but I did get free."

"You killed them?" someone in the crowd asked.

"I did." I swallowed hard. "I killed them and then I torched their bodies, and I walked away." The mumblings in the pack were disconcerting, but I needed to finish this. "The reason that I share this with you is because we know that the Pack Council covered this up." The mumbles became shouts. "I know you have no reason to trust me, and I have said nothing this afternoon that makes you *want* to trust me, but you need to hear this. Bale owns the Pack Council—I don't know how or what he has over them, but he *owns* them. So when you think about avenging your alpha, my brother, or both, you need to know that the Pack Council is on *his* side, and we need to fight that too."

Vic whistled low as he looked around. "You got anything else you want to share?"

I thought about it. "Probably, but I reckon my mate's going to throttle me as it is."

Strong arms wrapped around me, and I felt Cannon kiss the top of my head. "She may be a handful," he told his pack, "but you can't say she holds back."

Looking up at him, I saw the affection in his eyes. "Are you mad at me?"

"No." Dropping his head down, he kissed me briefly. "It's more than I would have said right now, but it needed to be told."

Rising up on my tiptoes, I kissed him back. "I do love you."

Cannon grinned at me, squeezing me softly. "You better." Straightening, he looked out over his pack. "Well, that was more than you probably bargained for," he said with a casualness I envied. "We'll give you tonight to think about it."

"I don't need a night," Vic said as he looked around him. "Doubt many of us do. I'll fight with you, Alpha. For the crime against you, for crimes against another alpha"—he looked at me —"and the crimes against my alpha's mate."

"Thank you," I whispered.

"I was ready to fight before the reason why," Ned spoke gruffly from the back. "I've been in another pack. Alpha Cannon picked me up out of the dirt and showed me what a true pack is." Ned met my questioning look. "We aren't all that different, Alpha Zia, but hearing your hardships, you have my loyalty and my fists whenever you need them." He added with a wry grin, "And I've seen you fight in those human rings. You need all the fighters to protect you because, girl, you can't fight for shit."

"Ain't that the truth!" Leo bellowed behind me, and I laughed out loud along with the others as the tension eased in the room.

Cannon quieted us all down, his steely look serious. "You sure?" The chorus of yeses was deafening. "All right, you know what to do. We leave in two days."

As the pack broke down to discuss and plan, I watched Royce and Nikan work their way through the crowd. Leo went as well, and it looked like they were giving orders.

"Two days?" Kris asked from beside us.

"Probably one too many," Cannon agreed quietly, "but they have a lot to process. They need that time." His look was thoughtful as he scanned the crowd. "They were already alerted to a threat; this has just clarified our intent."

"Where do I go?" Kris asked, looking uncomfortable. "I know the pack, but I don't know the place where Kez was. I'll go wherever you think best."

"You stay with me," Cannon told him. "You fight beside me. Okay?" Kris nodded once and Cannon clasped his shoulder in some manly bro hug-type thing. I still didn't know how they had become so close, but I was glad that they were.

"And me?"

Cannon looked at me, his lips drawn into a thin line. "You stay behind."

"Absolutely not." I noticed my brother taking a step back, but I was too focused on the caveman in front of me. "I go too."

"No. You don't."

"Cannon!"

"I said no, that's final."

"You said that we would do this *together*." I knew I was glaring at him. "Me staying here, is *not* together."

"We will do this together, and you staying here and protecting the pack that stays behind, is helping us both." He glanced at Kris, and I saw my brother's head dip in agreement.

Yeah, we'd see about that.

CHAPTER 21

Cannon

MY PACK WAS ONE TO BE PROUD OF. I KNEW IT, AND I knew I probably shouldn't be as boastful about it, but they were my pack.

Mine.

Not the leftovers of my father's pack, but wolves that belonged to this pack who were strong and had a sense of justice. Luna knows they had seen too much injustice in my father's days.

I walked among them with pride, and I saw that pride reflected back at me. It was an honor to be their alpha, and I knew I would spend every day of my life making sure I was the best alpha I could be.

Which is why the white-haired firecracker in front of me was causing me heartburn. Kezia was ignoring me.

It had been three or four hours since the meeting with the pack, and for reasons only my mate could tell me, she had hitched onto Ned and was following him around as he got ready to fight.

She was so obvious it was painful.

After catching a few knowing looks from Willy and Vic, I decided that enough was enough.

"Kezia?" I called out as I approached and watched her pretend not to hear me. "Kezia, you're fooling no one."

Bright blue eyes glanced my way before she stubbornly turned her back on me. Ned looked my way and turned his head quickly but not before I saw his shit-eating grin.

"Ned?" He turned back to me, and I saw the amusement in his eyes and fought the urge to grab her and throw her over my shoulder. "Can you give me a minute with her?"

"Sure thing."

I ignored his laughter as he walked away. Kezia was folding blankets, badly, that were to be put into packs.

"You've never folded a blanket in your life, have you?" Taking the blanket off her, I redid it, making it a tight, military square. "Did you see what I did there?"

"I'm not talking to you."

I snorted. *No shit, babe.* "I got that." I tried to keep my voice reasonable. "Do you need me to show you again how to fold these so they take less room in a pack?"

She nodded once and I hid my grin. Stubborn she may be, but she was always willing to be taught. "You take this corner here." I demonstrated slowly. "Then this one." I took the opposite corner diagonally across from it. "You then take this corner and fold it like this, see?" She nodded once more, stepping closer to watch. "Then go back to this corner and bring it to meet this one." I held up the corner I meant. "Place them together and then bring this corner over, and..." The blanket folded in on itself. "See?"

"Again."

I repeated the demonstration with another two blankets

217

before she tried it herself and then shook that out and did it again. When she had it, the two of us folded blankets in silence.

"How long before you think you'll speak to me?" I asked as we neared the end of the blanket pile.

Silence.

"I thought you were very brave to be so open to the pack earlier." I didn't look at her as I spoke, but I felt her interest as she pretended I wasn't there. "No one can ever doubt your bravery, Kezia. But you are my mate. He's targeted you before, and I won't let the fucker get you again."

"It's not your decision."

"Yes, it is." I packed the last blanket. "And if you're hurt or in danger, then we have a whole other threat to face, and I can't fight two wars at once, Kezia. Tell me you understand that?" Her hands stilled and I saw her turn her head away. "Kezia?"

"Why don't you call me Zia?"

It was such an unexpected turn that I didn't have an immediate answer. "What?"

"I prefer Zia."

"I don't."

"Why?" she challenged me.

She *always* challenged me. "Zia is the shifter who fights in human rings, defies pack laws, and unfairly battles weaker opponents. I don't like Zia. Zia cheats."

"Wow. Say what you really think," she muttered.

"If you don't want the answer, don't ask the question," I snapped back at her. "Why are you even asking me this?"

"I like Zia."

"Your parents named you Kezia. The woman I know..." I hesitated. "The *Kezia* I know is strong and courageous." I ran my eyes over my mate's body. "Zia is a fraud, Kezia is real."

"My brother calls me Kez."

"He's your brother; he's allowed to call you anything he wants."

"Of course, there would be a different rule for Kris." She blew hair out of her face in exasperation, and I tugged her towards me.

"Okay, this is stupid. What are you really asking me, Kezia?"

"Why does he get to go, but I can't?"

"I explained this. There will be pack left behind, they need someone to lead them just as much as the pack that goes with me." I saw her eyes narrow. "Plus, Kris isn't carrying around an uncontrolled spirit who is trying to take over his body."

The very fact that she rolled her eyes at me when I said that made me love her more. Insolent and challenging. Life was never going to be dull with my mate in it.

"I can control her."

"You gave yourself over to her." I started stacking the packs. "I don't think she is going to be too amused you rescinded on that when she comes forward next time." Side-eyeing her, I tried to remain casual. "Have you felt her presence?" Kezia shook her head, avoiding eye contact. "Do I need to ask again, Kezia?"

"She's dormant."

"You sure?"

"Yes!" Finally, eye contact. "I don't lie to you all the time."

"Just some of the time?" My mate stuck her tongue out at me, and I laughed despite her nonsense. "You drive me crazy."

"Good, you deserve it." She feigned a scowl, but the corner of her mouth was already tugging upwards in a smirk.

"Do you understand why you can't come?"

Kezia sighed. "I do..."

"But?" I repressed my own sigh as I waited for her reasoning.

"But I think I'm in more danger of her coming out when you aren't here."

The lightness I'd been feeling slipped away like oil on water. "What do you mean?"

Piling her hair on her head, Kezia looked at me and shrugged. "Being with you, near you, I don't feel her. My wolf and I are content, but when you aren't here, I don't know... before when you were gone, she would feel more present."

Frowning, I scanned the crowd for Doc. No, not Doc, he had fucked up. I would forgive him—I basically already had—but I didn't want him near Kezia with this. "Come on, we need the shaman." I took her arm and started walking.

"We do?"

"You think we don't?" I asked over my shoulder, and seeing her agreement, I hurried us through the crowd.

I met Royce near the front door, and he looked at us both with concern. "What is it now?"

Kezia and I exchanged a sheepish look. "I didn't know we had a *now*," I tried to tease, but it sounded more petulant than I would have liked.

"Well, neither did I, but it's a thing." He folded his arms across his chest as he looked between us. "Out with it."

"I need to go see the shaman, that's all."

Royce looked at Kezia with concern. "She back?"

"Not yet."

He looked relieved and I saw Kezia straighten as she noticed his reaction too. Her eye caught mine and I saw her reluctant acceptance of what I had been trying to tell her. "I saw him earlier with Kris's mate."

"Cass," Kezia said with a scowl of disapproval. "Her name is Cass."

Royce wasn't in the least bit ruffled. "Yeah, well, until she proves she's as loyal as the rest, she can stay a stranger."

Reaching back, I took hold of Kezia's hand. "Come on, you can fight this battle another day," I murmured as we headed out of the hall. "You got this?" I asked Royce over my shoulder.

"Always."

It felt good to know my beta was so reliable. I'd already seen Nikan organizing one group of shifters. I was a lucky alpha to have such a loyal pack.

"Where's Kris?" Kezia asked as we walked the empty streets.

"Last I saw of him, Leo was learning the layout of the Anterrio Pack."

"Learning? Or interrogating?" Kezia asked dryly.

"Never quite sure with Leo," I told her with a grin. "Can't fault his enthusiasm."

She didn't say anything as we walked to my house, and under any other circumstances, it would have been a pleasant evening.

"Do you think we will win?" Kezia watched me expectantly.

"I don't think we'll lose."

"Is that not winning?"

"Fighting pack against pack is never winning. There's enough shit in the world without shifter against shifter."

As we reached the front yard, Kezia pulled at my hand, bringing me to a sudden stop. "That's exactly what makes you a good alpha," she told me quietly. "It's why I fell in love with you."

Bending down, I kissed my mate slowly. As I pulled back, I

looked her deep in the eyes and smiled. "Nice try, mate, but you're still not coming with me."

Kezia growled as she pushed me away, storming into the house ahead of me, leaving me laughing behind her.

I found her in the kitchen. The shaman was there, with a whole lot of herbs and things I didn't recognize spread out in front of him.

"Alpha Cannon," he greeted, completely at ease as my mate hugged him as she passed.

"Shaman." I tried to remember my studies, but having never had a shaman in the pack, I hadn't paid too much attention to herbs. "Do I want to know what you're making?" I *did* remember that sometimes it was better not to ask.

"A drink for Cassandra," he said happily. "Some herbs for my Kezia." Reaching out, he patted her hand. "A few tricks for your pack to hide their scent in the coming days."

"Scent erasers?" I leaned forward eagerly. "They work?"

The old shifter chuckled. "Of course they work; why do you think Kris asked me to make them?"

Kezia looked at me smugly. "My brother is sneaky," she reminded me.

"Like his sister," I teased back.

"But you're not here for sneaky," the shaman said soberly. "Are you?"

I felt my own smile fade, and I shook my head. "No. We need to know about Moonstar."

The shaman put his herbs down and sat quietly. "The Goddess has shared nothing with me," he told us softly.

"Do you need a sacrifice?" Kezia asked him, leaning forward and taking hold of his hand. "Deer? Rabbit?"

"I do like rabbits," the shaman said with a wry smile. "But

no, a sacrifice won't work this time. The Goddess is quiet. It's not the right time to ask."

"When *is* the right time?" I didn't mean to sound sharp and I saw Kezia's eyes widen in warning, but I shrugged it off.

"The Goddess does not answer at our beck and call," the shaman chided. "I am her vessel on earth. I'm not the one who rules; I am only a messenger."

"Can you send a message to her? Ask her for help?"

"Cannon!" Kezia scolding me for being inappropriate was new.

"What? We need to know this. We are going into a fight with a pack that is ruthless and dangerous. I can't take you with me in case you get hurt—or worse, captured—and you tell me that I can't leave you behind in case your *passenger* hijacks your body. Some help from the Goddess would be appreciated."

"She stirs within you?" the shaman asked Kezia.

Shooting me a glare, my mate turned to the shaman. "No, she has been quiet since we completed the mate bond. But..." She sighed loudly. "She has always been more dominant when Cannon isn't near me."

The shaman frowned as he thought about what she had said. "Hmm, the alpha's Will is strong."

"Not strong enough to get rid of her," I muttered.

"You will never have that power," the shaman told me sagely. "The spirit chose the wolf, not the other way around. Moonstar will need to *want* to leave. Kezia is much like myself in that regard; she is a vessel for the spirit of another."

"I don't want to be."

The shaman chuckled lowly. "No, I imagine you don't, but she has saved you more times than harmed you, child, remember that."

Kezia slid off her stool and walked to the fridge, grabbing herself a bottle of water and one for me. "I do remember," she said as she put the water back, taking a beer instead, and handing it over to me. "I also remember the months I lost because of her help. I sound ungrateful, I do, but it's my body. Not hers." Opening her water, she took a sip. "It's possible that I could have survived without her." Avoiding looking at either of us, she tried to act indifferent. "Women survive attacks every day and can be stronger for it. Maybe I make myself weak by calling on her for aid."

"Maybe I've never heard such bullshit in my life," I told her.

"I can fight. I should have fought harder, and I didn't."

"You didn't fight harder because of Moonstar. You couldn't fight harder because you were weak and overpowered," I snapped at her. "The humans beat you and shot you with silver, Bale beat you and weakened you with silver, and the only way you survived that was *because* of Moonstar."

"You're the one who wants her out of me!"

"Of course I do!" I yelled in exasperation. "She no longer *wants* to be with you, she wants your body, and I refuse to let my mate go no matter how grateful I am to the one who has saved her over and over. You are *my* mate, not her. I will not lose you, Kezia."

Her eyes were swimming in tears, yet she didn't break my stare. "What if you have no choice?"

"I don't accept that." I looked over at the shaman. "I will never accept that. There is always a choice."

The shaman rolled a flower bud between his thumb and forefinger. "You sound like you do not want to destroy her, Alpha."

Blinking back my anger, I shook my head. "Destroy her?

No, I owe my mate's life to her." Throwing my hands in the air in frustration, I barked out a laugh. "Mine too. I just want her somewhere that isn't *inside* Kezia."

The shaman tutted and I worried I had said the wrong thing until he spoke. "Keep her spirit but put her somewhere else? Is that what you are suggesting?"

"Yes?" Was I? The more I thought about it, the more I realized I was. "Yes. Can you do that?"

The shaman laughed. "You ask it like it is as simple as plucking a dead leaf from a branch." He crushed the bud between his fingers. "However, replacing the vessel may be easier than eradicating the spirit completely."

"I don't want her to be eradicated," Kezia spoke up. "She's only ever been my ally." She walked across the kitchen to stand with me. "I want her gone but not gone forever." Kezia slipped her hand into mine. "I want her to be free."

"I'll need a rabbit."

Kezia was already nodding, kicking off her shoes. "Dead or alive?"

"What's going on?" I asked as my mate pulled her jeans off.

"The shaman needs a rabbit."

As I looked between the two of them, the complete bizarreness of the whole thing struck me, and I started to laugh. I laughed so hard I cried.

"What is wrong with your mate?" the shaman asked Kezia.

"I think he's freaked out," she told him thoughtfully. "The bond feels...confused." I saw her shrug. "I don't think he was expecting the sacrifice to be real."

Being talked about like I wasn't in the same room as them made me laugh more.

"Fix him," she said.

"He isn't broken, pup." The shaman continued to make his potions. He spilled some herbs into a cup of water and then handed it to Kezia. "Make him drink this."

I downed the concoction without even asking what it was. My laughter disappeared as my mouth swallowed the pungent potion.

"What was that?" I gasped, downing my beer to get rid of the foul taste.

"Nothing but a horrible drink of water," the shaman told me smugly. He handed another drink to Kezia. "You need to drink this."

"Why?" She was still half-dressed, but she took the drink.

"I seek a white rabbit with red eyes. This will help you find it." I watched as she drank the potion in one go, my protest dying on my tongue. "Alpha Cannon, she should not go alone."

For the first time, I wanted to snap at the old shifter. "She was never going alone."

"Just checking." He smiled serenely, and I wasn't sure if he was teasing me or not.

Cass walked into the kitchen, eyeing me with distrust. "Alpha. Kezia." She leaned against the counter, watching the shaman. "Is my drink ready?"

The shaman had lost his easy laid-back way and pushed a packet of herbs over to the young female.

"It's not mixed?"

"Two spoonful's in a half cup of water," he told her.

Cass sighed dramatically, and I saw Kezia dip her head to hide her frown. "You couldn't make this for me?"

"You can't make it yourself?" I asked, ignoring the jab in my ribs from my mate.

Cass looked flustered. "Well, the shaman's here; he's the shaman."

"I'm aware of who he is."

"The shaman makes the potions." Cass looked at Kezia for support, but my mate was suddenly very interested in her nails. "Kezia?"

"Mm-hmm?" Kezia looked up. "Just add it to water yourself, it's no big deal."

"But..."

As I watched the pampered and spoiled girl in front of me flounder, I worried if Kezia and I looked as alien to others, because the concept of Cass and Kris being mates was alien to me. Kris was blunt and straightforward, and this girl was everything but that.

"White with red eyes?" Kezia asked the shaman, who nodded, while Cass made her potion. Kezia tugged my hand. "Come on."

In my boot room, Kezia rose to kiss me. "We fit."

Blinking in surprise, I didn't hide my confusion. "What?"

"I can feel you, through the bond," she told me, pulling off her shirt. "We fit perfectly. I promise." Turning her back to me, she took off her bra. Looking over her shoulder, her back bare and her hair spilling loosely over her shoulder, she watched me drink her in. Kezia winked at me. "You ready to hunt?"

Stupid question. She already knew the answer.

Because we fit.

Perfectly.

CHAPTER 22

Kezia

EVERYTHING FELT BETTER WHEN I WAS MY WOLF. I had said it all my life, and I would continue saying it until the day I died: there was nothing that beat being a wolf.

Nothing?

Are you going to tell me that sex is better? I asked my alpha as he ran beside me.

Are you seriously *going to tell me it isn't?*

He may have a point. I wasn't letting him know that though, so I chose to say nothing. It didn't matter—his massive black wolf nudged me playfully and sent me tumbling. I was back on my feet instantly, racing after him as he ran ahead, both of us relishing the run and being free to be with each other.

I should have felt guilty. I knew that these were serious times, but the sense of freedom and rightness as we ran together couldn't be dented by something like guilt.

Cannon saw the white rabbit first, about the same time as it sensed him, and by the grace of the Goddess, it gave us a wild run. The chase was exhilarating, both of us working together almost seamlessly as we hunted down one rabbit. When

Cannon finally had his jaws around the beast, I waited for the snap of its neck, which never came.

Did you forget how to kill?

The shaman never stated if it was to be dead or alive.

Shit. I remembered asking, but I didn't remember the answer. I had a more pressing problem, I realized, when I felt an urge rise inside me that only my alpha could satisfy.

Shifting to human form, I looked around the lowland brush that we were in. "If I make a cage, we could keep it alive."

Turning to look over my shoulder, I saw that Cannon had already shifted. He held the rabbit by the scruff of the neck as he watched me. His body was hard and inviting, his cock resting heavily against his thigh. The sight of it made me lick my lips. I remembered tasting him earlier.

"Kezia," Cannon growled. "Keep looking at me like I'm dinner, and I'll let this thing drop."

"That's why I am looking for a cage," I explained. Pulling twigs off a bush, I tried to make them form a weave. All I did was scratch myself. I felt his warm body behind me, one large hand ran down my back and over my hip. "I need to make the cage."

"You're not making a cage," he said gruffly. Pushing my hair aside, Cannon kissed along my shoulder to the crook of my neck. "The rabbit's gone."

Spinning around, I faced him. "What? *Why*?"

"Didn't have red eyes. Wasn't the right one."

"Are you sure?"

Cannon's kiss took me by surprise. Pulling me tightly against him, his hand settled on the small of my back, pressing me even closer to his body. I could feel the strength of him all around me, a strength that almost made me nervous, but I knew he would never hurt me. The thought made me bold as I took his cock in my hand and stroked his length. His groan made my knees weak, but still, he never broke the kiss.

Opening my mouth, I pushed my tongue between his lips, parting them, tasting all of him as we kissed. The scent of him made my mouth water, and I wondered if I would ever get enough of this male. Cannon drew back slightly, breaking our kiss, the look in his eyes enough to make my blood heat.

"Kezia?"

"I need you," I told him simply. "Right here, right now."

"The rabbit?"

"Can go fuck itself." His burst of surprised laughter made me grin. "Sorry." I bit my lip. "Nope, not sorry. I'll say it again, I don't give a fuck about the rabbit right now."

Cannon pulled me closer. "In that case, I say stop talking."

He kissed me deeply, almost forcefully, exploring my mouth as if he had never tasted me before or would never get to again. His fingers stroked against my throat before cupping my chin, holding my head in place, exactly where he wanted it. I didn't want to escape his hold, but even if I did, I doubted I would be able to. The kiss was all-consuming, it took my breath away, and I knew without a doubt I was a fool to have let another male kiss me.

My body was on fire. Heat was gradually building in my center and slowly spreading outwards. My nails dug into his shoulders as Cannon laid his claim on my body. The sensation of his touch was burning hot in my veins, and I needed to quench the fire. Wetness pooled between my legs as the pressure built deep in my core, and I knew only having him inside me would ease my craving.

"Cannon." It could have been a groan or a whisper, or I may not have even spoken. The ache for him was everywhere.

He moved us and I felt rough bark press against my skin. I didn't care, so eager to have him inside me. I pulled my leg up his thigh, my body slick with sweat. Hooking my leg over his hip, I pulled my mate into me. So desperate, I ignored everything around me.

"Fuck me."

The frantic need to be filled by him was overriding all my senses. I felt wild and out of control. All I wanted was his cock pushing inside me, stretching me, making me his.

"Fuck, Kezia," Cannon groaned against my neck when I bucked my hips against his hard length, eager for him to take me. "So eager for me, my mate."

He pushed inside in one thrust, taking me hard, knocking the air from my body, and both of us groaned in appreciation. There was no finesse. No lovemaking. Cannon fucked me hard and deep, and I begged for more. We had lost control, acting on pure instinct, which only made me crave him more.

My legs crossed behind his back, pulling him into me as hard as I could. I needed to feel his strength against me; I needed to feel almost squashed against his weight as he drove his cock deeper and deeper into me. My fingers were tangled in his hair, pulling his head down so I could kiss him, lips crushing mine as we lost ourselves in each other.

Cannon ground his hips against me, increasing his speed. His moan of approval as I angled my body to take more of him only made him take me harder. So hard it was almost brutal, and still, it wasn't enough.

We'd had sex before, but he'd never been this uncontrolled.

EVE L. MITCHELL

This rough. It felt as if he was giving me all of him, all his force, uncontrolled and wild, and I wanted it.

I needed it.

As his thrusts became more punishing, I knew I'd wear the bruises, and I relished the pain as well as the pleasure.

"More, Alpha," I grunted against his skin.

"I'll give you more," he snarled, eyes wild with lust. Grabbing my hands, he pinned them above my head, using the tree to push off against me as he picked up his punishing rhythm.

My entire body was strung so tight I knew my orgasm was going to ruin me. His thumb stroked over my clit once, and my orgasm hit me so hard I may have blacked out. My teeth sank into his skin where his shoulder met his neck, and I felt my alpha's body still as he spilled inside me.

Cannon rested his forehead against mine as we both panted, desperate for air, our gazes locked.

"Holy Goddess, what the fuck was that?" he asked me with a shaky breath.

"Sex." My voice was rough, hoarse sounding. "Good sex."

"*Great* sex."

"The best sex," I agreed. Cannon moved back slightly, and all my muscles screamed in protest. "Ow!"

"Are you hurt?" He cupped my jaw, concern in his eyes. "Did I hurt you?"

"Hurt me?" I grinned up at him. "I think you tried to split me in two." Gingerly I dropped my legs from around his waist, and on shaky feet, I tried to stand. "Ow, ow, ow."

Cannon half turned to show me his back. "Feel like I've been shredded. Have I?"

His back was a mess of bloody scratches, and with a glance

at my hands, I saw blood under my nails. "Um...I think you need to shift, to heal."

Cannon kissed me softly. "Savage little mate."

"What the heck was in that potion the shaman gave me?" I asked ruefully as I stretched my arms over my head. "That was... unexpected."

Cannon shook his head from side to side, almost as if he was shaking his head clear, before coming to a complete stand-still. "Kezia?"

"Mm-hmm?"

"There's a very big fucking rabbit with red eyes, eyeing us as if *we're* dinner," he spoke quietly.

Following his line of vision, I held back the gasp. I'd never seen a rabbit so big. "Did we just screw that into existence?"

Cannon's snort of laughter broke the stare off. The rabbit turned on its heel and ran for it. The alpha and I both shifted at the same time, and soon we were running after it.

What a wild and crazy day this had been, and as we chased down the biggest rabbit ever seen, I knew I wouldn't have changed one moment of it.

"THAT'S A BIG RABBIT." Royce eyed the beast thoughtfully. "Is it supposed to be eyeballing me like that?"

Drinking my coffee, I leaned casually against my alpha's chest. We were on a couch in the study, he was sitting behind me, and I was using him as my support as I leaned against him. "It runs quicker than a wolf too."

"No shit? Really?"

"Almost broke my neck trying to catch the darned thing,"

Cannon said, sipping his coffee. His head bent to speak in my ear. "You comfy there?"

"I'm deliciously comfy," I told him as I burrowed in deeper.

"You two make me nauseous."

"Liar," I teased Royce. "You love it."

He gave me a look that told me I was right, but he wasn't admitting it. "The pack's ready to move when you give the word, Alpha."

I felt Cannon tense slightly, but then he relaxed once more. "I'll check everything over before I give the order."

"Of course," Royce murmured.

Sitting up, I turned to look back at Cannon. "Are we ready?"

Lifting me off his lap, Cannon stood. "We are ready. I'm up-to-date with all the preparations. I've given my orders, and most of them have been followed."

"Most of them?" I hesitated. "You've done what? How are you up-to-date? You've been with me the whole time!"

"I'm alpha to my pack, Kezia. Because I'm with you doesn't mean I am not with them."

"Huh?" The mindlink meant that he could talk to any of his pack. "Are you *always* with them?" My gaze darted to Royce, who was studiously examining the bookshelves.

"Not all the time." Cannon winked at me, and I knew I was blushing.

"Why is the rabbit in the study?" Royce asked suddenly, obviously keen to change the subject.

"Because the shaman told us to put it somewhere until he needed it," I told him, leaning back on the couch, which was no longer as comfortable without my alpha to lean on.

"So...we're keeping it? Like a pet?"

Cannon and I exchanged a look. "We don't know," Cannon admitted. "It's as unknown to us as it is to you."

"Have you asked him?"

"Have we *asked* him?" I slapped my forehead. "Cannon, *why* didn't we *ask* him?"

"Okay, fine, I get it, stupid question."

"We asked him," Cannon told him, shooting me a look of reprimand, and I stuck my tongue out at him. "He deemed it wasn't pertinent to answer yet."

Royce was once more looking between us with confusion. "That means what?"

"We don't know." I got off the couch, wandering over to the window where the alpha just *happened* to be standing. Cannon pulled me into his side, and I felt content once more.

"Do you ever not touch each other?" Royce asked us.

"You make it sound sordid," I admonished him, sharing a smile with Cannon.

"Do you even know you're doing it?"

"If you don't want to look at us, don't keep coming into the house."

"*Kezia.*" Cannon nudged my hip, and I glowered at him. He ignored me as he spoke to his beta. "It's still new for us," he reminded him. "I am sure in time, we will be like any other married couple. Until then, I'm not going to not touch my mate in case it makes people uncomfortable."

Royce flushed and, for once, looked put out. "You know I don't mean it like that," he spoke to Cannon directly. "But you plan to lead us into a pack war. Your pack is ready, and you haven't been exactly...present."

I felt Cannon bristling behind me, but before I could come to his defense, he spoke first. "You're right. I need to be seen."

Turning me to face him, Cannon kissed the tip of my nose. "Do you want to come check the pack with me? Or stay here with... it?" We both looked over at the rabbit, which was still watching us.

"Don't leave me alone with it."

"Agreed."

And that was how the three of us went on pack patrol. Cannon told me not to call it pack patrol, but since I had coined the phrase, it was firmly implanted in my head.

We met Kris deep in conversation with Ned, and I loved how easily my brother fit into this pack. I didn't love the fact that Cass still hadn't told him she was pregnant. A fact I decided I was going to rectify right then.

"I need to go back to the house."

Cannon's look of surprise faded when he saw me looking at my brother. "Kezia..."

"It happens today." My voice was firm, and he gave a slight dip of his head in agreement.

"Kris, I need you."

My brother's head snapped up, and he looked at me with concern. "Why? What's happened? Are you hurt?"

Luna, I loved this man. Why had I been such a brat to him when I was younger? "No, I'm fine. I just need you to come with me."

"But—"

"Just humor me, okay?"

Kris mumbled his goodbyes, but like a good brother, he followed me as I made my way to the house.

"You sure you're okay?"

"I've never been better," I told him truthfully. "You?"

"I could be better," he said with a tired sigh. "I feel guilty for wanting more. I have my mate, my sister is happy, and we all have our health, but…"

"But we're still going to fight a pack war and overthrow a Pack Council?"

Kris chuckled as we walked. "Yeah. That."

"We can do this," I told him with a confidence I was sure I was channeling from Cannon.

"We better, it's death otherwise."

I stopped in the street. "Death?"

Kris frowned as he turned to face me. "Obviously, Kezia. You think we *just* get our knuckles rapped for rebellion?"

"They *kill* us?"

"Why are you freaking out? You know this!"

I gawked at him before I found my voice again. Pointing at my face, I glared at my brother. "Does this *look* like the face of someone who *knew* this?"

Kris scratched his jaw. "What did you think would happen?"

"He said we would be exiled, and I said I would be exiled with him." I had given absolutely no thought to the consequences of our actions if we failed. "Everyone dies?" I whispered.

"Most likely just the alphas, the betas, other important instigators."

Once more, I was gaping in horror at my brother. "Luna, Kris! Why didn't you tell me this?"

He stared back at me in confusion. "Why didn't you *know* this before you ran around talking about rebellion?"

"Oh my Goddess! You know me almost better than anyone. Have you ever, *ever* known me to think through things first?"

"No, but you have a mate now."

"You think Cannon is thinking for me?" I snapped.

"Well, he better be thinking of his pack!"

"Why are you both shouting in the street?" Nikan asked casually as he joined us. "You're loud." He gave a tight-lipped smile. "It's not a good look for the pack leaders."

"Nikan," I breathed out loudly, hoping the tension in my chest would ease now Nikan was here. "What happens if we don't win?"

"We die." He looked similar to his brother, his hair lighter, the green of his eyes not as deep, his face almost boyish, but still, the no-nonsense attitude was exactly the same.

"You say it so casually."

Nikan shrugged. "It's war, Zia, people die."

Looking at my brother, I almost kicked him in the shin when I saw his *I told you so* look.

"I don't accept that."

"Then you're an idiot."

"Nikan!"

He shrugged. "What, Zia? We're not going to exchange pleasantries and share a cup of tea. They tried to kill my brother. They beat and tried to rape you. If they aren't dead by the end, it means we will be. *That's* what fighting is. That is war."

Taking a step back from them both, I shook my head. "Not everyone has to die."

"True." My brother held his hand up to stop Nikan from speaking. "But the ones responsible for *all* of this, for what happened to our parents, to us, Cannon, Cass, fuck, even Landon..." His eyes softened. "Their mom, Claire. They need to be held accountable. The Pack Council needs to be held accountable for the wrongs they have let slide because money was being put into their hands. They chained us with silver, Kez. They put silver into the hands of the humans and *let them hunt us*." Kris licked his bottom lip as he looked away. "They need to be stopped. We *will* stop them."

"Or die trying?" I snarked back at him.

"Or we die trying."

My head was reeling. Was I so naive? Probably. I was rattled and I couldn't think properly, but I *could* focus on what I could fix. "You need to go to the house."

Kris looked at Nikan and then sighed in defeat. "Cass will tell me when she's ready."

I blinked. Had I heard right? "What?"

Kris reached out and ruffled my hair. "I know, Kez. She's my mate. Of course I know."

"She hasn't told you though."

"She'll tell me when she's ready."

Weirdly, I wanted to cry. "I think I'm overwhelmed."

Nikan slung his arm over my shoulder. "Welcome to the Blackridge Peak Pack, Zia. You're in for the ride of your life." He dipped his head into mine. "And I don't mean when my brother's rocking your world."

When *my* brother punched him for his smart mouth, I laughed out loud, and just like that, the world was right again.

We had right on our side, and I had faith in the Goddess that she knew that.

CHAPTER 23

I'D SENT A TEAM OUT WITH THE BACKPACKS DURING the night, scouts I knew and trusted to move without being seen. We'd approach the Anterrio Pack as our wolves. Some of us would fight on two legs, some on four. The packs were for those of us who would choose to fight in our human form.

They had supplies of clothing, weapons, provisions, and medical kits. The blankets that Kezia and I had folded were in there too.

Standing at my kitchen counter, I heard the faint footsteps as she approached from the stairs. It was the dead of night; she should have been sleeping. Instead, she looked surprised to see me standing in my kitchen.

"Cassandra. Can I help you?" It amazed me how she was friends with Kezia. Kezia, who was so fearless, so ready to tackle anything, and this young wolf was just...*none* of those things. They said she was just as mischievous as Kezia, and I just couldn't see it. She jumped at her own shadow, whereas my mate would have already been challenging it to a fight.

"I just wanted some water, Alpha." She spoke with her eyes down, and it was that which pissed me off more.

"You can call me Cannon," I reminded her sharply. "After all, we're practically family."

Cass looked up in surprise and quickly looked away again, her lips twisted into a semblance of a smile, but there was no humor in it. "Of course, one would be an alpha, and the other mated to an alpha."

Resting my butt against the counter, I crossed my arms over my chest as I watched her. "You sound as if you don't approve."

Cass took a few steps closer, still indecisive, but it seemed the darkness of the kitchen gave her courage. "I love my mate with everything I am," she told me huskily. "I've always been drawn to Kris. Dad knew it and hated it." She snorted lightly as she looked past me once more. "Now that I hear all these horrible stories about who my dad is, I guess I know why."

"Stories?"

Cass let out a shaky breath. "Stories. Facts? I don't know what to believe anymore."

Reaching over to take a tumbler out of the cupboard, I placed it on the counter. "Get your water, Cass, and go back to bed."

Surprisingly, she didn't move, her timid stare became bolder. "Why Kezia?"

"Why Kris?"

Rubbing her lower belly, she shrugged. "The Goddess likes to fuck with us all. Right?" She saw me watching her hand, and she dropped it immediately to her side. "I can't help it."

I heard the tears in her voice, and if she was one of my pack, I would have offered her comfort. But she wasn't, and as much as I respected Kris, I didn't trust his mate one bit.

"You regret this?" I indicated her abdomen, and she shook her head so quickly that my worries about her intent eased slightly.

"No." With a shaky laugh, she once more placed a hand over her stomach. "This is *perfect*." I saw the tears trickle down her face.

"But?"

"But my father is a psycho, and no one knows if they can trust my twin." She sniffled loudly. "And my mom is dead. He let my mom *die*."

I wasn't sure she meant Bale or her twin and chose not to ask. "You've had a lot to deal with, it's true."

Cass sent me an exasperated look, and I fought the smile. *There* was the attitude they told me she had. "And Kez has been beaten, and my dad was going to have sex with her—"

"Rape." I met her watery stare with a hard one of my own. "*Have sex* implies she had a choice."

With the heel of her hands, Cass wiped away her tears. "What if..." She swallowed hard, shaking her head as if to clear her thoughts. "Never mind." Walking quickly forward, she grabbed the tumbler and ran the faucet, filling it up. Taking greedy gulps, she dipped her head as she passed me. "Sorry for intruding, Alpha."

I watched her walk away from me, and I could almost feel Kezia's stare boring into me, even though I knew my mate lay spent in our bed, demanding me to reach out to her best friend. *Fuck, Kezia,* I grumbled, blaming her when she was, for once, blameless.

"What if your child is like your father?" I should have worded it better, but subtlety wasn't my strongest trait. "Is that what you were going to say?"

Cass stopped, looking at me over her shoulder, and she looked so much like her twin I had the irrational urge to punch her.

"Yes." She turned back to me, glancing at the stairs to ensure we were alone before she spoke again. "Or my brother. What do I do?"

"You doubt your brother's part in this?" I knew I sure as hell did. No one was that good an actor.

Cass rubbed her nose, reminding me very much of the big red-eyed rabbit taking up half of my study. Another *guest* in my home I would rather not be here.

"Landon is complicated."

"Is he?" I scoffed.

Cass glowered at me, and I had zero fucks to give if I upset her. "He wants my father's approval above all," she told me quietly. "Kez...she has never been his." Cass sipped her water. "I mean, you know *that*, what I mean is that he was never interested in her like that *at* all." Cass took a few steps back towards me, her voice lowering. "You have to understand, our dad, he wasn't this person he is now. He never even *hinted* at being this...horror."

Horror. An apt description.

"I hate to break it to you, it seems he was."

Cold, Cannon. So cold.

Cass was nodding, staring at the floor. "Yup, seems so." Tiredly, she lifted her head and met my guarded look. "Tell me, *Alpha*, what the fuck do I do now?"

"You tell your mate your fears, your concerns, your hopes. You figure your shit out." I shrugged. "Be better parents, learn from the mistakes."

"Mistakes?"

"I'm going to be honest with you, Cassandra, okay?"

"Are you ever anything but honest?"

Her dry tone almost made me smile. Almost. "You and your brother are spoiled little shits that got away with far too much because you were raised in a pack ruled by a tyrant and a bully." Her eyes widened and her skin turned whiter than Kezia's hair. "Your brother is a prick. He's been a prick long before we knew your father was a murdering asshole. Every pack knows that Landon of the Anterrio Pack gets away with far too much because he is Pack Leader Bale's son. He's fucked his way through many a pack and not given a shit about his actions or the consequences. He's a dick and an entitled little shit that needs a good beating." I didn't stop even though I saw her flinch at my harsh words. "Why do you think your mate dislikes him? It has nothing to do with his supposed interest in Kezia. It's because he knew that Kezia would be nothing more to Landon than a notch on the bedpost."

"He's not that bad."

"He isn't that bad, he's worse." My hands gripped the counter behind me as I spoke to her. "It's hard to hear home truths. Your father is a terrible pack leader. He extorts his pack for his own gain. Your people, who get *nothing* from him, have to pay him to live. The bakery and the stores in your town have to pay Bale a portion of their income. He leaves your pack almost penniless because they have nowhere else to go and no provision to do so. He makes me sick." Cass looked away as I continued. "There isn't a pack in these mountains or beyond that *wants* to join your pack. It's rotten and corrupted, and the pack that stay there and *accept* that rule are no better."

"Are you finished?"

"No." Pushing off the counter, I stepped closer to her.

"And then there's you. The little princess who does absolutely nothing. You don't help with pack chores. You don't contribute. In a pack where technology is forbidden, you walk around with a cell phone and tablet, flaunting your *superiority* like it's a medal of honor. Only you have none. You do nothing and get everything. You are spoiled, entitled, self-centered, and selfish. You want to know how to ensure your child doesn't turn out like you or your brother, *do* better. *Be* better."

"I..."

"You know it's true. There are perks in being an alpha," I told her. "The *decent* alphas don't exploit them. They don't take from their pack for their gain. *Everything* I am is for my pack. I *serve* my pack, they don't serve me. They never will. A pack is strong because of its loyalty to one another. Not one ruled by fear." Looking down at her, I shook my head. "You have a lot of growing up to do, little girl, a child to raise and protect. Be grateful the Goddess gifted you a mate as true and fair as Kris. She's given you a second chance. Use it."

Cass was sobbing quietly, and when I stepped back, she turned on her heel and ran to the stairs.

"And, Cassandra?" I called after her. "Tell your mate you're carrying his child. Stop being selfish and grow up. In a very short time, you'll be responsible for someone else."

She didn't answer me, and I heard the bedroom door close. Pissed off even more, I left the house before I had to punch Kris when he came charging down the stairs to avenge his mate. I'd take that punch and then ask him if anything I'd said to her had been untrue.

I walked the deserted streets of my town under the watchful gaze of the moon. Nikan had said I wasn't to be alone since the attack, but what kind of alpha was I if I couldn't even walk my town alone?

I felt a rumble of discontent through the mate bond and rolled my eyes. The sniveling little fool hadn't gone to Kris, she'd gone to Kezia. *That* was a fight I didn't need. Kezia was blindly protective of Cass, and I really had no idea why. Was it purely a loyalty that arose because the twins were the only two who had befriended her in that useless pack? Surely not.

You've never been lonely. You don't know what it's like.

Glancing at the moon, I almost flipped off Luna despite the thoughts being mine. Shoving my hands in the pockets of my jeans, I walked every street, enjoying the serenity of my home. Some houses were in darkness, while some still had lights on as pack members made their final preparations or relished the nights of peace.

I should have been surprised when I stopped outside the house, but I didn't question it when Barbara opened the door and stood back to let me in.

"Can I make you a drink? Tea, Alpha?"

"No, thank you." I took the seat she offered and watched as she poured herself a glass of milk. "I don't know why I'm here."

"Restless feet mean restless hearts."

I waited but when she said nothing more, I frowned. "My heart isn't restless." How could it be? I had Kezia. She was everything I ever wanted. Which still made me marvel at the will of the Goddess.

"Restless mind then?"

I huffed out a non-answer, and the older shifter smiled as she sipped her milk. "Want to talk about it?"

Did I? Why would I be here? Why this female? "Why am I here?"

Barbara hesitated. "I thought we just established we never knew that."

"I mean, why would I come to you?" I studied her. She was so utterly unassuming. I'd spoken to her twice before that afternoon Kezia found her.

Barbara widened her eyes as she shrugged. "You can leave?"

I barked out a laugh when she grinned at me impishly. "Yeah, I could." Instead, I leaned back on her sofa. "My feet took me here, Barbara. I don't know why, but I feel that I need to be here. Why is that?"

"The moon's almost full," she answered. "Luna may be weighing on your mind."

"Luna is always on my mind," I told her glibly. She put her glass of milk on the table, and I chewed my inner cheek as I watched the milk that coated the glass run back down. "Barbara..."

She was already on her feet. "Milk and some cookies?"

Milk and cookies. I wasn't a pup, but damn if that didn't sound delicious. "Please."

I watched her fill her glass, pour me one, and place a plate of cookies beside me. They smelled fresh and delicious. "We need to keep Kezia away from these," I told her seriously as I took a bite. "She'll want them every day."

Barbara flushed happily. "Kezia can have what she wants whenever she wants it."

I was already shaking my head in denial. "No, that's the worst thing to say ever. She will exploit you mercilessly."

"Your mate would exploit me?"

"When it comes to food, yes."

Barbara's laughter was light and free, and it made me smile.

"I think I was too harsh on Cass." When she looked at me in confusion, I clarified. "Kris's mate."

"Ah." Barbara ran her hands over her pants. "Andrea's son."

"He hasn't come to see you, has he?" I guessed, watching as she shook her head briefly. "He will."

She didn't look like she believed me, but simply took another drink. "You regret what you said to her?"

"No."

"Then I don't understand."

"Me neither." Dropping the half-eaten cookie onto the plate, I leaned back. "Were you waiting for me?"

"I didn't know that I was," she answered honestly. "I too was restless. I knew I didn't want to sleep, and I knew I wasn't going anywhere"—she gestured to her blouse and pants—"but I didn't want to change clothes."

"So you were restless waiting for me, and I was restless and came to you?" We both looked out the window. "It's almost a full moon," I murmured. When I looked back at her, I gave a wry smile. "Your pack wasn't rogue, was it?"

Barbara didn't smile, just watched me steadily. "Not always."

"Your mate was a druid?" Cocking my head, I studied her. "Or you were?"

"I was."

And I understood why I was here. "You sent Moonstar." It made so much sense. "You knew Bale would never stop looking for Andrea, and you sent a guardian to watch over her." Barbara sat straighter with her hands clasped on her lap primly. She looked like a schoolteacher. I couldn't imagine her dancing under the moon, invoking the incantations of the Goddess.

"I sent a gift of protection."

"She's threatening Kezia's very existence."

Barbara nodded. "The spirit was never to enter the vessel, especially if the vessel was Kezia."

"The vessel?" The milk sat sour in my belly. "You mean Andrea?"

"A protection spell, that's all it was." Barbara looked at me calmly. "When I met Kezia that day, I felt the other's presence. So strong. I knew what she carried inside her."

"How do I get it out?"

"You have a pack war to fight, Alpha. The spirit will not harm."

"The spirit *has* harmed!" I exploded as I burst to my feet. "She takes *over* her body. She *wants* to keep her body, her wolf. She is no longer protecting her! She wants to *eradicate* her!"

Barbara looked up at me, still calm. "I can put a stop to that, for now."

"For now? You mean not permanent?"

"I'll need time. And the aid of a shaman."

"A shaman, I can give you," I muttered. "Although how *that* conversation is going to go beats me." Druids and shamans served Luna, but both had very different approaches. Druids believed in the spirit world, reincarnation, and the Otherworld, and while they practiced the relationship with flora and fauna, they relied heavily on natural spirits and the sense of specific places. The shaman was the voice on earth for Luna. The spirit they sought was the Goddess herself, wielding the power of the Goddess through sacrifice and trance.

"We can work together if we have the same goal," Barbara spoke reasonably.

"How will you get her out of my mate?"

"I will work on that with the shaman."

So she wasn't going to tell me. I knew not to push. I was ignorant of many things that concerned both practices, but I wasn't so ignorant that I didn't have respect for them. "Seems Luna had a plan for me after all, tonight."

"I know why I was called here," Barbara mused. "But I don't think this is all you are here for."

I was tired. Sleep suddenly weighed heavily on me. Looking at the milk and the cookies, I raised my head to meet her steady stare. "What did you do?"

"Trust me, Alpha, I do this for you both."

I couldn't keep my eyes open, and as I slumped forward, I remember being surprised at the strength of the female in front of me as she caught me, and then it all went dark.

CHAPTER 24

Kezia

WALKING THROUGH THE TOWN, I TRIED TO KEEP MY face free of the anger currently coursing through my veins. I waved and smiled at the pack who, had I not been burning with fury, I would have noticed were casting me strange looks. They were preparing for a tactical strike, the whole pack was subdued, and I was waving at them like I was ready to go on a picnic.

Had anyone asked me why I seemed so overtly cheery, a phrase that had never been associated with me before, I would not have been able to lie. Because *I* was an *honest* and *fair* person.

Unlike the brute that was my mate.

And when I found the male whom I was bonded to, I was going to tear strips off him. Cass woke me last night, sobbing her heart out, and when I finally had her calmed down, she told me all the horrible things that Cannon had said to her.

When she had finally settled, I had gone in search of my mate...only to find the fucker wasn't in the house.

Where was he? I hated that my first thought went to Koda, and I gave myself a stern talking-to about *that*. He may be harsh and cruel to people I cared about, but I knew he would never do *that*.

But still, it burned deep within me that he was not home and that I couldn't reach him through the mate bond. I couldn't *ask* anyone either. Because I was his mate, and I had a hotlink right to him.

Or I was supposed to.

He had blocked me.

Blocked me.

I was going to make him suffer for this. No sex. Not even a hand job. He was going to feel my frustration until I was sure he was as furious as me.

I saw Hannah approach me, her daughters in tow, and I pushed the rage down so I didn't snarl at her when she said something nice about my mate. Because she would; she was his number one fan.

Ugh.

"Morning, Kezia," she greeted. "I'm just taking these two to the hall to help prepare the last of the packs." She wasn't smiling, and she smelled anxious. "Their daddy went out last night and hasn't come back yet, but when he does, he'll need some extra packs."

Fear penetrated my anger. Her fear, and I focused on something other than kicking my mate in the nuts. "Royce went out with the team?"

She nodded, pulling her youngest daughter into her hip. "Yeah, he always does. If Cannon doesn't go, Royce does." Anxiety was tight across her eyes.

"They need to be thorough," I reminded her, having no idea if that was the right thing to say. "You know Royce, he'll be so thorough he'd rather take that extra time now than lose it later." Which was complete speculation on my part, but Hannah nodded.

"I know." She blew out a low breath, careful not to alert her girls she was freaking out. "But..."

"You worry." I smiled, pretty sure all I did was bare my teeth at her, but she gave me a small smile back. "As soon as I find Cannon, I'll ask."

"Find him? Where is he?"

Fuckity fuck fuck. "Helping."

Hannah looked at me expectantly, and when I didn't say anything else, she looked down at her girls quickly. "Helping? With what? I thought everything was more or less ready?"

It was?

"Yeah, but you know him, he's..." Stumped, I rocked back on my heels.

"Thorough."

We both looked down at Hannah's oldest daughter, who was looking up at us with wide eyes the same color of brown as her father's.

I felt guilty and I hadn't even done anything. "That's right, he is, just like your daddy."

Her lower lip trembled, and then she was crying, which made her sister cry, and I had no idea why or what to do, so I looked helplessly at Hannah, who was also fighting back tears.

Luna's grace, this was not a situation I should be in front of. I had no people skills at all.

"Hey, who's crying?" Nikan scooped the youngster into his arms and bounced her into his arms. "Why are you crying, little wolf?" The tears stopped almost immediately as she beamed at him. "Where's Cannon?" Nikan asked me quickly as he dried the tears from the girl's face.

"Being thorough."

"Huh?" Nikan looked between the two of us. "Am I missing something?"

Yes, your idiothead brother. "Nope. Cannon's busy being all alpha-ey."

"Alpha-ey?"

"Oh my Luna, why is everything you say to me this morning a question?" I snapped, causing the girl to cry again. Pinching the bridge of my nose, I blew out a breath. "I can't do this. I need to go."

Without another word, I left them in the street. Both girls were crying again, and I fought the urge to run from them. "I swear, Luna, you make me a mother too soon, and we'll have words. I can't deal with all that, yet."

I swear the breeze that swirled around me was the sound of her laughter.

"Kezia!"

Nope. No. Not now.

Instead, I turned and greeted Leo. "What's up?" Sliding my hands in my back pockets, I hoped it hid the fact my hands were shaking. "Why aren't you out dropping packs?"

Leo looked at me blankly, my question catching him by surprise. "Err...I was running ops?"

Running ops? Sounded contagious. "Oh, right. Of course, you all done?" I searched the streets for my mate as Leo spoke.

"Yeah, everything is set up, and I think we have most of the terrain covered. There's a few blind spots—"

"Aren't there always?" I murmured.

"Well, yeah, but if you know where they are, then it's not so bad, right?"

What? "Yeah." I hesitated. "But if you know where they are, why can't you cover them?"

Leo flushed. "You're right, of course. I'll go run them again."

He hurried off and I wasn't sure what I'd said to make him redden with embarrassment. I started walking again, and someone else stopped me. When I'd answered their questions, which usually started with *where's the alpha?* I listened to the reason they wanted him in the first place.

It went like that for the next few hours, and in the end, I was crouched low, hiding behind a wall that ran around a pack member's house. I was exhausted. All the questions and constant reassurances drained me. I still hadn't found my mate, but I was no longer angry at him. I was looking for him because now I knew why he was sometimes short-tempered and blunt.

All the questions. How did he get through the day with all of this pack looking to him for answers? I felt a flutter in the bond, and when I stood up, I saw Cannon striding towards me, a storm brewing in his eyes.

Shit. What had I done this time?

"Where have you been?" I asked him, ready to defend whatever bad advice I had given. With my hands on my hips, I was giving him attitude just from the way I was standing. I wasn't expecting him to grab me and kiss me. Don't get me wrong, I wasn't complaining either; I would never complain about *this*.

Cannon didn't give a damn that we were in the middle of the street, albeit a secluded corner. His hands cupped my ass, lifting me slightly to meet him, and I happily went, my arms looping around his neck as he kissed me deeply.

When he pulled back, I looked up at him, worry replacing my former agitation. "What is it?"

EVE L. MITCHELL

"Your friend Barbara has some explaining to do."

"Barbara?" Sinking back onto my feet, I didn't let go of him. "What did you do to her? Is it like what you did to Cass?" My temper was back.

"Cass? She needed to hear the truth. You and Kris shelter her for no reason."

"You were a dick."

"I was honest."

We stared at each other, both of our eyes narrowing as we got ready to argue. Sounds of the pack getting ready to fight a pack war drifted in between us. I let out a sigh.

"You could have been kinder."

Cannon's lips twisted into a sneer but then smoothed out just as quickly. "Maybe I could have."

We held each other's stare. "That was almost mature of us..."

Cannon grinned. "An adult conversation. Us?"

I returned his grin. "Wow, who knew that being bonded meant we wouldn't scream and shout at each other?"

Cannon scoffed. "Barbara."

"Huh?" Looking around, I thought she was near. "What happened with her? Is she okay?"

"She's a druid."

If he had led a conga down the street naked, I would have been less surprised. "She's a what now?"

"A druid." The storm was back in his eyes. "She's also the reason you have a *passenger*."

"Wh-what?"

He nodded grimly. "And she *drugged* me with milk and cookies."

My burst of laughter died under his icy stare. "Sorry." I

smothered my smile behind my hand. "Are you okay?" His glare intensified, and I knew it was because I was trying not to laugh. "Why would she drug you?"

"She said it was for both of us."

"I didn't have any milk or cookies." I knew I was laughing at him, but he was just so *big*, and milk and cookies? Seriously?

"Shut up." He turned to look up the street, his cheeks flushing.

"Where's Barbara now? Making more sugar cookies?"

"You're evil," he told me with a smile playing around his lips. "No, actually, she's gone."

I gave him a worried look. "What do you mean? Gone?"

"I mean she drugged me and then ran for it."

"But you're fine." He gave me a flat look and I rolled my eyes. "Your ego's hurt." I checked him worriedly. "Right?"

"Maybe." He refused to meet my eyes, and I knew I was going to laugh again.

"Then why would she run?"

"I don't know. If she comes back, we can ask her."

I snickered. "Your face is a picture."

Cannon growled at me, but he was looking around the empty streets. "My pack's quiet."

I choked out a snort of derision. "Quiet? All morning they've asked me a hundred thousand questions."

"What kind of questions?" Taking my hand, Cannon walked us back to the main part of town while I told him all the things that I had answered this morning in his absence.

When he pulled me to a stop in the center of the town, outside the gate to the house, he was smiling so brightly that I stopped talking to stare at how gorgeous my mate was when he was happy. I mean, when he was all mean and moody, he was sexy and lickable, but happy...Luna, I didn't think I was prepared for that. I was almost drooling.

"What is it?" I asked him carefully, his smile infectious, causing me to smile too.

"Don't you see what you've done today?" he asked me softly, his thumb brushing across my cheek. "You led the pack. Like an alpha. No...*as* an alpha."

"I did?" I had? I had! With a squeal, I launched myself into his arms and laughed when he swung me in a circle. "Oh Goddess, what if I gave bad advice?"

Cannon kissed me soundly. "Then we'll fix it." He kissed me again. "But I don't think you have." He beamed at me. "Thank you for looking after them."

Now I wanted to cry. My emotions were all over the place today. "They're our pack."

"Yes, they are." His kiss was gentle. "Come on, we need to make sure everything is ready." We walked up the path, the sense of urgency returning as the fight drew nearer.

"We go tonight?"

"I do, yes." As I tugged on his hand, he didn't look back. "No. You need to be here. Too many will be left behind. You need to make sure they are safe and you proved today that they will listen to you."

Cannon pushed the study doors open, almost coming to a stop when he saw Kris, Royce, Nikan, and Leo waiting for him. "A welcoming committee," he greeted them curtly.

"Where've you been?" Royce demanded. "Now is not the time to go on solo missions."

I caught Cannon's eye and shook my head slightly. Barbara and her druidness could wait. Was *druidness* a word? I tried to focus on the solemnness of the males in the room.

"I had things I needed to do," Cannon said, with his eyes on me. "Kezia has served the pack well in my absence."

When my brother looked at me in surprise, I pulled a face at him, causing him to scowl. "You can see why I doubt Alpha Cannon," he deadpanned.

"You were absent to get the pack used to Kezia?" Leo asked with a look of understanding. "Clever." Pride for his alpha was strong.

I almost, *almost* blurted out that I stepped up because their *clever* alpha had been duped by a druid who came bearing milk and cookies. But I held my tongue because I was a mature pack leader.

Alpha. Cannon's warm voice sounded in my head. *You're a mature-ish alpha.*

Mature-ish?

We all saw you stick your tongue out at your brother.

Go drink some more milk.

His huff of laughter enveloped me, making me feel warm and tingly.

"Everything's set," Royce was telling us both, and I forced myself to pay attention. "We move on your command."

"How many stay behind?" Cannon asked, his full focus on his beta.

"Twenty-three."

"Including my mate?"

Royce glanced at me. "Twenty-four."

"See! Even Royce thinks I should be with you!"

"Royce does not think that."

I pointed at the beta. "He's right there. *Ask* him if he thinks I should be with you!"

Kris spoke over us both. "You will stay here."

I turned to look at my brother. "I'm *mated*. You can't boss me around anymore."

"And you will stay here with my *mate*." His blue eyes narrowed. "My *pregnant* mate, who is fragile and emotional because I am going to war against her father and possibly her twin brother."

Sneaky, duplicitous asshole. Making me feel guilty like that.

"The shaman will be here," I countered.

Kris raised his eyebrows. "Kezia..." he warned.

"That's so underhanded." I crossed my arms grumpily. "You're a turd."

Leo laughed, trying and failing to cover it with a cough.

I pouted in the corner while they discussed war tactics. Pissed off with them all, I knew why Cannon wanted me here. His fear that Moonstar would come forward was a battle he couldn't fight at the same time as waging a war against the bastard Bale.

It didn't matter that I hadn't felt her since the bond was completed. He wasn't ready to risk it.

Risk me.

"Where's Doc?" Silence filled the study. As I looked at each of them, none of them met my eye. "Cannon?"

"Doc was compromised."

"Mal?" My attention flicked to Royce, who studied his hands. "The Doc, Mal? Was compromised?"

Cannon cricked his neck. "He knows how to break the mate bond." When I went to speak, he held up his hand. "He told Koda."

Looking over at my brother, I saw his lips pressed into a thin line. I filled in the gaps they left out. "And Koda told

Landon didn't she?" Cannon nodded once. "Holy shit, that jealous bitch."

"I'm sorry."

Looking at Cannon, I blinked. "Why are you sorry? You didn't tell her." I had noticed that I *hadn't* noticed her around town. "I wondered where she was. She in hiding?"

"Exiled," Nikan told me. "We no longer let shifters stay who mean ill will to our alpha, or his mate."

Exiled? That was huge. "Wow." I wasn't sure what to say. A heaviness lay over the study, and I didn't want them to feel that, especially over a petty female who deserved her punishment. I tried to lighten the mood. "I hope you revise the whole *ill will to his mate* thing."

"Why?" Royce asked curiously, but when Kris looked up and saw my smirk, he smiled slightly, knowing me well enough that I was going to say something ridiculous. I did not disappoint.

"Well, I can cook...but not *that* well. If the pack gets the shits because I was on cooking duty, I'm just saying...you may have a *lot* of ill will towards *this* mate."

It broke the tension as I hoped, and they finished discussing their final plans with lighter hearts despite the seriousness of the topic.

"You have twenty minutes," he spoke to the room. Cannon looked only at me. "Say your goodbyes quickly."

I was surprised when Royce hugged me before he left the study, then Nikan, and even Leo, and I returned each hug warmly.

My brother looked down at me. "She's pregnant with my child," he reminded me.

"She finally tell you?"

261

Kris gave me one of his looks, then kissed my cheek. "Protect her."

"Consider it done."

I watched him leave, the doors closing behind him, and I turned to look at my alpha. "Eighteen minutes left?" He made a noncommittal noise. "Wanna do it?"

Cannon's head tilted back as he laughed loudly. "Goddess, I love you, Kezia." Wrapping me in his arms, he looked down at me. "You'll lead the pack while I'm gone. They'll listen to you. Barbara's trick proved that." He scowled in remembrance. "She told me it was for the good of us both. I never thought it was for the good of the pack."

"Showing me I could lead, and showing you that they will listen to me?" I guessed.

"Showing me that they trust you. That *I* trust you." He kissed me. The kisses led to more, and soon our clothes were on the floor, and I was gasping his name.

Which was fortunate, because he didn't need to realize his trust was misplaced. Not yet. They were leaving in under twenty minutes, and I fully intended to be with them.

CHAPTER 25
Kezia

I STOOD ON THE EDGE OF THE PACKLANDS AS I watched the pack leave. They left in groups. Cannon was the first one to go, and I'd had no embarrassment as I kissed my alpha goodbye and told him to come home quickly. The shaman had blessed them with Luna's grace before they left, and then Cannon had shifted, and I'd watched the massive wolf lead his pack to war.

Kris had been with him, and I didn't think I had ever been as scared as I was right then when my brother and my mate left me behind to go fight a battle that I was at the center of.

I felt helpless, but not for long, I vowed.

Royce led the next team out. *Team* was probably the wrong word, but they looked like they were split into teams, so that's what I was calling them. Royce went in a different direction, and I didn't need to ask, because I knew the plan of attack.

I *knew* all of it, which if you thought about it, was Cannon's own fault when he found out I had followed him.

Leo and his team left next, in human form, which surprised me because I knew how fast Leo was as a wolf. His cheery grin and wave as he left made me smile. The big bulky shifter Ned was with him. He didn't smile or wave, but the wink he gave me was as good as.

It was dawning on me that perhaps Cannon's pack had more than a touch of eccentricity running through their veins.

Your pack.

My breath caught as I heard him through the link. *How far out before we lose this?*

Not being a radio frequency, I can't answer that.

My huff of laughter had the shaman looking at me curiously. "Pup?"

"Nothing." I watched the last team disappear over the horizon before turning to the shaman again. "Have you seen Cass?"

"She chose not to come down," he told me quietly. "I believe she's resting."

I saw Hannah talking to some of the pack who were left behind. There were twenty-four of us, and we had our orders. A perimeter around the town was already in place, and the children and older shifters were in the hall together. Keeping us contained and together.

I was to regularly check on all aspects of the *guard* Cannon left behind. Hannah was well-versed in what to do, so I wasn't feeling too guilty about my plan to ditch them. Which wasn't true at all—I felt like shit—but he was my mate, and Luna knew he wouldn't be sitting back if it were the other way around.

Feigning patience while my insides screamed at me that I needed to move fast, I went back to the house on the pretense of checking in on Cass.

The shaman was heading to the hall when he stopped and looked back at me. "There are herbs on the counter, take them."

"I'm good, thanks." My pulse had spiked, and I felt like I'd been caught even before I did anything.

"Kezia, *take* the herbs."

I was glad he was partially sighted so he didn't see my eye roll, but I grumbled my agreement, and with urgency snapping at my heels, I made my way to the house. Running up the stairs, I yelled out to Cass that it was only me and then threw myself into Cannon's bedroom.

All of my things had been moved in here from the guest bedroom where I had stayed at first. This was now our bedroom. He'd explained about the hole in the wall, and we'd both reflected somewhat sheepishly at how hardheaded and *stupid* we'd been about fighting the mating bond. If we had just completed it sooner, would any of this have happened?

Stripping off my shirt, I pulled on a formfitting black T-shirt. Kicking off my jeans, I pulled on a pair of leggings. The door opened and I turned quickly to see Cass leaning against the doorframe.

She looked me over and smiled. "Knew I could count on you." It was only then that I realized what she was wearing. A black shirt, black jeans, and a black hoodie.

"What are you doing?"

"Coming with you." She pulled her long blonde hair into a high ponytail. "You think my mate is going to war against my father, who wants to kill us, and I'm going to sit here and bite my nails?"

"You're pregnant."

"Even more reason why I will not let my mate go without me."

I watched her as I reached for my own hoodie. "You marked him?"

Cannon and I had made the mate mark the night we completed the mate bond. I'd noticed, almost by accident, that Kris and Cass had no mark. They were mated, there was no doubt, but they hadn't marked each other.

"I told him I was pregnant," Cass said, with a flush in her cheeks. "Your brother was *very* happy."

I grinned. "Nice." I frowned as I realized what I had said. "Ugh, ew, no. *Not* nice."

Cass smiled wider before she turned serious again. "I won't lose him, Kez. Tell me you're defying your mate's order too?"

We shared a conspirator's smile. "Does a bear shit in the woods?"

Together we hurried down the stairs, and I directed Cass to the back door. We'd need to be quick to get out of town and then make it past the perimeter guards. Grabbing her arm, I pulled her to a stop as we passed the kitchen counter.

A pitcher of water sat between two cups, both of which had herbs in them.

"What?"

"There." I pointed to the cups. "The shaman..." I reached for the water.

Cass gripped my arm. "What if it's to knock us out?" she hissed.

Pushing her hand off me, I rolled my eyes. "Don't be ridiculous," I scolded her.

"He's on the *alpha's* side."

Looking at Cass incredulously, I fought the urge to slap her. "*We're* on the alpha's side, dumbass."

She looked stumped momentarily before knocking my hand away again from reaching for the cup. "Not on this. They want us here. We don't want to be here. He could be working with them."

"Has pregnancy made you stupid?" I poured water into my cup. "This better work cold." Swirling the mixture, I watched as the water changed color, and then knowing the shaman's potions better than I should, I held my nose as I drank the concoction down.

After a few moments, I beamed at Cass. "See? Not dead. Or unconscious. Come on, drink, we're wasting time."

Cass took longer to drink than I did, but she wasn't as familiar with all of the shaman's concoctions as I was. She was still gagging when we got to the back door. Looking at her over my shoulder, I had a twinge of guilt as I took in her pale, drawn face.

"Are you up for this?" I glanced at her stomach. "It's not just you anymore."

Cass's lower lip trembled, but she nodded firmly. "This is my family."

"Yeah, but half of your family could be trying to kill us."

"My dad," she choked. "Pack *Leader* Bale killed my mom." Tears welled in her eyes, but they didn't fall. "Even if he didn't administer the blow, he left her in a cell to die. *Alone.* My brother? I know he's got his issues, but he would *never* put a silver collar on my neck. I know it in my soul. Your alpha and his pack see him as an enemy—he isn't. I *know* it, Kez. I *need* to do this for my mate and my brother. My unborn child. It's my *family*, Kez."

"*Our* family," I corrected her. "Landon's shady, he's up to something, but I agree...he'd never hurt you."

"Or you." I could argue, but I merely looked away. Her hand on my arm caused me to look back at her. "He knows what you can take. He may have pushed, but he wouldn't. Unless..." She swallowed. "Unless he's desperate. He's desperate, Kez. I need to get to him before he does something so monumentally stupid..."

"He is stupid," I agreed. "This wasn't supposed to be a rescue mission for Landon," I scolded her as I eased the door open.

Cass scoffed. "Course it was. He's your best friend."

"I thought that was you," I snarked as I peeked out onto the street.

"I'm mated to your brother; I'm your sister now."

Looking at her over my shoulder, I saw the twinkling laughter in her eyes. It was the first time she'd looked happy in days.

"Yeah, well, something happens to you, and my brother is going to kick my ass, so you better be ready to remind him how much you love and *need* your sister." The street was clear. "Okay, let's go. Act naturally."

We walked out the door, closing it firmly behind us, and headed towards the bunker. We didn't see anyone and I didn't hear a sound.

It was almost too good to be true. Right up until we reached the bunker, and Doc was sitting in front of a Jeep, a gun in his hand.

"Doc?" I asked warily.

He shook his head as he looked us both over. "I told Hannah she was stupid to doubt you, that you would listen to your mates, and she told me to sit here anyway and prove her wrong."

"Hannah?"

He straightened. "Yup. Seems like I'm the stupid one."

"What's the gun for?" Cass asked cautiously.

Doc looked at it as if he forgot he had it. He placed it on the hood of the Jeep. "I'm on perimeter duty."

"So not for us?"

I shot her a withering glare. "Doc isn't going to shoot us, dumbass. He's on our side." I looked back at him. "Right?"

He shook his head. "No, I'm on Cannon's side, always." He frowned slightly. "But I also know *you*," he told me. "And you're getting out of this town no matter who stands in your way, so..." He walked to the passenger door, opened it, and pulled out two of the black backpacks. "I was told to make sure you had everything you needed."

Gratitude swelled within me. "Hannah?"

"Also knows how stubborn and reckless you are," he said with a small smile.

"If you don't agree, why are you letting us go?" Cass asked suspiciously as she took a pack off him.

"Because I fucked up." He shrugged. "I got too into my own head and wanted to fix a problem, a scientific problem. Only I was reminded not that long ago that there's magic in this world, not just science. I made a mistake. This will not make up for it; in fact, it's going to get me thrown out of this pack, but I'm not messing with the magic."

I took the offered backpack. "He won't throw you out," I told him softly. "I won't let him." Reaching up, I kissed the Doc's cheek. "Thank you, Mal."

He rubbed his cheek, a blush in his cheeks. "Told you it's best to call me Doc."

"Doc is for the pack," I told him, putting my backpack on. "Mal is my friend."

He watched me for a minute and then chuckled. "Well, it's a nice thought. Won't stop the punch though."

"I'll help nurse you," I told him with a wink. "Or we just don't let him know."

"Right." He checked Cass over. "You're in your first trimester; you need to take care. Nothing too strenuous, no heavy lifting, keep hydrated." Leaning back against the hood of the Jeep, he sighed. "I'd say try not to stress, but I honestly don't think you can avoid that right now. Whether you're here or following them, I reckon your stress levels are pretty much shot."

Cass actually laughed. "Yup. I weirdly feel calmer doing this than I would sitting not knowing." She looked at him thoughtfully. "You're an actual doctor?"

"I am."

I watched my bold friend become suddenly unsure. "Um, when I come back, could you, would you..."

Doc looked more sure of himself. "I can give you a full medical, check the baby if you like."

Cass nodded, and her bottom lip trembled as she rubbed her belly. "I do like. Please."

"Are you going to cry all the time?" I demanded. "Stay here with Mal, get checked now. I can't have you weeping all over the place."

Cass's eyes hardened. "You're not a nice person," she scolded. "I told you *we're* doing this. Come on, you're holding us up."

She beamed at Mal like they were sudden bosom buddies, and then set off, leaving me staring after her.

"I think Kris would want you to make sure she's okay," Mal prompted.

With a curse, I ran after her, ignoring his low laugh behind us.

We moved at a steady run. Cass may not have done a lot of chores at home, but she trained and hunted and liked to run in both human and wolf form. After my third time of asking, when she told me to stop asking her if she was okay or she'd punch me, we ran in easy silence, both of us watchful of our surroundings.

It was a trek I had made three times now, so it was familiar to me, and I had the advantage of knowing the attack plans from listening to the meetings.

We stopped after a few hours. Cass needed to rest, even if she wasn't saying it. She downed her water bottle, and I gave her some of mine too. There was a fresh spring further up the mountain, and I told her we would refill there. We both ate some dried beef and shared a protein bar.

We spoke little and, when she nodded, we set off again. I knew they were a few hours ahead by now. The pack would be moving at a much faster pace than us, but that was my hope. That they were so far in front that, by the time Cannon realized we were there, he couldn't send us back.

When we reached the place where Landon had taken me, it was fully dark. I pulled Cass away from the direct path to the Anterrio Pack.

"What? Why?" she whispered.

"The place Landon took me, it wasn't at the pack. It was somewhere else. I think it's this way."

"You think?" she hissed.

"Don't hiss at me, Cassandra. It's your father's hidden pack; why don't *you* know where it is?"

"Snappy much?" she grouched.

Inhaling deeply, I rubbed my eyes. "Sorry, I'm on edge."

"I know." Cass slipped her hand into mine. "We've got this, Kez."

Did we? I was beginning to doubt my great plan to swoop in and save my alpha.

"Kezia?" Firm hands grabbed my face, turning me to her. "I need you for this. I need the badass bitch who struts into illegal fighting rings and kicks ass. I need her."

I nodded. "You got her."

"Yeah?"

Pulling free from her hold, I nodded. "Yeah." I took a calming breath. "Yeah. Come on." I nodded to the west. "It's this way."

We kept in low crouches as we moved over the terrain. I couldn't sense any other shifter nearby, and that was beginning to freak me out more than I wanted to admit.

Together, we went lower down the mountain until I heard the faint snarls on the wind. "Cass?" I whispered.

"It's already begun?" she guessed.

"Quickly!" We stood and ran towards the sound of the fighting, our feet flying over the uneven ground as we stuck close together.

Cass grabbed me, bringing me to a halt when the clouds suddenly parted to reveal the full moon high above us, which lit the world in sudden brightness.

I almost fell backward at the sight.

In front of us was more than a pack war.

It was complete and total bloodshed.

CHAPTER 26
Kezia

IT WAS LIKE SOMETHING FROM A MOVIE. A REALLY BIG Hollywood blockbuster movie, where special effects took the budget over the quality of the acting. The moon's light cast eerie shadows, illuminating the scene in front of us.

Wolves fought with tooth and claw against men and their weapons. I saw the glint of silver in some hands, but amidst the noise of fighting—snarls of rage, cries of pain—it all melded into the earsplitting sound of battle.

A cacophony of growls echoed in the air, accompanied by the desperate cries of humans and the metallic clash of weapons meeting fur.

Fueled by instinct, each movement was a swift and purposeful blur, figures clashing in a brutal struggle for domi-nance. They vanished and reappeared in the shadows, taking advantage of the moon's intermittent cover. The air was thick with the scent of blood and damp fur, intensifying the savage atmosphere. I watched on in mounting horror as the primal instincts of the fighters took over, blurring the line between human and animal, and shifters fought fiercely in the sudden almost pitch-black darkness.

Reaching out, I took Cass's hand. "Come on."

We ran towards the fighting, while somewhere in the back of my head, a small voice was telling me to run *back*, away from it all, but I plowed onwards, Cass right beside me.

I pulled her to the side of a building, its musty scent filling the air as we hid in its shadows. I'd never seen it before, and judging by the look on her face, neither had she. We looked around wide-eyed as I tried to figure out who was who.

"What the fuck is this?" she whispered as she pressed close to me.

"Bale's *other* pack," I grunted, flattening against the wall.

"This is insanity," Cass muttered. "How am I going to find Landon?"

How were we going to find anyone?

"We have a problem," I murmured to her quickly.

"What?"

"I don't know *all* of Cannon's pack."

"And?"

I winced. "I may not know who is who," I confessed.

Cass cursed but I heard her take a deep breath. "Then we avoid them all. We just need to get to Landon." She gripped my wrist. "Then find Kris. We'll be okay when we get to Kris." She said it almost like a prayer of hope.

I wasn't convinced that this would be as straightforward as she believed. Seeing the battle, witnessing the savagery, I knew why Cannon didn't want me near this.

This wasn't a barn fight.

This was *war*.

It was so much more than I was expecting. I wasn't

prepared. I didn't know how to fight like *this*, and my unease grew as I realized the mistake I'd made by coming here. Cannon was going to be so pissed, and he was right to be.

"You're freaking out," she accused me in the sudden darkness.

"You're not?" I asked her incredulously.

"Yes, but the longer we stay here like freaked-out pups, the quicker we'll be caught."

She was right. I needed to pull it together. "Stick to the edges. I was in some kind of giant cabin-like compound thing. We find it. We may find...someone."

Thankfully, Cass said nothing as we crept along the side of the building. We edged backward away from the fighting, and then we were once more in the rough grass.

"Stay low. No matter what you see, stick with me," I instructed her.

"What if I see Landon?"

Rage raced through me. "If you see your brother fighting my pack—"

"I get it, okay. Let's just...let's just get him."

As the battle unfolded before me, the knot of fear tightened in my stomach. With a racing heart, I frantically tried not to look around the chaotic brawl, trying desperately not to seek out a familiar face. The thought of encountering a friend amidst the chaos sent shivers down my spine. The fear of seeing someone I cared for amid the battle frenzy made my heart pound and my palms sweat. The fighting raged on ahead of us, an unsettling landscape where the fate of my loved ones teetered on the edge, filling me with a constant worry that followed me with every step as I skirted the edge of the fight.

A body came flying through the night towards us, and I

grabbed Cass, frantically pulling her out of the way. He landed with a thump and a sickening crunch, making us both wince. I almost didn't want to, but I peeked to see if he was one of my pack. The relief I felt that he wasn't almost knocked me over. He was the guy from the showers, and when Cass tugged on my hoodie to get me to move away from him, I went.

"There!" I pointed to the two-story building. "It's there."

Cass looked at me and the building. "We're not getting in *there*."

She was right. It was surrounded, the fighting heavier here, and my heart stopped when I spotted a familiar black wolf right in the middle of the fight.

"He's not here," Cass whispered.

I couldn't take my eyes off my mate, fighting as his wolf, ripping through Bale's pack as easily as a knife slices through paper. With an unstoppable momentum, Cannon cleaved through the enemy, leaving a trail of destruction in his wake. On the battlefield, his movements displayed raw power, each action executed with precision and calculation. In the madness, he stood tall and unyielding, a formidable figure that demanded both respect and fear.

Holy Luna, my mate was phenomenal.

"*Kezia*." Cass's urgent hiss broke my trance. "We need to *move*."

Nodding, I started to inch forward, but my gaze kept returning to Cannon. "Stop." I yanked her to a halt. "This is stupid. We need to let them know we're here. We'll find Landon together."

Cass pulled me down lower, crowding me. "Are you insane? Kris told me what Landon did. You think your *mate* will let him live?"

I blinked at her in surprise. "You think Cannon is the threat here?" I asked incredulously.

"Do you think he'll save him?" she asked, tears falling rapidly. "Landon's dead either way, whether it's my father because he brought you here, exposing this"—she waved her hand frantically—"shitshow, or Cannon because Landon *brought you here.*"

I took a calming breath, which was really fucking hard when a battle raged around you. "He won't harm him. He knows Landon could have been playing both sides."

"*Kezia*!"

"*Stop* screeching," I hissed. "Your brother may have played fast and loose with the truth, but I don't believe he meant harm. Not a lot of harm." She was glaring at me. "He was a douchebag, okay? But he wasn't a murderous one," I added grudgingly.

Cass peeked over my head. "Well, we can't walk into *that* and say surprise."

"We're fucked." Rubbing my temples, I shared a look with her. "Fine, we find your stupid twin." Gnawing my cheek, I looked at her. "Any idea?"

"Kris and I were underground."

I gaped at her. "You tell me this now?"

"I don't know *where* we were, but we were in tunnels. I thought they may have them here."

I was going to hit her. "How in the name of the Goddess am I going to find *tunnels* when there is a damn pack war on the ground?"

Cass bit her lip as she stared at me. "I didn't think about that."

"How you two got this far amazes me."

We both jumped and a hard hand over each of our mouths stopped us from screaming. Leo glared at us, and I almost wept with relief that it was one of my pack who had found us.

"He's going to go fucking insane when he sees you, you know that, right?" he told me bluntly, and I saw the hard anger in his eyes. "This is beyond irresponsible." Leo pushed us both down into the grass. "Why are you here?" He let my mouth go. I noted that he kept a firm grip on Cass.

"Landon."

Leo's eyes widened in disbelief, but he said nothing. Looking at Cass, his scowl deepened. "Did she talk you into this, Kezia?"

"No. I was coming anyway."

He looked undecided for a moment, and then his face was grim once more. "This is for your own good."

I didn't get the chance to ask what; the howl of rage had me shrinking into the ground, wishing it would open and swallow me.

It was moments, seconds really, but it felt like an eternity, fear filling me with dread before I felt him looming over me.

The black wolf was furious. It rolled off of him in waves, and I was too chickenshit to look up at him.

Kezia!

Wincing, I forced myself to lift my head.

Are you out of your mind?

I didn't have an answer. I was beginning to think I was. His eyes were burning an electric blue, and I felt so incredibly small and foolish as I crouched at his feet.

I'm sorry.

Sorry isn't good enough. Cannon turned from me, surveying

the scene behind him. He turned back and looked at Leo, who nodded once.

"Come on, you two, let's get you back."

"No!" Cass was on her feet, bolting for the main building, not caring who saw her. I heard a howl I knew, and I knew my brother had spotted his mate, along with every other shifter in the vicinity.

"Fuck!" I went to run after her, but the black wolf knocked me off my feet.

Do not even think *about it.*

Cannon shifted to his human form, blending into the shadows between Leo and me, and he crouched low. "Leo, get her out of here. I don't care what she says. Gag her if you have to."

"Alpha," he said with a nod.

"Cannon!"

He turned to me, his eyes turquoise. "I will deal with you later."

I was crying and I didn't care. "I shouldn't have left, I know. I realized the moment I got here. I'm so sorry."

"Sorry from you means nothing." He looked at Leo. "Can you scent her?"

Leo looked surprised and then shook his head. "No...I can't sense her at all. I found them because I just killed some fucker and was checking he was dead. I saw two shadows that didn't look right and closed in on them, thinking they were the enemy."

Cannon looked at me, and I answered quickly. "The shaman left a potion."

"Take her."

I reached for him, but he pulled away from me. "What about Cass?"

He looked at me with such coldness it was as if he was a stranger. "She has a mate. She's *his* problem."

My throat closed with fear. He wasn't going to help them?

Cannon shifted. *Leave now.*

I watched as he bounded back to the fight, his attack more brutal, more savage. The pain in my chest was throbbing.

"Come on," Leo murmured. "We stay here much longer, we'll be exposed."

"My chest," I told him, clutching it.

"You fucked up," Leo told me harshly. "The alpha's angry. We can all feel it." Gripping my bicep, he pulled me across the ground. "We stay low and we move fast." He eyed me angrily. "Got it?" I nodded once. "You won't give me any shit?" I shook my head, my throat too swollen with holding back tears. "Let's move it."

I followed Leo dutifully. I knew I'd fucked up. Cannon might never talk to me again, and I'd taken one of the pack's prime fighters out of the fight. I didn't lift my head, I didn't turn to look at the melee, I just followed Leo's lead.

We were hundreds of yards from the fight, almost clear completely, when I heard Cass scream.

My whole body whipped itself around, and I was running back to the fight, not hearing Leo's savage curse or giving any thought to who could see me. Cass screamed again, and I shifted to my wolf.

I dashed into the fray, feeling the adrenaline surge through my veins. With each stride, a surge of determination pulsed through me, my shifter instincts heightening my physical capabilities, making me stronger and faster. Amidst the turmoil, the sharp odor of blood cut through the air, blending with the cries of my comrades and foes, only fortifying my resolve. My focus zeroed in on the sole objective: to get to Cass.

I felt others reach for me, but I was too swift, too evasive. I deftly navigated the battlefield with astonishing ease, skillfully evading any attacks that came my way.

I saw her ahead, in the doorway of the compound, on her knees with her father's hand wrapped in her hair, holding her in place. Keeping her down. Beside her lay the unmoving body of her twin. Bale didn't see me, his focus to his left, and when I looked, I saw the body of a broken tawny wolf.

No.

With a thunderous roar that echoed through the air, I sprang at Bale, unleashing my sharpened claws. I bared my teeth as I went for his neck. He turned just as I landed on him, jerking his head back, my fangs narrowly missing his neck. With a loud thump, we landed in a heap on the unforgiving ground, our bodies tangled together. I lunged for his throat, my claws tearing through his flesh with a sickening sound. As he shifted, the brute strength of the pack leader knocked me back.

Shaking my head, I got to my feet. We circled each other warily. Every movement was measured, every step calculated, as we assessed each other's strength and determination. As we crouched in anticipation, our muscles coiled tightly like springs, every heartbeat seemed to resonate with the ancient, instinctual rhythm of the hunt.

Bale leaped forward first, and I surged to meet him. Claws dug into my side, and I bit into his shoulder, tearing at his fur. His hind leg dragged down my belly, slicing me open, and I yelped in pain. Agony ripped through me, but I refused to yield, my resolve unbroken even as my blood spilled freely. With a roar of rage, I fought back, driven by an unwavering determination to protect myself from his relentless attack. I fought on despite the overwhelming pain, refusing to let him get the best of me. Not again.

Bale's teeth circled my throat, and he flung me aside, and I went crashing to the ground. He stood over me, saliva dripping from his fangs. I tried to push myself to my feet when the black wolf soared over me, knocking Bale off of me.

Cannon.

The black wolf pinned Bale to the ground, and in one sudden violent move, he ripped the pack leader's throat open. Turning to look at me, Cannon had blood dripping from his mouth, and I fell back as all my pain came rushing back into my awareness.

Cannon rushed to me, shifting mid-run and landing on his knees at my side. "Kezia, you need to shift. You need to shift and shift again. Right now, Kezia." He reached out to touch me, hand pulling back as if he was scared to touch my fur. "Shift *now*, Kezia."

I felt the alpha's Will and I screamed as the shift forced my human body to endure the immense pain.

Shift.

I did, with his help. My wolf was panting, my heart racing.

Again.

I was sobbing so hard I could hardly breathe. Blood poured from my human body faster than it should have.

SHIFT.

His Will once more surrounded me, and I was my wolf again. His hands were in my fur, his forehead against mine. "One more time, sweetheart, one more time," he pleaded.

I shook my head and he gripped my fur tighter.

Shift.

The pain didn't ease. It was still so much...*so* much. My fingers dug into the ground as I tried to crawl away from the intense agony.

"Shift again." Cannon looked away from me for a moment. "Bring him," he barked.

As my wolf, I tried to get closer to my alpha. A tight hold on my neck, he held me back. "Not yet, I need you to shift one more time."

I could feel the healing power of Luna as I lay on the ground, but there was so much pain. It had lessened some, but not as much as it should have.

I shifted once more to my human form, the fight to shift taking more of my strength. I knew I was still bleeding. I was burning.

"She's still bleeding," he said to someone close by. "Why is she still bleeding?"

Someone stood close to us, the echoes of the fighting distant but still around us. "Cannon, his claws, they're tipped with silver."

I heard Cannon's roar and I closed my eyes. I could feel it within me, and I knew I was too weak to resist it this time. I'd lost too much blood. The wounds were too deep.

"Kezia, sweetheart, shift for me."

And I couldn't. I knew I'd had my last shift. Opening my eyes, I met his green ones. They were almost glowing in the darkness.

"Hey," I whispered. "Did we kill him?" Warmth trickled down my chin, and I knew it was blood.

"Don't speak." He pressed a kiss to my forehead.

Someone pressed into my side, and with effort, I turned my

head and saw my brother. He was bloody and looked wrecked, but he was alive.

"Hey."

As Kris reached out to stroke my hair back, I could feel him recoil at the touch of my bloodied hair. "You're so grounded," he muttered.

"I'm—" I coughed and it sounded wet. "I'm mated now."

"I don't give a fuck."

He looked over my prone body to Cannon. "We need to combine our Wills."

"Wha—" My eyes closed. I was so tired. Peaceful darkness tugged at me.

"Stay with me, Kezia," Cannon ordered, and my eyes snapped open.

If we combine our Wills, we can force the shift.

Who was talking?

Show me.

That was my alpha, I'd recognize that bossy tone anywhere.

Pressure surrounded me. Forcing me into a hole I couldn't squeeze into. Pain that had numbed me erupted anew, pouring through my veins like molten lava.

I screamed in agony, my back arching off the ground, as suffocating weight pressed all around me, and then there was nothing.

CHAPTER 27
Cannon

WALKING DOWN TO THE KITCHEN, I WASN'T surprised to see Royce making coffee. "You're up early." He grunted as he filled the filter with grounds. "You sleeping okay?"

He gave me a flat stare. "Sure."

I nodded. Right. "Yeah, I know." I took a stool and watched my closest friend make the morning coffee. Was it morning? I hadn't looked outside in days, not since we had returned to the pack. Beaten, battered, but not broken.

My bunker had far more prisoners in it than it was accustomed to.

"Any change?" Royce asked gruffly as we waited for the coffee to brew.

"I think her eyelid flickered." He said nothing and I didn't blame him. It wasn't really a conversation starter. "You speak to Doc?"

"Yeah, his jaw healed faster than I thought."

I nodded. I had punched him when I learned that he had let the two of them walk past him. Hard. It cracked something, but

I was more inclined to believe it may have knocked some sense into him.

Maybe.

"He got anything?"

"A guilty conscience," Royce snorted. "Hannah too."

I didn't meet his penetrating gaze. Doc's actions came from Hannah's insights, and I felt therefore that she was equally to blame. I had *not* punched Hannah. Not because I was a good male who didn't hit women or some human reason—we were shifters, we fought—I didn't hit Hannah because Royce had stepped in front of me and blocked her from me.

"Shaman?" he asked.

I shook my head. "He moves between the three rooms like a wraith, but nothing changes."

"I sent out search parties for the druid."

"Who was able to join a search party?" I asked sourly. The fight with the Anterrio Pack had been brutal, and while we had won, who was I fooling? No one. We didn't win. We defeated Bale, but we lost.

We lost so much.

Almost too much.

"Leo," Royce told me with a look I knew well. It meant he didn't approve, but he wasn't in a position to say no. "Ned."

"Luna," I huffed out a laugh. "That's a search party I want to avoid."

"Nikan."

I nodded, breaking eye contact. "Of course."

Royce placed a mug of coffee in front of me and picked up his own. "Do you think you will be able to see some of the pack today?"

"No."

"Cannon..."

"I can't." I shook my head. "I walk out that door and—" I cut myself off as I took a sip of coffee.

"You aren't abandoning her if you go outside."

Placing my cup down on the counter, I stood. "Being down here is too far from her." I gave him a shrug as pitiful and as hopeless as I felt. "I can't." I made to move to the stairs.

"Take the coffee with you," he reminded me.

Silently I picked up my drink and slowly climbed the stairs, making my way to my room, where my mate lay in a dreamless sleep. Her body was unresponsive. She wasn't even breathing on her own. Doc had hooked her up to a ventilator, and she just lay there. Doc told me her brain activity was low. He hadn't said anything else, but I knew what he meant.

Kezia was barely hanging on. If she was even still in there.

Closing the door behind me, I settled into the chair that sat beside the bed, and I took her limp hand in mine. Every time I looked at her, I saw her body torn and ripped open, saturated in blood. I heard her screams as the silver embedded deeper into her bloodstream, her agony as we forced the final shift.

Leaning back in my chair, I tilted my head back and looked at the ceiling, not seeing the white paint but instead the night of the battle as it played on a constant rerun in my head.

After our first attack, the night we broke Kris and Cass free, Bale had ramped up his security. It wasn't enough to stop us in our assault, but that didn't mean they weren't waiting for us. Leo's patrol made first contact, and Bale had not taught his pack stealth. They had charged out of the compound like human brawlers from a pub.

With them being so unruly and undisciplined, the rest of us had charged in, and we'd clashed in a battle of ferocity and hate.

Despite everything I had said to my mate, I had gone looking for that prick Landon. Kris too. It was an unspoken agreement between us. I had *left* my pack to find the limp dick twin.

He'd been chained to a wall, naked, sitting in his own filth, with a silver collar around his neck, two silver cuffs on his wrists, and so badly beaten his face was a swollen mess. Neither Kris nor I could break him free. Kris had shifted back to his human form, and using soiled blankets, he had used them as protective wraps for his hands.

It took both of us—with a lot of strength, cursing, and sheer brute force—to free him.

Kris had slapped him several times to get him to wake up and then forced him to shift. It was obvious he would need to shift several times, and Kris had told me to go back to the fight.

I'd been eager to leave. Landon was not and never would be my priority. I'd done this for my mate, and when she asked me, I would be able to tell her I got him. That was enough.

In wolf form, I had fought several of Bale's pack inside the compound, separated from my pack. I had held my own as I searched the halls for Bale himself. He wasn't there, and I had gone outside, ready to tear the place apart until I found him, vowing to myself that he would never hurt my mate again.

When I heard Leo tell me he had Kezia, fury unlike any other had descended over me. What the fuck was I fighting to keep her safe for if she was willing to throw herself into danger?

She'd left my pack defenseless. She was an *alpha* now, and I had *trusted* her to serve my pack as I did.

I still remembered her guilt and regret as she cowered at my feet. Part of me knew I was harsh, but my pack was everything. They were here fighting *for* her, and she had thrown it back in their faces.

My eyes closed as I remembered the way she had looked at me. If I had been softer, gentler, and kept her *with* me, she wouldn't be lying in this bed, unmoving and lifeless.

When I had left her, I'd seen Ned struggling with three pack against him. I saw the glint of silver, and I'd charged forward. When I got there, another two enemy shifters attacked me. I heard Cass scream.

I snorted in the quiet of the room. *Luna herself would have heard Cass's scream.*

A wolf almost as big as me had taken a chunk from my leg, and as I spun to face him, I saw her. A white wolf streaking across the battleground. She dodged and evaded everyone. She was mesmerizing. I fought to see what she was racing towards, and I saw Bale with his children defeated at his feet, and then I saw the crumpled form of Kris's wolf.

I had no recollection of how the shifters who fought me died. I saw Kezia pounce and tackle Bale to the ground, and I fought like a man possessed to clear a space to get to her. Royce told me later that I took down so many he'd never seen anything like it, but I could only see Kezia. When Bale threw her away from him, I saw nothing but his death.

He should have been taken prisoner.

We should have contained him.

He needed to answer for his crimes against pack law. He held the answers to so many questions, but when I saw her white coat turning red with blood, all I'd seen was his death.

I didn't regret the fact I'd killed him. I'd kill him over and over for what he had done to my mate. But I couldn't. He was dead and Kezia lay unmoving beside me.

Her body... I rubbed the heels of my hands into my eyes, trying to erase the sight of her broken and bleeding in front of me, but the picture wouldn't fade no matter how hard I tried to rub it away.

I'd made her shift. Over and over. I didn't think of the silver. The weapon he had used against *all* of us, and I had *forgotten* about the silver. His claws were tipped with it. I didn't know how that was possible, I didn't want to know how it was possible, and yet it was.

When he had sliced into her tiny body, again and again, he'd poisoned her with silver.

Silver binds.

It was a miracle I got her to shift as many times as I had, and then when she was unable to shift again, Kris told me we needed to combine Wills. I didn't know we could. I doubted he did. It was a move of desperation, and I wasn't sure it worked.

She'd shifted to her wolf, and the magic of Luna healed more of her body, and we'd forced the shift back, but when we did, Kezia was gone. I didn't know where her spirit was.

Where was my mate?

The body that lay in the bed was a shell.

Her soul was gone, and I had no idea how to get her back.

I WOKE up to see the shaman in the room. He looked frailer, older. He looked like he had fought the pack war.

"Any change?" I asked him, straightening in my chair.

"It's been two weeks, Alpha," he told me, crushing herbs with a pestle and mortar. "I'll let you know when there's a change with Kezia."

I bit my tongue. He was older and frailer and also grumpier. He'd also unhooked her from the ventilator and snorted when

Kezia breathed fine on her own. Doc hadn't returned after witnessing that.

"Your pack is restless."

"My pack is fine."

He looked at me with a disapproving stare. "Your pack needs their alpha."

"I'm right here," I snapped. Drawing a breath, I looked at him. "Sorry." He said nothing but continued to crush his herbs. I watched him in silence. I'd never asked him why he had let them go. He had given them a potion to mask their scent, and while I was grateful they had been undetected, I was still pissed that he *hadn't* given them a potion to knock them on their asses and keep them in the safety of my pack.

"Your anger towards me is justified."

My head jerked up and I looked at him. Had I spoken aloud?

"I can sense it," he told me with a small smile. "I am Luna's vessel." He gave a sigh, placing his tools down. "As I have done with so many things, I followed the signs and never questioned. The belt buckle. The need to protect two young wolf cubs. Teaching a young wolf how to be an alpha in a pack that had a weak ruler. Leaving a potion for two strong-headed females who could cause trouble in an empty den."

"You did it for Luna?"

If he could have, he would have rolled his eyes. "Everything I do, I do for the Goddess."

"Why?"

He pointed at himself with a smirk. "Shaman."

I actually chuckled at his attempt at a joke. "Why would Luna want them there? They were safe here."

"Were they?" He shrugged. "Kris tells me not all of the

Anterrio Pack have been recovered." He picked his tools back up again. "Where are the others? The fighters? Only women and children remain in the pack we called home. Where are the soldiers, Alpha?"

I studied him for a long time. "How is Kris?"

"He healed quickly. Cass is more delicate. She maintains her own bedside vigil."

I pressed my lips together to stop my sneer. Landon still suffered the ill effects of the silver. He was still unable to shift to heal. Kris had tried to will him to shift, but as he was not his recognized alpha, it hadn't worked. Kris had tried to force him, but Landon had made such a fuss that Cass had begged her mate to stop. Even when he was incapacitated, Landon was an ungrateful prick.

Tapping my fingers off the armchair, I shook my head in defeat. "A vessel of Luna you may be, old one," I said as I got to my feet. "You're still a sneaky meddler."

The shaman smiled widely. "I serve the packs."

At the door, I hesitated. "If she..."

"When Kezia is ready, she will wake," he told me solemnly.

"Will she?" I heard my doubt and I hated it.

"We have to believe that she will."

Right. I left him to sit with her and walked down the hall, rapping my knuckles briefly against the door before opening it and seeing Kris and Cass both turn to look at me. Landon lay in a deep sleep; the shaman kept him drugged as his human form healed slowly.

"Kezia?" Kris was on his feet.

"No." I glanced at Cass, but it was hard to look at her and not want to shake her. "Got a minute?"

Kris looked at his mate, dropped a kiss to her temple, and

left the room with me. In the hallway, he looked at me with something akin to relief.

"Hard going?" I asked him quietly as we went downstairs.

Looking over his shoulder, he checked we were alone, and as the doors of the study closed, he let out a loud sigh. "I swear the fucker's milking it."

His frustration echoed my own, and it made me smile properly for the first time in weeks. "He's a deceptive asshole. It wouldn't surprise me."

Slumping into a chair, Kris looked up at me. "What do you need?"

"My mate awake and shooting off her smart mouth?"

He nodded sagely. "Never thought I'd want one of her eye rolls."

We mulled in silence until I remembered what I'd dragged him away from the twins for. "The shaman tells me we're missing some of the Anterrio Pack?"

Kris sat up straighter. "Yeah, I asked Royce if he could ask your scouts to find them, but so far, they've seen nothing." He looked slightly uncomfortable. "I hope that was okay? To ask?"

I waved it off. "We need to find them. Ned and Leo and some others brought everything they could find at the second location back here." It was my turn to be uncomfortable. "I haven't gone through it yet."

"Other things on your mind," he said, brushing it off, then coughed. "But..."

"When the Pack Council arrives, and they will, it would be nice to have the evidence we need to overthrow them." Scratching my head, I tilted my head back and groaned. "I've neglected my pack."

"Your pack is more than able to function without you for a

few weeks," Kris said gently. He then looked at me with his own guilt. "I need to be back at Anterrio Pack and explain *something* to them, but..."

I laughed. "What a pair of *alphas* we are, right?"

He stood. "We should be better."

"Yeah." I looked out the window. "I'll call for the others."

The speed with which my brother, Royce, Leo and Ned arrived shamed me. I watched Ned look around, obviously feeling out of place. It was rare I took him into these meetings. He was more a follow-orders-and-not-question shifter, but he had been an invaluable help at the compound. He'd kept his head when I had lost mine.

"Sit," I directed him. Kris hovered near me and eventually retook the chair he had been in when he first came in. "I owe you an apology," I started. "She's..." I swallowed. "She's the same, no change. But my pack has changed. We have faced losses." Five of my pack hadn't made it back. I had gone to their families, but I recalled very little of what I had said, my concern for Kezia overriding everything. "We uncovered a mess, we confronted it, and I have failed to clean it up."

"You've had a lot going on," Royce said gruffly.

"Yes," I agreed. "But I need to remember I am an alpha, this is my pack, and my duty remains to my mate and my pack."

Nikan watched me. "What do we need to do?"

"We need to find the missing pack members of Anterrio, we need to go through the documents Ned brought back, and we need to *go* to the Anterrio Pack and try to clean up the mess Bale left behind."

Leo looked at Royce and grinned. "Sounds doable."

"We also need to put out feelers to the other packs, see who will talk to us, who knows anything, and anticipate when the

Pack Council will come and try to try us all for violation of pack law."

"I've already sent out communications to a few packs," Royce said.

"I've been documenting the shit from the compound," Ned told me. "It's in some kind of code. I'll get it though."

Kris looked at him. "Code?" He flicked his gaze my way. "We used a code in the security team. I might be able to help."

Ned nodded slowly. "Appreciate it."

"You're wary of me," Kris told him bluntly. "Cassandra is my mate. She is the only one of Anterrio Pack I am interested in protecting."

Ned looked around the room and grinned. "Good."

"I can form search teams," Leo told me. "Nikan and I have been scouting, but it's a vast mountain range, and they had those tunnels—"

"They could be anywhere," I agreed. "I'll join you."

"And the Anterrio Pack?" Royce asked with a glance at Kris.

I met my beta's stare. "It's my first stop."

CHAPTER 28
Cannon

TWO WEEKS LATER

Entering the house, I stopped short when I saw Cass in the kitchen. Her pregnancy was showing more, and in shorts and a simple T-shirt, she looked healthy. Turning, she jumped when she saw me. Our interactions were tepid at best.

"Cassandra."

"She's the same."

I dipped my head in acknowledgment. "And your brother?" I didn't manage to keep the scorn from my voice, but Cass ignored it. It seemed to be our thing: I ignored all the things about her I didn't like, and she did the same to me. It was a shaky truce, but it was a truce nonetheless.

"He's getting stronger. He may be able to shift soon."

I said nothing, but I was sure I didn't need to. My face was incapable of being blank when Landon the Prick was mentioned. "Good."

It *was* good. It meant the little shit could be out of my house soon.

"Is Kris with you?" Cass looked past me, hoping that the reason we remained civil to each other was here too.

"He's in the bunker again," I told her. Walking to the fridge, I opened it, searching for my dinner from last night that I hadn't had a chance to eat. "Where's my food?"

"Oh." Cass was bright red. "Was that yours?" She saw my scowl. "Um, Landon was hungry."

"*I'm* hungry," I snapped at her. "Tell the lazy shit to get up and get his own food."

"Cannon!" Cass gasped. "He's still healing!"

"*Humans* heal quicker than him!"

"Hey, guys." Hannah walked into the house through the front door. "Good time?"

Cass practically deflated with relief when she saw Hannah. For some reason best known to my friend's reasoning, Hannah and Cass had formed a friendship.

"Is it ever a good time?" I mumbled as I returned to the fridge. "I assume Landon also wanted the leftover chicken?"

"Um, no. That was me. The baby, really."

Shutting the fridge closed with more force than necessary, I smiled humorlessly at both of them. "Excellent." I gave Hannah a tight smile as I passed her and headed upstairs to see Kezia.

"How did it go?" Hannah called after me. "At the Anterrio Pack?"

Pausing on the stairs, I looked down at her. "They're dense, bigoted, and beyond help," I told her flatly. "But Kris thinks they're getting better, so"—I shrugged—"who knows." Resuming my climb, I made my way to my bedroom. Kezia lay exactly as I left her, laid out on her back, her white hair around her, her skin as white as the bedsheets, and her eyes closed. Dropping down, I brushed her pale pink lips with mine.

"Hey, sweetheart," I greeted her. "Your old pack are a bunch of fools," I told her as I stripped off my clothing. "They have been *liberated* from a tyrant, and they act like they've lost a martyr." Kicking off my shoes, I pushed my jeans off. "How you lived amongst them amazes me."

Kezia never answered.

"Kris is going gray trying to deal with them," I carried on. "I can practically *see* him aging. I do *not* know why he keeps trying." Grabbing a towel and wrapping it around my waist, I carried on. "Actually, I do. He thinks he owes them. He *owes* them nothing." I went into the bathroom, got my toothbrush, started to brush my teeth, and came back out again. "Nikan and Leo finally caught up with the missing pack," I added. I brushed the other side, taking the brush out to tell her more. "Rounded them up and added them to the bunker. There are so many cells now." I grinned at her. "You'd have lots of company."

Going back into the bathroom, I rinsed my mouth, switched on the shower, and returned to the room.

"We have thirteen held." I hadn't expected the Pack Council to take so long to come for retribution, if I was honest. I had thirteen prisoners, and although they said little, I still couldn't kill them, as they were my proof that Bale was a psycho. "I don't think Doc will cope if we find any more."

I watched her as she lay there. With a sigh, I went into the shower, washing away the day's fatigue.

Two weeks ago, I took charge of my pack again. With a plan set, my closest confidants and I cleaned up the aftermath of the pack war.

Ned had cleared the compound so thoroughly that we had a lot of evidence against Bale and the thirteen we held. Kris hadn't known the code Bale had used, but he was familiar with his thinking, and he and Ned had decoded some damning evidence.

Nikan and Leo led teams of scouts and flushed out the remaining enemy pack from the mountains. I'd been a part of some of the scout teams, and pummeling my fists into Anterrio Pack faces had been a great stress reliever.

Royce and I had received word from some of the closer packs that Bale had been causing them trouble too. They had been willing to talk, and Hannah and he had gone and met with them. They were warier of me, and while I needed their cooperation, I had stayed away. I didn't want to spook them when they could testify in front of the Pack Council.

Doc had driven through many of the towns in the state and neighboring ones and uncovered a lot of Bale's fighting rings. As a male who passed for more human than shifter, he hadn't raised any alarm bells. He had documented it all, taking pictures, and he'd even snagged a ledger of fights.

I had a mountain of evidence and no Pack Council to show it to.

Of their deception and corruption, I had found no proof, and I was beginning to doubt that they were involved at all. However, the fact that the murder of the three humans had been covered up so well, kept me suspicious of them, but I was now considering only some were corrupt, not all.

Stepping out of the shower, I dried off, ran my fingers through my wet hair, and pulled on fresh sweatpants. I was starving and wanted to head to the food hall before it got too busy.

My pack hadn't judged me for my absence, but I still felt guilty that I had chosen to wallow when they were in pain too.

Coming back into the bedroom, I wasn't surprised to find the shaman there.

"You're back."

"You miss nothing," I joked. Opening a drawer, I got a gray T-shirt out and pulled it on. "It's been a few days." While I made sure I was here every night, I didn't always see the shaman.

"I've been restless," he admitted.

Taking a seat, I watched him closely. "Why? Kezia?"

He shook his head, his frail old hand taking hold of hers. "No, I...I don't know." The simplicity of his uncertainty concerned me. "I tested her blood yesterday. The same."

He'd started drawing blood from Kezia a few weeks ago, and while I wasn't a fan of the practice, it was very similar to what humans did in hospitals for patients. Kezia was similar to a patient in one of those hospitals, only her malady held a little more of the magic variety than the common human illness.

"Luna?"

His mouth turned down in a frown. "I know the touch of my Goddess."

We sat in silence, and I opted to miss dinner and keep him company. Keep them both company. But as time passed, I couldn't deny I was hungry, and my mind wandered to what they were serving tonight in the food hall. I wanted a big bowl of stew.

"What did you end up doing with that rabbit?" I asked suddenly.

The shaman startled in his chair. I wasn't sure if I'd woken him. "Rabbit?"

Leaning forward, I rested my elbows on my knees. "Yeah,

you sent us to find a big white rabbit with red eyes. We put it in the study. What did you do with it?"

The shaman was watching me with a keen alertness. "Nothing."

Leaning back, I frowned. "You let it go? I almost broke my neck catching the damn thing."

The shaman let go of Kezia's hand and stood. "I didn't let it go." He motioned to me. "Get up."

Pushing to my feet, I followed him wordlessly as he hurried down the stairs and out of the house. The shaman had taken a small cottage on the outskirts of the town, and his speed surprised me as he hastened through the street. I'd pushed my feet into sneakers as we headed out, but while I tugged them on as I followed him, I saw a few of my pack watch us curiously.

He opened his door with a bang, and I felt my unease grow as I followed him into the one bedroom cottage. "Care to share?" Closing the door behind me, I looked around. The room looked similar to his cottage at the Anterrio Pack. It hadn't surprised me that he chose to remain here. Whether it was because Kris and Kezia were still here, I wasn't sure, but I knew a lot of my pack were hoping he would stay.

The shaman placed his hands on the kitchen counter, his milky eyes watching me with unnerving intensity. "Strip."

I blinked. "What?"

He was nodding to himself, muttering under his breath. Turning, he started to pull out bags of herbs, a rolling pin, and what I was sure were chicken bones. Looking up at me, he frowned. "Take your clothes off." I remained in place, jumping when he smacked the rolling pin off the counter. "Clothes, Cannon, *now!*"

I quickly undressed. "Why am I getting naked?"

"The rabbit!"

Folding my clothes, I looked at him. "You need to give me more, old man."

"Luna sent you both to get that rabbit, a white rabbit with red eyes."

I nodded. "Yup, I was there." I'd also had amazing sex with my mate during the hunt for it.

"You had a *druid* in your pack," he told me with a sneer. "Tricky things, druids."

I remembered Barbara's *trick* with the cookies, but neither of these incidents made sense together. "I'm still not following."

The shaman looked at me as if I were dense. "Rabbits can be seen as *guides*. These guides can assist individuals in navigating their spiritual paths and accessing their inner psyche, their inner wisdom." He looked at me expectantly. "*Rabbits*, Cannon! In certain druid and even shamanic traditions, a *rabbit* can be associated with intuition and *transformation*."

It took me a moment, and then I was sure I was the one who was looking at the shaman as if he were dense. "The rabbit... No?"

He was nodding as he made a potion. "The rabbit has her spirit." Crushing petals into a thick gloopy mixture, he was still nodding. "The Goddess sent you to find a vessel; the druid performed the rite."

"Kezia's spirit is in the rabbit?" I asked him again dubiously.

Thrusting the drink out to me, he nodded. "Yes, drink this."

I must be as crazy as him, but I drank the potion in one go.

"Find it, bring her home."

"The rabbit?"

The shaman swatted me with the rolling pin. "Get my Kezia

and bring her to me and her body. I should be able to put her back."

I left his cottage and shifted immediately. I stood indecisive for a moment and then realized it had been one month since she was gone from me. Looking up at the darkening sky, I knew it was the full moon and I was a creature of Luna, and if the Goddess wanted me to hunt rabbits, well...I was hunting rabbits.

I sent a vague holding command to Royce, and then I did my best to retrace my steps all those weeks ago when Kezia and I had chased down a massive white, red-eyed rabbit.

I was a good hunter, one of the best in my pack, and as I searched high and low for an elusive white rabbit that may be holding the spirit of my mate, I found my patience wearing thin.

Hours later, I sat on a bluff overlooking a town I'd been to only once before. Cautiously, I approached, my wolf too big to be natural, and the option of running through the woods naked wasn't an option. Picking my way through the dense under-brush, slinking low, I found myself at the back of some log cabins.

Night had fallen long ago, and I was grateful it allowed me to blend more into the darkness.

The door opened and the old woman stood uncertainly in the doorway, a blanket in one hand and a shotgun in the other.

"You coming out?" She dropped the blanket. "Door's open." She went back inside.

Luna, grant me your grace.

Wrapping the blanket around my waist, I went inside. She'd been watching me from the window and grinned.

"Well, you're a fine looking thing," she said with admiration.

My day had been crazy, and now a woman old enough to be my grandmother had just openly objectified me. "Lottie? Right?"

"Yup." She smacked her lips together, still openly appreciating my bare chest.

"This is going to sound strange—"

"The rabbit's out back."

She walked past me, back out the back door, and led me to the smallest of the cabins. "Zia stayed here the first time around," she told me easily as she unlocked the door. "Thought this would be the best place for it."

Inside, she closed the door firmly. "Never seen anything like it."

"A rabbit?" I asked cautiously, searching the dim cabin.

"Oh, it's not just *any* rabbit," she told me and flicked the light on.

"Holy Luna..."

It was as big as I remembered, only its coat had changed, now streaked with black. Its eyes were no longer bright red, but deep burgundy. It watched me with an intensity that would have been unnerving if I hadn't experienced it before.

"It's her, isn't it?"

I had no answer.

"I know it is," Lottie continued. "Won't eat a scrap of my cooking."

It was the most bizarre thing to say on an already bizarre day, and it made me laugh. The old woman said nothing and just eyed me warily, but as I wiped my eyes of the tears of laughter, I edged closer to the cage the rabbit was in.

"Why the cage if it's in here alone?"

"Slippery fish escaped twice now." Lottie sniffed. "Comes back right enough, but still, it's a tasty meal for any *predators* out there." She gave me a pointed look. "You took your time."

"I'm sorry." I was speaking more to the rabbit.

"So? Is it my Zia?"

Looking at the older woman, I looked back at the cage, at the rabbit that stared at me patiently. "I have no fucking clue," I told her honestly.

"You gonna take it?"

"Yes."

"All right then, I'll get some carrots."

I blinked. "It eats them?"

"Nope. But you look freaked out, and I thought I'd give you some time to pull yourself together."

I snorted another laugh. "I know now why she keeps coming back to you."

"I'm her family, that's why." She closed the door behind her, and I turned back to the rabbit.

"Kezia?" The rabbit didn't move. "I've lost my mind. I'm so desperate to believe you'll come back to me that I think you're a rabbit." Opening the cage door, I hissed when the thing bit me. "Luna, if this is a joke, it isn't funny," I muttered as I grabbed the rabbit by the scruff of its neck and lifted it out of the cage.

I held it up to my eye level, and it squirmed and struggled, but my grip was firm. It was the same rabbit, but different. "Fuck it, you're coming home with me."

Walking outside, I met Lottie's skeptical stare. "You carrying her back like that?"

I looked down at the rabbit in my hand. "Pretty much." I

handed it to Lottie. "I need to shift. When I do, keep a tight hold of it. I need to grab its scruff."

"You're going to eat her?"

"No!" I told her hastily. "Here." I demonstrated the loose skin around the rabbit's neck. "My wolf can travel quicker than me. I need to carry it, and it'll be easier for me if you hand her to me like this." I demonstrated. "My wolf is big. I need a little help to take hold."

"You won't harm it?"

"Never."

Lottie held the rabbit protectively as it squirmed in her arms. I shifted, ignoring her protests about her ruined blanket. She took a few steps back when she saw how big I was up close. After a long pause, she took hold of the rabbit as I showed her. With great care on my part, I secured the rabbit in my teeth.

Lottie stepped back. "Well, I seen it all now," she murmured. "Bring her back when she's herself again."

I couldn't answer, so I simply turned and started the long trek home, with a white rabbit dangling terrified from my mouth.

The run was quicker given I was headed back to the pack in as straight a line as possible. I had a few encounters with some predators who thought the rabbit was an invite to fight for it, but I either ran over them or avoided them.

As my packlands came into view, I slowed to a stop as a thin, murky gray wolf stepped out of the tree line.

Druid.

I've been waiting. Come, it is time.

CHAPTER 29
Kezia

I'D BEEN FLOATING FOR A VERY LONG TIME.

It wasn't even peaceful floating. It was like the feeling of being suspended but not dropping. When I was younger, Kris used to carry me in his mouth, and this was the same. I was weightless but felt as if I was in the maw of something much bigger than me.

The pain had stopped, and at first, I thought I had died. But I was too aware to be dead, and after floating endlessly for days, I decided I was too stubborn to die.

Cannon would be so pissed if I died.

Cannon was going to be pissed at me no matter what.

I remembered his fury. I remembered I deserved it.

I remembered the pain.

Above all, I remembered the pain.

It had been everywhere. Burning through my body, eviscerating me with its intensity.

Then pressure, immense pressure that made me think my skull was going to crack, squeezed me relentlessly. My bones had felt shattered under the weight of it, and I had screamed for it to stop.

Then it did.

And I was floating.

And now it was nothing.

Sometimes, there was a flash of light. A noise. They made me jump. I'd never been scared really as a child, but flashes of noise and light now had me jumping like a ninny. Kris would laugh at me.

Kris.

My brother hurt me.

No...my brother would never. But the pressure? I felt *him* when the horrible pressure was there.

Sadness slipped over me like a blanket.

Had I died? If this was the afterlife, I wanted a refund.

I rolled through nothing as I thought about my life.

Everything that had happened to me in my life had been because of Bale.

He killed my parents.

He took us into his pack and forbade me to shift, treating me like a leper, so his pack did too.

He operated illegal fighting rings, sending killers after me when he learned I was fighting in them.

I paused. Had he? Maybe not. But he had *always* known where I was.

He kept me from my mate.

He gave the order to kill my mate.

He kept me chained to a wall with silver and hurt me.

He was the reason Cannon fought for justice.

Bale was dead. I'd seen Cannon rip his throat out. It shouldn't have filled me with as much satisfaction as it did.

I moved through nothing some more.

Cannon.

I wanted my mate.

I missed him.

Would he forgive me?

Where was he?

Why couldn't he find me?

Where was I?

The panicked feelings eased as I floated.

I jerked in alarm when the bright light snapped into the darkness and was just as quickly gone.

Turning fearfully, I searched the inky blackness.

Who was there?

Where was I? Moonstar?

"KEZIA? SWEETHEART? CAN YOU HEAR ME?"

That voice was familiar. My heart beat faster in my chest. Darkness shrouded me still, but that voice...I knew it.

"Kez? Wake up, little sister."

A rush of familiar warmth seeped through me. I knew this voice too.

A touch so light caressed my cheek. Was it my cheek? I felt weightless still. But the touch, I knew that too.

"Breathe, pup, breathe deeply."

I did. I inhaled until I couldn't hold any more air in my lungs, and I heard a whisper of *she's doing it*, and I exhaled a long drawn-out breath.

I lay on something soft but firm. I could feel it. I was lying down.

309

"Kezia? Open your eyes."

I wanted to open my eyes, I wanted to see the ones that belonged to these voices, ones that I knew. Light burned my eyes when I tried to open them, so bright that I shut them again.

"I know it's bright, Kezia, but you can do it."

They had such faith in me. I wanted to see who believed in me so much. It shouldn't even be hard to open my eyes. They were mine after all.

"Kezia, I'm waiting, I've been waiting, open your eyes."

Him. I knew him.

"Cannon?" My voice was drier than leather left in the sun. I knew what leather in the sun felt like. I opened my eyes. Green, so deep, like the forest, stared down at me. "Cannon."

He lifted me off the bed almost into his lap, cradling me in his arms, his head burrowed in my neck, and my alpha sobbed. I was crying too. I clung to him as he held me, my head turning, my lips searching for his. He kissed me and I felt my body strain to get closer to him.

He pulled away from me, and I saw others. My brother, the shaman and—

"Barbara?" I focused on the small, demure woman, settling back onto the bed, my alpha still holding me. "What the fuck did you do to me?"

Kris swooped down, hugging me tightly, even though Cannon wasn't letting me go.

"Never, I mean *never* do that to me again," my brother scolded. "I *should* ground you."

It felt vaguely familiar. "You can't ground me, I'm mated." Looking to the side, I checked Cannon was still there. He was, and I reached for him once more. His lips pressed to mine, and I welcomed the kiss. I leaned back into him as I searched the familiar faces.

"How do you feel?"

I looked at the shaman. "Surreal. What happened to me?" Again, I fixed on Barbara. "You did something to me."

"I saved you."

Cannon scoffed so loudly that it reverberated through me. "Kris and *I* saved her," he said with barely concealed contempt. "You stole her."

"Where have I been?" I demanded, pushing myself up the bed, taking advantage of the fact I could snuggle in against Cannon more. Trying not to be obvious about it. I felt his contented sigh, and I knew I was busted. I also knew I didn't care.

"It's quite a complicated story," the shaman told me carefully.

"Okay...I can keep up."

By the time they finished telling me, I wasn't sure whether to laugh at the sheer ridiculousness of it or get down on my knees and thank Luna over and over.

"I was a rabbit?"

"Your *spirit* was housed in a rabbit," Barbara explained once again. "I needed a vessel just in case. The signs were so ominous for you, Kezia, I had to be prepared."

"A rabbit?" I glanced at Kris, who was tight-lipped and trying to mask his anger. "I'm a wolf. Why wouldn't you put my *wolf* spirit in a wolf?"

"Why did you need to be *put* anywhere?" Cannon grumbled.

"I interpret the signs of the Goddess," Barbara explained once more. "This was the right thing to do."

I wasn't convinced. "That was a really ugly rabbit." Cannon tried not to laugh, but I was a *wolf*; I *hunted* rabbits.

"You're back now," the shaman declared, attempting to be diplomatic. "Your friend the doctor is coming to check on you."

"Why?" I twisted in the bed, my elbow digging into Cannon's ribs.

"Oof, what are you doing?" he asked me as I tried to look at my butt.

"Do I have a fluffy tail?"

"Kezia!" Barbara snapped, finally losing her patience. "Your body is the same. You have some added scars, but you were injured very badly. Your spirit was in a vessel of the Goddess. You are *not* a rabbit."

I eyed her suspiciously. "Cannon, check me over."

"Oh, I plan to."

My body heated with anticipation as we shared a loaded look. Kris cleared his throat loudly, and my cheeks burned as I remembered there were others in the room.

"Is Cass okay?"

Kris nodded. "She's good. The pregnancy is treating her well."

Reaching out, I grabbed his hand. "Good. And Landon?" Three grown males avoided my eyes. My eyes narrowed as I looked between them. "What have you done to him?"

"He's resting," Cannon said with so much contempt I turned to look at him in question. "He's a big, fat faker."

I laughed. "He's okay then?"

"More's the pity," Kris grumbled.

I switched my attention back to Barbara. "A rabbit?"

She sighed and looked at us all with such profound disappointment I felt guilty. "None of you have asked the most important question."

"The tail?" I asked with dread.

"Moonstar," Kris said at the same time.

"She's gone," Barbara said smugly.

I searched my inner self, my wolf spirit was there, but otherwise...I was empty. "Where?"

Barbara clasped her hands in her lap as she spoke. "The spirit was sent to protect your mother, not possess you. It took time, a *lot* of energy, but I coerced the spirit out of you."

We sat in silence for a long time before I had to ask. "Is she now the rabbit?"

Barbara stood fluidly. "When you're over the fixation with the rabbit, come see me."

She left us and I grinned at Cannon and Kris. "I think she thinks I'm ungrateful." Pulling Cannon's arm around me tighter, I settled back. "Tell me everything, again."

I grew tired quicker than I liked, but the three of them insisted I sleep, even though I'd been sleeping for a month. As the bedroom door closed behind Kris and the shaman, Cannon promised me more visitors the next day. He climbed under the covers with me, wrapping me in his arms.

"Why haven't the Pack Council come?" I asked him tiredly.

"I don't know," he said into my hair as he pulled me closer. "It worries me too."

"We'll deal with it when they do come." I linked our fingers together. "I'm so sorry I broke your trust."

"As Kris said, never put me through this again, and we'll call it even."

Turning my face up to his, I searched his eyes for any lingering doubt. "I will never. I'm truly sorry."

313

After dropping a kiss on my nose, he sighed in contentment. "I know."

We lay holding each other as the night darkened. It felt so strange to be back in my body but also right. It was my body and it should feel right to be here. My mind went over all the things I had learned since waking. So much had happened in my absence, but still so much had to happen.

"I can hear the wheels turning," Cannon teased as his lips skimmed my ear.

"We have so much work to do," I told him.

"We do." His hand glided over my arm. "How do you feel?"

"Sleepy."

"Go to sleep, sweetheart."

"Sweetheart," I mused, "I never liked terms of endearment like babe or baby, but since the mating bond, I have to admit, I like it. I like when *you* call me sweetheart." His body stilled beside me so suddenly I turned to face him. "What is it?"

"Barbara..." He cleared his throat. "The *druid* isn't sure, but she *thinks* the bond may be broken."

I sat bolt upright in bed, my hands reaching for his collarbone, demanding he put on a light so I could see. The mark, the mating mark, was so faded that I could hardly see it.

"Cannon!"

Large hands clasped mine, bringing them to his lips as he kissed my knuckles. "It's okay," he soothed me. "I love you with or without the bond."

Pushing off him, I shook my head. "No! I *am* your mate! Your bonded mate!" Tears spilled and Cannon pulled me into his body.

"Kezia, it's okay, we can test the bond when you're stronger, and if it's broken, we'll be fine."

"What if we aren't?" Scrambling over his body, I pulled my shirt off. "We need to have sex, now."

Cannon pulled me close once more. "Kezia, you just woke up after a month in a dreamless state of limbo. You need your strength. This is something we don't need to fix right now. Rest."

"The bond's definitely broken," I told him flatly. "I'm half-naked on top of you, and you want me to sleep."

Cannon tugged me down towards him, and the kiss he gave me was so thorough, so *hot*, I was panting by the end. "I will always want you," he whispered against my lips. "But I *need* you to sleep."

A wave of exhaustion washed over me. "Fine, but you better screw me into next week tomorrow."

His low laughter caused me to smile in the darkness. "My mate...the sex addict."

"You know it."

I drifted off to sleep in his arms, worry gnawing at my gut that my bond to my mate was gone.

CHAPTER 30

Kezia

HE DIDN'T HAVE SEX WITH ME THE NEXT DAY. Instead, Doc gave me a thorough examination, and between him and the shaman, I was given a clean bill of health.

With Doc's supervision, I visited Landon, finally hearing the whole truth of his subterfuge. In true Landon style, he'd tried to play both sides. Not for an advantage but so he could figure out what the hell was going on. His dad knew him better than he thought, and when Landon insisted he capture me, Bale became even more suspicious.

Landon hadn't been lying; he truly thought I could help free his mom and sister. He believed that Cannon would be hot on my heels. He hadn't known the plan to kill Cannon, hadn't counted on it at all, and then was left scrambling about what to do with me since he'd dragged me into the mess. When he had disappeared, saying that he was at Cannon's funeral, he'd been locked in a cell until he was persuaded to go along with the lie. He told me Bale thought Tev would kill Cannon, they were expecting his death, but when I hadn't reacted like someone who had just lost their mate, they knew Cannon lived. Which is when they locked up Landon.

He also had never suspected his father's true hatred for me. His horror as he relived his last days within the compound made us both cry.

I knew that Cannon and Kris were fed up with him, but I knew why Landon lingered in the bed—he feared he had nowhere to go. I promised him he was welcome in my pack, but I was sure he would go where his twin settled.

Cassandra was blooming. There was no other word for it. She looked radiant, and I felt drab beside her. Pregnancy suited her, and with the threat of the bond gone between me and Cannon, I admit, I felt slightly broody when I left her.

Doc argued heavily against it, but I left the house and went out to see my pack. Cannon had been called to an emergency at Anterrio Pack, and from his grumblings, I guessed it was a regular thing. He'd left this morning with the warning I was to rest.

In the streets, I was swarmed with my pack. They let me go at my own pace, and they were never far from me in case I got tired, but their love surrounded me, and I felt so blessed to have found this pack.

My pack.

When Cannon came home, he found me in the food hall, surrounded by friends as I caught up on all I'd missed.

"I thought I said *rest* when I left this morning," he murmured as he sat beside me.

"You did say rest," I told him as I stole a chicken wing from his plate. "I've rested enough." He went to argue, but I leaned over and kissed him softly. "Our pack walked beside me and made sure I had company. I have spent the day with our pack, my love, I was fine."

His eyes searched my face, but he said nothing further about it. Instead, he dipped his head and brushed his lips over mine. "My love?" he said, a smile hovering over his mouth. "I like that," he told me, kissing me more firmly this time.

When he leaned back, he reclaimed his stolen chicken wing, winking at me as he bit into it. The pack watched us, smiling at our open playfulness. As Cannon began to eat his meal, he lifted his arm in invitation, and I eagerly snuggled into his side content to be close to him as we spent an enjoyable evening with the pack.

Days passed and my strength and color returned. Cannon and I had made love, slow, sweet, and tender, and I had cried halfway through at how gentle he was, at how much he *loved* me. I was healing, but one thing still bugged me, and it would bug me until I had an answer.

"A rabbit?"

Barbara sighed as she swung her door open. "Come in."

I marched inside, wearing jean shorts and a tank, presenting less like an alpha every day. Taking a seat, I glared at her. "Dish it."

She blinked, then went to her kitchen and returned with a plate of scones. "Tea?"

"I don't mean serve me, I mean *tell* me the truth."

She opened her mouth to speak and snapped it closed. With a wry smile, she rolled her eyes. "The shaman had the rabbit, so I used what was available."

"So you never sent Moonstar to my mom as *a rabbit*?"

"Good Goddess, no!"

"Then *why* tell me you did?"

She looked at me in confusion. "I sent the spirit to Andrea for protection. I never said she was in *any* form."

She hadn't? I scowled at her. She met my look calmly. "Where is Moonstar? I know she isn't in some rabbit."

"When I committed the ritual to save *your* soul, I was able to separate you both. You need not worry about Moonstar ever again."

"I don't even know how you did it. No one tells me; did you tell them?" When I saw her steady unblinking gaze, I got angry. "You told them *nothing*. You capitalized on the fact they would be so desperate to get me back they wouldn't question *how* you did it at all."

"You are free. Isn't that all that matters? You don't need to worry."

I frowned. "But I *am* worried. What happens to her? Is she gone? Is she...dead? I need to know she is all right."

Barbara watched me. "She is happy. She is free." When I went to speak, she shook her head. "I will tell you no more."

"Why did my spirit need to be taken? It was my *body* that was broken, so why even take me out of it?"

Barbara rubbed her forehead. "Kezia, I am a servant of the Goddess. These were the signs she sent me. I did what I did as I was told by Luna. For her. For *you*."

"So you don't know?" I glowered at her. "I was in a rabbit for a *month*, and you *don't* know why?"

She took a deep breath. "Your body had been through a lot of trauma. You were dying, Kezia; I wasn't there, but I felt it. I knew you were barely holding on. I took your spirit so that your body could heal."

"How did you feel it?" Leaning forward, I scowled at her. "You don't know me *that* well, Barbara. I will not give up until you have given me answers."

She sighed and looked away. "Are you sure you don't want a drink?"

Milk and cookies.

Pushing myself to my feet, I gaped at her. "The bond. That's why you think it's broken. You drugged Cannon, my *mate*, and you did something to him. To *our* bond. He told me..." I was muttering as I paced. "He told me you said you did it for us both..." Looking up, I saw her watching me, her focus intent. "It wasn't to show him I could lead this pack; you did something to the bond. What did you do?" Leaning over her, I felt like screaming, but I remained calm. "*What* did you *do* to our bond?"

Barbara sniffed delicately as she looked away. "Sit down and I will tell you."

Taking a seat, I couldn't stop glaring at her. "Speak."

Barbara watched me while she adjusted her sweater, leaning back in her chair slightly. "They tell me that not that long ago, you were seeking to break the bond—"

"Things changed."

She gave me a look of disapproval. "*If* you would let me speak..." When I said nothing, she continued. "I heard you went to the scientist." Her lips curled with scorn. "What would *medicine* know about a spiritual gift?"

"You knew how to break it?" I asked her quietly.

"I do." Barbara gave me a small smile. "It's why I came here. I knew you were running. Running from it. I wanted to see for myself if you *truly* did not want to form the bond, and if not, I would help you break it." Wearily she leaned back even more, getting comfortable. "But you were both so blind to each other. Anyone could see how you both needed it, wanted it."

I couldn't stop the smile as I remembered the fools we had been. "We were stupid."

"You are stubborn," she corrected with a gentle look. "Both of you. I could have left, but I liked it here. He is a good alpha, your mate." Barbara looked around her room. "It is hard to be a druid. Many shun us, preferring the blindness of a shaman to see what they cannot see themselves. I keep my calling to myself, but I am always at the service of Luna."

"She made you stay here?"

Barbara shook her head. "No. I would like to stay here. It feels like home, and I..." She licked her lips nervously. "I would like to remain close to you." Seeing my eyes widen, she hurried on. "I know you have no trust in me, but I care for you, Kezia." She broke my stare. "Your mother would kick my ass if I left you now."

I didn't know how I felt about that. She *had* saved me, but she had also lied to me. I had had enough of lies; it didn't matter who they were from. Not anymore. My trust levels were low.

"Tell me what you did," I hounded her.

"Luna sent the signs. I knew something bad was coming, more than war. Cannon felt it too. He came to me. It was my house he stood outside. Luna called him to me. When I answered the door, I didn't know what she wanted. Cannon and I talked, and I could feel your newly formed bond." She broke off with a faraway look in her eye. "It was so new, so strong, I could practically see it."

"See it?"

Barbara nodded quickly. "There was an aura around him; it was almost golden."

Royce had said Moonstar had healed Cannon with magic that was golden. An uneasy feeling churned in my belly. "Golden?"

Barbara gave a soft laugh. "Silly, I know. A bond is not physical, it cannot be seen." Blowing out a breath, she continued. "I know how to break a bond. I know that, while it cannot be seen, it can be felt. I *also* know that a strong bond can be"—she looked at me quickly—"stretched."

"Stretched?" There was a dangerous undertone to my voice I didn't recognize, but Barbara did.

"I pulled the bond between you, and I tethered part of it, just a small part, to me. So that *if* anything were to happen to you, I would know and I would be ready."

"Ready for what?"

"To save you, Kezia."

"I was healed within days, so why keep me away for so long?" She said nothing and I watched her through narrowed eyes. "Moonstar? She fought you. She didn't want to go, did she?" She still said nothing, but I pushed on. I knew I was right. "Moonstar was still *in* my body, wasn't she? You *tethered*," I spat the word out, "*my* bond to Cannon to you, but that left Moonstar in my body." Anger thrummed through me. "*Where* is she?"

"She is gone. She is safe."

"Where?" I demanded.

"I will not tell you." She met my look squarely, and I knew in this, she would not bend. "It is so good to see you healthy, alive...demanding."

I snorted, but in truth, I didn't know if I should argue with her. I was back, wasn't that all that mattered?

No. Moonstar mattered. She mattered a whole lot.

Looking at Barbara, I knew I'd need to figure it out another day. "So, my mate bond is broken?"

"Can you feel it?"

"I think...maybe?" Uncertainty swept through me. "I don't know if it's wishful thinking."

She shifted her eyes down. "You need your heat to determine that."

"Make my heat come."

Another impatient frown. "I can't do that, Kezia."

"Yes, you can. You meddle with all of Luna's cycle; meddle with mine."

"It would be a *false* heat." Reaching over, she patted my knee, and I fought the urge to rip off her arm. "Be patient." Standing up, she looked down at me, tenderness in her gaze. "I know you do not trust me, but you will see, I only did what was best for you, Kezia."

I left her house feeling grouchier than when I went in, and I still had a list of unanswered questions.

The highlight of my day came when Cannon woke me, slow and sure, from an unintended nap. He covered my body completely with such possessiveness that I was beginning to think it didn't matter if the bond was broken, but I knew that it did. I wanted my mate to be *my* mate.

I wanted the silvery mark on his collarbone to tell everyone he was *mine*. He wasn't the only possessive one in our relationship.

Later, we were in the kitchen, having coffee, having just come back from a run. I'd shifted to my wolf for the first time knowing there was no danger of Moonstar coming forward, and I hated to admit it, but it was liberating.

The shaman greeted us as he came in and handed a rather intricate-looking envelope over to Cannon.

"What's that?" I asked as I ate a handful of nuts.

"A letter for the alpha, from the Pack Council."

CHAPTER 31

Kezia

NERVES SWIRLED IN MY BELLY AS CANNON TOOK THE letter, opened it, and read it. I saw his frown deepen, and then he seemed to read it again.

"Kezia, get Kris."

"Fuck off, tell me what the letter says."

He gave me a look of exasperation, which was so familiar I grinned. "Get your brother."

At the bottom of the stairs, I shouted for Kris. I ignored all the protests that sounded when I shouted for Landon to come down too.

In the kitchen, we gathered, spilling over into the dining area, and when Royce came running into the house, it was only then that Cannon read the letter, by which time I had already threatened him with violence.

"Alpha Cannon and Alpha Kris," he began reading aloud.

I saw the look of shock on Kris's face.

"While your investigations into the Anterrio Pack have uncovered some unsightly and worrying facts, and we are aware of your efforts to clean the corruption from the pack by the removal of the pack leader and his loyal followers, we, the Pack Council, have also had the opportunity to conduct our own investigation."

Cannon cleared his throat before he continued.

"We find that corruption and greed can be uncovered anywhere. After much reflection, debate, and contemplation, we have considered the crimes of the Blackridge Peak Pack and pass the following." Cannon looked at us all. "You ready?"

I think we all nodded at once.

"Kezia of the Anterrio Pack is absolved of any crimes and violations of pack law while residing with the humans. All pack are entitled to defend themselves, and we find her actions that of self-defense. Should Kezia of the Anterrio Pack wish to be recognized as the bonded mate of Alpha Cannon, an official mating ceremony will be performed by a shaman of their choosing."

I was sure my brother was holding me up—my knees had left me as my relief was so overwhelming.

"Alpha Kris of the Anterrio Pack will take the Anterrio Pack as his own. His hard work, dedication, and loyalty to the pack puts him in the best position to take the pack forward. Should he wish to rename the pack, his submission should be made to the Pack Council in writing after achieving a unanimous vote from the Anterrio Pack."

"What if I don't want them?" he muttered as he shared a look with the shaman.

"I don't think you get a choice," the shaman answered solemnly.

Cannon continued. "Should Alpha Kris of the Anterrio Pack wish to be recognized as bonded mate of Cassandra of the

Anterrio Pack, an official mating ceremony will be performed by a shaman of their choosing."

Cass looked at me and winked. "Double wedding?"

Landon's snort was ignored by everyone but Cannon, who shot him a look of warning. "Shaman of the Anterrio Pack, your counsel is necessary to aid Alpha Kris; you will remain with the Anterrio Pack." The shaman shrugged as if it wasn't a big deal, but I felt like crying. "Landon of the Anterrio Pack, you will report directly to the Pack Council and provide a detailed and thorough account of your father, Bale, Pack Leader of the Anterrio Pack, until we are satisfied with your account."

"What does that mean?" Landon asked warily.

"Sounds like an interrogation," Royce told him quietly. "If you have nothing to hide, you have nothing to lose."

I watched as Landon stared sullenly at his shoes, but he nodded once in acceptance.

"For our inner investigations, we have been found wanting. In conclusion, there are now three empty seats on the Pack Council. Alpha Cannon and Alpha Kris are invited to come forward to take their place."

"Holy Luna, *what*?" I screeched. "No. Nuh-uh. No way."

Cannon and Kris exchanged a look.

Cass was beaming at Kris. "Pack Council? That's a huge honor. And you're both so young, that's..." She beamed with pride. "A huge honor, Kris." She glanced at Cannon. "And you, Alpha."

I stared at her as if she was insane. "The Pack Council that was corrupt and evil."

"They cleared the garbage out," she said primly.

"How do you know they didn't kill the only good ones left and leave all the baddies?" I demanded.

"Because we are Pack Council," the shaman spoke quietly.

My jaw dropped along with everyone else's.

"You?" I couldn't speak. "You!"

"What do you think a shaman is?" He smiled at us all as he looked around the room, his milky white eyes seeing little. "I serve all packs. How many times do I need to say it before you believe me?"

"*You're* on the Pack Council?" I demanded.

"I serve them, yes."

"You could have stopped all of this?" Kris asked as he stood closer to me. "You could have told them at any time how much we needed them."

"The Council was facing their own struggles. Only with the evidence you have all diligently presented in the last few weeks could changes be made."

"I can no longer keep up," Royce declared, looking around at everyone. "Can anyone?" His gaze settled on the shaman. "We're good? The pack, the alpha's? Kezia?" The shaman nodded. "Right then, I need a drink."

"Second that!" Cannon said, handing the letter to Kris. "I might need two."

"Or twenty," Kris muttered, following him to the study. The others trailed after them, many looking back at the shaman with wariness and speculation. The shaman stood back, a serene smile on his face.

"You have questions, pup?"

"You lied to me."

"When?"

"I don't know..." I was struggling, *really* struggling. "Bale? He knew that you were so close to them?"

"He did. I believe that's why he took me and held me in the cells when he truly lost his mind to greed and rage."

"All these months." I shook my head. "All these months you could have done something."

"I did do something. I was here by your side as you grew into the amazing woman you are, with a pack and an alpha who love you. Who *deserve* you."

I was still shaking my head. "I don't know." With my hands on the side of my head, I stared at him. "I don't know what to do with this."

"I do." Reaching over, he took my hand. "Let's get drunk."

WHO KNEW an old shifter as frail as the shaman could hold so much liquor? My head was pounding, and my bed was empty. Daylight streamed through the window, and I knew Cannon was no doubt on pack business.

With a groan, I rolled out of bed, landing on the floor with a thump, knowing I needed a shower and a run as my wolf to get rid of this hangover. I didn't even know it was possible to get a hangover, but I definitely had *something*.

Moaning, I got to my feet. The shaman's *special blend* of whiskey was to be avoided from now on at all costs, I promised myself as I stumbled down the stairs and headed to the boot room.

"Luna, my head hurts," I grumbled as I bounced off a stool in Cannon's kitchen, still unsteady on my feet. "What the hell was in that whiskey?" Opening the door, I shifted and ran out of town. I made sure enough of the pack saw me; I was never sneaking away from my alpha ever again.

My run took me up the mountain, far from the Blackridge Peak Pack, but the fresh air and breeze as I ran kept me going. At a high point on the mountain, I looked down.

Whoa, that is a long way down.

I shifted back to human form. Looking around, I didn't care that I was naked. I *knew* this place.

"Where are you?" Turning slowly in a circle, I searched for her. "Moonstar?"

Shaking my head, I moved forward, ready to search for her. "I know you're here. I know this place. This is where you took me." I shivered in the cool air. Swiftly I shifted back to my wolf, needing my wolfskin to keep me warm. Uncovering nothing, I stubbornly sat down.

Fine. I'll wait.

I must have dozed, or maybe I was still feeling the shaman's lethal blend of alcohol, but I woke up when I felt the presence of another. I shifted back to my human form as I watched her approach me.

Her hair was black. I hadn't expected that. I'd always envisaged her to have hair the same color as mine. Her skin was ivory pale, her rosy lips the only color on her face. Her eyes were white.

Hello, child.

I burst into tears, and her arms surrounded me, but there was little substance. Still, I clung to her as I wept. Finally, I pulled back and looked at her.

"How?"

Moonstar smiled serenely, looking up at the darkening sky.

I was bound once. She looked down at me. *When I felt your pain all that time ago, I did not think. I hoped the strength of my spirit would keep you alive. When I entered your body, I think we merged.*

"Merged?"

Moonstar nodded. *So eager to heal you, I ignored the tightness of your hold on me. When I knew you were better, both of you, I tried to leave, but you had a claim on my spirit, and I could not break free.*

Scooting back, I looked her over warily. "Are you telling me that *I* did this? That *I* bound *you* to *me*?"

Her hand ran over my hair. *You have always been so strong. So fierce. You were always so sure you relied on my strength...* She drew her hand away. *I think I relied on yours.*

"Moonstar...I'm..." I gulped back tears. "I'm so sorry."

Child, you never need apologize. Her gaze returned to the sky. *I was bound for so long I forgot who I was. I wanted to be free so much, but—*

"But I kept you." My voice was filled with bitterness. "I did this to you!"

You were scared. Nothing more than a child. It is not your fault.

But I couldn't get over the immense feeling of guilt. "Why didn't you tell me?"

She looked at me, her face one of calm and peace. *I did not know the words. I did not know until I was free.*

Standing, I moved away from her. "They were all so desperate for you to be gone, sure I would *lose* myself, when I was the one who *took* you!"

I guarded you of my own free will, child.

"And I kept you with mine," I snarled with loathing.

I am free now. You freed me.

Squinting, I looked at her. "I did what now?"

331

I am free, child.

"I don't think I can take the credit for that," I told her dubiously. "You owe your thanks to a druid and a *really* ugly rabbit."

A druid? Moonstar laughed and it was the lightest laugh I had ever heard. I could have sworn it sounded like wind chimes. *A druid can do nothing to me.*

Wow. She sounded smug.

"You sure?"

She beamed at me fondly. *Only the one who binds can grant freedom.*

Blowing out a breath, I sat on the ground, my butt protesting at the cold earth. "Barbara, she said…" I thought about it. She *hadn't* said anything. She told me she'd never tell me. "She didn't tell me because she didn't know."

Moonstar watched me curiously as I ran through all the scenarios and conversations. "I gave you your freedom," I started slowly. "I told you, if you could heal him, you could take over."

I healed the alpha as you asked.

"*I* gave you your freedom that day. In the compound, I gave you control. I…" I stared at her blankly. "I let you go."

You let me go.

"But you stayed?" Tears filled my eyes. "You couldn't take control of me anymore because I let you go. You could have left, but you stayed near?"

I was no longer bound, but I knew you may need me still. There was so much danger surrounding you.

"The fight?" I was crying again, tears streaming down my face. "Bale? I…I heard you?" She nodded as she watched me.

"Why? Why help me? After all these years I've held you prisoner?"

Why? She frowned. *I love you, child.*

I started sobbing again, uttering over and over how sorry I was. When I finally stopped crying, I looked up at her.

"What happens now?"

I would like to wander. Her eyes turned north. *I wish to remember the taste of the land.*

"You can go," I said softly. "You don't need to stay for me anymore." Scrambling to my feet, I rubbed my arms. "I'm safe."

I know. Her hand cupped my cheek. *He is strong. He will be a fine mate.*

I was nodding, too choked up to speak. Moonstar turned from me and I grabbed her arm. "I still don't know why that rabbit bugs me so much."

She frowned.

"Barbara, the druid," I explained hastily. "She put my spirit in a rabbit when Bale almost killed me." Moonstar was watching, alert but confused. "She put my spirit in a stupid rabbit while she tried to..." I grappled for words. "Exorcise you."

Moonstar didn't look like she knew the word, but she still looked pissed off.

Standing back, I held my hands up. "Sorry, you don't need this. It's nothing. It's all fine now, it's..."

Something.

Relieved, I nodded. "Yeah, it's weird."

Her head tilted, and I studied her as she thought about it. *A rabbit can be a conduit for transformation.*

The shaman had told me this also. It made no more sense when Moonstar said it. She cocked her head again as she watched me.

My spirit was free.

"But only you knew that," I whispered. We shared a look. "They didn't know." I scoffed. "*I* didn't know; how the heck were they supposed to know you had left?"

A misunderstanding?

I'd lain in that bed for weeks because Luna forgot to send the signs to her *vessels* that Moonstar was free of me.

It was almost funny.

You will be safe, child.

It wasn't a question, it felt like an order. "I'll do my best." Rubbing my nose, I exhaled loudly. "You can come visit?" She watched me silently. "I mean, you've got tons of other things to do, but if you're ever near here..." I was babbling. "I mean, my mate bond is broken. You never know, Luna may send him someone else, and I..."

Her hand once more cupped my cheek. *Hush, child.*

She was eager to go. I could tell by her energy, and she had waited long enough.

"I'm going to miss you."

I felt a kiss on my brow. *And I you, little one.*

Epilogue

It was a week after all the crazy revelations, decrees from the Pack Council, and my farewell to Moonstar. I'd only told Cannon and my brother that I had met with her. I returned in the early hours the next morning, dawn was just breaking the sky, and both of them had been waiting for me. Both pissed off and frustrated with me for being gone for so long, alone.

I was too broken to lie. Piece by piece, we figured out what happened. Barbara had linked herself to our bond. With it, she knew if either of us was in danger. When she felt the strain on the bond, she had yanked me out of my body, thinking she was saving me. Not knowing the bond of friendship between my mate and my brother, their Wills combined gave them the strength to heal me.

It had taken them a while, but they had done it. By then, Barbara thought the only thing in my body was the spirit of Moonstar. Not being close enough to my body, she hadn't sensed it was empty.

The shaman would have but he thought the druid had put us *both* in the rabbit.

That fucking rabbit. If I ever saw it again, I was going to eat it.

I would never tell Barbara or the shaman where Moonstar was. That she was truly free. It was a secret I would keep from them, and I made my brother and my alpha do the same. Cannon worried Barbara might search for her, but I decided that Barbara was content to stay here, close to me and Kris. She seemed to like it here, and after Cannon had a private conversation with her, she was happy to stay.

The Blackridge Peak Pack had no shaman, but it did have a druid *and* a doctor. Magic and science blending as one.

Kris was getting ready to reclaim Anterrio Pack permanently and move back there. Cass was delighted to be returning home, but nervous too, knowing she had the chance to change. To *be* better. Cannon's words to her that night months ago may have been harsh, but they resonated more than perhaps he even realized.

Life was almost *normal*. I was ready for normal.

I was folding laundry when the first stab of pain shot into my abdomen, and I doubled over in agony. The second pain made me cry out. The third followed swiftly, and I pulled myself towards the study, where my mate was carrying out pack business.

I looked up and saw he was already at the doors, his eyes burning with desire as my heat swept through me.

"Kezia?" His voice was a low growl, and my core tightened with need.

Running my hand over my abdomen, I tried to smile through the pain. "Want to re-form a mate bond?"

Cannon was already taking his clothes off. "I thought you'd never ask."

About the Author

Eve L. Mitchell is a USA Today Bestselling author who writes Contemporary Romance, and New Adult Romance but also dabbles in Paranormal Romance.

If you like a morally grey alpha-hole, then chances are Eve's got a male character for you to claim as your next book boyfriend.

As an avid reader from a young age, Eve still considers herself a reader first. She believes there is nothing better than getting that new book either on your e-reader or in your hands, and the fact she may bring that excitement to a fellow reader fills her with wonder. She writes under a pen name; otherwise, her Secret Agent status will be revoked.

Eve lives in the North East of Scotland, with her three coffee machines and her significant other, Mr. M. She enjoys NFL Football, music (played loudly), and having long conversations with the voices in her head, which sometimes turn into the stories she writes.

How to Connect with Eve:

Join my newsletter and keep up to date with the latest news and updates on my books and releases: http://bit.ly/Eves newsletter

Connect with me on Facebook: http://bit.ly/evesfacebook page

Also by Eve L. Mitchell

<u>CONTEMPORARY ROMANCE</u>

The Boulder Series

Unbroken Devotion (Boulder Series Book 1)

Dark Heart (Boulder Series Book 2)

Unbroken Bonds (Boulder Series Book 3)

Dark Soul (Boulder Series Book 4)

A Very Boulder Christmas (A Holiday Novella)

The Denver Series

Her Greatest Mistake (Book 1)

Beautifully Broken (Book 2)

Keeping Harmony (Book 3)

The Ruthless Devils Series

Ruthless Heart (Book 1)

Ruthless Desire (Book 2)

Ruthless Charm (Book 3)

Ruthless Devil (standalone)

Torn & Broken Duet

Torn by Grace

Broken by Faith

A Collection of Short Romances: Volume 1

THE BOULDER SERIES

The Boulder Series is an interconnected series that explores the relationships between friends, family, and the family you choose...with some love, heat, and underground fighting along the way!

The series covers tropes of forbidden romance (ex-boyfriend's older brother), enemies-to-lovers, friends to lovers, opposites attract and second-chance love.

The Boulder Series will take you on a rollercoaster of emotions. You will laugh, scream, feel the characters' excitement, and it's possible you may throw your e-reader (just make sure it lands somewhere soft).

A complete four-book series that has all the feels. What's stopping you from jumping into Boulder?

The series includes **Unbroken Devotion**, **Dark Heart**, **Unbroken Bonds** and **Dark Soul**.

GET THE SERIES
WWW.EVELMITCHELL.COM

THE DENVER SERIES

The Denver Series is a three-book mafia romance shared world series. Each book is a standalone, featuring cameos from the other books. Although it is recommended that the books be read in order, it is not necessary to do so.

The series covers tropes of opposites attract, enemies-to-lovers, and forbidden romance (stepcousins).

The Denver Series is a steamy contemporary romance series that dabbles in the mafia romance genre, with book one hinting at it and the other two exploring the darker side of this much-loved genre.

A complete three-book series where sassy heroines meet and fall for their dark alphahole heroes.

The series includes **Her Greatest Mistake**, **Beautifully Broken** and **Keeping Harmony**.

GET THE SERIES

WWW.EVELMITCHELL.COM

THE RUTHLESS DEVILS SERIES

A college sports romance series following twin brothers and their cousin. Three football stars who have it all: looks, money, talent and the world at their feet. No one messes with the Devils. Each book deals with a different Devil and their love interest who will either make them or break them.

The series covers tropes of enemies-to-lovers, second-chance romance and forced proximity.

This is interconnected three-book series with an underlying story arc that carries through from book one to book three, and therefore the series must be read in order. The series deals with some elements that sensitive readers may find triggering.

This series includes **Ruthless Heart**, **Ruthless Desire** and **Ruthless Charm**.

GET THE SERIES
WWW.EVELMITCHELL.COM

TORN & BROKEN DUET

The Torn & Broken duet is a duet with a twist. You can read either book as a standalone. *Torn by Grace* was written first and one of the female side characters in that book is the main character in *Broken by Faith*, however, you don't need to know what happened in *Torn by Grace* to enjoy *Broken by Faith*. There is a little bit of crossover, but no spoilers.

Torn by Grace is a second chance, enemies-to-lovers, brothers-best-friend romance.
Broken by Faith is an enemies-to-lovers, forced proximity, fake relationship romance.
The series includes **Torn by Grace and Broken by Faith.**

GET THE DUET
WWW.EVELMITCHELL.COM

THE WATCHER SERIES

The Watcher Series is a paranormal romance trilogy that will take you on a journey where you will get lost in a world that will hold you in its depths. With a blend of steam, humour and angst, be ready to buckle up for the ride.

With demons, devils and one sassy, clueless witch, what more could you ask for? Join Star as she gets a crash course in what not to do when you get involved with the Watchers.

An enemies-to-lovers story that has all the emotions packed between the pages as the heroine deals with love, betrayal, loss and so much more.

This series is a trilogy and must be read in order. If you love cliffhangers, this series is for you. If you hate cliffhangers, don't worry, the next book's already written.

The series includes **A Glow of Stars & Dust**, **A Flame of Stars & Midnight** and **A Blaze of Stars & Dawn**.

GET THE SERIES
WWW.EVE-MITCHELL.COM

THE BLACKRIDGE PEAK SERIES

The Blackridge Peak Series is a wolf shifter series about rival packs, hidden secrets, a little bit of magic, and a girl who's trying to find her way amongst a pack that doesn't want her. Kezia is an outsider, and when given the chance she leaves the pack that never truly accepted her. But trouble follows Kezia and she soon learns that only an alpha can protect her.
An alpha who may be her mate.
The series includes **Wolf's Gambit, Wolf's Betrayal, and Wolf's Endgame.**

GET THE SERIES
WWW.EVELMITCHELL.COM

THE AKRHYN SERIES

Creatures of evil roam the shadows - the Drakhyn. They may look like humans, but their taloned hands and razor-sharp teeth serve one purpose only; killing.

A Sentinel's purpose is to patrol and protect. They are highly trained soldiers with superior skills and abilities. Whether they be Vampyres, Lycan, Castors or gifted Akrhyn, their purpose is the same; hunt the Drakhyn and rid the world of their evil presence.

This fantasy trilogy covers tropes of chosen one, fated mates, good vs evil.

The series includes **Into Darkness**, **Lost in Darkness** and **From the Darkness**.

GET THE SERIES
WWW.EVELYNMITCHELL.COM

355

THE ORDER OF THE RAVENS SERIES
written as Ava Speirs

The Order of the Ravens Series is a traditional epic fantasy series where the focus is on action and adventure.

Bastian dal'Leif is a Knight of the Order, an Order that has fallen into distrust. The Order of the Conclave which were once seen as warriors of the Gods and a beacon of hope, are now cast in shadow.

Bastian and his men remain true to their Order but are forced to become mercenaries, selling their swords for coin.

In the halls of his Order, Bastian is entrusted with a mission. A mission he is reluctant to accept.

The mission is so dangerous and deadly only a fool would take it...and only a coward would reject it.

The series includes **Knight of Sword & Shadow, Knight of Sacrifice & Shade, Knight of Dagger & Darkness, and Knight of Trials and Twilight.**

GET THE SERIES
WWW.EVELMITCHELL.COM

Printed in Great Britain
by Amazon

42940612R00209